The Becket Approval

Duncan Falconer

© Duncan Falconer 2019

Duncan Falconer has asserted his rights under the Copyright, Design and Patents Act, 1988, to be identified as the author of this work.

First published in 2019 by Lume Books.

Table of Contents

Chapter 1	7
Chapter 2	9
Chapter 3	28
Chapter 4	47
Chapter 5	51
Chapter 6	64
Chapter 7	80
Chapter 8	83
Chapter 9	90
Chapter 10	99
Chapter 11	108
Chapter 12	125
Chapter 13	135
Chapter 14	141
Chapter 15	151
Chapter 16	157
Chapter 17	175
Chapter 18	203
Chapter 19	212
Chapter 20	224
Chapter 21	234
Chapter 22	253
Chapter 23	262

Chapter 24	278
Chapter 25	310
Chapter 26	312
Chapter 27	326
Chapter 28	353
Chapter 29	367
Epilogue	383

To my dear brother, John

'Will no one rid me of this turbulent priest?!'

King Henry II, referring to Thomas Becket, overheard by his knights who promptly did just that!

Chapter 1

A fawn army beret lay on a cold, stone floor, bottom up, as if begging for a coin, the cap badge a winged dagger, the words 'Who Dares Wins' floating across it. The walls were blocks of hewn stone, blemished by centuries of soot and blood. An ancient oubliette. A log fire crackled in an iron grate. A bulb glowed on a stand, its cable clipped to a car battery.

Shadows stretched up the walls, cast by two dozen men and three women standing around the beret. Silent people. At ease and with a shared reverence. Toughened by age and battle like ancient gladiators. Hardened hearts. Weathered masks. Eyes that would not flinch from horror. Bonded by an ancient pedigree and shared purpose.

The sound of footsteps on stone broke the silence. A man at the back eased his way between the others. Albert Peters, aged seventy-three, craggy features, gnarled hands, hardened by life.

He stopped above the beret. In his hand a crisp, white envelope. He placed it in the beret, hands slightly shaking with age, a decision made, right or wrong. He was satisfied. It was done. He made his way through the gathering to the only door into the chamber, pulled it open, hinges creaking, and closed it behind him.

The only sound was breathing, a gentle cough, the wheezing of an old man, the crackling of the fire.

Another man stepped forward, a large, powerful man in his forties. He plucked up the envelope, considered its significance and his own response and, with a final decision left the room.

His footsteps could be heard along a corridor. Before they fell silent, the others filed out of the room.

It was done.

One man remained. Jack Henderson, in his sixties and, like the others, tough and worn. He picked up the beret with reverence, folded it in half and half again and tucked it into his inside breast pocket.

He turned off the light plunging the room into darkness but for the glow from the dwindling fire and headed for the door, closing it behind him.

The latch came down with a clunk.

Chapter 2

Devon Gunnymede marched along a sterile corridor, escorted by a barrel-chested, steel-eyed corrections officer, the badge on his crisp uniform a white eagle on a globe encircled by the words 'State of Georgia Correctional Facility'. The sound of their heels hitting the glistening concrete floor in unison echoed off the shiny grey-painted walls. Gunnymede was heading for the exit four years, eight months and twelve days after entering the place. But he had little to be pleased about.

They passed through an electronically-operated steel door into an airlock that shut behind them with a decisive clunk. A loud buzzer sounded. Another door opened. Gunnymede squinted as he stepped into sunlight onto a red brick pathway that divided a manicured lawn and led towards a squat building the other side of a gate in the outermost perimeter fencing. He was wearing jeans and a shirt, the clothes he'd arrived in, and carrying a canvas jacket. The shirt was tight in the chest and shoulders where he'd added muscle. A daily gym session and boxing training which had come in handy mitigating the occasional altercation with bully-boys when avoidance techniques failed had toughened him mentally as well as physically. Coldness and unappeasableness had combined with the bitterness and resentment he'd brought with him to form a guarded knife-edge of uneasy tolerance. Needless to say, he was not quite the same man who had entered the place.

Gunnymede walked into the reception hall where he was invited to finalise his release document. His automaton escort remained in the centre of the small hall, his large hairy arms crossed over his ample stomach.

Gunnymede took his copy of the document, tossed it in a bin, pushed his way through the glass entrance doors and stepped outside into what, for any other con, was freedom. The door closed behind him as he stared coldly ahead. A road passed along the front of the penitentiary grounds, straight as a laser. A white sedan was parked in a lay-by the other side of it. He noticed another nondescript car further down the road and, standing beside it, a tall, thin grey-haired man in a black suit looking directly at him.

The doors to the white sedan opened and two men in suits climbed out, crossed the road to Gunnymede, showed him their FBI badges and asked him to put his jacket on and turn about. As Gunnymede's hands were cuffed behind him he saw his corrections officer behind the glass doors watching him. He was escorted to the white sedan. The man in black down the street was still watching him as they drove away.

It was late evening by the time the agents escorted Gunnymede to the doors of a British Airways Boeing 787. His handcuffs were removed and he was formally handed over to a British police officer in civilian clothes. He was handcuffed again, this time in the front, and led through the plane to a window seat near the back.

The last person to walk on board was the thin grey-haired man in black. Gunnymede watched him take a seat a few rows ahead on the other side. Gunnymede didn't know him, but there was something familiar about his aura. And he was pretty sure he knew what it was. He couldn't give a damn enough to wonder why the man was tagging along.

An hour into the flight, a stewardess came by with a drinks trolley and asked Gunnymede what he'd like. Gunnymede asked for a whisky which his police officer took pleasure in denying him. Bastard. Gunnymede closed his eyes and tried to shut the world out. Prison had taught him how to clear his mind and let time pass without stress but he wasn't successful on this occasion and opted to watch a movie. A meal helped pass the time. When he finally felt like dropping off, an intercom voice announced the aircraft would soon be landing.

When the plane came to a halt in its parking bay and the passengers got to their feet, Gunnymede's escort remained seated. They waited until everyone was off before the officer ushered him to move out. Gunnymede passed the man in black who had remained in his seat. Another plain-clothes officer was waiting for them at the end of the air bridge and the three headed through the terminal towards immigration. Before they reached it, the officers stopped at a security door and punched a code into a key pad.

A man's voice came from behind them. 'Excuse me, officers.'

It was the tall, thin man. He was holding out a badge for them to inspect. Gunnymede recognised it. His suspicions had been correct. The man offered them a folded paper. The security door opened and a senior uniformed officer stood in the doorway. The man in black redirected the paper to him. He read it, looked at the badge and begrudgingly nodded to his men.

'Remove the cuffs,' the man in black said in a croaky voice that had the hint of a foreign accent.

They obeyed.

'Come with me,' he said to Gunnymede.

The officers watched them walk away as if they'd been verbally abused.

As they approached an immigration officer directing passengers into the appropriate passport queues, the tall man showed his badge again. The officer removed a barrier and invited the pair to take an empty fast track lane that led to an immigration officer in a cubicle. The badge was presented once again along with another piece of paper. Gunnymede noticed his picture on it beside an ornate Ministry of Defence logo. The immigration officer read it, glanced at the badge, at Gunnymede and nodded them through.

When they stepped outside the terminal building a vehicle was waiting for them. They climbed into the back and off it drove.

'What's this about?' Gunnymede asked.

The man ignored him.

Forty-five minutes later, the car came to a stop in the backstreets of the Temple and they climbed out in front of a building a stone's throw from the Thames that Gunnymede recognised.

'Harlow?' Gunnymede muttered, somewhat surprised.

His escort led the way into the building and up a flight of stairs to the first floor where Gunnymede was invited to step into a Georgian-style ante-room. Every surface was wood or leather coated, with books packed onto the shelves lining the walls.

Gunnymede recognised the secretary who managed the gateway to Harlow's office. He couldn't remember her name though, if he'd ever known it. She was that classic severe, mature, unattractive matronly type. Harlow didn't permit the distraction of a female pleasing to the eye to hold that position.

It wasn't long before the secretary opened a door and settled her gaze on Gunnymede. 'You may go in now,' she said.

Gunnymede got to his feet and entered. Harlow was seated behind an ornate desk scribbling something. The office hadn't changed as far as Gunnymede could recall. All wood and leather, like the ante-room. Dark green and brown. The formal twat looked the same in his dark, expensive suit. He always reminded Gunnymede of a thin Churchill. There was even a cigar in the ashtray beside a crystal glass containing an amber liquid.

The man in black joined them and closed the door.

Harlow regarded Gunnymede with the slightest of smiles, as if he was enjoying the visitor's discomfort. 'Thank you, Aristotle,' he said.

Aristotle, Gunnymede thought. Odd moniker.

'Devon Gunnymede,' Harlow said, savouring the name. 'I expect you're surprised to find yourself in here. Have those five years flown by as quickly for you as they have for me? How was your American jail time? You look very well on it.'

'It was boring.'

'Yes. I suppose that's the point of these things, isn't it? Take a seat.'

Gunnymede sat in a chair the other side of Harlow's desk.

'Can I get you a drink?' Harlow asked. 'Scotch is your poison, isn't it? Single Malt. Would you be so kind, Aristotle?'

The tall man walked over to a dresser with a large crystal decanter on it and poured a finger into a glass.

'A touch of water,' Harlow added, confidently.

Aristotle added the water and handed the glass to Gunnymede.

Gunnymede looked at the drink. Harlow had never offered him one before. He put the glass to his nose and savoured the aroma. Nice. He took a sip. Nectar.

'You're wondering what you're doing in your old boss's office sipping whisky when you should be awaiting transfer to one of Her Majesty's prisons in order to complete the UK portion of your sentence. Another five years, I expect.'

Gunnymede stared at him. All of the above was correct.

'I'll get right to the point. Spangle's back and the game is in play once again.'

Gunnymede shifted in his seat. There were so many implications to what had just been said it was overpowering.

'Not a great deal has changed since you left us. We still don't know who Spangle is. We've narrowed the list to Kanastov, Reeshekov, Malakov, Siskiv. Three kovs and a kiv. My money's on Malakov. Jervis thinks it's Siskiv. Aristotle doesn't think it's any of them. We're all agreed it can't be a woman because Spangle has to be highly connected, has to be former Russian Federation, council of ministers, a cabinet member or military intelligence and at a level that no woman has yet reached in the Russian government. We used to believe Spangle was all about heroin but it may be a lot more than just narcotics this time.'

'So, why are you here in between jail sentences and talking about Spangle?' Harlow continued. 'The answer is we're putting a new operation together and we can't think of anyone better positioned than you to join it.' He looked at Gunnymede for his reaction. 'We want you to come back in.'

Gunnymede did his best to hide his shock.

'You have many qualities that we need. You know the players. The environment. The rules. The smell. The fabric. But most importantly, even though you're filthy dirty, you're clean as fresh laundry for this task. Not only have you been tucked away for the last five years, everyone is expecting you to be tucked away for another five. In short, you not only have your freedom, but your old job back. What do you say to that?'

Gunnymede could only sit and watch while digesting as much as he could.

'Of course, you'd have to play by the rules,' Harlow added. 'Scrutiny will be severe. Things have changed quite a bit since you left. Accountability has tightened. If you're not a good boy, you'll find yourself back behind bars. Let me re-phrase that. If you're not a successful boy, you'll be back in lock-up.'

Gunnymede finished his whisky and put the glass down. Harlow stared at him. Gunnymede appeared to be contemplating.

'What do you say?' Harlow asked.

Gunnymede got to his feet. 'You can shove your job up your arse.'

Harlow chuckled. 'You do talk a load of bollocks, Gunnymede.'

'You don't know me as well as you think.'

'Oh, I think I do. Not that I have to. Even a fool would take this opportunity.'

'Take me back to the police,' Gunnymede said to Aristotle.

'I don't see the disadvantages. Give me one reason why you would refuse?'

'It stinks. You're setting me up.'

'How?'

'I can't see it right now but it's there.'

'You were never this paranoid.'

'Of course I was.'

'This is the only chance you'll get.'

'Fine.'

'Once you step into that police station you'll be stuck in the judicial system and we won't be able to get you out.'

'Fine by me.' Gunnymede headed for the door.

Harlow watched him step through it and out of sight. But he wasn't quite finished. 'You haven't heard from Megan recently, have you?'

It was a long few seconds before Gunnymede looked back into the room.

'You wouldn't have heard of course,' Harlow continued.

'What?'

'I have some bad news, I'm afraid. Megan's in hospital.'

'Why?' Gunnymede asked, trying not to look too shocked but deep down he was.

'She's in the Hammersmith and Fulham mental health unit. She was assaulted. In a bad way I'm afraid. Would you like to see her?'

The answer was pretty obvious.

'Aristotle will take you.'

Gunnymede left the room. Aristotle glanced at Harlow with what appeared to be a look of disapproval. Harlow waved him out.

Less than an hour later, the two men arrived at the hospital.

'They're expecting you,' Aristotle said before Gunnymede got out of the car.

Gunnymede had been anxious for the entire journey. 'What happened?'

'The worst thing that can happen to a woman.'

Gunnymede stared at him, controlling his anger. 'Who did it?'

'The police have no suspect.'

Gunnymede wondered about Aristotle. What was his role? He climbed out, walked up a ramp through the main entrance and across the lobby to the reception desk where he was asked to take a seat and wait to be called. He was filled with concern.

A pair of heavy doors leading into the main hospital mechanically opened and a male nurse stepped through at a very slow pace alongside a young man who was physically and mentally challenged. An older couple sitting near Gunnymede got to their feet and, with broad, painful smiles and outstretched arms, greeted him as if he was their most precious belonging. The young man didn't respond other than to stare at the floor as they held him, cooing softly.

Gunnymede was too engrossed to hear his name being called.

The receptionist tapped him on the shoulder. 'You can go through, Mr Gunnymede,' she said. 'Turn right and Ward 6 is at the end.'

Gunnymede walked into the main block and along a corridor to a pair of doors that were electronically locked. A sign above declared it was Ward 6.

He took a moment to prepare himself. Was she badly injured? Disfigured? Was it life changing?

He pressed a button on the wall and pushed the doors inwards. It was a large room with a collection of beds, chairs and tables randomly placed. A dozen patients were in various stages of activity or inactivity. A couple of nurses hovered. A teenage boy nearby rocked from side to side on his feet making a whining sound, unaware of anyone else.

Gunnymede saw Megan the far side of the room sitting alone by a window. She was wearing a simple dress, her hands were folded on her lap. She was staring at nothing, a blank expression on her pretty face. Gunnymede's heart ached for her.

He walked over and stood in front of her. She didn't appear to be damaged in any way. Other than being spaced out, she looked normal. Her long, dark hair was shiny and combed. So young, so innocent, so vulnerable.

'Megan?' he said softly.

He hoped she'd look up at him, spring to her feet and with a broad smile leap into his arms as she so often did. He could taste her soft lips, feel her fingers in his hair, look into those big brown eyes. But she didn't move. Not a stir. As if she was locked into position.

'It's Devon,' he said, pulling a chair around to sit in front of her.

There was no response. Her eyes were open. It was as if she'd been switched off or he wasn't even there. He took a hold of her hand. Her fingers were warm and limp. Lifeless, like her eyes.

Gunnymede was startled by sudden loud voices. They were the amplified drones of a soap opera coming from a television high on a wall. A nurse headed across the room, took the remote control from a patient and turned it down.

Megan hadn't flinched, as if she were deaf. Gunnymede kissed her hand and placed it against his cheek. He'd never felt so helpless in his life.

When he eventually left the ward, Aristotle was waiting for him in the reception hall. Gunnymede stopped beside him without looking at him, still in a mild state of shock. 'Stuporous catatonia with mutism, according to the nurse,' Gunnymede said. 'Probably permanent. She'll never be normal again.' He walked away, lost in thought, out of the building.

A man climbed out of a car as Gunnymede walked past it. 'Gunny,' he called out.

Gunnymede didn't hear him. The man called out again, jogged over and grabbed his shoulder. Gunnymede spun around, pushing the man's hand away, his face locked in a menacing grimace, fists ready to strike.

'Easy, Gunny!' the man exclaimed, putting his hands in the air in a sign of non-aggression. 'It's Charlie. Charlie Gibson.'

It took a few seconds before Gunnymede recognised him.

'We used to work together,' Charlie said. 'Down at the Fort. I was with 22 back then.'

Gunnymede put the name and face together. 'Right. Charlie. Sorry. I was somewhere else.'

Charlie seemed to understand. 'That's alright, mate.'

'This isn't a great time.'

'I know. I'm sorry about Megan.'

'You knew Megan?'

'Before you,' Charlie said. 'Not in the same way a'course. Her dad, Jack, was my sergeant major in 'G' squadron. I'm a civvy now. Got out a few years ago.'

Gunnymede looked past Charlie to a lump of a man he recognised climbing out of a car.

Charlie followed his gaze. 'You remember Boris the bull. One of your lot.'

Gunnymede knew of Boris. Beyond his Neanderthal physique, an unimpressive man.

'You and Boris've got somethin' in common,' Charlie said with a smirk. 'He was also kicked out for a little extra curricular while on task.'

Gunnymede remembered the story. Boris learned of a cash shipment flying into Kabul International bound for the United Nations HQ while he was assigned to the British Embassy in Afghanistan. A couple of hundred thousand US dollars. He tossed CS into the vehicle while it was passing through the city and grabbed the money box. What Boris didn't know was that it was standard procedure to include a tracker in amongst the bills. Boris was a thick twat. When the transit team reported the robbery, UN security sent up a tracking drone and they found the money inside the British embassy where Boris had hidden it. He got three years.

'He couldn't resist the insider knowledge either. Not in your class a'course,' Charlie added with a cheeky wink.

'What do you want?' Gunnymede asked.

'Is there somewhere we can 'ave a chat?' Charlie asked.

'Not a good time,' Gunnymede said.

Charlie could sense Gunnymede's irritation. 'Look, I appreciate your situation but I just wanted to chat about something.'

'I don't mean to be rude but I do have to get going.'

'I'll get to the point. Don't you want to see it put right?'

'What put right?'

'This. What happened to Megan.'

'I don't understand,' Gunnymede said, his irritation increasing.

'No-one's paid the price.'

'What are you talking about?'

Charlie had to take a moment. 'What happened to Megan. The rape. I 'eard a rumour the police know who did it but they're not doing anything about it.'

Gunnymede could only stare at Charlie, disturbed by everything he was hearing.

'What would you do if that was true?' Charlie asked. 'If you knew who did it?'

Gunnymede continued to stare at him.

'Did you hear me? It's a simple enough question, Gunny – what would Megan want?'

Gunnymede became suddenly angry and took an aggressive step towards Charlie. 'If you and that retard go anywhere near Megan, I'll rip both your faces off. Do you understand me?'

Boris took an aggressive step towards them. Charlie held out his hand, commanding Boris to stay. Charlie stood his ground, not the type to back away from an aggression. 'Alright. Bad timing. But whatever happens, it isn't up to you. Get in touch with Jack. Alright. Something needs to be done.'

Charlie walked back to the car, climbed in with Boris and they drove away.

Aristotle joined Gunnymede, who sighed heavily as he fought to unravel his brain. 'I can't think right now,' Gunnymede said.

Aristotle watched the car drive away and put it out of his thoughts as he held out a phone to Gunnymede. 'I'm in the contacts,' he said. 'Take a walk. Think about things. You don't have much time. Jail or the game. Decide which one you want.'

Gunnymede put the phone in his pocket. 'You got any money?'

Aristotle took out his wallet and handed Gunnymede a few twenties. 'Harlow must know by this evening. Things are moving quickly.'

'That quickly?' Gunnymede asked, wondering what things.

'Yes.'

Gunnymede wondered who the man was. He nodded and walked away.

Gunnymede made his way aimlessly through the City, crossing roads barely mindful of traffic. The sun was setting when he finally came to a decisive halt in a busy commercial street and, for the first time since leaving the hospital, wondered exactly where he was. Nothing looked familiar. Not that he cared.

He saw a pub sign hanging from a building part way down a narrow side-street: The King's Head. It looked on the rough side, a grimy black painted exterior in need of a fresh coat and some filler. But a drink was a drink and he needed one.

Pushing open the doors, he entered an atmosphere of stale beer and cooking oil. Undeterred, he weaved between tables occupied mostly by hardened labourer types to arrive at the bar where an obese geezer plastered in moronic tattoos was cleaning glasses. The man looked at Gunnymede with an unwelcoming, gormless gaze that served as a request for his libation. Gunnymede pointed at one of the beer pulls, a random choice since he recognised none of them, and the bartender did the honours.

A lone barstool beckoned and Gunnymede sat on it. The pint was placed in front of him. He handed over a note and had a sip. It tasted good.

His mind was swirling with thoughts of Megan, her rape, his conversation with Harlow, prison, what it all meant. Several pints, a couple of whiskies and a greasy burger and chips left Gunnymede feeling carcinogenic. It was time to go. He dug the phone out of his pocket, placed it on the bar and searched for the contacts.

Three large men entered the pub, dressed in expensive street and bling, and made their way to the bar. Judging by the evasive moves from patrons, the men were not to be trifled with. They stood either side of Gunnymede while the bartender prepared their drinks without an exchange. The leader looked down on Gunnymede through dark sunglasses perched on a nose that had been broken more than once and allowed to heal without an attempt to straighten it. When Gunnymede ignored him, he removed his glasses and moved his face closer to emphasise his presence. To his dismay, Gunnymede remained blissfully unaware. The thug leaned heavily onto the bar and dropped his key fob down in order to pick up Gunnymede's phone.

'Ain't seen one of these before,' he said.

Gunnymede looked at him and remained unfazed by the intimidation. 'It's a mobile phone.'

The thug didn't miss the disrespect but chose to ignore it. 'I like the case. Very nice.'

Gunnymede pushed a fiver and change towards the bartender. 'Thank you for your service, kind sir, and please take this as a tip,' he said as he got to his feet. 'I'm leaving,' he said to the thug who continued to inspect his phone.

'Fuck off then,' the thug replied, tapping the phone on the bar to test the casing.

'My phone,' Gunnymede said.

'I like it,' the thug said. 'Thanks.'

'It's not mine to give,' Gunnymede said.

'If it ain't yours, then you won't miss it, will ya?'

Gunnymede glanced at the other two thugs who were looking at him coldly. The bartender wore a slight smile, enjoying the moment. Gunnymede took back his tip. 'Mind it doesn't bite you,' he said to the thug as he eased himself out from between them and headed away.

Gunnymede stepped outside and took a moment to get his bearings. To his surprise, Aristotle was standing a few metres away looking at him.

Gunnymede smiled. 'Socrates,' he called out, heading over to him. 'I was just thinking about you. Fancy a drink?'

'I don't drink.'

'That's okay. I just need your funding. I've spent my allowance. Where shall we go?'

'That's what I'm here to find out.'

'Of course you are. Well, let's just say for the time being I've decided to return to the fold.'

Aristotle nodded.

'Lead on,' Gunnymede said, swinging himself round in the opposite direction to the one Aristotle headed.

'We should celebrate,' Gunnymede said jovially, catching him up. 'There's a pub I used to frequent just off the King's Road. You can tell me all about the business these days and how you ended up with old Harlow.'

Back in the bar, the thug was playing with Gunnymede's phone when the screen flashed brightly enough to startle him. A second later a picture of his face filled the screen with a message stating THIS IS NOT YOUR PHONE! It was followed by a clock counting down from ten seconds. The thug dropped it onto the bar as if it might explode. When it reached zero the screen image crackled and went blank. As he stared at it he realised something was missing. 'Where's my car key?'

The thugs ran for the doors.

Aristotle and Gunnymede reached the top of the street where the MoD car was waiting. Aristotle felt a vibration in his pocket and took out his phone. The thug's face filled the screen.

'You know this person?' Aristotle asked, showing it to Gunnymede.

'Nope,' Gunnymede replied as looked at the thug's car fob in his hand. He pushed a button and a shrill double beep came from behind them. They turned to see a shiny, fully loaded Range Rover, its lights flashing, parked on a double red line below a sign that strictly forbade it.

Aristotle climbed into the back of the MoD car. Gunnymede got in beside him and as he closed the door he saw the thugs jogging up the street. He slid down the window and held out the car fob. The thug leader saw him. As the MoD car pulled away, Gunnymede released it.

The thug arrived at the kerb out of breath and looked down to see a drain and no fob.

His henchman took a photo of the departing car using his phone. 'I got the plate, boss,' he said, checking the image.

The leader's expression contorted into a one of hatred. 'Get me an address,' he growled. 'We'll pay that bastard a visit.'

Gunnymede sat back with a sigh. 'I can't say I've missed London. Where we headed?'

'Syria.'

Gunnymede looked at him as if he'd grown another head. 'Did you say Syria?'

'You, not me.'

Gunnymede had his full attention. 'What the fuck am I doing in Syria?'

'First you'll go to Dubai for some training.'

'Training? Training for what?'

'Before going into the field.'

'Field?! What field?'

'You were brought back to find Spangle.'

'To help find Spangle. Be a part of the team.'

'There is no team.'

'What do you mean there is no team?'

'You *are* the team.'

'What are you talking about?'

'Spangle will reach out to you. You're a crook. A thief. You stole from him.'

'What if he just wants to kill me?'

'Harlow thinks Spangle will want to use you, not kill you.'

'Don't you think he'll wonder why I'm not in prison? More than that, why I'm back with the firm?'

'That can be explained.'

'I look forward to hearing it.'

'It's more than just about heroin for Spangle. There's something else.'

'What?'

'We don't know exactly.'

Gunnymede contemplated the update. 'Why Syria?'

'We think Spangle has made contact with someone there. We cannot miss an opportunity to chase a contact with Spangle.'

'Who?'

'A member of ISIS.'

'ISIS?'

'His name is Saleem.'

'Saleem?' Gunnymede checked.

'He's British.'

'What has Spangle got to do with ISIS?'

'That's what you're going to find out. It's also an opportunity to let Spangle know you're back.'

Gunnymede looked out of the window at the shops flying by. Pedestrians going about their daily lives. 'I want to go back to prison.'

'No you don't,' Aristotle said with certainty.

He was right.

Chapter 3

Pandi Lako joined the Albanian Policia Kufitare, the border police, when he was twenty years old. His older brother and one of his uncles were already members and pretty much paved the way for his entry. Nepotism went a long way in the Albanian Policia Kufitare, in the Debar region at least, which was where Pandi was to spend his career, short-lived though it was.

Pandi had no skills to speak of. He'd successfully avoided popular apprenticeships such as plumbing and carpentry despite his mother's efforts. His brother and uncle were the ones who kept on at him about joining up. There were benefits for them too. Having family members in the force was always useful. In Albania, blood was trusted above all else. And the border police wasn't such a bad career. It was easy if one didn't push for promotion and it would always put food on the table. While there were borders, men would be required to police them. That was true of the Balkans at least.

The Lladomerice road to the Debar border crossing ran parallel to the Albanian-Macedonian border on the Albanian side for several kilometres. It was this geographical characteristic that made the border at that point popular with smugglers; anyone in fact who needed to cross to avoid the authorities. There was one minor disadvantage and that was that no roads along that stretch headed inland other than to local farms. A large range of hills created an imposing obstacle. A smuggler had to head some miles north or south in order to go west. This provided the border police with an advantage.

It was a fresh, early winter's morning when Pandi and the eleven other members of his patrol, designated K-17, arrived at Dontrav Pikë Kontrolli, a semi-permanent checkpoint, to take over from the men of K-23 who'd completed a twenty-four hour posting. It was one of the more popular locations with the patrols in winter because it had a cabin with a wood burner and room for everyone to cram inside, just about.

K-17 had three vehicles, two cars and a flatbed pick-up truck. The patrol was lightly armed, each man responsible for a Beretta pistol and an AK47 assault rifle. A PKM belt-fed machine gun fixed onto a post on the truck bed directly behind the cab was the unit's heavy firepower if such force should be required.

The road was rarely a busy one, the traffic mostly local with many of the vehicles and drivers familiar to the officers. It was estimated on average there were three illegal crossings per week along that particular stretch of border and more could be done by the border police to reduce this.

Apart from an ugly situation involving a United Nations lawyer and his bodyguard early on in the year, there'd not been a situation in a while where a gun had been used other than to fire warning shots at u-turners or to bag a piece of venison that happened to wander within sight. The incident involving the UN lawyer was an unfortunate day for his bodyguard. Pandi had no participation in the incident but saw much of it from outside the log cabin where he'd been cleaning his rifle. He saw the car stop and the driver approached. The passenger and driver got out. A few minutes later he heard raised voices and then a gunshot. The UN lawyer, a Brazilian, accused the border police of brutality and one in particular, Storen, of cold-blooded murder. The officers supported their colleague by claiming the bodyguard had been aggressive and, after assaulting Storen, reached for a concealed weapon whereupon Storen drew his pistol and shot the man in self-defence. In a bar some weeks later, while consuming two bottles of Rakia, Storen bragged that he hadn't liked the bodyguard and so he killed him. But with so many police statements providing evidence in Storen's favour, the incident would never go to trial. Pandi had submitted one of those statements after being coerced by his brother and uncle.

On this particular day, when the team arrived at the checkpoint, the sun was out and there wasn't a cloud in the sky. Pandi was leaning back against the cabin having a cigarette when an old BMW series 7 with dark tinted windows came into view. No-one recognised it and so it immediately dropped into the category of suspicious. Pandi's uncle was on stopping duty and walked into the road and signalled it to pull over.

The BMW came to a stop and the driver lowered his window.

Pandi's uncle leaned down to look inside. The driver was a heavy set man with a full head of black hair, well dressed and in his fifties. The woman beside him was of a similar age and looking pensive. Someone was in the back but Pandi couldn't make out much detail through the darkened windows.

'Open your windows,' Pandi's uncle ordered. 'All of them.'

The driver pushed several buttons on his console. The windows slid down.

'All the way down,' Pandi's uncle ordered.

'That's as far as they go on this kind of car,' the driver said politely, a forced smile in an effort to show he was friendly.

'Are you sure?' Pandi's uncle asked.

The driver suppressed his sigh and pushed the window control button with pantomime exaggeration in order to prove his point. 'That's as far as they go.'

Pandi's uncle looked at the person in the back. Pandi hovered close behind to get a look. It was a pretty girl in her late teens. 'Are you related?' he asked the man.

'This is my wife and my daughter,' the driver said.

'Papers?' Pandi's uncle asked. 'Everyone's.'

The driver gave him his ID, collected the others and handed them over.

Pandi's uncle went through them, each time comparing the face to the photo. 'How long have you lived in Albania?'

'I've always lived in Albania,' the driver replied.

'Always?'

'I've spent some time in Skopje and Sofia.'

'Macedonia and Bulgaria?'

'Yes. Skopje is the capital of Macedonia and Sofia the capital of Bulgaria.'

Pandi's uncle was quite able to absorb sarcasm without reacting. The comment seemed to increase the woman's discomfort.

'You have an accent,' Pandi's uncle said.

'What kind of accent?' the driver asked.

'A Serbian accent.'

In Albania that was tantamount to an accusation.

'That's rubbish,' the driver said, ruffled.

'Get out of the car,' Pandi's uncle ordered, stepping back.

The exchange had attracted the attention of other officers. It was not that they were particularly interested. Pandi's uncle was known for being antagonistic. Standing around a checkpoint all day was boring. Civilians were entertainment.

When the girl climbed out the officers' interest increased. She was very good looking with long brown hair, slender legs wrapped in tight jeans and a jacket short enough to reveal her pert bottom and open at the front to present a pair of ample breasts inside a tight jumper. She had just about everyone's attention.

'Where did you go to school?' Pandi's uncle asked her.

She was nervous and didn't answer.

'Doesn't she speak?'

'You frighten her,' the father replied. 'Tell him where you went to school. Don't be frightened. He thinks it's his job to be scary and insulting.'

The girl took the advice and stiffened. 'Qemal Stafa high school,' she said.

'Tirana?'

'Yes,' she said.

'You sound Serbian too,' Pandi's uncle said, much to the amusement of the officers.

One of them stepped forward. Jeton was his name. 'We'll talk with her separately,' he said, giving his colleagues a wink. 'Come here.'

The girl didn't like the invitation and looked at her father. He didn't like it either but indicated for her to obey them.

She held her jacket closed in a nervous, protective manner as she walked over to Jeton. All the border officers were looking at her, including Pandi, who had forgotten about his uncle.

'Open your boot,' Pandi's uncle commanded.

The father did as he was told. Pandi's uncle inspected the contents. The father looked at the officer with his daughter who was joined by another. They asked her a question and as she answered they eyed her up and down. One of them felt her hair. She pulled away.

The father didn't like what he was seeing but Pandi's uncle distracted him. 'Lift up the spare tyre,' he asked. 'I want to look underneath.'

The father removed the rug that covered the spare wheel.

'Take off your jacket,' Jeton said to the girl.

She refused, holding her jacket closed tightly.

'I said take off your jacket.'

'What are you hiding under there?' another officer said, amused by his wit as he mimicked her boobs to his appreciative audience.

'Come on, let's take a look,' Jeton said, tugging at her jacket.

She held onto it.

'If you don't take it off, we'll rip it off you.'

She refused.

He prodded her. 'Take it off I said!' He gave her a gentle slap on the side of her head. 'It will only get worse for you if you disobey us.'

She continued to refuse. He hit her on the head a little harder. She yelped. Pandi's smile faded, suddenly feeling sorry for the girl.

Her father took a step towards her but Pandi's uncle grabbed his coat. 'Stay,' he warned.

The father tried to yank free. Storen took out his pistol and pointed it at the father's face. 'Stay where you are.'

The father obeyed and watched the officers struggle with his daughter's jacket. 'Leave her!' he shouted. 'Savages!'

They succeeded in pulling it open. The girl dropped to her knees as they yanked it off completely. 'What are you hiding, bitch!' Jeton shouted.

'Pull off her jacket,' someone cried.

'Let's see her tits.'

'Take her trousers down.'

Pandi wanted to help her but it was pointless to try. His uncle and brother would be angry and so he just watched.

They lifted her up as if trying to get her to stand. She screamed and kicked out wildly. As she wriggled, she slid down until her breasts were jammed above Jeton's arms, much to the amusement of the others. The father wanted to go to her, but Storen threatened him with his pistol.

The border patrol commander stepped out of the cabin wondering what all the commotion was. He saw the girl struggling, the others laughing, and Storen aiming a pistol at the head of a civilian. 'What the hell is going on?' he called out.

'They're Serbian spies,' someone replied, prompting laughter.

What happened next was beyond surreal.

Jeton's head suddenly exploded! Blood and brains spurted in all directions. A bullet entered one side of his head and came out the other taking his brains with it. The only sound was a sharp, loud slap. The life went out of his limbs and he dropped to the ground in a crumpled heap. His head was shattered.

Some of the officers dropped to the ground while others remained frozen where they stood. Everyone was trying to process what had just happened.

The first managed response was from Pandi's uncle who snatched his pistol from its holster and aimed it at the father as he shuffled away from him, fully expecting to find a smoking gun in the man's hands. But both hands were empty. He switched to the mother, shuffling his feet as he'd practiced many times on the range, knees bent, bottom out in a sitting position, arms reaching in front of him, both hands clenching the pistol. The woman was standing with her mouth agape in utter horror, staring at the dead officer who's skull she'd seen explode. Her hands were empty and shaking.

The silence was broken by the girl's high-pitched scream, blood and pieces of brain splattered across her face. Heads snapped around, searching in all directions, all wondering where the shot had come from. Hands reached for guns, bodies crouched, torsos twisted on heels, fingers on triggers.

It seemed longer than sixteen seconds before the next bullet arrived. It struck the other officer who'd been holding the girl, entering the back of his head just above the neck and exiting through his nose. He dropped like a discarded puppet.

'It came from there,' the commander shouted, pointing towards the wooded hillside to the west. 'There!'

Everyone scrambled for cover except the mother who was catatonic, her eyes glued to Jeton's shattered head. An officer grabbed the girl and dragged her to the cabin. The father stumbled back into his car before realising his wife was just standing there. He yelled at her to get in. She didn't respond. He pulled himself across the passenger seat, reached out the door, grabbed the bottom of her coat and pulled her inside.

The other officers all found a tree to hide behind.

'Pandi!' Pandi's uncle shouted. 'Get down!'

Pandi realised he hadn't moved and scrambled as quickly as he could to a tree where he hugged the base of it.

'Anybody see a shooter?' the commander shouted.

No-one had a clue. The ground to the west of the clearing went sharply downhill from the edge of the clearing for eighty metres to a narrow gully before turning steeply back uphill for another thousand. The first few hundred metres were bracken and shrubbery turning into uncultivated woodland the rest of the way to the top.

'They must be in the woods,' someone shouted.

The commander peeked around his tree as much as he dared to get a look. 'Did anyone see anything?' he shouted. 'Anything at all?'

Silence followed.

'Does everyone have their rifles?' he shouted.

'I don't,' an officer called out, his pistol in hand.

'Me neither,' shouted another.

Pandi realised he didn't have his weapon. 'Mine's in the cabin,' he shouted. 'It's with my body armour.'

'It's no good to you there, is it?' the commander yelled.

'So's mine,' another shouted.

'Go get it,' one of the officers called out.

'I'll get shot, you idiot,' came the reply.

The commander considered the situation and came to a conclusion. 'It was a long shot from that wood. The targets were standing still. No-one can hit a moving target from there.'

'He's right,' one of the others said. 'They won't be able to shoot you if you run.'

The officer without his rifle, Eni, absorbed their comments. He wanted his weapon, not badly enough to get shot, but he felt he needed to show he wasn't afraid.

'Go on, Eni,' a colleague shouted encouragingly.

'You can do it, Eni,' another called out.

'Fuck you all!' Eni shouted. But he wanted to do it anyway. He blew out his cheeks in an effort to get himself ready. He could see the sense in the argument that no-one would be able to shoot him from so far away if he ran. 'I'm going for my rifle,' he announced.

Everyone looked at him. He was nervous but confident.

'I need to get mine too,' another announced. 'It's in the truck.'

'Go at the same time,' the commander called out. 'You'll confuse the shooters.'

'If they're still there, which I doubt,' Pandi's uncle offered.

'I agree,' the commander said. 'They will have run by now.'

The assumptions only increased the general confidence of the runners. Both tensed in preparation.

'Ready?' Eni called out. 'Go!'

The two men propelled themselves forward. The one heading for the truck had taken hardly a second step before a bullet struck the side of his body, in the ribcage below his armpit, tearing through him and dragging tissue and blood out the other side. His legs buckled, he collapsed to the ground and after several spasms he lay still, his eyes open.

Eni had seen his colleague go down and put the brakes on. Panic set in. He couldn't decide whether to go on or turn back.

'Keep going!' the commander shouted.

Eni half turned, changed his mind and took off towards the cabin. It was unlikely that either selection would've saved him. The distant crack announced the arrival of the bullet that slapped through Eni's neck severing the vertebrae and he hit the ground.

Everyone was stunned. They pressed themselves tighter into their trees. One started to pray. Another began to cry.

The commander pressed his forehead against his tree, afraid to look towards where he thought the shots had come from. 'Did anyone see anything?' he asked.

'I saw Eni and Marko shot while they were running,' came a reply.

'No-one move,' the commander ordered. 'Stay where you are.'

'No shit,' someone else muttered.

'He can see me here,' an officer shouted.

The commander was unable to see him from where he was. 'Who said that?' he called out.

'It's me. Duno.' He waved briefly. He was beside one of the cars. The front of it was facing the shooter and he was down one side between the wheels.

'You're fine,' the commander shouted.

'No I'm not,' Duno shouted back. 'It's alright for you to say.'

'If he could see you, he would shoot you,' the commander argued. 'You're good where you are.'

Duno wasn't buying it. 'That's what you told the others and look what happened to them!'

Duno reached up, gripped the door handle and unlatched it, opening it a little. So far, so good.

He opened the door fully, crawled onto the seats, twisted onto his back, hooked his foot under the door handle and pulled it shut. He made it.

A shot rang out, striking the car with a metallic slap. The door eased open and Duno's feet fell out limply.

'Duno?!' the commander shouted.

There was no reply.

The commander felt utterly trapped. He checked the signal on his cell-phone even though he knew there'd be none. The only radios they had were short range. He was going to have to wait until it was safe and then send someone up the road to where they could get a signal and report the incident to headquarters.

Pandi hugged the base of his tree where he planned to stay until it was dark. The girl was still sobbing as she lay on the ground against the cabin. She wanted to join her parents in the BMW. The vile border police were as much a threat to her as whoever was shooting at them. They were going to rape her, or worse. None of them were taking any notice of her. She got to her knees and into the sprint position. An officer nearby happened to look at her and realised her intentions.

'No!' he shouted.

His warning had the opposite effect. She leapt forward. The officer managed to dive and grab her leg. She fell as he hung on and fought to pull away. His grip slipped to her foot. She cried out, unable to go any further.

They all looked towards her as she called out. The officer holding her was also exposed. He suddenly realised his vulnerability, released her and scrambled back to cover. She took off towards the BMW, ripped open the door and dived inside into her father's arms.

The commander had the same thought as the rest of his men. The officer hadn't been shot which meant the shooters had gone. He needed to get on their trail as soon as possible. There was no time to lose. First thing was to find the ambush location. Before he could get started of course, he had to be sure the ambushers had indeed gone. That meant someone stepping out of cover. That someone was going to have to be him. He couldn't order one of his men to stand in the open. They'd refuse and ask him to do it anyway. He had to accept the responsibility. The only other option was to remain where they were until darkness.

'Throw me your rifle,' he said to an officer hidden behind a pile of logs.

The commander holstered his pistol. The officer held his rifle in both hands and threw it. The commander caught it neatly.

He checked the gun was loaded and the sights set on maximum range. He stepped back from the tree while remaining behind it, put the butt into his shoulder, aimed at the woods and shuffled back. He was partially exposed. He fired a dozen shots at various parts of the woodland. The gun was deafening and hurt his ears but when no fire was returned his confidence increased.

He shuffled from side to side, exposing more of himself and then went for it. Keeping the weapon aimed at the wood, he bravely stepped away from the tree and moved to where he was in the open. He scanned the woodland through the weapon sight, beads of sweat forming on his brow. With every passing second he became convinced the attackers had made good their escape.

'It's clear,' he shouted.

No-one else moved. Not immediately. A couple poked their heads from cover to search the hillside. Pandi decided not to look just yet. Confidence increased throughout the others that the ambushers had indeed fled the scene. One of them stepped from cover. Then another. Pandi decided he didn't want to be the last and eased into the open.

The commander went to the nearest victim to see if he might be alive. 'Check the others,' he ordered.

It was pretty obvious they were dead. Three had their brains shot away and the eyes of the other one were open, his tongue hanging out.

Pandi's uncle opened the door to the police car to see his nephew lying dead inside. Pandi joined him to look at his brother. His uncle put a hand on his shoulder to comfort him. Pandi wasn't particularly close to his older brother. But they were brothers after all. He would have to tell their mother. She'd be devastated. He was her favourite.

'Close in everyone,' the commander ordered. His officers made their way to him. He looked towards the BMW, unable to see the family inside. 'Hey. You inside the car.'

The driver's door opened and the father looked at him without getting out of his seat.

'You stay there,' the commander ordered. 'Don't go. I have your vehicle details. If you drive away you will be considered an accessory to this and hunted down.'

The father knew well enough to take the commander seriously.

'Now listen in,' the commander said, facing his men. 'We have experienced a great atrocity here today. Two things must happen immediately. Someone must drive to where there is a phone signal and report what has happened and get a response team down here right away. The other thing that must happen is we have to find the ambush position and in which direction the ambushers went. We have to find out as much as we can so that when the response teams arrive they can immediately start to track them down. Is that understood?'

None of them said a word.

'I can go make the call,' Pandi's uncle offered.

'No,' the commander said. 'I need you to help search for the ambushers. Pandi is the youngest and least experienced so he can go and make the call.'

'I'd rather help search for the ambushers,' Pandi said.

'And last time I checked I was in command here and you will do as you are ordered. Let me tell you all one thing in case you have not considered it. This is going to be the most high profile incident that has happened to this force in many years. I can't even think of anything like it, other than during war time. Everything that happens, every action we take, every word we say will be recorded and examined by every authority in the country, all the way to the top. Is that understood? So from this moment on, stay sharp, do your duty and keep your mouths shut unless you are asked.'

Judging by the expressions that faced him, the commander was satisfied his exhortation had been well received. 'Okay then. Let's get organised. All of you get your gear. Make sure your weapons are ready for use. We're going up the hill to search those woods. Go!'

'Do we have to wear our body armour?' one of them asked. 'It's very heavy and that's a steep hill to climb.'

'What would you prefer if someone starts shooting at you?' the commander asked sarcastically.

The man shrugged, not looking entirely convinced. 'The ambushers have gone,' he said.

'Idiot! Go! Wear your armour!'

The men walked off.

'Shall I take the car or the truck?' Pandi asked.

'The car. And have all of your equipment. Make sure you have your weapons ready. Look sharp. Do you know who you are going to talk to?'

'Our headquarters.' Pandi shrugged as if it was obvious.

'Who?'

Pandi shrugged again, this time because he wasn't sure.

'The highest possible rank you can find. And what will you tell them?'

'That this happened. Five of our men shot dead by unknown ambushers.'

'Correct. Ensure you report that I am in immediate pursuit and that we need as much support as possible. Tell them to send the army. Remind them that as we are near the border the attack could involve foreign nationals.'

'You mean it could have been Serbians?'

'Anything is possible. But don't say that in your report. We have no idea who it was until we find evidence. Get going.'

Pandi hurried off to get his gear while the commander joined the others who were ready to go. He was handed his body armour which he pulled over his head, grabbed his rifle and walked to the edge of the clearing that opened up to the vista. 'Move out! In a line!'

The men got into position either side of him.

'We walk down to the bottom then up the other side. When we reach the trees I'll give fresh orders. Keep your eyes open. Concentrate. We're looking for any signs. If you see fresh tracks or anything you think could be evidence, call out and we'll stop and assess what we have. Any questions?'

The men were looking at the ground ahead, some thinking about the hard work it represented, others worried about meeting the killers.

'Let's go,' the commander ordered and he set off down the slope.

Pandi left the cabin with his gear and headed for the police car. He glanced over at the BMW to see the father sitting in the open door. As Pandi reached his vehicle there was a single, sharp gunshot. His immediate thought was that his colleagues had engaged the ambushers. He heard voices. Shouting. There was a scream of extreme anguish.

Pandi dropped his stuff except for his rifle and ran to where he could look down on the others. They were halfway down the slope, in short shrubbery, scurrying around. One of them was lying still, face down in bracken.

Another shot echoed across the open ground and one of the men flew back as a bullet blew out between his shoulder blades. The others started to run back up the hill the way they'd come.

Pandi felt helpless. He aimed his rifle at the woods but couldn't see anything to shoot at. Another shot rang out and another officer fell dead. Three seconds later a shot killed one more.

Pandi considered running to the car and driving off to get help as the commander had ordered. But that would mean deserting his colleagues. That was one of the things his brother and uncle had lectured him on; the patrol was a family. Everyone looked after each other. That meant not only drinking together but also fighting together.

He looked down the slope to see two men left – his uncle and the commander. They still had a way to go to reach the top. He knew what he had to do.

He ran to the truck, scrambled into the back and to the PKM machinegun. It wasn't loaded. An ammunition box was on the floor. His hands trembling, he ripped it open, pulled out the long belt of linked bullets, raised the top cover, slapped the bullets onto the feed tray, dropped the cover, wiggled the bullets because the tray wouldn't shut properly, raised the cover a little, adjusted the bullets, slammed the cover back down where it clipped into place. He pulled back the cocking lever against its heavy spring, aimed at the trees and pulled the trigger! The burst of power shook the weapon and his entire body as bullets spat loudly towards the woodland and empty casings flew into the air around him. The sound was deafening. He was on full automatic, like the weapon. He kept hold of the trigger, letting loose an endless stream of copper coated lead, holding on with all his strength. He could see branches snapping and bits of debris flying up as bullets ravaged the trees. All he could hope for was to distract the ambushers enough for the others to get back to the top of the slope. If he was lucky he might hit one of them. Every fifth bullet was a tracer that shot into the wood like a laser, lasting a couple of seconds.

Pandi was unable to see that the commander and his uncle were already dead, face down in the bracken with holes in their backs. The commander had managed to get within a few metres of the top of the slope before being hit.

Pandi reached the end of the belt and everything went silent. His blood was up and he wanted to continue. He would keep firing until he ran out of ammunition or the men appeared. He grabbed the remaining belt from the box, loaded the tray and pulled the cocking lever back. As he gripped the trigger a bullet slammed into his chest and he flew back onto the bed hitting it hard.

Pandi lay there looking at the sky, trying to breathe. He knew he'd been shot. It burned like hell. He could feel liquid filling his throat and began to choke on it. He coughed, spurting blood from his mouth and the hole in his chest. It was filling his lungs. And suddenly he couldn't breathe. He was drowning. Within seconds it went dark. Pandi lay still, his glazed eyes open. Blood trickled from his mouth.

The father in the BMW had watched Pandi throughout his last half minute of life. When silence fell he reached for the ignition key and turned it. The engine gunned to life. He floored the accelerator and fishtailed across the dirt until the tyres reached the road and tore along it.

Chapter 4

Bethan Trencher faced the full-length mirror in her bedroom and examined herself in her black business suit. On the bed was a suitcase filled with enough comfy clothes to last a week, notably devoid of socialising garb. Scrummy jumpers, pyjamas and thick, long socks. She placed it on the floor, smoothed over the bed cover, checked all was in order, picked up the case and left the room.

She stepped into another room, a spare bedroom turned office. A wall was covered in pictures, notes, sketches, pieces of cloth, all connected by a complex web of coloured strings. It was the pictures that were disturbing. Young girls mostly, smiling, posing, selfies, happy, disfigured, mutilated, bloody and dead. At the top of the matrix was a man in his thirties.

Clenching her teeth she ripped his picture down and screwed it up as if crushing his very soul, folding and pressing it until her fingers hurt. She tossed it inside a black plastic bag and tore at the rest of the matrix, pulling it off in chunks. She worked with enthusiasm and aggression in order to remove every little piece of it.

She took a deep breath when it was over. But it wasn't over. That would come later in the day.

She left the room, carried the suitcase down the stairs, grabbed her laptop bag and a box of files and left the house. It was a bright afternoon in Hampstead. Leaves were shoved around by a gentle breeze as she put her stuff into her car, climbed in and drove off. Two hours later, she was sitting in a packed courtroom near the Aldwych. Beside her was her boss, Detective Chief Inspector Andrew Dillon, brow furrowed as he concentrated on the proceedings. Bethan was staring at the man in the dock, his hands chained. It was the man in the picture at the top of her matrix.

'You are an evil man, to be sure,' the judge said. 'There is no place for you in civilised society, nor is there any likelihood of that being the case in the future. This court sentences you to whole life imprisonment without possibility of parole.'

The sentence was met with stony silence. It was no surprise to anyone. Bethan was satisfied and sighed deeply without realising how loud she'd been. DCI Dillon put a gentle hand on hers. Bethan wasn't sure if it was intended to calm her or to share a moment of victory. She wanted to stand up and applaud and wondered whether, if she did, how many people would join her.

Bethan was more than ready to leave when the court was dismissed. She wanted to get on the road, away from the City and into the countryside. She could already taste the solitude. As she headed along a corridor towards the main entrance, she heard her name being called. It was Dillon. He was doing his official bit, chatting with various people, receiving plaudits and discussing police business but he wanted to speak to her.

'Well done,' he said, genuinely cheerful. 'Your father would have been very proud.'

'Thanks,' she said. She appreciated the comment.

'Enjoy your week.'

'I will.' And she headed out the door.

Five hours later, Bethan was driving along a narrow lane that burrowed its way into Dartmoor. There was wide open countryside as far as the eye could see in every direction with pockets of trees behind her and nothing but moorland in her windscreen.

She turned onto a gravelly lane that curved down into a dip where a neat old farmhouse nestled surrounded by a dry stone wall. The place was well maintained, made easy by its simple stone paths, gravel surrounds and indigenous flora. It had long since given up its farming status in exchange for private residence. Rain speckled her windshield as she drove inside a former stable and turned off the engine. Silence descended. And with it came a sense of relief. Isolation at last. Freedom.

There were still some minor adjustments needed before the transition was complete. A change of clothes. A roaring fire. Add a glass of whisky and she would have truly arrived. She sighed in anticipation. A week off with nothing to do but long walks, books, finishing the report – which she kind of enjoyed – and read a new case file.

There was something obvious missing of course. Companionship. Bethan pushed the thought aside before it took hold, dragged the suitcase out of the boot along with a bag of groceries and headed through the light shower to the house. Within an hour she was plonked in front of a crackling fire wearing pyjamas, a thick jumper, woolly sock slippers and clutching a glass of whisky. She made herself comfortable on the rug, exhaled deeply, inhaled the moment and began the process of exorcising the serial killer from her bones.

She hadn't realised how deeply tired she was until she woke up in darkness several hours later. The fire had gone out and she was cold. She picked up the empty whisky glass, the contents of which no doubt contributed to her snooze, put the contents of what was supposed to have been supper in the fridge and trudged off to the bedroom. Within minutes she was under a thick duvet and ready to sleep. She questioned why she was lying on one side of the double bed and forced herself into the middle in an effort to make it feel normal. But it didn't.

Stop thinking about everything, she told herself as she curled into a ball, closed her eyes and concentrated on clearing her mind.

Chapter 5

Gunnymede sat comfortably in a shallow scrape wrapped in a camouflaged windproof with a thick fleece lining. An icy wind roamed an ocean of sand to the horizon in every direction, like lumbering waves, frozen still but for the fine spray that left their crests. He was wearing a military issue Davy Crocket bonnet with long, woolly ears against the relentless granules riding the northwest Shamal and pelting his face. Stars were everywhere, all the way to the ground, as if he was inside a vast snow-dome. There was a man-made addition to the heavenly display. A light show coming from the west. Miles away, someone was getting a pounding. Sharp flashes. Silent explosions. On a still night a rumble might've been heard, but not with the Shamal blowing.

A figure trudged towards Gunnymede's back. Gunnymede reached for his pack and pulled out a sand-coloured metal flask. He filled a cup with tepid coffee and took a sip as Granger plonked himself down and placed his assault rifle across his lap with an exaggerated sigh.

Gunnymede handed him the cup.

'All good in every direction,' Granger announced, taking a sip. 'No sign of a sandstorm either. Not that those buggers can't appear in a minute of course.' He looked west through his thermal imager. 'That glow's the village on the sat phot, right?'

'Must be.'

'Could be some nomads set up camp.'

'I think it's the village.'

'I think you're right,' Granger said, taking another sip before handing the cup back to Gunnymede. He pulled out a single meal ration pack, tore it open, dug a plastic spoon into it and savoured it. 'Boring, boring, boring,' he said as he took a plastic box from a pocket and spooned some powdery spices over the meal.

Gunnymede watched with curiosity as Granger sampled it again.

'That's better – want some?'

'I'm good, thanks.'

'Your loss. I'm a master field chef.'

'Then I'd better try some,' Gunnymede said, more out of politeness than curiosity.

Granger filled the fork and handed it to Gunnymede who nibbled at it as if he was an official taster. 'Very entertaining. Do I detect a suspicion of tarragon?'

'The man knows 'is 'erbs,' Granger said, pleased with himself. 'These Yank meals are good but they can get a bit bland. I like my spices. Bit heavy on the turmeric though,' Granger decided after another taste.

'Good for inflammations.'

'Indeed,' Granger agreed and sat back to watch the distant flashing light show as he ate. 'Must be Homs.'

'Probably.'

'Pretty, isn't it? I mean, I know some poor rag 'ead is getting a beating but, you know what I mean. Syria's version of the northern lights,' he quipped with a chuckle. 'What's it called?'

'Aurora.'

'That's it. Aurora ... bore ...'

'Borealis.'

'That's it.'

Gunnymede couldn't see the pretty but there was no accounting for tastes. 'Where's your accent from?' he asked.

'I'm a local lad.'

'Syrian?'

'Fuck off. Hereford. Born within sight of Lord Hereford's Knob.'

Gunnymede hadn't a clue.

'It's a prominent erection in the Brecons,' Granger explained.

'So you always wanted to join the Regiment?'

'I s'pose.'

'What was your parent unit?'

'1 Para. Four years. Did selection eight years ago. Time flies.'

'Depends what you're doing with it,' Granger mumbled. 'So what do you reckon? About this lot?'

'What lot?

'Saleem?'

'I don't know.'

'Come on. You're the int man. This is your op. I'm just your baby sitter. You must know something.'

'I don't know anything more about Saleem than you do.'

'Bollocks.'

'He talks to some Russian dude. We don't know who or what he talks about. That's why we're here.'

Granger shook his head. 'That doesn't make any sense. We must have an idea what he's talking about and that it's bloody important enough for us to be here.'

'Very true,' Gunnymede said. 'But my point is, I don't know.'

'So why does he come here regularly to the same location to make a phone call? I mean, why the same place? It's a sat signal. He can talk from anywhere. He doesn't have to drive all the way out here?'

'Validation.'

'What?'

'If he makes the call from a predetermined location it confirms to the recipient who the caller is. Not many people can make a call from the middle of the Syrian dessert these days.'

Granger thought about it. 'Makes sense I s'pose. But whoever he's calling would need to be able to locate the exact position of the sat phone.'

'Correct.'

'And to do that you'd need sophisticated IT which would suggest a government.'

'Or someone who has access to state technology.'

'Why doesn't he call from anywhere and just send a code?'

'He probably does. Two-step verification. The code plus the location verifies it's Saleem.'

'And how do we know when he's coming out here?' Granger asked. 'We know every time he leaves his compound to come on one of these secret chats.'

'No idea how that triggers. We must have a friendly somewhere.'

'Okay. But why this Saleem bloke? He's nothing but a low ranking Daesh foot soldier. He's like the equivalent of a corporal. His commanders live in the same camp as him. Why aren't his bosses talking to this Russian? I mean. Who the hell is Saleem?'

'A conundrum to be sure.'

'Shh!' Granger's eyes darted to the sky. He removed his hat to hear better.

Gunnymede looked skywards as he concentrated.

'That's air,' Granger said.

The sound grew. They got to their feet, hoping to see something amongst the millions of stars.

'Not a drone?' Gunnymede said.

'No. That's a fighter.'

They followed the sound as it moved in a wide circle around them.

'This patch is out of bounds while we're in it,' Granger said. 'They can't be friendlies.'

The rumble continued to move around them.

'There,' Gunnymede said. 'Orion's Belt.'

Granger found the constellation. 'Seen. Two fighters.'

They watched the planes continue to circle.

'They're hunting,' Granger said.

Half a minute later the gentle roar grew quieter. Seconds later the only sound was the wind playing with the sand.

The men sat back into their scrapes.

'Russians having a sniff about I expect,' Granger said checking his watch. 'Three and a half hours till first light.'

'More coffee?'

'Why not.' Granger produced a packet of cigarettes while Gunnymede opened the flask. Granger lit his fag using a tactical lighter and blew out the smoke, savouring it.

'Can I have one of those?' Gunnymede asked.

'Didn't know you smoked.'

'Only on special occasions. And when I'm pissed.'

Granger offered him one and they sat back and enjoyed the moment.

'Your first time in the sand box?' Granger asked.

'In the field, yeah.'

'More adept at five star hotels and long legged spies I expect.'

55

Gunnymede glanced at him, realising the man had no idea about his recent past. 'I wish.'

'I trained some of your lot down the Fort last year. Pistol and SMG work.'

'I haven't been there in a while.' Gunnymede had a thought. 'Do you know a 22 lad called Charlie Gibson? Former I should say. G squadron. He used to do some training for us at the Fort.'

'Gibbo? Yeah, I know Charlie. He's been out a few years now. Bit of a wide boy but a good enough lad.'

'I bumped into him in London the other day. We didn't have time for much of a chat. Do you know what he's up to these days?'

'No idea what Charlie does these days.'

Gunnymede drew on the cigarette. 'What about Jack Henderson?'

'Former Sergeant Major, G Squadron. Knew him well enough to say hello. I heard something happened to his daughter. She was attacked or something.'

Granger noticed Gunnymede pondering. 'You knew her?'

'Yeah. I went to visit her in hospital.'

'She alright?'

'No.'

Granger sensed something in Gunnymede's tone. 'Knew her well then, did you?'

'Yeah. Charlie was there.'

'At the hospital?'

'I can't imagine why though.'

Granger took a draw of his fag and blew the smoke out after holding it in for a while. 'Was Charlie there to see her or you?'

'Me, I think.'

'How'd you leave it with him?'

'I wasn't in the mood to talk.'

Granger studied Gunnymede for a moment. 'All I'd say is tread carefully with that one.'

'Why?'

'It might be your cup of tea or maybe it ain't.'

'I don't understand.'

'It doesn't matter.'

Gunnymede wanted to know what he meant. 'He said the police have a suspect. But the police say they haven't.'

Granger drew on his cigarette while he mulled over something.

'Why would he say such a thing?' Gunnymede asked. 'That's why I asked what he was up to. Would he say such a thing if it wasn't true?'

'What was she to you?' Granger asked.

'Megan was my girlfriend.'

'Seriously?'

'We were engaged.'

Granger let out a deep sigh and tossed the butt of his cigarette. 'I see. Daughter of a SAS man would do it. Girlfriend of a field spy would back it up.'

'Do what?'

'Ah. It's just a rumour.'

'Come on Granger. Don't play about.'

Granger took a moment to consider his next words. 'You ever heard of the Becket Approval?'

Gunnymede looked at him. 'I heard the phrase some years ago. I don't know what it means though.'

'Ask Charlie. He'd know.' Granger sat up and put his hand out for quiet.

'What would Charlie know?'

'Shhhh!,' Granger urged. 'Here we go!'

The rumble of vehicle engines drifted to them on the wind. Granger scanned the darkness with his thermal imager and found the source a kilometre away. The heat from the wheels and engines outlined the vehicles. All lights were off, driving by starlight.

'Two vehicles,' Granger reported getting to his feet. 'Looks like the little bastard's arrived. Get the drone up.'

Gunnymede jumped up, removed a large plastic box from his pack and opened it to reveal a drone in pieces. He snap-clipped the rotor arms to the body, attached a swivel camera to the underside, unfolded the slender legs and rested it on the sand.

Granger watched the vehicles draw closer, the engines growing louder. They passed a hundred metres across their front. A Land Cruiser and a Hilux. The Hilux came to a stop and the Land Cruiser continued on for another fifty or so metres before stopping.

All engines went dead.

'Right on station,' Granger said. 'Don't we just love creatures of habit?'

Gunnymede flicked a switch on the drone and the propellers hummed to life. A touch of the joy stick and the drone rose off the ground into the night sky and disappeared amongst the stars, sight and sound.

Granger kept his eyes on the vehicles. 'Bods climbing out the Hilux. No movement on the Cruiser.'

Gunnymede hit a memory key on his sat phone and plugged his throat mic into it. A moment later a short buzz indicated a connection.

'Charlie, Charlie. We're green, green,' Gunnymede said as he piloted the drone while watching a bird's eye thermal image of the vehicles on the console monitor.

Eleven hundred and fifty miles south east of their position, the Dubai operations room displayed the drone's view on a massive screen filling a high wall of a modern military operations room packed with electronics. The image occupied one section of the multi-split screen, the others showing weather fronts, aircraft patterns and an eye in the sky of the operational area pinpointing Gunnymede and Granger's position using graphics. Half a dozen personnel managed the room, five British and an American female colonel, all wearing military fatigues, most of them busy in front of computers.

There was one other person in the room, at the back, in the shadows, detached, observing; Neve Murray, pretty woman dressed in civvies. She looked up from her coffee as Gunnymede's voice broke the silence, smiling thinly to herself as she focused on the satellite view of the two operators, pinpricks in a sea of sand.

'That's a de-bus,' Gunnymede said.

A dozen thermal figures climbed out of the rear vehicle. Several moved away to urinate, the warm liquid outlined as it pooled before soaking into the sand. The heads of others suddenly flared as if exploding as they ignited cigarettes. A couple set about making a fire.

'Do you have the drone?' Gunnymede asked.

'Acquired,' a controller replied.

'Anything on those aircraft a few minutes ago?' Granger asked.

'Russians,' the British SAS Major who was operations officer said. 'They're still in the sector.'

'We good to continue?' Granger asked.

'Affirmative. Let's do it,' the ops officer said.

'The drone's all yours,' Gunnymede said.

'Let's take a look at the lead vehicle,' the ops officer said to the drone operator.

The drone operator moved a joystick and the drone's point of view shifted from the Hilux to the Land Cruiser.

Granger and Gunnymede made cursory checks of pouches and pockets, reminding hands where spare magazine and toys were stowed. Grenades were felt, release catches thumbed. Pistols touched.

'You good to go?' Granger asked.

'Yes.'

Granger gave Gunnymede a look.

'What?' Gunnymede asked.

'You up for this? Could get nasty.'

'I'd rather be buying a drink for a long legged spy in the American Colony in Jerusalem.'

Granger smiled. 'I'd rather be 'ere,' he said as he touched his throat mic. 'Green green is foxtrot.'

'Roger that,' the Ops Officer replied.

Granger moved off at an easy pace, Gunnymede behind and to one side. The surface of the higher ground they occupied had a hard, wind-packed crust with softer sand beneath it. Some parts were thick enough to support a man's weight while others gave way, their feet breaking through to the soft sand below up to their knees.

By the time they dropped down onto hard packed ground between the dunes the vehicles had gone out of sight. They slowed as they closed on the edge of a rise. The Land Cruiser came into view. The wind continued to be the only sound as they stepped into the open. The Hilux was in view further away, the men standing around the fire focused on making a brew. None would be able to see Gunnymede and Granger even if they looked straight at them, their night vision blanked by the fire.

Granger paused to study the Cruiser through his imager. 'Two occupants. Driver plus one in back,' he reported.

'Red for Charlie,' a voice came over Gunnymede's earpiece from the Dubai operations room. 'They're on comms now.'

'You want me to take out the driver?' Granger asked Gunnymede.

'I'll manage.'

'And if Saleem doesn't want to come?'

'He'll come.'

'And if he doesn't?'

'I'll whack him and grab the gear.'

'Don't get into a conversation with him.'

'We had this discussion back in Dubai,' Gunnymede complained.

'Just making sure. You ready?'

'Yes.'

They brought their rifles into their shoulders, placed their fingers on the triggers and walked towards the Cruiser. The wind picked up a little. The cab light was on. The driver was turned in his seat to face the man in the rear.

As Gunnymede reached for the door a voice came over his earplugs stopping him dead.

'Red, red! Aircraft! Standby!' It was one of the controllers in Dubai, her voice betraying her concern.

Granger and Gunnymede looked at each other and then skyward.

'Two birds,' the ops controller continued. 'Turning towards your location.'

Their ears picked up the sound of the jets above the wind. Getting louder. The Land Cruiser's doors opened and the two men scrambled out to look skyward. Daesh fighters were very sensitive to threats from the air. The sound of aircraft was the herald of death to them.

The one who'd climbed out of the back suddenly realised someone was nearby. He turned to look directly at Gunnymede. It was Saleem. Their eyes met above Gunnymede's rifle barrel.

A thunderous explosion wiped out the Hilux in a massive fireball. The Cruiser was next. Everyone ran for their very lives.

There was no cover in any direction. Just sand. Distance was Gunnymede's only hope. The vehicle was the bomb magnet. The further he could run from it the greater his chance of survival. Every metre counted. But each pace felt like slow motion. As if he was running through molasses. He pulled his knees up and slammed his toes down, one step after the other, thrusting as hard as he could. But it all seemed too damned slow.

The missile struck the Cruiser, penetrating the roof and detonating inside. The explosion ripped it apart like paper, sending it somersaulting into the air in a fireball. The shockwave followed, radiating in a widening circle towards the fleeing men.

The tip of the wave caught Gunnymede and flicked him up off the ground like an insect. He somersaulted several times before landing hard, bouncing and rolling until he came to a stop. Shrapnel zinged past, ricocheting off the ground around him. Debris followed, landing in chunks.

He lay on his back, breathing hard. He wondered how badly he was hurt. He couldn't be certain his head was still attached to his body. He felt no pain. Just disconnected from life and hanging by a thread of consciousness. He could see the stars. Not clearly. A blur. His eyes blinked against the flecks of sand blowing into them. And then, as if a dimmer switch to his mind was slowly turned down, everything darkened. The last thing was a high-pitched ringing in his ears before it all went dark.

Neve got to her feet, horrified as the screen flashed where the Land Cruiser had been, figures moving away from it in different directions. When the screen recovered from the burst of light there were heat signatures dotted around the large one which was the cruiser. It was impossible to say which was Gunnymede. One thing they all had in common. None was moving.

Chapter 6

Gunnymede jolted back to consciousness as hands harshly gripped the length of his body. He was being carried. His bearers were in a hurry. Laboured breathing came from above as he was ferried over rugged terrain. A leg was dropped, his heel dragging along the ground before being picked up. He tried to open his eyes but the sun directly above was too bright. His body felt like a lifeless hulk attached to his brain. His backside hit a bump as they went up a rise. A voice barked in Arabic and Gunnymede was jolted higher, the voice as urgent as the pace.

The sun disappeared as they went into shadow. He could see the faces of those carrying him. Dark-skinned, bearded males. Children amongst them were trying to help. The men shuffled along, out of breath but undeterred. Intermittent structures broke up the light. Mud walls. Corrugated metal roofs. Reed fences. It suddenly went much darker and cooler as he was taken inside and lowered onto a rug on the earth floor.

The men stood back and watched him. A soft word was spoken here and there as they waited. Gunnymede fought against his weakness and struggled to lean onto an elbow. He squeezed his eyes, trying to get them to focus. They began to improve. About half a dozen men were standing inside the small hut. Arabs. Villagers. Poor, grubby, emaciated people. Curious children squeezed between their legs to look at the stranger. An elder shooed them out.

The men's demeanour conveyed concern as well as curiosity. Gunnymede could also sense their fear. He took a moment to gather himself. To think. He put himself in Syria, on the operation. The drone. Dubai. The Daesh vehicles. The helicopter flight and drop off. Saleem. The air attack.

The pieces fell into place.

He went through the events that led to the attack. Remembered running before the Land Cruiser exploded. 'Granger,' he said out loud.

Gunnymede looked around, behind the men's legs, hoping to see his partner. 'Where ...?' he started to ask, but his throat was dry and he struggled to release the words. He swallowed and tried again. 'Where's my friend?' he began again, his voice croaky.

The men simply looked at him. One made a sign to another who went to a corner, filled a mug with water from a plastic container and held it in front of Gunnymede. He gripped the mug in trembling hands and took several gulps.

He lay back, drained by the effort although he could feel life coursing through him. His concern for Granger remained. If they'd gone to all the trouble of bringing him to their village, they would've most likely done the same for Granger. That didn't mean the man was dead of course. Maybe he was on his way with another group. Maybe he was somewhere else.

Gunnymede pushed himself onto an elbow again and another effort sat him up. He shuffled back so that he could lean against the mud wall.

He looked around for his gear. His pack. Rifle. Webbing. No sign of any of it. His hands snapped to his shoulder holster to discover his pistol still in it.

He had to find Granger. He couldn't lie there a moment longer.

With a supreme effort, he rolled onto his knees, an action that alarmed the men. The elder urged him to stay down. Gunnymede ignored him and, using the wall, rose unsteadily to his feet. The old man kept talking as if trying to reason with him.

Gunnymede made hand gestures aimed at easing his concerns. 'I'm okay,' he said. 'Ana bikhayr.'

He leaned back against the wall, letting it take his weight while he checked his pockets, taking an inventory. He pulled his satellite phone from a thigh pocket. A piece fell off it. The screen was broken. Bits inside moved.

His emergency beacon looked okay. That was the life-saver. But he couldn't activate it. Not yet. He needed to find Granger. He might be lying somewhere badly wounded.

Gunnymede faced the hut entrance and took a step forward. The men parted. Physically, he felt better. When he got to the opening he looked outside. Half a dozen children hanging around a narrow path between huts stopped what they were doing to look at him.

Gunnymede made his way between huts until he reached open ground in the centre of the village. Several women were caught off guard and wrapped their scarves around their faces as they grabbed children and hurried away. Gunnymede carried on to the edge of the village. The men followed at a distance. He walked beyond the huts to where he could take a look at the surrounding landscape. Everything was parched, the land nothing more than sandy gravel. Goats roamed nearby, nibbling at sparse, brittle vegetation.

He activated his watch compass. The village might be the one they'd seen the evening before. If so the attack was a couple of clicks south east. He couldn't see anything in that direction. There was nothing more for it. He had to go back to it.

He felt his spare pistol mags in a clip on his belt. Some comfort at least. He was far from fit but confident he would brighten once he got going. Before he could take more than a couple of steps a sound floated to him on the wind. An engine. The villagers took to their heels and scurried into their huts. Within seconds they'd gone.

A pickup truck broke over a rise five hundred metres away. Three more closely followed. The backs were filled with men. Gunnymede knew it was Daesh. It couldn't be anyone else in this area. He had serious problems and not many options. Hiding in the village was a waste of time. There was nowhere to go outside of it either. Fighting ensured his death. The only sound option was capture. That also meant death of course, but perhaps not immediately. Where there was time, there was hope. Getting caught by these clowns was a subject that had not escaped discussion back in Dubai. The general consensus was to kill as many as possible but to save the last bullet for oneself. The logic was obvious since, based on history, a western soldier wouldn't survive if captured by Daesh.

Gunnymede removed his pistol from its holster. It would be quick and easy to put it to his head and pull the trigger. Life would be over in a second. He'd be spared the torture. But Gunnymede wasn't the type. He was too much of an optimist. As the vehicles closed, in he dropped it to the sand.

The trucks came to a stop either side of him. The fighters climbed out, curious about the man standing alone in the open who was clearly a western soldier.

The Daesh fighters were heavily armed with AKs, RPGs, grenades, knives, axes and machetes. Bearded. Unwashed. Sun-baked. Grim. Intolerant. These people were getting battered from one side of the Iraq Syria plains to the other and didn't look like any had been on R&R of late. Much as they knew he was the enemy and hated his very being, their self-control kept them from tearing him apart. Discipline was still evident amongst the ranks of this lot at least.

A man stepped from one of the trucks wearing a bloody bandage around his forehead. Gunnymede recognised him immediately. Saleem.

As soon as the Arab saw Gunnymede he smiled, recognising him from the night before. A reversal of fortunes. The irony was not lost on either man.

Saleem looked him up and down. 'It's you, innit?' he asked in a London accent, his voice deeper than one might expect from his frame size. Saleem was a few inches shorter than Gunnymede, thinner, wiry and tough with a menacing coldness that could not be concealed even behind his broad grin. 'I can't believe it's you. How lucky is this? Allah has the best sense of humour, I swear. So you survived. Amazing. Just you, me and Mustafa 'ere.' Saleem indicated a man Gunnymede recognised as the driver of Saleem's vehicle the night before.

Mustafa stared at Gunnymede with cold malevolence, a fresh, bloody wound down the side of his face.

'You Brit or American?' Saleem asked.

Gunnymede kept silent.

'You gonna play the strong silent type?' Saleem asked, smiling confidently as if it was a puerile challenge.

'Brit,' Gunnymede said.

'What unit? You ain't a regular. Not out here with just your mate.'

Gunnymede decide to keep quiet.

Saleem smirked with obvious contempt for Gunnymede's silence. 'These people help you? These villagers?'

'I got here just before you did,' Gunnymede said.

'Is that right? Where's your gear then? Your pouches with all your little toys an' stuff? Not like you lot to go walking off without your rifle. I came 'ere looking for you. I thought this lot would 'elp you. They'd do anything for a chance of a food parcel.'

Mustafa whispered into Saleem's ear. Saleem nodded.

Mustafa barked a command and most of the men set off into the village. Shouting followed. Women screamed. A gun was fired.

'Don't worry,' Saleem said, as if reading Gunnymede's concerns for the villagers. 'We need these people for what little farmin' they do. We'll punish one or two. The leader will be hung. That's all.' He looked for Gunnymede's eyes. 'Look at me,' he said.

Gunnymede obeyed.

'What you doing here?'

Gunnymede merely blinked.

'You'll tell me,' Saleem said, confidently.

He barked an order and the remaining men grabbed Gunnymede, searched him, putting his gear into their pockets. His hands were tied behind his back and he was shoved towards one of the pickups, his back turned to the vehicle, legs picked up and thrown over the side and onto the flatbed where he landed hard. When he opened his eyes he found himself looking at Granger's face inches from his own.

His partner's eyes were dry, his face streaked in flaking scabs and coated with sand.

Poor bastard had been dead for hours.

Gunnymede lay silently in the sun facing Granger long enough to begin to doze before the men climbed back in and sat around him as the engine fired up. Granger and Gunnymede were shoved tightly together into the centre so the fighters could use them as foot rests.

It was a painful journey as he bounced over the endless ruts. The engine transmission vibrated through the metal floor and his entire body. The most strenuous part was keeping his head off the bed each time they went over a bump to prevent his skull from being cracked open.

The journey lasted several hours and included a stop to refuel and relieve bowels. Gunnymede was left with Granger without a sip of water.

He suspected they'd arrived at their destination when the men clambered out, the engines died and the air was filled with voices like a crowded market place. A sack was placed over his head and he was manhandled off the truck and shuffled through crowds of people. His shoulder hit something immovable. His guide pushed him onwards. All thoughts of his partner faded as the question of his own fate took pole position.

He was yanked around a corner and it suddenly went darker. The cacophony dropped away. The air became cooler. Sounds echoed. He brushed a stone wall with a shoulder and a few steps later brushed another with his other side. His nostrils filled with the smell of musky carpets.

He could make out lights above his head through the sacking fibre. A string of lightbulbs. The ground dropped steeply away and he almost fell down several stone steps. He reached the bottom and the back of his shirt was harshly grabbed to halt him. The stairway had led into a small chamber with lights on the walls. The sound of keys jangled. A lock was turned. A door creaked open.

Gunnymede was shoved through and his hood removed. He blinked the dust from his eyes to find himself standing in a damp, windowless, stone room that looked medieval. A couple of bulbs on cables provided the only light. Half a dozen other people were in the room, sitting or lying on the dirt floor in chains.

Gunnymede's guide slammed him in the gut with a wooden rod totally winding him. A second blow to his back forced him to his knees. The guide then left, closing the door behind him. The heavy lock turned with a clunk followed by the muffled jingle of keys as they were removed.

Gunnymede could sense someone behind him and turned enough to see a fighter, presumably the guard, sitting on a wooden chair beneath one of the dim bulbs. He looked at Gunnymede coldly.

Gunnymede took a look at his new home. The room was long and narrow with space for many more guests. Each man had his own piece of wall to sit against. Their feet were shackled, their hands free. But their greatest restraint appeared to be their lack of physical well-being. They looked malnourished. A foul smell came from them. They were all sitting in their own shit and urine.

Gunnymede's mouth was bone dry and he looked around for any sign of refreshments. 'Water?' he said to the guard.

The guard jutted his chin towards a bucket in a corner. Gunnymede shuffled over to it. A wooden bucket half filled with water with bits floating in it. He leaned down to smell it. A bit musky but he wasn't in a position to be choosy. He lowered his face into it and sucked up as much as he could in case he didn't get another chance.

When he straightened up again he looked around the accommodation, saw a space, made his way over to it and sat back against the cold, uncomfortable wall, his hands still tied behind him. He regarded his fellow inmates, heavily bearded and gaunt. The Count of Monte Cristo came to mind. Two were asleep or unconscious, or worse. It was difficult to assess in the poor light. The others looked at him. Two were white. The other two looked Latino or Middle Eastern. All were in a sorry state. Their poor physical condition was a reminder that if an escape attempt was to be made it had to be sooner rather than later.

Three of the men went back to whatever daydreaming they did while one continued to look at him. Gunnymede felt the man wanted to say something.

'How long've you been here?' Gunnymede asked.

The guard immediately sprang to his feet and lunged at Gunnymede with his wooden rod. Gunnymede instinctively fell to his side in an effort to avoid the blow, squeezing his eyes shut, bracing for it.

It didn't come. He opened his eyes to see the rod in the guard's hand inches away.

'No speak,' the guard said.

He walked back to his chair and sat down.

Gunnymede shuffled back into a sitting position. The man opposite hadn't moved. Gunnymede searched for a question in the man's eyes, an expression perhaps, any kind of meaning. But as he stared he realised there was nothing in them but despair. He wasn't trying to communicate. He was simply looking at someone new who would soon be like him.

Gunnymede dropped his head back against the wall and sighed inwardly. The ceiling was covered with small stalactites, formed by centuries of moisture seeping from above. His thoughts went to Granger. What were ops doing? Did they have any idea what had happened to the pair? Did they know where Gunnymede was?

He suddenly felt exhausted. Sleep encroached, rolling over him like a heavy cloak. He didn't fight it.

When they came for him, Gunnymede had no idea how long he'd been asleep. He jerked awake as hands grabbed his clothes and hauled him to his feet. He hadn't heard the door open or the men come in.

He was in a daze as he was shoved out of the room, up the stairs and along a dark, dank corridor. His hands remained tied behind his back. He was wide awake by the time they left the cool, damp, musty stone building into the suffocating sunshine. Gunnymede's handlers were two armed fighters, one behind, one in front who kept him moving with purpose. The sun had gone past its high point putting the day at mid to late afternoon.

They turned a corner through an arch into a courtyard packed with stores and equipment; vehicle parts, weapons and ammunition, fuel and tinned food. There were no clues as to what town they were in.

At the other end of the courtyard, they passed through another stone arch into a sand field of Roman ruins. Everywhere were slabs and plinths, some with the remains of statues, sections of what were once tall pillars topped with flared capitals, some upright, others lying on the ground, the remains of an ancient city that looked as if it had been blown apart. Corinthian.

Gunnymede wondered where he was being taken. If they wanted to interrogate him they could've done that in the dungeons. This felt ominous.

They arrived at a clearing where a wooden scaffold had been constructed. Four men were standing on upright logs with nooses around their necks attached to a horizontal span above them. Saleem was sitting in a tatty leather armchair under a canvas awning, facing the scaffold, his legs crossed on a stool, a plastic bottle of water in his hand. A dozen fighters lounged around passing the time. As Gunnymede got closer, he could see that the men standing precariously balanced on the upright logs were uniformed Kurdish soldiers, their hands tied behind their backs.

Gunnymede was brought to a halt by the scaffold. He looked up at the faces of the Kurds. All were sweating, clearly stressed as well as hot, helplessly awaiting their fates. One in particular looked more precarious than the others, his crotch soaked in urine, with trembling knees that threatened to unbalance him.

Saleem wore a thin, superior smile and gestured for Gunnymede to be moved to the end of the line of Kurds. There was a space beneath the scaffold waiting for him. A short noose was attached directly above a narrow log like the ones on which the Kurds were standing. Gunnymede was helped up onto it. His hands remained tied behind his back. When he was able to balance on the log without assistance the fighters released him. One climbed onto a chair behind him, fixed the noose around his neck, tightened it, gave it a tug to ensure it was secure, jumped down and walked away with the chair.

Gunnymede was now a full member of the hanging team.

Saleem climbed out of his chair and went to a slab of stone where the stuff they'd found on Gunnymede was laid out. He selected a device and showed it to Gunnymede. 'Emergency beacon?'

Gunnymede remained silent.

'You flip this switch and hit this button?'

Saleem walked over to Gunnymede. 'Welcome,' he said, as if making an official start to the proceedings. 'We're joined today by Amanj, Nebez, Karzan and ... Eja? Eja, yes?'

The Kurd didn't respond.

'We'll go with Eja. Let's go on with the chat we were having earlier. I asked what group you're from. Your unit?'

Gunnymede swallowed, the noose a little too snug around his neck.

'For every question you don't answer I'll top one of the Kurds,' Saleem said.

Gunnymede looked into his eyes. The man was cold as a fish.

'Your unit?' Saleem asked.

Gunnymede paused before opening his mouth.

'Too slow,' Saleem shouted as he kicked away the Kurd's log. The man fell a few inches and the noose slammed tight around his neck. He shook violently as he choked, his face turning bright red, eyes bulging, tongue sticking from his swelling lips as he fought for air. His legs bucked, trying in vain to find a purchase. A minute later his efforts reduced to a twitch. The man would

75

remain alive for a few minutes more, a residue of consciousness until his brain was starved of oxygen. His eyes remained partially open, his tongue hanging from his mouth, his face swollen and turning cyan.

He swayed gently beside Gunnymede, the rope creaking rhythmically. The fighters watched the death with the usual fascination. Watching someone die was never boring.

'Your unit?' Saleem said as he stepped in front of the next Kurd.

'Army Int Corps' Gunnymede said.

Saleem nodded as he pondered the answer. 'The Int Corps? Bollocks. What was your mission?'

'You.'

'What do you mean?'

Gunnymede was reluctant to answer.

Saleem placed his foot on the Kurd's log. 'We've got plenty more 'a these. We can play this game all week.'

'We want to know who you're talking to,' Gunnymede said.

'Who do you think I'm talking to?' Saleem looked at the Kurd, who was sweating profusely.

'We think Russian but we don't know.'

'What do you think we're talking about?'

'We don't know.'

'You must think it's important to go to all the trouble of coming out here to get me.'

'Yes.'

'And you have no idea why?'

'That's right.'

'Sounds like a load of bollocks to me.'

'If someone knows any more than that, I don't.'

Saleem smiled and closed in on Gunnymede so that only he could hear him. 'Shall I tell you?'

Gunnymede blinked as he looked into his eyes.

'If I tell you, promise you won't tell anyone.'

'I can't guarantee it.'

'I can,' Saleem chuckled, keeping his voice too low for any of the fighters to hear. 'I'm going to England as soon as Baghdadi approves the plan, which he will because it's brilliant. Thousands of Londoners dead in one go. No guns, dirty bombs, nuclear, gas, bio or chemical. Just pure engineering brilliance.' Saleem put the toe of his boot against the top of Gunnymede's log. Gunnymede braced himself as the log moved.

'But now that I've told you I'll have to kill you. Those are the rules. Sorry you won't be around for the big day.'

Saleem made ready to kick the log away.

'Untazar!' a voice called out. It was Mustafa. 'I want to do it,' he said in heavily accented English as he walked over.

Saleem looked between Mustafa and Gunnymede with a grin. 'Mustafa wants to be the one to kill you. He used to work for the British Army. In Basra. How long for?'

'Two year,' Mustafa said.

'SRR wasn't it?' Saleem asked.

'Special Reconnaissance Regiment,' Mustafa said.

'He worked in the kitchen. Mustafa was going to kill a bunch of 'em but he was laid off before he could. He's a bit of a thug is Mustafa.' Saleem removed his toe from Gunnymede's log. 'One last thing. What was your mate's name?'

'Granger.'

'When we found Granger he was still alive. Straight up. He was wounded. He couldn't walk. But alive.' Saleem raised his hands so that Gunnymede could see them. 'I strangled him with these. I wrapped them around his throat and squeezed until he died.'

Gunnymede stared at Saleem as the man held up his hands and for a few seconds he forgot his own life was literally hanging by a thread while wanting to tear the Arab apart.

Saleem stepped away and Mustafa put his boot against the log. Back to reality. Gunnymede's hands strained in vain to break the bonds, his throat braced against the noose. Where was all the pomp and ceremony? The video. The banner with armed fighters in prayer. Didn't they want more information out of him? Surely this wasn't it.

Mustafa moved the log a little.

A Daesh fighter came running from the courtyard and between the ancient stones. 'Aircraft!' he shouted.

The air was suddenly filled with the sound of fighter jets. As one, every man ran as fast as he could. The best place to be during an air raid was the catacombs of the building Gunnymede had just left. A jet screamed overhead with a deafening roar and a rocket slammed into a building. Explosions detonated in rapid succession. Saleem took off as fast as he could. A nearby strike shook the ground. Gunnymede felt it quiver up the log and through his legs. He and the Kurds fought to stay balanced.

But Mustafa had not run. He remained, looking at Gunnymede for a second. Gunnymede could see the death in his eyes. Mustafa kicked the log away as another rocket struck nearby and broke into a run. The log fell beneath Gunnymede's feet and the noose slammed tight around his neck. He swung inches above the ground, his feet kicking out in desperation to find anything to step onto. He pulled frantically against the bonds that tied his hands. His face turned red as he choked.

Death was seconds away.

Chapter 7

The week in Dartmoor dragged by as Bethan had hoped it would. With no-one to talk to and a poor internet connection, she made her way through two novels, half a bottle of scotch, two bottles of wine and covered some thirty miles of moorland. She'd been so chilled that she'd forgotten to complete her case report or read the file she'd brought with her.

By Saturday afternoon, her need to organise and tie up loose ends steered her towards her small dining table by the window where she'd placed her laptop and work papers. A gust of wind hit the window with a gentle thud and she looked onto the moor, never tiring of its prehistoric beauty. It was a cold, blustery day with a sweeping wind that stroked the tops of the heather in swirling waves. Rain sprayed against the glass as grey shadows eased over the folds of land like whale ghosts.

Her phone chirped on the table. Who dared to interrupt?

She checked the number. DCI Dillon. Anyone else and she might've ignored it. 'Hello boss,' she said in a cheery tone.

'How's your leave going?'

'Well, you told me that I deserved it. Vigorously pursue diversions was your command. Forget all about work. Cleanse it from your mind. Yet you call.'

'Your leave ends tomorrow,' Dillon said. He was in his office in Scotland Yard, the River Thames outside his window.

'Which is not today.'

'Have you finished the Macaw report?'

'Almost,' she said.

'Accounts need it to finalise the budget.'

'Monday for sure.'

'Did you get to the Carlton case?'

She eyed the unopened file on her desk.

'Not a problem if you haven't,' he said. 'I have something else for you.'

'That's a shame. It was going to be tonight's bedtime read.'

'I'm sorry to hear that.'

'Why are you sorry?'

'I meant I was hoping you might be otherwise distracted.'

'It's not your place to hope for such things.'

Dillon suddenly realised he'd been inappropriate. 'What I meant was ... I'm just being fatherly,' he said, backtracking.

Bethan was amused by his stuttering. 'Fathers don't usually hope their daughters are distracted at bedtime in the manner you meant.'

He fought to recover. 'I worry about you at times, that's all. You work very hard and I don't like to think of you without companionship.'

'I like being alone,' she said, wistfully, picturing him rolling his eyes.

'Okay. See you Monday.'

'Why exactly did you call me?'

'Oh, yes. You're off to Albania.'

'Albania?'

'As in the Balkans.'

'When?' she asked, frowning at the thought.

'Monday morning. Early. Don't be late. The weather is warm but dress with cultural sensitivity. It's seventy per cent Muslim.'

'If you were culturally sensitive, you'd send a man.'

'You're the best man I've got for this particular task.'

'What is it?'

'I'll tell you when you get here.'

'Anything else?'

'Don't forget your passport.'

Dillon disconnected.

Bethan put down her phone. What was happening in Albania that required Scotland Yard?

The week suddenly felt as if it had come to an end.

Chapter 8

Gunnymede entered the cavernous arrivals hall of London Heathrow Terminal 3 amongst a stream of people, trolleys and luggage. As he moved with the flow, he glanced along the line of cards in the hands of drivers and greeters waiting behind a long, steel rail. None bore his name or a phrase that meant anything to him.

Gunnymede had no baggage. All his clothing, including a garish t-shirt bearing some inane slogan across the chest partially covered by an oversized jacket had been purchased from a market stall in the Green Zone in Baghdad two days before. The embassy staff member who'd bought it had either poor taste, a small budget or a wry sense of humour. Gunnymede had no say in the matter. As soon as he arrived at the embassy he had been taken to the infirmary where his wound was cleaned and stitched and immediately after he was shown into the bubble room with a tray of tea and sandwiches where he was connected with Dubai operations and debriefed on the failed operation. Gunnymede had been anxious to report not only Saleem's survival but his threat to carry out a major attack on London. But Ops hadn't seemed particularly interested in the attack. Gunnymede supposed their lack of curiosity was justified. Saleem was a low level fighter. It was one thing for him to make such threats and another altogether to carry them out. The fact he was in Syria and had a slender chance of getting out of there alive decreased the priority. In short, Saleem had been all talk.

Gunnymede omitted the part where he'd actually been hanging by his neck, swinging off the ground and choking to death seconds before he got away. He put it down to security reasons, protecting something other than his dignity. It was in fact the truth. He was protecting the existence of his saviour.

When Mustafa kicked away the log and ran, Gunnymede was, to all intents and purposes, a dead man. He had seconds to live. But as the noose tightened and he began to lose consciousness he hit the ground. At first he thought the scaffold had been felled by an explosion. They seemed to be going off all around. But then the rope was removed from his neck and the bonds cut from his wrists. An explosion nearby threw a load of sand over him. Gunnymede was turned onto his back. He fought to focus on a man looking down on him. It was one of the Daesh fighters. The Arab looked around, wide-eyed, afraid. 'Can you hear me?' he shouted.

Gunnymede was still dazed.

The man slapped his face. 'Can you hear me?'

Gunnymede raised his hands against another blow. 'Yes.'

'Run!' he shouted. 'Run! Get out of here! Or we're both dead!'

And with that the man sprang to his feet and took off.

He was a friendly. He could only have been an undercover operator. There was no other explanation. He'd taken a huge personal risk in saving Gunnymede. And Gunnymede had to respect that to the point of not even telling the Dubai team. The spy was above their level and probably only known to his handler. Gunnymede would be eternally grateful to him whoever he was.

As the spy ran off, Gunnymede struggled to his feet unsteadily and set off at the run. But with his first step came a searing pain in his side. His hand was covered in blood after inspecting it. It was not the time or place to worry about a mere flesh wound. He looked back to see if he was being pursued and caught sight of the Kurdish soldiers he'd shared the scaffold with, all hanging limply by their necks. He ran on as hard as he could. The air raid was coming to an end. The fighters would soon emerge from their hiding places.

He pushed on, holding his bloody side, through the remnants of the ancient city. He paused to get his bearings using the sun and headed due west. Lebanon was that way. How far, he'd no idea.

A mile from the Daesh compound he came across a farmer loading goats into the back of an old truck. Without being seen, he crawled inside and hid amongst the animals. It wasn't long after the truck was on its way that Gunnymede realised they were heading east not west. Towards Iraq.

It didn't matter. He didn't care at that point, as long as they were moving away from Daesh. His wound had stopped bleeding but it was going to need stitches. After patching it up with strips of his clothing he explored his confinement.

As the truck bumped along the sand road Gunnymede moved between the goats and found the mesh back door was held shut by a twist of wire. Hanging by a hook was a plastic bag containing old clothes. Gunnymede removed his military fatigues and exchanged them for a grubby pair of trousers and a shirt. He looked like a beggar, which would do perfectly. He was reluctant to give up his boots though. The alternative was bare feet. But there was so much military gear lying around the desert these days the boots would not attract any particular attention.

Gunnymede made himself as comfortable as he could on the grubby floor and spent the next few hours keeping the goats from falling on him whenever the truck jolted. Several hours later they arrived at a market town. He lay flat in the middle of the bed, the goats surrounding and concealing him. Daylight was fading and when the truck came to a stop he had no problem slipping away. He found some much needed water and made his way to a vantage point from where he could get a look at the place. He had no idea if he was still in Syria or not until he saw a police station with an Iraqi flag hanging outside. There were no border checkpoints in this area.

Being weathered and unwashed helped disguise his western features. Not that they'd stand out as unusual in Western Iraq where the British Army had been in occupation for long enough in the 1920s to contribute to the gene pool. He walked through the town to find something to eat. A man preparing falafels saw him staring hungrily and scraped up a pile of offcuts, wrapped them in a sheet of unleavened bread and gave it to him. He ate hungrily. The next objective was to find a ride to Baghdad. He repeated the name of the city to the driver of every truck making ready to leave the market and eventually one allowed him to sit in the back. Before dawn he was on his way.

The most challenging part of his journey was getting through the Iraqi checkpoint into the Baghdad Green Zone. It was crowded with people coming in and out, mostly labourers, domestic and government staff and shopkeepers. It was a struggle to get the guards to even acknowledge him the way he looked. After some barracking, the guard commander was eventually called and as luck would have it the man spoke some English. Gunnymede gave a false name and explained he was a British businessman who'd been visiting an oil facility when he had a car accident after which criminals robbed him of everything including his identification.

Gunnymede was driven to an army office where he spent more time waiting around and being questioned. Eventually, a tall white man arrived and introduced himself as a member of the British embassy. Not long after, Gunnymede was taken to the embassy where he revealed his true identity. After his debriefing he was given a room where he could clean up and rest while his documentation was prepared and transport organised. While in the shower, his rags were removed and replaced with the cheap civilian garb.

Gunnymede's only possessions were a new passport and change from a few quid given to him to buy a cup of coffee and a sandwich while waiting in Amman airport for his connecting flight to London. The only sign of his ordeal was some weathered flaking around his face and a nasty rope burn across his throat from one ear to the other.

After getting to the end of the line of greeting cards he decided the rendezvous system had failed until he saw a familiar figure standing back beyond the main body. Aristotle. The tall, grey man set off towards the exit and Gunnymede followed on an interception course. Aristotle spoke into a phone as Gunnymede joined him and by the time they reached the road outside the terminal a car had arrived and they climbed in.

The car pulled away. Gunnymede waited for Aristotle to say something but after several minutes of silence he couldn't help himself. 'I'm fine, thanks,' he said.

'Don't be so attention seeking.'

'It was a comment on your lack of social graces.'

'I read your report,' Aristotle said. 'I know you're fine.'

Gunnymede sighed and sat back in silence. He looked at his cheap sandals and white socks, looking forward to getting out of them. 'So, where do I live? Hopefully not with you.'

'You have one of the firm's apartments in Docklands.'

That sounded nice.

Aristotle held out a package to him. 'Your new phone. Don't lose this one or you'll be charged. There's a credit card with a five thousand pound limit, for operational use only.'

'What about money? Cash? Wages? I assume I'm being paid.'

'There's two hundred pounds in cash in the bag.'

'That's my wages?'

'An advance. You'll have a bank account in a few days and a cash card.'

'I need to buy some things today.'

'What things?'

'Living things. Things that make life comfortable. Clothes for instance.'

'I bought you some clothes.'

'*You* bought me clothes? Why did *you* buy me clothes?'

'Because you don't have time to buy them for yourself.'

'Why don't I have time to buy some clothes?'

'You're going to Albania.'

Gunnymede turned in his seat to look at Aristotle. 'Why am I going to Albania?'

88

'You're helping the police.'

'The police?!'

'Scotland Yard.'

Gunnymede processed the revelation. 'And this has to do with Spangle.'

'Everything you do has to do with Spangle.'

'What has Albania got to do with Spangle?'

'That's your job to find out.'

Gunnymede shook his head in disbelief. 'This is ridiculous.'

'It's the business you're in or have you forgotten?'

'I seemed to remember getting time off between operations.'

'Harlow told you things have changed. We're now getting our money's worth out of the field spy department.'

Gunnymede shook his head. 'You have to be kidding me. I can't go – I'm wounded.'

'The task does not require anything physical. You should be back tomorrow.'

'Can't you put it off for twenty-four hours? I'm knackered.'

'You're pathetic.'

Gunnymede looked at him angrily. 'And what if I tell you to shove this job up your arse?' Gunnymede spat.

'You'd rather go to jail for five years than a day trip to Albania? I don't think so.'

'I think you need me and I don't like the way you're pushing me around.'

'You're going to Albania today or you're going to prison. Make up your mind.'

Gunnymede frowned as he sunk back into his seat. This was bullshit.

Chapter 9

Saleem sat in his sterile room, the bare plaster walls severely cracked, the glass long since blown out of the windows that looked down onto the Daesh vehicle compound. His simple furnishings were a metal hospital cot, a chair and a desk. Hanging from hooks on the door was his meagre wardrobe including a well-worn AK47 rifle and ammunition harness. A gnarled copy of the Koran rested on the desk in the top left corner, a stack of paper neatly piled beside it, a couple of pens. Spread over the rest of the desk was a frayed map of the City of London.

Saleem closed his eyes, reached for a piece of paper, placed it on the map to cover it, opened his eyes, took a pen and began to draw a long curving line. He drew another curve parallel with the first. A section of the River Thames. He drew a bridge. And another. Roads followed the course of the river, specifically the north bank. He was attempting to replicate major streets and landmarks between the Thames Barrier and Blackfriars. He drew a small circle and an underground train station symbol and wrote the words Temple beside it. A line from the station followed the river to Blackfriars Station.

There was a knock on the door. He quickly folded the map and placed it inside the desk drawer.

Another knock. 'Saleem? It's Araf.'

'Yes,' Saleem said.

The door opened and a young Arab stood in the doorway. It was the man who had saved Gunnymede's life. 'Alright, mate?' he asked cheerily in a South London accent, a smile on his bearded face as he looked around the room. 'Rajik wants to see you?'

'What for?'

'He didn't say. Fat bastard doesn't tell me anything.'

'You shouldn't talk about 'im that way,' Saleem said, placing his chair tidily under his desk.

'Why not? He's a fat wanker.'

'You should have respect for our superiors. Without respect, we'll fall apart.'

'We're already falling apart.'

'You think this is the only place we're at war?' Saleem was calm and preachy.

'Well, I'd like to go somewhere we're winning.'

'Stay alive and maybe you will.' Saleem walked out of the room and waited for Araf to exit.

'You know we're neighbours,' Araf said, stepping into the corridor.

'Neighbours?' Saleem closed the door and walked on.

Araf followed him along a dilapidated corridor racked by the violence of bombardments. 'I'm from Clapham. You're from Wandsworth, right?'

'Not a good idea to get nostalgic, mate.'

'I ain't. I don't expect to see the place again. I just thought it was a coincidence, that's all.'

They walked down a creaking, unlit staircase illuminated by daylight from below.

'Is Rajik in his office?' Saleem asked.

'Where else would 'e be? Bomb-proof basement, next to the food store. Fat fucker.'

They reached the ground floor then continued along a short corridor and down a narrower, dingy stairwell lit by bulbs that dimmed rhythmically to the uneven purr of a generator beyond the walls.

Araf led the way along a narrow corridor to a door that was slightly ajar and knocked on it.

'Come in,' a man's voice called out in Arabic.

The two men stepped inside Rajik's office which was crammed with crates and boxes of equipment and foods. Rajik, a fat, sweaty man with a long black beard, greasy face and wearing a black turban sat behind a desk finishing off a tin of beans with a plastic spoon. Evidence of the beans and past meals was in his matted beard. He dumped the empty tin in a nearby bin, burped as politely as he could, licked the spoon clean and wiped his mouth on his sleeve, all in one swift action. 'Ah. Saleem. Come in. Come in. Can I offer you something?'

'I'm fine, thanks,' Saleem said.

Rajik placed a slender bar of confectionary on the table in front of Saleem as if it was some kind of award. 'That's for you.'

'Like I said, I'm fine,' Saleem said dryly.

Rajik lost his smile, miffed by the rejection. Araf made eyes at him in an effort to convey that he'd happily accept the sweet. Rajik put it back in a box.

'Sit down,' Rajik ordered.

There was only one chair, the other side of Rajik's desk. Saleem sat on it.

'Well,' Rajik said. 'You are in much favour, it seems.'

'I am?' Saleem asked, looking hopeful.

'Al-Baghdadi himself has sent you a message.'

Saleem controlled himself but deep down he was electrified.

'I am annoyed with you for communicating with higher command without going through me,' Rajik said, giving

Saleem a scolding look. 'But I cannot punish you now that you have the ear of our leader.'

'It wasn't my intention to offend you. But secrecy is of extreme importance.'

'What's the secret, Saleem? Come on. You can tell me. I am your commander, after all.'

Saleem's eyes darkened at Rajik's stupidity. 'What is the message?' he asked coldly.

'You're not going to answer my question first?'

Saleem did all he could to mask his distaste for the fool. 'Will you refuse to pass me our leader's message if I do not?'

Rajik smirked at the unsubtle threat. 'Don't you think I could be of assistance to you?'

'Please give me the message,' Saleem said, making an effort to be polite.

Rajik gave up and sat back. 'Your request, whatever it was, has been granted. You are to be given all assistance.'

Saleem calmly exhaled, disguising his immense relief. 'Anything about timings and travel?'

'Won't you miss your frequent trips into the desert to talk with your Russian friends?' Rajik asked, slyly.

Saleem's eyes pierced Rajik's at the disclosure of one of his secrets. 'Who told you that?'

Rajik grinned with satisfaction. 'You have your secrets and I have mine. The Russians are our enemy and yet you talk with them. Frequently. And then they blow you up. What's going on, Saleem? It's a very curious situation.'

Saleem wanted to tell Rajik to go to hell but chose to exercise restraint.

'And then there's the map of London on your desk,' Rajik added.

Saleem's mouth opened, about to lose control. Rajik smiled with a nod to Araf who returned the smile, clearly the source of that snippet.

'Intriguing,' Rajik said, revelling in Saleem's discomfort. 'Russia. London. And what's in Afghanistan?'

'Afghanistan?' Saleem asked, knowing nothing about the relevance of that country.

'That's where I'm to send you,' Rajik said. 'Mahmoud?!' he suddenly shouted at the top of his voice giving Saleem a jolt. 'Come here!'

Footsteps could be heard hurrying along the corridor and a young Arab entered the room.

'You know Mahmoud?' Rajik asked Saleem.

Saleem turned in his seat to look at the lad. 'No.'

'He's English like you,' Rajik said. 'He just arrived. A new recruit.'

'I'm from Balham,' Mahmoud said.

'Too many English here,' Rajik grumbled. 'Be good to get rid of some of you. You see how Mahmoud looks like you?'

Saleem took another look at Mahmoud. 'There's a resemblance.'

'I didn't ask. I have my own eyes. Mahmoud is to become you and go to Turkey while you become someone else and go to Afghanistan.'

'But I just got here from Turkey,' Mahmoud complained.

'Shut up! You will do as you are ordered.'

'It took me months to get over the border,' Mahmoud continued.

'One more outburst and you'll be impersonating Saleem as a dead man.'

Mahmoud got the message.

'You both leave right away,' Rajik continued. 'Vehicles are waiting for you in the courtyard. Take all of your belongings. Neither of you are coming back.'

'For fuck's sake,' Mahmoud mumbled.

Saleem got to his feet.

'Wait,' Rajik said. 'There's something else.' A plastic folder was on his desk, bound in a strap and sealed in a manner so that it could not be opened without revealing it had been. Rajik pushed it towards him. 'This is for you. It's from Al-Baghdadi.'

Saleem took the folder and began to put it in his pocket.

'You're to open it immediately on receiving it,' Rajik said. 'Those were *my* strict instructions.'

Saleem used a knife to cut through the seal. He opened it and removed a single page.

Rajik watched greedily as Saleem read the note. 'Why you, Saleem?' he asked. 'You're a nobody,' he added with a sneer. 'I don't understand why they chose you.'

Saleem looked at him. 'You want to know what it says?' he asked.

It was obvious Rajik desperately wanted to but he couldn't give Saleem the pleasure of refusing him.

'Take it,' Saleem said, holding the piece of paper out to him.

Rajik took it and began to read. His brow furrowed as he quickly reached the end of the short sentence. His eyes darted to Saleem in instant fear. Saleem removed a pistol from inside his jacket and fired a single bullet into Rajik's head. Rajik dropped forward onto his desk, hitting it like an engine block.

Saleem turned the pistol on Araf and fired a bullet into his brain too. The young Arab slumped to the floor.

Mahmoud leapt back with his hands up, expecting to be next. But Saleem put the gun back inside his jacket and picked up the piece of paper. 'Get your gear and be ready to leave right away,' he said to Mahmoud.

Mahmoud realised he was going to live and lowered his hands.

'Go!' Saleem ordered.

Mahmoud headed for the door, keeping as wide a berth from Saleem as he could. 'Why'd you kill them?' he asked.

'Al Baghdadi ordered me to snuff anyone who knew too much.'

'I don't know anything except I'm going to Turkcy as you,' Mahmoud assured him.

'Which is why you're still alive. Get going!'

Mahmoud hurried away. Saleem made his way back up through the building towards his room. He didn't like being called a nobody. But the pig had a point. Why indeed had he been chosen? He knew how he'd come to the attention of the high command. During the retreat from Mosul, he'd been ordered to execute a dozen Iraqi policemen who'd been incarcerated since the taking of the city. Instead of just lining them up and shooting each in the back of the head in the usual manner, Saleem decided to make sport out of his assignment and save ammunition at the same time. He ordered his men to find half a dozen kitchen knives and threw them in front of the officers. Their hands and feet were untied. The men were in a sorry state, malnourished, injured and weak from regular beatings. Saleem told the officers that they were to fight each other to the death and the sole survivor would be set free.

The policemen refused at first but Saleem was confident it would take only one of them to start. And that is precisely how it began. The largest officer as it happened, who clearly fancied his chances, suddenly lunged for one of the knives. Before he could reach it another officer barged him aside to get it for himself. The others instantly realised that solidarity was not going to work and that survival was up to the individual and they threw themselves at the blades that were fewer in number than the hands that grabbed at them.

The fight was frenetic and brutal with officers slashing at the nearest body. Those fighting over a single knife were stabbed by others. Bodies were stuck randomly, punctures bleeding profusely, screams and moans as those mortally wounded capitulated. Within minutes only four officers remained. They circled, lunging at each other randomly, hoping to make a significant cut. One of them stepped back too far from the epicentre of the battle and a fighter shot him in the leg. As he yelled and staggered in pain a colleague took advantage and shoved his blade through his eye. Another dropped to his knees, unable to stand any longer having lost too much blood, and was quickly despatched by a stab in the neck. The two remaining policemen were in a sorry state, both covered in oozing wounds. It was obvious neither was going to survive for long. Not that Saleem intended to keep his word anyway. The officers wrestled each other to the ground, thrusting and slashing. Neither could defend, both sticking the blades into any piece of flesh relentlessly. A carotid artery was eventually slashed and blood spurted. The recipient of that fatal cut knew he was finished. He released his knife and lay back, exhausted. The force of the spurting blood gradually reduced to a trickle. The victor watched his colleague die and then collapsed beside him. Within seconds he breathed his own last breath.

Saleem stood over the bodies, fascinated. Brothers and friends had turned on each other like wild animals. The spectacle had been watched by two men who were not in Saleem's command. Saleem knew one to be a senior member. He was to discover the other was a member of Al-Baghdadi's inner circle who was looking for something and seemed to find it in Saleem.

Three weeks later, Saleem was summoned and briefed on an operation. He was to drive into the desert, to a precise GPS location, and call a number on a satellite phone. A man would answer. A Russian. The man would give Saleem a piece of information. Saleem was not to take notes. Just listen and remember. He was to tell no-one the contents of the conversations, not even Baghdadi's officer who was giving him the orders at that moment. There would be several of these meetings at the exact same location. It was during the last of those conversations that the jets attacked. But Saleem had received enough information to know what the task consisted of and exactly how those thousands of Londoners were to die.

Saleem returned to his room and closed the door. He sat at his desk, removed the map of London from the drawer and spread it out. His journey was to begin. Afghanistan was clearly a part of his route to the UK. The powers that be saw great potential in the plan. They would put their best efforts into ensuring it was a success. And why not? It had the potential to eclipse the Twin Towers, in numbers of dead and theatrical splendour.

Chapter 10

Bethan pushed her way in through the main doors of Scotland Yard pulling a wheelie bag. As she crossed the busy lobby, a woman's voice called out her name. She headed towards a matronly lady behind the reception counter who smiled sweetly as she approached.

'Hello, Bethan,' she beamed. 'How was your leave?'

'Short,' Bethan replied, feigning sadness.

'Bliss. Aren't they all?' The receptionist directed her gaze towards a far corner of the room. 'Got a chap here to see DCI Dillon. Perhaps you can take him up. He's been cleared and has his pass.'

Bethan looked at various people the other side of the room, unsure which one she meant.

'The one in the budget khaki jacket looking out of the window,' the receptionist explained. 'He's got a rash.' She pointed to her own throat. 'He could also benefit from an exfoliation treatment.'

'I'll take him up.'

'Bliss,' the receptionist said as Bethan headed away.

Bethan approached Gunnymede's back. His clothes were outdoor casual, inexpensive indeed with sharp creases where they'd been shop folded.

'You're here to see DCI Dillon?' Bethan said.

Gunnymede snapped out of a daydream as he faced her. 'Yes,' he said.

His shirt was open at the top revealing the rash which Bethan did her best not to look at more than two or three times.

'I'll show you to his office,' she said.

Gunnymede picked up his holdall and followed her to a security door which she accessed with an ID card and they carried on to some elevators. They were joined inside by several people and the elevator ascended. Gunnymede followed her onto the third floor and into a large room bustling with personnel, most of them in police uniform.

She pointed to several offices with opaque glass walls at the far end. 'DCI Dillon's office is the one on the right.'

Gunnymede gave her a nod and headed away. She watched him go, certain he wasn't a police officer. She checked her cell phone and listened to her messages as she went to her desk and sorted through her in-tray.

The elevator doors opened and a man in retro civilian clothes with long hair and several days facial growth stepped into the room. Serpico came to mind to those who didn't know him. Something less flattering came to those who did.

He saw Bethan and made his way towards her. 'Bet, honey bunch!' he said loudly, long before he reached her.

Bethan groaned inwardly and forced a smile as he arrived. 'Jedson, honey bunch,' she echoed with feigned delight.

'Congratulations,' he said with over-the-top enthusiasm. 'Great result. You are the most amazing profile analyst in the entire force. They're gonna be calling you Trencher of the Yard.'

'All I did was his profile.'

'Without which they'd never have followed him to his last victim. Brilliant work.'

'A bit over the top but I'll take it.'

'How was your week off?'

'Perfect,' she said, examining a file.

'I called you.' He sat on the edge of her desk, uncomfortably close to her, his legs wide apart.

She inched away from his crotch. 'I missed it.'

'I left a message.'

'That was my work phone.'

'I don't have your private number.'

'Which is where it gets its name from,' she said, scribbling a note and sticking it to a file.

'I was going to take you out to celebrate.'

'My loss, then.'

She looked up as DCI Dillon stepped out of his office and, seeing she'd caught his eye, signalled her to come over.

'First day back, pile of work to do, must rush. Excuse me,' she said, getting up.

He eyed her body lasciviously as she moved past him. 'Bet? I'm completely harmless you know.'

'It's your least attractive quality,' she replied as she picked up her phone and headed away.

As he watched her go an eraser flew through the air and bounced off the side of his head. He quickly turned to see who had thrown it but everyone had their heads down in work mode leaving him no clue as to the culprit.

Gunnymede was sitting outside Dillon's office as she entered it and closed the door. Dillon was at his desk absorbed by his screen.

'Who is he?' she asked.

Dillon looked for who she was referring to. 'Who? Oh, that's Devon Gunnymede.'

'Who?'

'Devon Gunnymede. He'll be going to Albania with you. He's your expert advisor, on loan to us from Military intelligence.'

'Military intelligence?'

'Indeed. It's a mystery.'

She looked at Gunnymede through a gap in the smoked glass. 'Why choose such a ridiculous cover name?'

Dillon hadn't thought of that. 'You don't think it's his real name?'

'Devon Gunnymede? Please ... Advisor of what? Certainly not couture.'

'I'm sure all will be revealed,' Dillon said, getting to his feet and opening the door. 'Would you come in please, Mr Gunnymede?' Dillon winked at Bethan.

Gunnymede walked into the office.

Dillon closed the door behind him. 'Thank you for coming. I understand it was at very short notice for you.'

Gunnymede smiled unconvincingly.

'This is Bethan Trencher, our profile analyst. She'll be going to Albania with you.'

'We've met,' Bethan said smiling politely.

'Have you been travelling, Mr Gunnymede?' Dillon asked. 'You look ... weathered.' Dillon regretted the question as soon as he'd asked it. 'Well. We don't have a lot of time,' he quickly went on. 'You have a plane to catch. Shall we get straight to the job in hand? Albania. What we know, which isn't a great deal. There was a shooting incident on the border with Macedonia. Serious enough to make world news. A dozen fatalities, all Albanian border police. There were no British victims, however the Sherbimi Informativ Ushtarak,' he read carefully from a document, 'Albanian military intelligence, acronym Shiu, S H I U, has requested our assistance in the investigation. They've not given us much detail. All we know is that they have "interesting subjects" they'd like to discuss with us. And those who we must obey have consented to send representatives to provide that assistance, notably the both of you.'

'Do you speak Albanian?' Bethan asked Gunnymede.

'No,' Gunnymede replied.

'You've been there before?' she asked.

'No.'

'You're a specialist in Balkan politics?' she hoped.

'No. In fact I don't know anything about the Balkans. I know where Albania is,' he added. 'Roughly.'

Bethan looked at him, in particular his rash, wondering what he was doing there.

Dillon picked up a file and handed it to Bethan. 'Your Shiu contact is one Ardian Kostaq. His details are in there as well as the case file. He speaks excellent English.' Checking his watch. 'You'd better get going. You can abreast Mr Gunnymede on our protocols while on your journey. Good luck and let me know if you need anything.'

Dillon sat back down and delved into his computer.

Bethan opened the door for Gunnymede who left. She paused to say something for Dillon's ears only. 'Why am I doing this?' she asked.

'Because you're not entrepreneurial enough to be self-employed,' he replied.

'I meant this task. I'm not a detective.'

'Someone upstairs thinks it needs your particular skills,' he replied. 'Success breeds opportunity.'

She walked out and closed the door. 'I'll meet you by the lift,' she said to Gunnymede and headed to her desk.

As Gunnymede walked to the elevator Jedson stepped beside him. 'Hello, mate.'

Gunnymede looked at him enquiringly.

'You the MI lad?'

Gunnymede's prat detector vibrated.

'I'm a UCO, just in case you're thinking I'm the cleaner,' Jedson said with a forced chuckle. 'Under Cover Operator. What happened to your neck?'

'I was recently hung by Islamic terrorists?' Gunnymede said.

Jedson chuckled. 'Yeah. Right. Need to know. Understood. Well, gotta go. Bad guys to catch. Off to the range to do some pistol shooting. Oh, and, look after our Bet. She's great. Nice bit of stuff. And hands off, ha! She's mine. Or I'll have to shoot you.'

Jedson shot Gunnymede with his fingers and walked away.

Bethan packed her laptop and files and was ready to go when Jedson blocked her way.

'The strong silent type,' Jedson said, referring to Gunnymede.

'Love the last bit,' she said.

'Let me know if he gives you any trouble.'

She sighed and skirted around him without touching him. Jedson watched her go. An eraser bounced off the side of his head and he looked around angrily to see who it was but all heads were buried into work.

Bethan joined Gunnymede in the elevator. She gave him a polite smile and the doors closed.

Two hours later, Bethan led the way down the aisle of a commercial aircraft to their seats and opened the overhead locker. 'Do you mind if I have the aisle seat?' she asked.

'Nope,' he said, stuffing his jacket and bag into the locker.

As he leaned forward to get to his seat she accidentally struck his side with her laptop bag and he winced painfully, grabbing his wound.

'I'm so sorry,' she said, surprised at his sudden pain. 'Are you okay?'

'I'm fine,' he said, recovering and sitting down.

She put her laptop into the locker and sat beside him.

The plane was three quarters full and they settled in as the crew prepared for take-off.

'I take it you're not enthralled to be on this job,' she asked.

'I was trying not to be obvious,' he said, propping the pillow behind his neck and closing his eyes.

She rolled her eyes and sat back.

When they reached cruising height the seatbelt signs flicked off with a ping. Bethan got to her feet, removed her laptop bag from the locker and as she was about to sit back down she saw a large patch of wet blood on Gunnymede's side.

'Mr Gunnymede' she said, trying not to be loud despite her concern. He remained fast asleep. She prodded his shoulder. 'Gunnymede!'

Gunnymede sprung awake and for a second had no idea where on earth he was. As reality returned, he looked at her quizzically.

'You're bleeding,' she said, indicating his side.

He looked at his bloody shirt, frowned and unbuckled his seatbelt. He stepped into the aisle, took his bag out of the locker and walked away.

She watched him enter the toilet and sat back down somewhat perplexed.

Ten minutes later he returned wearing a clean shirt. He placed his bag into the locker and got back into his seat.

'Are you okay?' she asked.

'I'm fine.'

'What is it? What's wrong?'

'Nothing.'

'Don't you think I should know what it is? That was a lot of blood.'

'It's just torn stitches. Nothing serious, I wouldn't be here if it was.'

A stewardess arrived pushing a refreshments trolley. 'Can I get you a drink?' she asked him sweetly.

'I'll have a scotch,' Gunnymede said. 'A double.'

'They are doubles,' the stewardess said.

'A double double, then,' he said forcing a smile. 'With a little water.'

The stewardess handed him a glass and two miniatures.

'I'll have a single double, please,' Bethan said.

The stewardess handed her the drink, dropped a couple bags of nuts onto her food tray and moved on.

They poured their drinks and savoured them.

'Have you ever worked with the police before?' she asked.

'Yes.'

'As a technical advisor?'

'No.'

'Have you worked with Scotland Yard before?'

'No.'

'Okay ... well. Scotland Yard protocols. They're simple enough for something like this. Whatever we find technically belongs to the Albanians but information sharing is the prerogative of those I – we – work for.'

He nodded and finished his drink. 'I don't mean to be rude but I've had a long couple of days.'

He lowered the back of his seat as far as it would go and closed his eyes leaving her to enjoy her drink alone.

Chapter 11

A black Mercedes saloon drove along a wide country road snaking through a vast forest that carpeted a hilly terrain. Gunnymede and Bethan sat silently on the spacious black leather rear seats. Ardian Kostaq of the Sherbimi Informativ Ushtarak was in the front beside his driver.

Gunnymede stared at the tree line as it strobed past, set back from the crumbling edge of the tarmac road, the gap in between filled with rubble, weeds and trash. They'd been driving for almost three hours since leaving Tirana. Kostag had said little beyond his greeting. He was pretty formal. He and his driver both smoked cigarettes and between them pretty much had one going throughout the journey. Bethan opening her window for fresh air didn't appear to encourage any consideration on their part. Gunnymede didn't seem to mind.

The car began to slow on a straight, broad open road with no other traffic in sight. Kostag said something to the driver as he pointed ahead. A vehicle was tucked into the trees on the left. As they got closer, more cars and people came into view.

The Mercedes pulled over and came to a stop. Kostag turned in his seat to face the others. 'This road runs north south, north being that way,' he said, pointing in the direction the car was facing. 'The border with Macedonia runs parallel a kilometre inside those woods.' He pointed to the right side of the car. 'What you're going to see now is the site of an atrocity. A massacre. We have no motive. No suspects and a small collection of evidences.'

He climbed out and looped a satchel over his shoulder.

'Take these,' Bethan said to Gunnymede, offering him a pair of latex gloves.

In the clearing was a local police car, several uniformed officers, two border police cars and a truck. Another border police car was ominously alone, deeper into the clearing with its driver's door open. A stand with a small red flag was inside the open door.

As Gunnymede followed Kostag he could see other numbered markers placed around.

'K-17 was here for maybe an hour when they were attacked,' Kostag said. 'Officers were checking a car, here. Three Albanians, father, mother, daughter. They are the only witnesses. One by one, the officers were shot dead.'

'Did the Albanian family have much to offer?' Bethan asked.

'They saw nothing other than the carnage.'

'And they were not shot at?' she added.

'Untouched,' Kostag said. 'We must assume the killer could have shot them but he was only interested in the police.'

'Killer?' Bethan asked. 'Just one?'

'We are certain,' Kostag said.

'And male?' she asked.

Kostag shrugged. 'He or she. I would suspect a he, but we will keep an open mind. You're the British military specialist,' he said to Gunnymede, addressing him directly for the first time since they'd met.

Bethan looked at him as if looking forward to the answer herself. Gunnymede gave a nod that Bethan didn't find very convincing.

'Can I ask where you would expect to find the sniper position?' Kostag asked him.

Gunnymede took a moment to contemplate the question before walking from one marker to the next. When he reached the far side of the clearing he looked down into the ravine and back up to woodland the other side. Bethan stopped beside him to see the five body markers on the slope.

'There,' Gunnymede said, pointing to the woodland across the ravine.

'What range do you think he could make these shots from?' Kostag asked. 'Do you mind if I say he?' he said to Bethan. 'We'll accept that for now it could be a he or a she?'

'Of course.'

'What was the calibre?' Gunnymede asked.

The intelligence officer signalled his driver to come closer. He had followed them across the clearing carrying a long canvas bundle. The driver unwrapped it to reveal a sniper rifle.

Kostag took a hold of it, raising it into his shoulder to look through the scope. 'You know this weapon?' he asked. 'We're pretty sure the killer used one just like this.'

'Dragunov,' Gunnymede replied. 'Basic, but gets the job done in the right hands.' He gauged the distance to the wood. 'Were there any head shots?' he asked.

'Four out of twelve,' Kostag said. 'Armour piercing. Their body armour was of no use.'

'Eight hundred metres would be respectable with a Drag on a good day,' Gunnymede said, estimating the distance.

'It was a good day,' Kostag said. 'The firing point was much higher. One thousand two hundred and fifty two metres to this edge. Twelve bullets. Twelve kills. More than a respectable shot, wouldn't you say?'

Gunnymede had to agree. He held the Dragunov out to Bethan who was taken by surprise and had to make a concerted effort not to drop it, holding it like a large fish.

'Are you okay to walk up there?' Kostag asked Bethan, seeing she was wearing a sturdy pair of trainers.

'Lead on,' she said with confidence.

'Shall I take that for you?' Kostag asked and she handed him the rifle and he handed it back to his driver. Kostag secured his satchel over his shoulder and led the way down the slope.

'Are you a sniper?' she asked Gunnymede as they set off behind him.

'No,' he replied.

'But you obviously understand the business.'

'I've worked with guys who are snipers and picked up a thing here and there. Sniping is a speciality. It takes natural talent as well as training. A headshot at twelve fifty with a Drag is very good I'd say.'

'What makes a good sniper?' she asked. 'Apart from training and natural ability?'

'Lots of practice.'

She found the comment interesting.

They crossed the ravine and headed up the other side. It was steep and lumpy with Bethan the most walking fit of the three. Kostag wasn't fit at all and was clearly feeling the strain as his breathing became severely laboured.

A policeman stepped from the trees as Kostag approached. He'd obviously been dozing as he brushed the dust off his backside and smartened himself up.

They entered the wood which was not as dense as it appeared from the clearing. Another fifty metre climb and

Kostag stopped to rest, his hands pressing heavily on his knees. Sweat trickled down his face and off the end of his nose. A police tape connecting a line of trees was a few metres beyond. Gunnymede and Bethan waited politely. The Albanian didn't take long and soon pressed on, ducking under the tape.

Another thirty metres and they came to a double line of tape. Kostag stepped under them and stopped again, taking a moment to dab his face with his shirt sleeve. He pointed to a patch of scorched foliage blackened by fire. 'You call this a hide in English, right?' he said, inhaling and exhaling audibly between each couple of words.

Gunnymede moved to get a better look. The side of the slope had been scraped away to form a level area long enough for a person to lie on. The ground and immediate foliage was heavily charred.

'This is how we found it,' Kostag said. 'The officer who was first on the scene was smart enough to make sure the area was not trampled.'

Kostag indicated another police tape that traversed the slope. 'It looks like the shooter came and went along this way.'

Gunnymede plucked a blackened blade of grass and inspected it. There was a deposit of white powdery substance where the charcoal ended. 'Phosphorous,' he said.

Kostag nodded. 'He used a phosphorous grenade to destroy everything. No evidence. No DNA. All burned.' Opening his satchel, he removed a plastic evidence bag with a charred metallic object inside and handed it to Gunnymede. It was the burned out phosphorous grenade.

Gunnymede scrutinised what remained of the factory markings. They were obvious enough.

'British army issue,' Kostag said. He produced another evidence bag. Inside was a small plastic container twisted by heat.

Bethan examined it. After a moment she shook her head, unable to identify it.

'Our forensics laboratory said it's a combination of ground turmeric, cumin, cardamom seeds and chilli powder,' Kostag said.

'Curry powder,' Bethan said.

'Yes. Based on the deterioration of the foliage we estimate he was here for five days.'

Gunnymede looked towards the clearing the other side of the ravine, assessing the sniper's point of view, the officers and vehicles quite visible.

'In that time, three different patrols occupied that clearing,' Kostag said. 'Each patrol spent between eight and twelve hours in position.'

'You said K-17 was in position for less than an hour when the first officer was shot,' Bethan said.

'Yes. The sniper was specific about who he wanted to kill. K-17 was his target. All of them.'

Gunnymede moved around the back of the hide and looked beyond it, further up the slope. 'What was his route out?' he asked.

'That's not clear,' Kostag said. 'We traversed in both directions but found nothing. I assumed he made his way to the road at some point. Perhaps he went directly to the border and crossed into Macedonia.'

'What about directly uphill?' Gunnymede asked.

Kostag looked up the steep slope. 'Why would he go that way? It's just a more difficult route out.'

Gunnymede moved in that direction. Kostag joined him. There was a barely discernible path through the foliage.

Blades of grass were disturbed in one direction, away from the hide.

'Any of your people go that way?' Gunnymede asked.

'I don't think so.' Kostag moved uphill to get a closer look. 'It could have been an animal.'

Gunnymede indicated a twig at shoulder height that had been broken and bending away from the hide. 'How tall are the deer around here?'

Kostag took his point. 'So let's check it,' he said, stepping off.

'Wait,' Gunnymede said.

Kostag ignored him. 'Let's just see where it goes.'

'Stop!' Gunnymede said firmly.

Kostag stopped to look back at him.

'Maybe he wouldn't want anyone following him,' Gunnymede said moving past him. A couple of metres up the hill he crouched to inspect something.

Kostag looked over his shoulder. 'What is it?'

Gunnymede plucked a long twig and reached out with it. Kostag focused on the end of it. A slender length of wire running across the path.

'A trip wire?' Kostag said, shocked.

Gunnymede followed the wire to the base of a tree where something was concealed by foliage. He removed the leaves to expose a black plastic device.

'What is it?' Kostag asked.

'A PAD – perimeter area defence. A directional mine.' Gunnymede looked back to see where Bethan was. 'We're all in the kill zone,' he added.

Kostag swallowed. 'Let's all move away. I'll call the bomb disposal.'

'No need,' Gunnymede said.

'I must insist you do nothing.'

Gunnymede pulled on the latex gloves. Bethan remained where she was, strangely fascinated. Kostag looked back at her with an exasperated expression.

Gunnymede applied the device's safety catch, disconnected the rubber strap securing it to the tree, unhooked the trip wire, removed the detonator and offered it all to Kostag. 'You have an evidence bag?'

Kostag exhaled deeply, pulled a plastic bag from his satchel and held it open for Gunnymede to place the PAD inside.

'It's safe,' Gunnymede said. 'Careful with the detonator.'

Kostag held the bag with some reverence as Gunnymede moved on.

Ten minutes later, they were back at Kostag's car.

'The PAD. Is it British?' Kostag asked.

'Yes,' Gunnymede said.

'You think the sniper was British,' Bethan said to Kostag. 'Which is why we're here.'

'There were some pretty good snipers around here by the end of the Kosovo war,' Kostag said. 'That was over twenty years ago. Whoever did this had a lot of recent practice killing people. He was a soldier, for sure, wouldn't you agree?' He was looking at Gunnymede.

Gunnymede didn't disagree.

'What was the motive?' Bethan asked.

Kostag shrugged. 'Whatever it was, he had a hatred for K-17. There was no mercy here.' He closed the trunk. They climbed into the car and it set off back the way it had come.

It was dark as the Mercedes pulled up outside a hotel in the heart of Tirana. Bethan and Gunnymede climbed out as the driver opened the trunk, pulled out their bags and placed them at their feet.

Kostag climbed out and offered his hand to Bethan. 'Thank you for coming,' he said as they shook. 'If we find anything of interest I'll be in touch.'

'And the same for us,' Bethan said.

Kostag looked Gunnymede in the eye and held out his hand. Gunnymede took it and Kostag shook it firmly, as if it was a little more special. 'And thank you, Devon Gunnymede. It was, how you say, most illuminating. Have a safe trip back home.'

Kostag climbed back into the car and it pulled away.

Gunnymede and Bethan picked up their bags and headed for the hotel.

'Wheels up at ten?' Gunnymede asked on receiving his room key.

'Excuse me.'

'Ten am, ready to go?'

'Yep. Sure.'

'Have a good night,' he said and walked up the stairs.

She watched him go. That was abrupt. But oh, well.

Gunnymede reached the second floor, walked along a creaky corridor to his door, unlocked it and went inside. After locking the door behind him he took a moment to take in the renaissance styled room that could've done with a face lift. In the bathroom was a large old bath with piping hot water. It was the first order of play.

Half an hour later Gunnymede was cleaned up and placing a fresh dressing on his wound. As he applied the last strip of tape a floorboard creaked outside his room. His eyes moved to the bottom of the door. The gap wasn't large enough to show light from the hallway.

The creak came again. Same floorboard.

He pulled on a shirt as he moved to the door, took a hold of the key and doorknob and paused to listen. Another creak, further away. He opened the door.

Bethan was halfway towards the stairs walking away. 'I was going to knock but changed my mind,' she said.

'Everything okay?'

'The hotel doesn't have a restaurant. If you want dinner you'll have to walk into the town.'

'Okay – thanks.'

'Sorry to disturb you.' She forced a smile and went down the stairs.

Gunnymede stepped back into his room. He felt he'd been rude.

He went to the window and looked onto the hotel entrance as Bethan stepped outside. She paused to look left and right and headed away.

Gunnymede felt a tinge of guilt as he watched her go. Unable to fight it he quickly pulled on his socks and shoes, grabbed his jacket and headed for the door.

Bethan walked along a quiet residential street looking at the architecture of the three story terraced houses on either side. Lights were on in most of the homes with cars parked on the street. She came to a crossroads as a car drove past and looked in every direction as if trying to decide which one to choose. She took the right turn and walked for a few meters before stopping, deciding the way ahead looked too dark.

She went back to the crossroads and straight across but stopped again. It looked worse than the previous option.

'Do you have any idea where you're going?' Gunnymede asked, startling her.

'You made me jump,' she said, recovering. 'The concierge gave me directions to what he described as a nice family restaurant. Left out of the hotel, right, right, left. But now I'm not sure.'

He joined her to take a look at the options.

I haven't tried this street,' she said, pointing directly across. 'Would you care to join me?'

'Sure.'

They crossed the road and walked along a residential street that was grubbier than the last with few functioning street lamps. She glanced at him. When he caught her look she smiled politely and looked away.

'What do you like to be called?' she asked.

'Mister Gunnymede.'

She hoped to find a trace of humour in his expression which she did. 'Devon. Dev. Or Gunny perhaps?'

'Take your pick.'

'I like Devon. I like Gunny too. I can't decide.'

They came to another crossroads.

'I'm going with straight on,' she said.

He shrugged indifference and they crossed into the next street.

'You think British?' she asked.

'Yeh, I'd say British military trained.'

'Why?'

'The PAD mostly.'

'Perimeter Area Defence,' she remembered.

'Very UK SF. The curry powder was another strong indictor.'

She looked surprised.

'Ration packs can be boring. Brits like their curry.'

'Not an Asian sniper then?'

'Brit smoke. Brit PAD. Boobytrap escape route. It looks very Brit SF.'

'Why kill all of them?'

'Because he could.'

She looked at him enquiringly.

'He wouldn't have arrived expecting to get everyone. The ones on the slope looked like they were trying to get to him and got caught in the open. I don't think they were very good at not getting shot.'

The street grew darker. Gunnymede noticed someone in a doorway, the glow from a cell-phone exposing him.

'How long do you think it took?' she asked.

'Did you check your phone when you were there?'

'No.'

'There was no signal. As long as no-one got away to raise the alarm, he had all the time he wanted.'

A man turned a corner up ahead the other side of the street. He seemed to pause and look for Gunnymede and Bethan before crossing the road and heading towards them.

Bethan hardly noticed him but Gunnymede's danger meter began to blink. The man looked handy. When he was metres away he stopped squarely in front of the pair. Gunnymede stopped and held out an arm to halt Bethan.

The man produced a large, serrated knife. Gunnymede held his arms ready to respond. The man muttered something and held out his free hand.

Bethan reached inside her pocket and took out her purse. 'He can have this.'

Gunnymede put his hand on her purse, pushing it back to her, his gaze fixed on the man's eyes. 'He'll probably want more than that.'

The man lunged forward and swung the knife in a wide arc. Gunnymede yanked Bethan back as the tip of the blade nicked her jacket. Several bricks were within reach on a garden wall and Gunnymede grabbed one and hauled it at the man. The brick bounced off his shoulder and went through a car window. Before the man could react, Gunnymede grabbed another brick and ran at him, releasing it at a short distance with all his might. The brick hit the man squarely in the face which sent him back. Gunnymede grabbed the knife hand and kicked the mugger brutally in the crotch, buckling his legs. As he leaned forward, Gunnymede kicked him in the throat. The man released the knife as he fought to breathe. He dropped to the ground struggling for air. Gunnymede followed it up with another brutal kick to the man's solar plexus.

'Stop!' Bethan said as she grabbed Gunnymede's arm.

Gunnymede stepped back and looked behind them to see two men hurrying towards them. He grabbed Bethan's arm and pulled her with him. 'Come on!' And they broke into a run.

They didn't have to run far before the residential street merged with a main road. Gunnymede guided her around a corner and into the road. A car drove past. Gunnymede kept hold of her hand and they crossed behind it.

Music came from a seedy bar up the street. Gunnymede looked back as they headed towards it. The two men arrived at the corner and paused to assess the situation.

'Go inside,' Gunnymede said to Bethan as they reached the bar.

'What are you going to do?'

'Just get inside.'

She picked up a bottle, grabbed a lid from a row of dustbins and held it like a shield, ready for battle.

Gunnymede studied the two men, waiting for their move. The thugs took stock of the situation and after a brief exchange stepped back out of sight.

The door to the bar opened, a man fell out onto the pavement, struggled to his feet and staggered away.

Gunnymede regarded Bethan with her bottle and dustbin lid at the ready and took an immediate liking to her. 'We should head back to the hotel.'

'I wasn't that hungry anyway,' she said, putting the bottle in the bin, placing the lid on top and brushing her hands clean.

'You okay?' he asked.

'I'm fine. You?'

'Perfect.'

Fifteen minutes later they walked into his room and she slumped into the only chair releasing a heavy sigh.

'How are you with blood?' he asked.

Her eyes immediately flicked to his side.

'Not mine. Yours,' he said. 'You have a cut on your chest.'

She pulled open her jacket to reveal a clean cut a couple of inches long in the V of her jumper, a line of dried blood going down inside it.

'You need to clean it,' he said.

She removed her jacket. 'You're bleeding too. Usual place.'

He pulled off his jacket and shirt to check his old wound. 'Be nice if it had a chance to heal, between you and your laptop and Albanian muggers.'

She pulled off her jumper down to her bra and looked unsure what to do with her wound.

'Wash it with soap and water,' he said.

She went into the bathroom.

He stepped into the doorway holding a piece of gauze against his wound. 'Do you mind?'

'No,' she said, moving to one side of the sink.

He joined her and together they cleaned their wounds.

'Do I need stitches?' she asked.

He took a look at it. 'I'll tape it. Dry it off.'

He dug the tape out of his first aid bag, tore off a strip and faced her as she dabbed the wound with a towel. 'Move your hands.'

She was suddenly conscious of the fact her only clothing above her waist was a flimsy bra.

He closed the cut and placed the strip across it. A brief check satisfied him. 'Add cosmetic surgery to my skills.'

He went back to his own wound as she pulled on her jumper. 'I need a drink.'

'Couldn't think of a better reason.'

She went to the fridge and examined the contents. 'No scotch. They all look like local brands.' She selected two, grabbed a couple of glasses, unscrewed the bottles and emptied their contents into them. 'Here.' She offered him a glass.

They raised them in a brief cheers. She slammed hers back. He was surprised but duly followed her lead.

She inspected her extended fingers. 'Still shaking.' She went back to the fridge and dug out two more bottles. 'Ek-ri-ga or Maf-ou-sa?' she asked, reading the labels.

'You choose.'

'Same glasses okay?' She cracked the bottles and poured them anyway.

Another salute and they downed them in one.

'Has there ever been a better all-round medicine in the history of the world?' she declared, flopping into the chair.

He finished taping his dressing. 'I'm curious,' he said.

'About what?'

'In the street, outside the bar, you held a dustbin lid threateningly. What were you going to do with it?'

She swung her arms out and slammed her hands together mimicking the crash of cymbals. 'You know, hit him so hard on the side of his head he vibrates. I've seen it done somewhere.'

'The cartoon network?'

'Why'd you think they backed off?'

'Captain America. That's who you reminded me of.'

'Captain America's long lost sister,' she corrected, going to the fridge again. She read the labels on several bottles. 'Not sure if we should be drinking any of these without food. Or at all in fact. This stuff's probably illegal in most countries. Oh, my. These are perfect. Vomitka or sheet-pees?'

'Difficult choice.'

She hid one in each hand and held them out. He closed his eyes and tapped one.

'Sheet-pees. Excellent choice.' She unscrewed the tops and poured them into the glasses. She grimaced at the smell of hers and they emptied them in one.

'That's got to be ninety proof,' he winced, feeling it burn his throat.

She suddenly felt the buzz and found herself looking at his strong body, in particular a couple of scars. 'They all come with a story?' she asked.

He felt self-conscious half naked and pulled on a shirt. 'And they get better with each telling.'

'What's the story behind the rash?'

'Rash?'

'Your neck?'

'Oh. I was recently hung.'

'Is that one of those comments that's so bizarre no one would believe it when it's actually true?'

'Can't fool you, can I.'

'And the wound on your side?'

'A Russian fighter jet bombed me.'

'While you were hanging by your neck I suppose.'

'Too much?'

'Not after a shot of Albanian sheet-pees. What are you doing here? I mean, I have no idea what I'm doing here, but do you know why you're here?'

'I'm looking for clues.'

'To what?'

'A secret.'

She smiled and, feeling a little drunk she picked up her jacket. 'That about sums it all up ... I'm sorry about this evening. The walk through the town. It was reckless of me.'

'We survived.'

'I bet you say that a lot. Actually, I feel quite special. Not everyone gets into a scrap with a secret service man.'

'Or Captain America's sister.'

She opened the door and looked back at him. 'Bye, secret service man.'

'Tell the entire hotel why don't you.' He smiled.

So did she as she left the room.

He found himself still smiling after she'd gone.

Chapter 12

An unmarked police car drove through the City of London, Gunnymede and Bethan in the back. The driver pulled into the kerb.

'Thanks for dropping me off,' Gunnymede said as he opened the door.

'Will I see you again?'

'That would be nice. Give me a call if you need anything.' He grabbed his bag, climbed out and closed the door.

The car re-joined traffic. Bethan couldn't resist looking back. She was pleased to see him watching the car go.

Before it was out of sight, he walked away. Minutes later he entered the Fulham and Hammersmith hospital and went to the reception counter.

'I'd like to see Megan Henderson,' he said to the receptionist.

'Do you have an appointment?'

'No. I was here a few days ago. I think you were here. I'm Devon Gunnymede.'

'Let me just check,' she said, smiling sweetly and looking at her computer. 'One moment please.' She picked up the phone and keyed a number.

Gunnymede looked around while the receptionist talked on the phone. 'Mr Gunnymede? Would you take a seat and someone will be with you.'

'Is everything okay?' he asked.

'Someone will be with you shortly,' she assured him.

Gunnymede took a seat.

It was fifteen minutes before an administrator arrived and explained that Megan was receiving treatment and wouldn't be available for the rest of the day. Gunnymede left the hospital consumed by thoughts and walked the short distance to Hammersmith underground station. The realisation that Megan was quite possibly gone from his life was confusing. She had become an integral part of his world, the only human being to have stuck by him throughout his trial and banishment. The only thread to string a future too. She had not been a deep rooted part of his game plan before his freedom was cut short but her love and loyalty had earned her a permanent place in his life. She had won his loyalty too, if not his complete unconditional love. It was the loyalty component of their relationship that was most impacted at that moment. He didn't know how that was going to play out. He needed to get his thoughts in order. Find out what happened. But his anger was as dark as a night blade at that moment.

Inside the entrance, a man in a business suit and coat was looking at a street map on his phone, following the progress of a marker as it moved inside the underground station. The man looked up to see Gunnymede enter the same time as the marker. 'Devon Gunnymede,' he said as Gunnymede walked past.

Gunnymede stopped to look at him. The man was in his forties, a blond mop of hair neatly combed on top of a hawkish face. He was wearing a crisp, expensive white shirt and shiny blue tie.

'My name's Simons. I work for Jervis.'

Simons flipped open a small leather wallet to reveal his MI6 badge, similar to the one Aristotle had shown the police at Heathrow. They were special badges, small with ornate detail. Silver and gold inlaid in simulated ivory. No expense spared in their production. On it was an inscription requesting any authority in the land to extend assistance to the bearer on demand. His name was inscribed on the back of it.

'You remember Jervis, don't you?' Simons asked. 'Head of operations.'

'He's been there a long time.'

'It's a long-term job, if you do it right. Welcome back to the fold. I was in the neighbourhood and wanted to introduce myself. We could find ourselves working together in the very near future.'

Gunnymede didn't know what to say.

'How was Albania?'

Gunnymede shrugged. 'Albanian.'

'Anything of interest?'

'Not at first glance.'

Simons studied Gunnymede. 'We're all on the same team, Gunnymede. Remember that.' He forced a smile. 'You take care of yourself. See you soon.'

Simons walked away. Gunnymede watched him leave the station. Odd bloke. Odd conversation. As he dug out his company credit card to use on the ticket barrier his phone vibrated. He accessed a message. Harlow wanted to see him in his Temple office. Strange though it was, Megan was already being compartmentalised in his head. Shelved but not forgotten.

Bethan was at her desk when DCI Dillon crossed the room and dropped a file in front of her.

'Take a look,' he said.

She opened it. The first page was a picture of an Afghan in his fifties.

'Mustafa Lamardi,' Dillon said. 'Former Afghan National Directorate of Security. He retired to Macedonia two years ago after opening a fat bank account with funds of dubious origin transferred from his account in Dubai.'

'Is Macedonia a popular destination for retiring Afghans?'

'Perhaps for those who don't want to be found too easily. If that's true it didn't work in his case. He was shot dead outside his home in Skopje a week before your mass border killing in Albania.'

'Why am I looking at this?'

'Take a look at the forensic report.'

Bethan turned the page to a photo of a Dragunov rifle. 'He was killed by the same weapon used in the checkpoint killings. What's the connection?'

'We don't know yet.'

'A thousand and seventy-five metre headshot.'

'Sounds challenging.'

'Apparently it is with a Dragunov.' She turned the page. 'Nothing on the sniper.'

'The Macedonians have drawn a blank on him so far. If it wasn't the same sniper it was the same level of expertise. Professional hit, clean firing position, no tracks.'

'Did he booby-trap his escape route?'

'No. The hide was on a rooftop. There was only one way down. I'd look at the possibility he did the Skopje job and then three hundred kilometres and seven days later crossed the border and did the Albania killings.'

'He was five days in the Albania sniper hide.'

'There you go. Two days to get there. Ample time.' Dillon held up another, older-looking file. 'I also have this for you which I know you'll find particularly interesting. It was prepared by an analyst just like you, now retired.' He placed the file in front of her. 'It's a reference guide to a profile pool.'

She read the title page. 'Unsolved British military related homicides.'

'Created in 2007. If we assume the Albanian sniper was British and that he's connected to Mustafa Lamardi's killing in Macedonia, both cases would fall into this profile pool.'

'How did you know about this?'

'I didn't until this morning. I sent a summary of your report upstairs at the request of those who are all-knowing and this came down in response.'

She read the file's introduction. 'Twenty-four cases – it goes back as far as the seventies.'

'The first three are unsolved killings of IRA members.'

'Mysterious IRA killings. Sounds like military intelligence assassinations to me,' she said.

'Analysts aren't allowed to be conspiracy theorists.'

'Which I'm not.'

'The MoD would be shocked to hear such a thing. Take a look through them anyway. Something might jump out at you.' Just as he was about to leave he had a thought. 'And how was your spy?'

She glanced at him and quickly looked away. 'Fine.'

Dillon tried to get a closer look at her eyes, suspicious about her.

'What are you doing?' she asked.

'I was on the streets for fifteen years before they parked me in here.'

'They probably parked you because you weren't very good at reading people's eyes.'

'Quite the opposite in fact. And you are a billboard, my girl.'

She accepted the bust. 'He was a knight in shining armour. How many girls get to have one of those in a lifetime?'

'Seeing him again?'

'We are worlds apart.'

'Good thing too.'

'Why do you say that?' She looked at him with a frown.

'I was warned about him.'

'In what way?'

Dillon lowered his voice. 'When I was given his name for the Albanian trip I naturally wanted to know more about who I was sending you off into hostile environments with. I asked a friend at the club who's in the MoD and has something to do with military intelligence. He only got back to me this morning. What he said was a little disturbing. Mr Gunnymede has done time.'

'As in jail?'

'Yes.'

'You confirmed that?'

'I didn't want to go digging around in case I set any alarms off.'

'If that was true how could he be working for MI6?'

'Very strange indeed. Did he say why he was assigned to the case?'

'No. If I were to guess, I'd say he wasn't sure either.'

'Well, don't expect any help from his department,' Dillon said as he walked away.

Gunnymede sat waiting in the ante-room to Harlow's office. The secretary opened the door and served Gunnymede her usual accusing stare as he past her.

Harlow was stirring teabags in a pot. 'Gunnymede,' he announced. 'Can I pour you a cup of tea? One sugar, right?'

How does he remember such details? 'I won't, thank you.'

'Has Jervis been in touch?' he asked, pouring a cup.

Odd question. 'No – I met Simons though.'

'Simons? You not met him before?' Harlow sat back and sipped his tea.

'No.'

'Of course not. He arrived after you left for the Americas. Strange fish that one. What did he want?'

'I don't know.'

'Hmmm. So. Interesting time in Syria. What was your impression of Saleem?'

'He's the serious type.'

'Capable?'

'Probably. Likes his theatrics.'

'He went to a technical college in Battersea. Quite bright. Not creative but good at replicating. This plan to attack London. It won't be his idea but he'll be capable of following instructions. He'll need help of course. He won't be able to murder the numbers he's talking about on his own. He's not driving a lorry through a crowded market. He'll need support. Logistics.'

'We came under attack when I escaped,' Gunnymede said. 'He may not have survived.'

'He did survive.'

Gunnymede looked at him.

'We had someone in that compound,' Harlow said.

'An operator?'

'One of Jervis's people.'

'A British Muslim?'

'Recruited in London. He was the trigger for Saleem's desert excursions. Very useful chap.'

Gunnymede could see the young Arab's face. 'He must've been the one who helped me.'

'How did he help you?'

'Saved my life.'

Harlow nodded interest. 'He missed his last proof of life. Not a good sign.'

Gunnymede was disappointed to hear that.

'We think Saleem has left Syria anyway,' Harlow said. 'We've had a sighting in Turkey. We haven't pinned him down but we think we can. As soon as we find him we'll pull him.'

'But he's our lead to Spangle.'

'I'm not so sure about that. He might've been while he was exchanging calls in Syria. We can't risk him coming to the UK with his dastardly plan.'

Gunnymede looked sceptical. 'I don't buy this whole Spangle and ISIS connection. Why is Spangle talking to a bunch of Islamic fanatics?'

'You mean why would a Russian, possibly FSB or former, have anything to do with a major ISIS terrorist attack on London?'

'Yes, if he was working with FSB interests at heart. But Spangle isn't. He's a drug tsar.'

'Who knows what drives Spangle or what palms he has to grease to get what he wants. Assume the ISIS attack is important to his interests. His greater plan.'

'What about the Russian planes that attacked us?'

'Coincidence perhaps. Bad luck. No one is powerful enough to protect all their interests in every theatre. Not even Spangle. At least he knows you're back in the game.'

'How?'

'There's a leak in the Baghdad embassy. Low level. Administrative stuff. We've known about it for some time now. It's been quite useful really. We were going to use it to release your arrival anyway but even better that you turned up there in person.'

'What will Spangle know?'

'That you're back on the payroll. He'll put two-and-two together, match the incident in Syria with your arrival in Baghdad.'

'Yes, but, he knows I was in jail. He'll want to know why I'm back on the payroll.'

'There, you got there in the end.'

Gunnymede sighed. 'So what now?'

'We wait and see.'

Gunnymede stared at Harlow.

'What is it?' Harlow asked.

'You rarely look me in the eye anymore. You don't trust me at all, do you?'

'It's disappointment, Gunnymede. I used to rate you. Now you're just a thief. It makes no difference you didn't steal from the Crown. Which is the constant, the thief or his principles? Surely it's the thief. This return to work isn't an opportunity to redeem yourself. You're not doing us any favours. You're saving yourself from a long stretch behind bars. You may or may not succeed.'

Gunnymede could only stare at him.

'Mustafa Lamardi mean anything to you?' Harlow asked.

'Afghan National Security Director. Former. He compromised an operation and sold us out to the Taliban.'

'How many people did we lose? One of ours and one SAS trooper?'

'Two SAS. One of the wounded died a few months later. We could never prove it was Lamardi.'

'But everyone knew. It was the heroin. He could be relied on when it came to tactical operations. We should've known he couldn't be trusted when it came to money. You'll be pleased to know Lamardi has paid his debt. Shot dead outside his home last week.'

'What's Lamardi got to do with Spangle, apart from heroin?'

'Isn't that enough? How was Albania?'

'Why'd you send me there?'

'Didn't Aristotle tell you?'

'I couldn't find even a remote connection to Spangle.'

'Keep looking. You have a good day, Gunnymede,' Harlow said abruptly, getting back to his work.

Gunnymede got to his feet and opened the door. 'The undercover operator in Saleem's compound. Who was he?'

'I'll see what I can do. Oh, I meant to ask you. How's Grace?'

That stopped Gunnymede.

'Dear Grace,' Harlow said with a little too much drama.

'I haven't spoken to her. Not since I got out.'

'She doesn't know?'

'It wouldn't surprise me if she did.'

'Yes, she was always well connected. Do send her my very best regards.'

Gunnymede left the room.

Chapter 13

The law offices of Birch and Allenby were situated on the eighth floor of the Stanley building in Fenchurch Street in the City of London. The firm hadn't always occupied such prestigious premises. The original office, when the pair first set up the business, was in Tooting, South London. There was only one room, shared by the two partners and a secretary.

Birch and Allenby always had high hopes for the business, as one might expect of young entrepreneurs. Their ambitions were pinned to a particularly fruitful category of law, a subject they'd both gravitated towards during tenures at Nottingham University where they first met. Birch specialised in Business and Human Rights and Allenby in International Human Rights Law. Between them they wrote dissertations on a selection of modules including Religion and International Human Rights and the Protection of Refugees and Displaced Persons in International Law. Both men had recognised, in the light of current geopolitical events, the potential for a financial killing to be made in the defence of an individual's human rights, particularly when a government could be called to foot the legal bills.

They raised start-up funds with a business plan presented to an investor who specialised in litigation that focused on the Iraq and Afghan conflicts, which were coming to an end, and where cases of human rights abuses could be identified and, in many cases, even created. None of the victims were British subjects. All plaintiffs were Iraqis or Afghans. And all defendants were members or former members of the British military. It was a goldmine.

Birch and Allenby left their office at 8pm, pretty much the same time as every other evening of the week. It had been a busy month for them. A busy year in fact. But the last quarter had been exceptional. And MoD cheques had been plentiful.

They were a happy pair. Chipper. Basking in success. They walked out of the elevators, through the security gates with a nod to the guard and across the lobby to the front doors.

'After you,' Birch said.

'No. After you,' Allenby replied.

Birch gracefully accepted and stepped onto the street and towards the underground car park. A skinny, malnourished dog was at the entrance rummaging through a dustbin. The animal paused on seeing the two men, partly out of curiosity, partly wary should the men be a threat, but mostly in the hope they might be the source of a morsel or two.

As soon as Birch was within range he kicked out at the dog, connecting his foot with its behind. The dog yelped and scampered away. 'Hate strays,' he shouted. 'They make the streets a mess with their crapping and rummaging.

'I find that surprising,' Allenby said.

'Why's that?'

'Because you married one.'

'How droll, Allenby. That was below the belt.'

'No. That's where you keep your girlfriends.'

'My, we are on form tonight,' Birch said, laughing as he led the way down a slope towards the first parking level.

'What can I say,' Allenby said. 'Money makes me funny.'

'Then you should be a complete riot this month!'

Both men burst out laughing as Allenby did a little skip as part of his routine.

They walked on into the dark, cavernous car park almost empty of vehicles.

'The lighting is pretty poor tonight,' Allenby noted.

Birch inspected one of the non-functioning ceiling lights. The plastic cover was shattered. 'The lights have been vandalised.'

'There are just too many low-lifes these days?' Allenby said.

'Where did I put my car this morning?' Birch asked himself as he took his smart key from a pocket and clicked it.

The lights on a shining new BMW flashed at the far end. 'There she is,' Birch said, heading towards it.

They stopped in front of it, shocked by what they saw. The windshield had been smashed in.

'What the bloody hell ...!' Birch exclaimed.

'Someone's deliberately done that. They've taken a club to it.'

Birch looked around at the handful of cars nearby. 'None of the others have been touched.'

A burly man stepped from a dark corner wearing a black boiler suit, boots, gloves, a black ski mask and wielding a long metal rod. He stood between the two men and the route back to the ramp and tapped the concrete floor with the end of the pipe. The sound echoed throughout the parking level.

Birch and Allenby turned around to see the man, legs splayed, calmly watching them. The lawyers exchanged looks, wondering what was going on.

'Are you responsible for this?' Birch called out.

The man tapped the concrete with the end of the rod again.

Allenby was first to recognise the potential danger and rummaged inside his coat pockets to produce a small plastic device. 'You see this,' he said. 'It's a panic button. A close friend who also happens to be a police superintendent gave it to me. All I have to do is push this button and the nearest police officer will be straight here.'

The hooded man didn't appear to be remotely phased by the threat. 'There's an envelope on your car,' he said, his accent northern.

Birch saw there was indeed an envelope tucked into the air intake.

'Take a look,' the man said.

Birch plucked out the envelope and removed a single page. Allenby joined him to read it.

'What is this?' Birch asked the man.

'What does it look like?' the man said.

'It's a death certificate,' Allenby said.

'Recognise the name?'

'Roland Peters,' Birch said as he recognised it.

'And the cause of death?' the man asked.

They read the cause, but neither wanted to say it out loud.

'I asked you what the cause of death was,' the hooded man said, taking a step closer.

'Suicide,' Birch said.

'A suicide you caused.'

'That's utter rubbish,' Allenby cried.

'You created false evidence which caused him to take his own life,' the man said coldly, taking another step closer. He gripped the rod in both hands and raised the end up.

'We work for the Ministry of Defence,' Birch argued, somewhat desperately, taking a step back. 'We're public servants.'

'You paid Iraqis to falsely accuse British soldiers of murder and torture.'

'That's not true,' Allenby said, swallowing. 'The men were convicted by the courts.'

'And you got paid a lot of money for your part in it. You're worse than any terrorist.'

'What do you want?' Allenby asked.

'Have a guess,' the man said.

'We have money.' Allenby was desperate. 'We'll pay you.'

The man mimicked the 'wrong answer' sound of a TV game show and took a step to within striking distance.

Allenby dropped his panic button.

Birch raised his briefcase in sudden fear-inspired anger. 'Get him!' he shouted.

Birch threw his case at the man as he lunged forward. The man neatly sidestepped, swung hard and struck Birch on the back of his neck breaking the base of his skull and snapping his cerebral cortex. Birch was dead before he actually hit the ground.

Allenby went on the charge too but the man displayed the elusiveness of a professional fighter and swung at Allenby's leg, smashing the kneecap. The lawyer went down with a piercing scream. As he hit the concrete, his eyes met Birch's a few feet away. He could see his partner was dead and that he was in a most dire situation.

He rolled onto his back, breathing rapidly, filled with such terror he could hardly feel the pain of his broken knee. The man leaned over him. Allenby could see his pitiless eyes through the woollen slits.

'Whatever you want, I can give you,' Allenby said in desperation.

'I want you to apologise to the soldier who killed himself because you destroyed his life,' the man said.

'How can I?' Allenby said, starting to cry. 'I can't bring him back.'

'I know,' the man said. 'That's why I'm sending you to him.'

The man raised the rod and brought it crashing down onto the lawyer's skull.

Chapter 14

Gunnymede stood on his apartment balcony in the boxer shorts and t-shirt he had slept in sipping a cup of hot, weak tea. The sight of the old Thames barge in full red sail cruising past was a pleasant but minor distraction. He needed to try and clear his mind.

He stepped back into the living room where a pair of trainers and workout gear, their labels still attached, lay on a couch. Ten minutes later, he was pounding the riverbank at a comfortable pace. He came across a patch of green with an outdoor workout stance and dived into it, punishing himself with various exercises until he felt the pain. He was breathing hard and glistening with sweat but it wasn't quite enough. Heading back along the footpath he aimed for a distant lamppost and sprinted as fast as he could towards it, determined not to slow down until he reached it. He only just managed it and, dizzy and exhausted headed back towards the apartment building entrance as a powerful motorbike pulled up.

The biker removed his helmet and ran his fingers through his thick, grey hair. It was Aristotle. He climbed off the bike and unclipped a briefcase from the seat.

'I didn't peg you for a bike man,' Gunnymede said as he arrived and proceeded to stretch the back of his knees.

'I'm not. It's a pool bike. I hate London traffic. What do you have planned for the day?'

'Nothing planned. I wait to serve.'

Aristotle gave him a look and headed into the apartment building.

'Nice to see you too,' Gunnymede said sarcastically. His phone chirped. 'There you go,' he called out. 'Has to be work. I have no friends.' He pulled the phone out of his shorts pocket and looked at the screen. 'Maybe I have one friend,' he said as he put it to his ear. 'Bethan.'

'Devon.'

'My Albania buddy.'

'How's your wound?'

'Fine. Yours?'

'I'm suing you. It's crooked.'

'Can we settle out of court?'

'Sure. When are you free?'

'Just say where and when.'

'There's a case I'd like to talk to you about. Are you in London?'

'I am.'

'What are you doing right now? Can I pick you up?'

'Erm ... sure. Why not?'

'Half an hour?'

'I'll send you the address.'

'Perfect.'

He disconnected and stiffly hobbled into the apartment building. Half an hour later, he was on the corner of the street watching oncoming traffic, the collar of his weatherproof jacket turned up against drops of rain that had just begun to fall.

A car drew up to the kerb, Bethan at the wheel. Gunnymede climbed in and she pulled away.

She smiled on seeing him. 'All I could think of while driving here was our adventure in Albania. Probably nothing to you, but it was pretty cool for me.'

'I thought it was pretty cool too,' he said, buckling in.
'That where you live?'
'Yep.'
'Nice digs.'
'Company flat.'
'Free accommodation on the river. Can't be bad.'
She eased the car through traffic as the rain got heavier.
'Where are we going? I'm starving,' he asked.
'To a farm just north of London.'
'A farm? This is to do with Albania?'
'Kind of, maybe, sort of, possibly. Maybe not.'
'Those are the kind of clues I'm used to working with.'
'So when a case gets cold what we sometimes do is look for relationships with other cases.'
'Connectivity.'
'Exactly. For instance, I've got a pool of cases that are all homicides related to British military personnel.'
'Which the Albanian case could possibly fall into.'
'This farm also has a slim chance of a connection so I volunteered to check it out. And I thought it would be a nice opportunity to chat with you.'
'I'm glad you did.'
'I know a cafe on route where we can grab a bite to eat.'
'Perfect.'
She takes a turn into another busy street.
'There was an assassination in Skopje a week before the Albania shootings,' she said. 'Have you ever heard of an Afghan called Mustafa Lamardi?'
Gunnymede looked at her. Interesting coincidence. 'Yes.'
'You have?'
'He was a former Director of Afghan National Security.'
'You just know of him or you knew him personally?'

'I worked in Afghanistan on occasion. Lamardi was a liaison between Afghan and British special operations. What's his connection?'

'Lamardi was killed by the same Dragunov rifle used to shoot the Albanian border guards,' she said.

Gunnymede found that interesting. 'Same sniper?'

'We don't know. Possibly. Seven days before the Albanian border killings. Same level of professionalism. I was hoping you might have some knowledge you might share with me.'

'I'm sorry, I don't.'

'Don't or won't?'

'I would tell you if I did.'

'Would you?'

'Look, I'll be honest with you. There are things that I would not be obliged to share with you but up until now there's nothing about the Albanian case that I know and you don't.'

'Okay. I believe you.'

'I'd tell you if I was lying to you.'

She glanced at him. 'I'd tell you if I was lying to you?'

'Yeh.'

She shook her head in wonder. 'Amazing... Who'd want to kill Lamardi?'

'A great number of people would be pleased to hear he's dead.'

'What people?'

'He betrayed us; the British military. He used his privileged position to compromise an operation and caused the death of several operators.'

'Military intelligence operators?'

'And Special Forces.'

'Were you involved in the operation?'

'Not directly. I was in country at the time. I was in the ops room when the operation went bad.'

'What happened to Lamardi?' she asked.

'Nothing. We discovered his connection months later but couldn't prove it.'

'How sure are you it was him?'

'The operation was to destroy a large shipment of heroin. We believe Lamardi alerted the Taliban and by doing so got himself into the heroin business.'

She pulled into the kerb and turned off the ignition. 'Food.'

They climbed out and entered the café. Gunnymede chose a table by the window while Bethan went to the counter. Minutes later she returned with two mugs of tea. He emptied a packet of sugar into the mug and took a sip as he looked around the simple, classic greasy spoon, most of the customers wearing overalls. 'This doesn't seem like your kind of local.'

'It would be if I lived closer. Great bacon sandwiches. The bad guy in my last case would come here. He'd have a cup of tea, at this same table, looking out the window. He'd cross to that paper shop every morning. I knew he was our man before anyone else did. He was a creature of habit, but not the ones he showed the world. He created a routine but he wasn't the type to do routine.'

'A creature of habit but not routine?' Gunnymede queried.

'It can be a habit to not have a routine. He never read the newspaper. The family that owns the shop had a little girl. She was similar to the girls he'd killed before. The morning he didn't turn up for his paper was the morning we caught him.'

'Did you save her?' Gunnymede asked.

'Yes. Her body at least. I'm not sure about her mind though. We weren't quick enough. I wasn't quick enough. We thought we knew where he was taking her. But being a creature of habit he changed his routine. I didn't see it coming soon enough.'

The café owner came over with two bacon sandwiches.

'Classic doorstep,' Gunnymede declared.

Bethan covered hers in ketchup and they bit into them. She nodded approval as she chewed. 'Classic indeed,' she said with a full mouth as tomato sauce ran down her chin. She stifled a laugh at herself as she wiped her mouth.

'You know how to enjoy your bacon sarnie,' Gunnymede said, also with a full mouth, grinning at her.

They settled into their meals as they watched the sodden world outside.

'Tell me about where we're going,' he said.

'There was a double homicide in the city last night. Two human rights lawyers. Both heavily involved in the prosecution of British soldiers who served in Iraq. They worked with IHAT, the Iraqi Historic Allegations Team. We're going to see an old farmer who made death threats to both lawyers.'

'And this is linked to those related cases – British military homicides.'

'It smells like it to me.'

An hour and ten minutes later, Bethan brought the car to a stop at the gate to a farm and turned off the engine.

She opened the glove compartment in front of Gunnymede, pulled out a double taser gun and checked it was functioning.

'You expecting trouble?'

'Farmers have shotguns.'

'You said he was old.'

'Seventy-three.'

'That would probably kill him,' he said.

She thought better of it, returned the taser to the glove compartment and got out of the car. Bethan unlatched the main gate and led the way into the cobbled courtyard.

A wooden barn in need of repair was opposite an old stone farmhouse. Everything looked run down. There was no sign of any livestock. Not even a dog. An ancient tractor sat rusting. Various pieces of farm machinery lay about, poorly maintained. This was not a going concern.

Bethan crossed to the front door and knocked on it. There wasn't a sound from within. The air was quiet.

She looked at Gunnymede. He had nothing to say.

She knocked again. This time there was the sound of movement inside. Seconds later the door opened and an old man with a grey pallor stood in the doorway. He didn't look well as he stared at her.

'Mr Peters. Albert Peters.'

'Who wants to know?'

'My name is Bethan Trencher. I'm with Scotland Yard.'

'I was here all night,' he announced.

'You know why we're here.'

'Those bastard lawyers were on the news.'

'It's been on television?'

'Internet,' he said. 'I expected you lot to be along soon enough. They as good as murdered my boy. They got what was coming to them. What do you want with me? I was here all night.'

'Yes, you said. You sent them several death threats, Mr Peters.'

'So, what of it?'

'Do you know who murdered them?'

'If I did, I'd buy him a pint.'

'Did the internet say it was a he, and only one he?'

'A wild guess.'

He moved towards her. She stepped back as if he was going to hurt her. He had no such intentions and stepped past her into the courtyard.

'That's where my boy hung 'imself,' he said, pointing towards the barn. 'In there. He stood on a chair, tied the rope around his neck and kicked the chair away. That's how I found him.' A quiver of emotion ran through him as he relived the moment. 'He left a note telling me he was sorry he'd failed me. I was at the cemetery that morning, putting flowers on his mum's grave. I haven't been able to work the farm for some years now. Tom left the army when he got back from Iraq and took the place on full time.'

Peters faced Bethan, looking into her eyes. 'He was a strong lad, but he was more like his mother emotionally. And those bastards stitched him up. He never tortured anyone, let alone a bunch of filthy terrorists. Those lawyers caused us to go bankrupt.' He started to cough but brought it under control. 'They've paid for it now,' he stuttered.

He started to cough again, but this time couldn't control it. He moved past Bethan holding his mouth and went back into the house. He disappeared inside and they could hear him coughing violently.

Bethan stepped into the doorway, concerned for him. 'Mr Peters?'

She could hear the continuous coughing and headed inside. She found him in the kitchen, struggling to open a bottle of pills which he dropped on the stone floor. She picked them up and unscrewed the cap while he continued his coughing fit. She filled a cup with water and held it and the pills out to him. Peters grabbed the water with a shaking hand, took a tablet, shoved it into his mouth and washed it down. He took a deep breath and continued his fight to control the coughing.

Gunnymede walked in. Bethan looked around the room that hadn't been cleaned in a while. A pile of dirty clothing on the floor in front of a full washing machine. The sink jammed with soiled plates and pots, as was the draining board. The bin overflowing with empty tins. Empty beer and wine bottles littered the place. There wasn't a clean surface anywhere.

Gunnymede caught her eye and indicated a wall out of view from where she was standing. She stepped to where she could see several pieces of military memorabilia. One of them was an SAS plaque with an inscription. 'Albert Peters 'B' Squadron 22 SAS'.

Beside it hung an old fawn beret with the famous winged dagger cap badge. A vertical row of framed black and white photographs showed a motley collection of white men with several Omanis, all grubby, some with guns, smiling and pally. A young Albert Peters was amongst them. On the bottom of one of the pictures was the inscription 'The Battle of Mirbat, Dhofar War, July 1972'.

A dagger hung beside the pictures.

Peters finally managed to stop coughing, unaware they were inspecting his artefacts. 'There are some crimes the law can't do anything about,' he said. 'But what are we supposed to do? Let bastards like those get away with it? Most people have to. But sometimes justice prevails. You can't complain about that, can you?' He coughed a couple more times but brought it under control. 'I would've taken an iron bar to them myself if I had the strength.'

Bethan looked at the old man whose sullen eyes were set on hers. 'Details of the weapon were not released.'

Peters realised his error but smirked anyway. 'I'm just an old fool, aren't I. Arrest me if you like. I don't care about anything anymore.'

Gunnymede left the room. Bethan joined him outside and closed the front door. He looked at her and raised his eyebrows. She did the same and walked on.

They climbed into the car. She started the engine and drove away.

Chapter 15

The sun dropped out of sight as Gunnymede and Bethan drove into London.

'Do you have any plans for this evening?' she asked.

He wasn't sure about his answer.

'I'm not hitting on you,' she said. 'Well, maybe a bit. I find you interesting.'

'I'm not playing hard to get,' he said. 'My hesitation is a sign of a complicated life at the moment.'

'That's code for you have someone I suppose.'

'As I say, it's complicated.'

She turned off the North Circular. 'How long've you been in the job?' she asked.

'Nine years. On and off – you?'

'Not counting college and training, three and a half.'

'You don't have to take me all the way home,' he said.

'I don't mind.'

'Any underground will do.'

'Whatever you want.'

He glanced at her, considering something. 'Do you want to grab something to eat?'

'Sure. Actually, I'm not far from here. I could knock something up?'

'That would be nice. You don't mind?'

'Not at all.'

'I'd love a home cooked meal.'

'It won't be anything elaborate.'

'A homemade sandwich would be more than perfect.'

Twenty minutes later they were walking into her house.

He closed the door behind him and took off his coat. 'Nice neighbourhood.'

'A gift from my parents.'

'Very generous.'

'What I mean is they died. I'm an only child.'

She went into the kitchen while he looked around the simple but tasteful furnishings. A picture of a man in senior police uniform sat on a bookshelf that contained some high-brow books on philosophy and art. 'Is this your father?'

'Deputy assistant commissioner.'

'Impressive.'

'He might've gone all the way if the big C hadn't got him.'

'Was that long ago?'

'Five years now. Mum died three years before that.'

'Was he why you joined?'

'I suppose so. Bit of a family tradition. Granddad made chief superintendent.' She came in with a couple of glasses of scotch and handed him one. 'I've upgraded your sandwich to chicken and broccoli pasta. Is that okay?' she asked as she went back into the kitchen.

'Perfect.'

'Where are you from? You sound London-ish.'

'That's where it all started. Mother was Scottish. My father was military.'

'They still around?'

'Mother left him, and me, for a richer, younger model when I was three. Father then went and got himself killed when I was six.'

She paused to look at him. 'That's very dramatic. Did your mother take over when your father died?'

'Nope. I haven't seen her since she left. I don't even know if she's still alive.'

'You were never curious enough to look for her?'

'No.'

'How'd he die?'

'He was killed in Lebanon while serving.'

'So who brought you up?'

His phone signalled a message. His expression darkened as he read it. 'I have to go. Where's the nearest underground?'

'About a mile. Where do you need to get to?'

'Hammersmith and Fulham hospital.'

She could sense his deep stress as he grabbed his coat.

'I can take you.'

'I have to go now.'

She hurried into the kitchen, turned everything off, grabbed her coat and headed for the front door. Within a minute they were in her car, speeding up the narrow residential street where she lived to a busy commercial road.

'Let's go,' he said, calmly but firmly.

She gritted her teeth as she pushed her way into a gap. Gunnymede grew impatient with the congestion and reached for a switch he'd identified earlier. A siren burst into life along with an array of concealed strobe lights around the vehicle. 'Go,' he commanded. 'They'll get out of your way.'

The situation unnerved her but she put her foot down and swerved into the oncoming cars.

'I've never done this outside of training,' she said over the sirens. And she wasn't comfortable with it then, either. The first oncoming car veered out of her way, mounting the pavement. The car that followed turned sharply while

153

hitting the brakes and its back end slid round. Bethan swerved an 'S' turn to avoid them all and accelerated away. She was at the peak of her abilities and barely holding it together. Once past the congestion, she returned to her side of the road and accelerated into her next overtake position. Traffic lights ahead turned red but she didn't ease her aggression as she pushed into the junction. Cars either side stopped hard as she sped through.

The final turn to the hospital gates eventually came in sight. She took the corner and he opened his door before she came to a halt. Two flashing police vehicles were parked outside the entrance. She braked hard behind them and Gunnymede ran up the ramp to the main entrance.

A small crowd was gathered in the reception hall, aware something bad was happening. The receptionist saw him and tried to intercept him as he hurried to the double doors.

'She somehow got the keys!' she called out to him.

Gunnymede headed along the corridor, towards the congregation room, the only place he'd ever met with Megan. He pushed the entry button and barged the doors open to find the place empty.

He went back along the corridor to see staff hurrying up a staircase. He tore past them to the next floor, through a set of doors into another corridor. Several police officers and staff were focused on a door, trying to open it. A nurse was banging on it anxiously while another attempted to push a key into the lock.

Gunnymede arrived and assessed the door. It was solid. A small reinforced window was in its high centre. He leaned over the others to look through it. A white, sterile room, a table and chair. A pair of feet off the floor against the wall, unsupported.

He stepped back to think quickly. An officer shouldered the door followed by a heavy boot but it didn't budge. A few feet away, fixed to a wall, Gunnymede saw a fire extinguisher. He grabbed it, raised it as he went back to the door and without a warning slammed it into the small window, smashing it inwards. The officers and nurses jerked back in shock.

Gunnymede punched the glass until it fell away, reached through with bleeding knuckles and felt for the handle. He found the key in the lock, turned it and the door opened.

Megan was hanging by her neck, her swollen tongue out, eyes bulging. He lifted her up, knowing she was dead but he had to do something. The officers quickly joined him. A nurse stood on a chair and grabbed at the knot in the cable around her throat, the other end tied to a conduit. She couldn't untie it. An officer handed her a penknife. She cut furiously, the wires inside the plastic coating making it difficult. With a supreme effort she managed to sever it and they lowered Megan to the floor.

Her face was blue. Her expression glazed. Gunnymede stared at her in disbelief.

Nurses elbowed their way through and tried to revive her. It was their duty though all knew it was futile. One of them pushed down on her chest as an oxygen mask was applied to her face. A defibrillator arrived as Gunnymede stepped back. Seconds later someone cried 'release!' and the pads were fired.

Gunnymede knew when the light had left a person's soul. He'd seen it often enough.

Bethan stood in the doorway. She'd seen everything since Gunnymede pushed open the door - his pain when he saw her hanging, his despair when she was laid on the floor.

It was dark by the time Bethan left the hospital in search of Gunnymede. He was sitting on a low wall away from the main entrance.

She sat a few metres from him.

'Thanks for getting me here,' he said.

'I'm sorry.' She felt awkward.

'We were engaged but the truth is we were never going to get married. I knew we weren't. She believed we were. I was playing a game of survival. She was the only one to stick by me.'

He got to his feet. 'Aunt Grace,' he said.

She was confused by the comment.

'You asked me who brought me up. It was my aunt Grace.'

He walked away.

Chapter 16

Gunnymede wore a black jacket, white shirt, black tie, his hair combed neatly, face cleanly shaven. He was part of a small, solemn group of people surrounding an open grave as a priest spoke into it. A shiny wooden coffin lay in the bottom of the hole. Gunnymede hardly took his eyes off it, his thoughts filled with images of a pretty, happy Megan. Laughing. Caressing. Night swims. Sunday runs. A pub lunch by the river. Lying side by side on green grass looking for images in the clouds. The picture he wanted to erase and couldn't was her hanging by her neck.

A hand squeezed his arm. He snapped out of his trance to find he was the only one at the grave. Everyone else was walking away. It was Megan's father, Jack. 'Come on, lad,' he said softly as if not to disturb the spirits.

Gunnymede pulled himself away and walked alongside Jack on a narrow path that meandered through the grounds.

Jack sighed and shook his head. 'What I don't understand is how she was compos mentis enough to get out of that secure area, get a pair of keys, lock herself inside that room, do all she needed to do to rig the cable and do what she did. She showed no signs of being aware of anything and then she does that. I feel for you too, Devon. There was no-one who could've taken your place in her heart. I remember the time you two first met. You were in Hereford on some course or other.'

'Free-fall.'

'That was it. Your first HALO you accidentally pulled on leaving the C130 and spent an hour coming down.'

'Not quite accurate. Someone thought it would be amusing to set my auto height finder to twenty-five thousand feet.'

'A welcome to Hereford. There was a camp bash on one night. Someone's leaving party.'

'You came with Megan,' Gunnymede reminded him.

'That's right. She'd been to the camp a few times with me for the odd bash. She asked me who you were. Someone nearby said, he's a spy.' Jack grinned at the memory.

'Jack ... I don't know if Megan and I would've ever made it to where you think we were headed.'

'I know marriage didn't suit you. Megan always believed you would both end up together. She wouldn't have given up easily on you. She was patient. She would've waited. I also know you loved her. You can't deny that, right?'

Gunnymede struggled to answer. 'Of course I did.'

'What I don't understand is why you don't want to do something about it,' Jack said, his voice growing dark.

Gunnymede was confused. 'About what?.'

'Are you just going to keep ignoring it?'

'Ignoring what?'

'She was raped! And the bastard who raped her is still walking this earth!'

'She was found all alone, Jack. No witnesses. No evidence.'

'Says who?'

'The police.'

'Bollocks. He's out there somewhere and that's a fact. Phase one is having the will to do something about it.

Phase two is finding out who he is and where he is. Phase three is delivering justice. Jesus Christ, you do it all the time on the job!'

'What you're talking about is not what we do.'

'It's exactly what we bloody well do,' Jack said in a raised voice, stopping to face Gunnymede. 'It's what we were designed to do! We do it for our government, our Queen, the people. But they don't do it for us, do they. Not when we need them to. We can do it for ourselves though, can't we? Of course we can. We can do it for our bloody selves.'

'If the police knew who it was, they'd be in jail,' Gunnymede said. 'You know that.'

'No, I don't know that. And you were born yesterday if that's what you believe.' Jack stared into Gunnymede's eyes. 'Do you feel any guilt?' he asked.

'About what?'

'Of course you don't. Why should you? Because the guilt's all mine. She's dead because of me, Devon. Because of me.'

Jack was highly stressed and walked away.

As Gunnymede watched him go his phone vibrated in his pocket. He fished it out to look at the screen. Aristotle.

'Mr Jervis wants to see you?'

'Jervis? I thought you worked for Harlow.'

'Be at Legoland reception for 1700.'

Aristotle disconnected. Gunnymede checked his watch.

He looked back towards Megan's grave. The sadness wouldn't go away.

Bethan sat at her desk reading a file from 2004. A former IRA commander mysteriously died in New York City after he left a Fenian pub, shot through the back of the head as he entered his house. She was more than halfway through the unsolved cases and a theme was starting to show signs.

She put the report down as her thoughts drifted to Gunnymede. His pain had touched her. She looked at her computer screen. Her hands hovered above the keyboard. She pushed herself and went for it, hit a few keys and seconds later a tracking reference for Megan Henderson popped up. Bethan hit the link.

The preview page of a file appeared. A picture of Megan. Bethan clicked on it and, to her surprise, a banner appeared declaring access to the file contents was denied. She repeated the process with the same result.

She looked towards Dillon's office. He was at his desk. She walked over and opened his door. He looked up long enough to see who it was and went back to typing. 'Yes,' he said.

She stepped inside and closed the door. 'I'm looking at a case related to the British military homicides trend. While I was researching connections I ran into a restricted file.'

'If it's restricted there's normally a good reason.'

'What if it's related to the case?'

'What case?'

'The one I'm looking at. There's an SAS connection.'

'You're not making any sense,' Dillon said, pausing.

'I'm looking at a rape victim with an SAS connection.'

'The trending pool I sent you is homicide not rape.'

'This one's not in the pool. It should be though. The victim died a few weeks after the rape. It was a motivated suicide, so that makes it a homicide.'

'How old?'

'Recent.'

'None of the cases in the pool I sent you were recent.'

'A woman was raped and committed suicide. Her father was SAS. That pool you sent me, most if not all of the perpetrators are or could be British special forces.'

'That doesn't quite fit, does it? She's a victim whose father is military while the other cases are victims killed by military.'

'Most of those cases were revenge where British Special Forces were possibly the avengers. This rape could be the catalyst to the next revenge.'

'You're talking about a future victim?'

'Isn't that what profile analysts are supposed to do, predict? The trend relationship is that all the victims were murdered because they somehow escaped justice for one reason or another. Mostly due to lack of evidence. What I'm saying is, if the man who raped this SAS soldier's daughter avoids justice then he could become a victim.'

'Has he avoided justice?'

'Now you're all caught up. That's what I tried to find out. But when I tried to access the file I ran into access denied.'

'I see – what do you want me to do?'

'Pretend you're my boss and help me.'

'And now we come back to the beginning. It's restricted for a reason. I don't suppose you could get me a coffee, could you?'

'The rape suicide victim was a twenty-six year old. Her name was Megan Henderson. She's a former girlfriend of Devon Gunnymede. Gunnymede also knew Lamardi, the Afghan national security director who was murdered in Skopje with the same rifle that killed the Albanian border police.'

Dillon studied her while the revelations sunk home. 'Pure coincidence,' he decided.

'My father said there's no such thing as coincidences.'

'He never said anything like that to me. Of course there are coincidences. I warned you about having conspiracy theories and now you have a Secret Service conspiracy theory.'

She fought to manage her frustration. 'You can't ignore this. If I'm wrong then we have nothing to lose. But if I'm right we have a chance at opening up these cases. Maybe all of them.'

He sighed heavily. She could see she was getting through to him.

'Do you know anything about the rapist?' he asked.

'Nothing. Maybe he hasn't been found. Maybe he's dead already. Maybe it's a gang or a cult. Why is the file access denied? It would be nice to know.'

Dillon considered something. 'Why do you think MI6 wanted one of their people to go to Albania with you?'

'I have no idea. I'm certain Gunnymede knows more than he's telling us. But then he's a spy.'

'Do you know who placed the restriction on the file?'

'No.'

He took a few seconds more to absorb it all before facing his monitor. 'Spell the name?'

'Whose?'

'The rape victim.'

'Me-gan Hen-der-son.'

A new screen appeared. He accessed the file register. A moment later the file appeared with the same restriction banner. He typed an access code and another window appeared with the restrictor's code. 'S C & O 19.'

'The UCs.'

'I'll talk with them.'

'When?'

'Tomorrow.'

She wasn't satisfied, but it was the best she was going to get.

His mobile phone beeped. He looked at the message and got to his feet. 'Got to go,' he said as he left the room, holding the door open for her.

Before he walked away something occurred to him. 'Are you seeing Gunnymede again?'

'No plans to,' she said.

'Be wise to keep it that way, don't you think,' he said and walked away.

She watched him go thoughtfully.

Gunnymede walked through the main entrance to the MI6 building and encountered the first layer of substance detectors. On completion, he made his way to a reception counter and, after providing his details, was asked to wait in the foyer.

Two minutes later an intelligent looking young man in a blazer arrived on the other side of the internal security barrier and signalled for Gunnymede to come through. Gunnymede stepped into the secondary security layer, this time an array of more sensitive scanners. When he emerged on the other side, the young man greeted him. 'Hello Mr Gunnymede. My name's Bowden. I'm Mr Simons' assistant.'

Gunnymede forced a brief smile.

'Follow me, if you would,' he said, setting off towards a glass barrier.

Gunnymede looked around as he walked through the lobby, deciding not much had changed other than a cluster of sci-fi looking probes in the ceiling.

Bowden used a pin code to access an elevator. They stepped inside and it descended.

'How's your day been so far?' Bowden asked.

'Delightful,' Gunnymede said, trying not to sound sarcastic.

'Warmer than normal for this time of year, wouldn't you say?'

Gunnymede decided not to keep silent.

The doors opened and the young officer led the way along a corridor to a metal door where he navigated through another personal identification system before they were permitted into a sterile room. The door automatically locked behind them.

'Remove any metal,' Bowden said. 'Watch, phone, pen, coins, everything. Do you have a metal zipper?'

Gunnymede started to check and then remembered his trousers had plastic zippers. He removed his stuff and placed them in the tray. Bowden touched a button, a partition moved aside to expose a steel door with large, robust hinges.

'Bowden and Devon Gunnymede,' Bowden said out loud.

There was a soft clunk and the steel door opened towards the men. This revealed another similar door. A very fancy bubble room. The inner door opened into a large room with a glass conference table on one side, the other dedicated to several monitors. Jervis and Simons were the only occupants, Jervis talking into a phone. Bowden left, closing the door behind him.

'Gunnymede. Good to see you again,' Simons said wearing a professional smile. 'Can I get you anything? A cup of tea or coffee?'

'Tea, please,' Gunnymede decided.

Simons poured the tea from a flask into a china cup balanced on a delicate saucer, adding a few drops of milk and offering it to Gunnymede.

'Any sugar?' Gunnymede asked.

Simons handed him some.

Jervis put down the phone. 'There 'e is,' he said in his south London accent with a hint of enforced posh developed over the years. 'Been a while since we last met, Mr Gunnymede. You two have met?'

'We have indeed, Mr Jervis.'

'How was your time in jail?' Jervis asked.

'Fine,' Gunnymede replied.

'A new experience for you.'

Gunnymede smiled politely.

'I'll have another cuppa, if you don't mind, Mr Simons,' Jervis said.

Simons complied dutifully.

'Hear you had some fun in Syria,' Jervis said, accepting the fresh tea from Simons.

Jervis had always fascinated Gunnymede. It was probably his cockney accent that was the most interesting thing about him, so out of place among the upper class accents of the other SIS mandarins he'd met.

Gunnymede had heard the usual stories about Jervis when he joined SIS ops. Jervis was one of the few mongrels that had made it into the inner circle. A feat indeed. There were doubtless many in the firm who didn't care for the commoner, not just because of his accent. He had a dubious pedigree. Jervis was a common city fox but with some special qualities. His earliest years, his birth to his teens, were shrouded in mystery, the most popular theory being that he came from gypsies and had a criminal record. The reason why no-one could uncover the truth about Jervis's early life was because all documentation of it no longer existed, the result of either catastrophic bureaucratic failure or deliberate intervention by a highly placed government official. The most popular rumour on that subject was that his predecessor and mentor, Sir Anthony Jewel, RIP, was the one who'd removed Jervis's records. Sir Anthony had plans for his favourite pupil and clearly didn't want the man's past to interfere with his future. Jervis found his way into the Secret Service via the army. The Intelligence Corps to be specific. Way before Gunnymede's time in the Corps. His first documented proof of existence was on operations in Northern Ireland as a tout-maker, creating and managing informants using bribery, threats or money. It was one of the most dangerous jobs in the field in those days and where he first displayed his rare gifts. He had a photographic memory, was exceptionally clever and as courageous as he was ruthless. It wasn't long before he was recruited by MI6 and brought to London where his skills were applied to the post-Cold War counterespionage program. After his success in managing a particularly complicated task he came under the gaze of Sir Anthony, who was the current operations director. Jervis spent some twenty years working under Sir Anthony and when the man retired, Jervis took his place. Gunnymede wondered if Simons had taken on the role of heir to the throne.

'That's why you're here, my boy,' Jervis said. 'Syria. Or to be precise, the information you came upon.'

Simons returned to his seat at the table and logged into a keyboard.

'Mustafa Lamardi,' Jervis said. 'Know who he is?'

The third time in a week Gunnymede had been asked that. 'Yes.'

Simons brought up a picture of Lamardi on a monitor.

'You know he's deceased?' Jervis said.

'I heard.'

'Any thoughts as to why Lamardi was killed?'

Gunnymede shrugged. 'Revenge for the deaths of our operators in Afghanistan. Or something to do with his drug connections.'

'Indeed. Several possibilities. Lamardi knew he was on someone's death list,' Jervis said. 'He contacted us the day before he was killed. He believed it was us who wanted to kill him. I told him we don't have an assassination program. He didn't believe me of course. He couldn't begin to comprehend why on earth we wouldn't have one. Do you want your tea freshened up?'

'No thanks,' Gunnymede replied.

Jervis topped up his own.

'Lamardi said that if it wasn't us who wanted to kill him, could we protect him? He had something to offer us. If we ensured his safety, he said he'd supply us with information about a significant Daesh attack on the UK. Obviously that was of great interest to us and so we immediately put gears into motion to get him to a safe location. But sadly we weren't quick enough.'

Jervis paused to finish off his tea. 'That's a nice cuppa that, don't you think? Problem with having it in flasks is it quickly stews.'

'That's because they sometimes leave the tea bags in,' Simons said.

'Really? I didn't know that,' Jervis said. 'This one's still pretty fresh.'

He put his cup down and wiped his mouth with a napkin before continuing. 'We can't find a connection between Lamardi and your Daesh friend, Saleem. There probably isn't a direct one. But we believe they both refer to the same attack. Hours before Lamardi was killed, he sent us a message. A good will gesture. A teaser. A snippet he hoped would give us incentive to move our backsides and give him sanctuary. You're familiar with the Nouvelle Route de la Soie?'

'Yes,' Gunnymede said. The New Silk Road. French military intelligence was the first to map it out a few years back. It wasn't a road exactly. Not all of it. Not like the ancient silk roads. This was primarily a modern drug trade route consisting of planes, trains, boats, mules, tracks and roads linking Afghanistan, China, India, various Stans and Eastern Europe into the West.

Simons brought up a map showing the New Silk Road routes, varied and intertwining across Central Asia.

'Lamardi gave us a name,' Jervis said. 'Taz Yon. An Afghan Silk Road ferrymen. Looks like Taz Yon is bringing something west other than the usual shipment of heroin. And we need to find out what that is. Saleem's still in Turkey as far as we know, no doubt preparing to move West to the UK.' He got to his feet. 'I must fly. Good to see you again, Mr Gunnymede. Stay out of trouble. Enjoy your trip.'

Jervis left the room, the door sealing shut behind him.

Gunnymede looked at Simons who was pouring himself a fresh cup of tea. 'Enjoy what trip?'

'Taz Yon left Kabul two days ago,' Simons said. 'He's on the Silk Road with cargo as we speak and heading west. It's the cargo we're interested in. Heroin for sure. But what else? We know where he is at present because he's carrying three cellular phones and we have their MINs. But his MO is to ditch his phones along the route and pick up new ones. If we don't get the MINs of the new phones we risk losing track of him and therefore his cargo handover which could be anywhere in Russia, the Ukraine, Turkey or even further west.'

'Don't you need to be within a few K to get the MIN?'

'From the air, yes. But on the ground, one must be closer. He's heading through Kazakhstan, which means he's going to cross the border into Russia here. It's the last predictable point of his route west. After that, he could go anywhere. Which is why we need to be in this bottleneck here, just inside Russia.' He pointed to an area on the map between Volgograd and the Kazakhstan border.

'We can't risk putting up a drone. The Russians will detect it. It's a good location for us because of its remoteness. All we need to do is get within sight of this road, identify Taz's convoy, record every MIN and get the info to GCHQ who'll do the rest.'

So this is Jervis's trip. Gunnymede looked at Simons who was looking back at him with a thin, knowing smile.

'Easy enough, don't you think,' Simons said.

Gunnymede almost said that if Simons had any operational experience he'd know that was a stupid thing to say but he just about managed to hold his tongue. 'Is the kit already in country?' he asked.

'No. We have to take it in.'

'Which means avoiding a legitimate border crossing or entry port.'

'Correct.'

'When are you expecting Taz at the border?'

'Tomorrow afternoon.'

Gunnymede's look of surprise was instant and unguarded.

'Which means we'd like to be in position by early tomorrow morning,' Simons added.

'Tomorrow?! That's ridiculous. The only way to get there by tomorrow is to fly and you can't fly into that area without being detected.'

'Correct. An air drop is the only way in at such short notice.'

'You just agreed nothing can fly in there. So how can you do a drop?'

'By using a plane that has a legitimate reason to fly over the area.'

'What plane do we have has a legitimate reason to fly over Russian airspace, other than a commercial flight?'

Simons smiled knowingly, raising an eyebrow.

Gunnymede looked at him as if he was crazy. 'You've got to be kidding me. How does that work?'

'There's a new technique we've been working on,' Simons explained.

'A technique?'

'It's not entirely new. There was a similar program in the seventies. It wasn't successful for various reasons. The important thing is the Russians won't be expecting it.'

'I've got to hear this,' Gunnymede mumbled.

'Oh, you'll do more than just hear it.'

'You're talking about me doing this?'

'Why do you think you and I are discussing it?'

'And I'm going to use a regular commercial flight to drop into Russia?'

'Correct.'

'A parachute drop.'

'Correct.'

'So I catch a regular flight and, at the designated time, I get out of my seat, pull on a parachute, open a door, wave farewell to the passengers, who by this time are doing their best not to get sucked out with me, and leave?'

'Of course not. We're not idiots. We have thought it through. It's been tested.'

'What's been tested?'

'You won't be in the cabin with the passengers. They won't even know you're on the plane. You'll be in the front landing gear compartment. The doors will be opened at the appropriate location and you'll ... drop out. You'll be wearing the latest stealth fabric to hide your signature – your size actually. Your chute will pop below radar and you'll land and get on with the task. It's a damned good plan.'

'It's been done?'

'Of course.'

'In Russia?'

'No. We've done simulations here. We've only got one pop at this for real. The Russians will figure it out eventually but you'll be long gone.'

'You're serious, aren't you.'

'You've done over twenty HALO jumps with the SAS. This is the same thing. The only unconventional bit is the drop out of the wheel housing. Otherwise it's an ordinary jump.'

Gunnymede pushed his fingers through his hair as he struggled with the concept. 'That's not ordinary.'

'What's the problem?' Simons asked, getting testy. 'If you're not up to it, it would put us in a bit of a bind. We went to a lot of trouble to divert you from jail and get you on this task.'

'My task is to find Spangle.'

'Which is why you're doing this and no one else.'

'This is a simple MINs check. Anyone could do it.'

'You're forgetting the other reason you were selected. This needs to be kept tight.'

'Bollocks. You could send an SF operator and he wouldn't need to know why he was there.'

'This requires someone who knows why he's there. Things could change. It needs to be you – what is it you're so worried about?'

'All of it. How confident are you the Russians won't detect the free-fall?'

'At their best they won't understand the anomaly in the time it will take you to complete the task and get out of there.'

'And if you're wrong, I'll end up in a Russian prison.'

'If you don't go, you'll end up in a British one.'

'I'll take the British one, thanks.'

Simons was about to lose his temper when he managed to hold onto himself. He forced a smile. 'Gunny ... this is an extremely important task. We have to get to that convoy. It's highly likely there's a WMD on it. All evidence points to that. This could be our only chance. Thousands of dead Londoners. Isn't that what Saleem said?'

Gunnymede sighed heavily. He was trapped. He got to his feet. Simons watched him for any signs. Gunnymede changed his gaze to the ceiling. Simons sensed he was cracking.

Gunnymede finally looked at him wearing the frown of the defeated.

Simons smiled. 'Good man.'

Saleem stood in darkness on the side of the road at the Kazakhstan border checkpoint while he waited for Taz to complete his dealings with the captain of the guard post. It was an isolated crossing point situated on high open ground miles from the nearest human habitation. A perfect place to cross and not just because of its isolation. The guards were corrupt and looked forward to illegals as a way of adding a bonus to their meagre salaries. In this case, a healthy bonus.

An icy Siberian wind blew from the north east. Saleem was chilled to the bone despite the thick sheepskin jacket, heavy wool jumper and pakol he'd been given on his arrival in Toragundi, northern Afghanistan. In fact, he'd been cold since leaving Syria. Taz told him the desert had thinned his blood. Saleem was cold but he didn't fancy returning to Syria in order to get warm again. He would never be that cold.

They'd been travelling in a convoy by road for eight days since leaving Toragundi. Over two and a half thousand kilometres to the Kazakhstan Russian border. It was as if the powers that be in ISIS wanted to remove all scent of his trail from Syria by finding a starting point to the UK that was as isolated as possible. You couldn't get much more isolated than where he was. The convoy had begun the journey with eight vehicles; five Toyotas, an old British four ton Bedford lorry and two Renault vans. The lorry lost its axle the second day crossing Turkmenistan. The initial roads were pretty bad and the lorry, which must've been fifty years old at least, had finally given in to the hateful terrain. The roads markedly improved halfway across Turkmenistan. The two vans left them on entering Kazakhstan, diverting to the east of the country on their way to Astana. Two Toyotas headed north into Russia leaving Saleem with the remaining three. The plan was for Saleem to stay with Taz until they reached Kiev, where they'd unload their cargo. Saleem would then make his way to the Belgian coast. The final leg was a boat to England. And then on to the task.

One thing constantly niggled him, though. It was a private pain. There was one other person outside of the very tight circle of trust who had knowledge of his plan. Someone who shouldn't know. The enemy. Some British Army Intelligence Corps wanker named Gunnymede who should've been hung dead seconds after he learned of the plot. How the man had escaped was a mystery. But escape he did. Still, Gunnymede had no knowledge of timings or location, both of which were essential in preventing the operation. What he did know was Saleem. Saleem had to assume Gunnymede had returned to England with news of the threat. Which meant if the security services knew Saleem had left Syria, they would be on the lookout for him. If Saleem's bosses knew that, they'd pull him from the operation, there was no doubt of it. It was a risk Saleem shouldn't take. But he was compelled to. He couldn't let anyone else have the glory. This show was his. The only fear he had was of failing. What truly fuelled his excitement, and indeed confidence, was the sheer simplicity of the operation. The fundamental rule of planning was to keep it simple. And his plan could not be simpler, considering the mayhem it would cause. The next major obstacle was getting into England.

He looked towards the guard post, hoping Taz would be finished soon. He could then start the engine and get warm. Warmer at least. All Taz had to do was pay the bill for getting the vehicles through and pick up the new phones. But Taz was a great talker and was no doubt enjoying some smokes and a few shots of vodka.

Be patient, Saleem told himself. It would all come together.

Chapter 17

Gunnymede stepped into Legoland's underground car park where dozens of private and fleet vehicles were parked. Two black 4x4s were waiting to depart. Aristotle, dressed as if he was going to a funeral, stood beside one of them. He nodded on seeing Gunnymede and climbed into the back seat of the lead vehicle. Gunnymede got in beside him.

'You've gone through the equipment?' Aristotle asked.

'Yes.'

'The maps?'

'Yep.'

'You are happy with everything?'

'No.'

Aristotle ignored the answer, as if Gunnymede was a child.

The vehicles made their way through the garage, up a steep ramp and into an alleyway that led onto the main road where they accelerated away.

They passed a flashy black Range Rover parked across from the MI6 headquarters. Inside were the blingy thugs who'd taken Gunnymede's phone.

The thug leader looked up at the towering MI6 building. 'This is the address your bloke gave you for that car.'

'Yes, boss,' his underling said.

'This is MI6 headquarters.'

'Yeh, I know.'

'You fuckin' idiot.'

Aristotle unzipped a large holdall on the floor between their feet. Inside was a collection of transparent plastic bags containing various pieces of material and technology. He opened another to reveal a parachute.

'Did they show you footage?' Aristotle asked as he pulled out a pair of ski gloves and goggles.

'Of what?'

'The test runs.'

'Someone bailing out of the wheel housing?'

'There's footage of the drop and landings.'

'It wasn't mentioned.'

'It shows one of the early jumpers leaving the wheel housing and bouncing along the bottom of the fuselage. He hit it several times and was knocked unconscious.'

Gunnymede looked at him. 'Are you trying to wind me up?'

'He was fine. The automatic chute opening worked perfectly.'

'Otherwise he would've creamed in.'

'What?'

'Hit the ground at terminal velocity.'

'Yes. Let's go through your equipment.' Aristotle pulled out items from the holdalls. 'Weapons. Suppressed assault rifle, pistol, ammunition for both. Altitude meter. Oxygen and mask. Helmet. Solar phone charger. Goggles. Earplugs. Water bladder. Snacks. Med-pack. Emergency map and compass. Passport. Travel docs and money. For tracking, we'll use your phone. And of course the Raptos which you will need to acquire the phone MINs.' He checked his watch. 'You should put on the stealth suit now.'

Gunnymede removed it from the bag and unfolded it. It was big. After a struggle to figure out which end was which he managed to manoeuvre himself into it. When he was finished he looked like a giant caterpillar.

'Where we flying out of?' Gunnymede asked.

'Gatwick.'

Gunnymede sighed and dropped his head back.

'Are you nervous?'

'Of course I'm nervous.'

'It will pass when you are in free-fall.'

'Why, because I'll be knocked unconscious after bouncing off the fuselage?'

'I have done worse than this.'

'Oh, yeah? Like what?'

'I had to jump from a plane into a snow drift without a parachute.'

'Deliberately?'

'Yes.'

'I mean, it was a planned drop?'

'Yes.'

'You weren't pushed?'

'Of course not.'

'You volunteered?'

'Yes. It was an operational requirement.'

'Fuck.'

'Exactly.'

'What I mean is, that was more stupid than this jump.'

'And I survived.'

'Are you sure?'

Aristotle gave him a cold look.

The vehicles entered the airport perimeter at a private checkpoint and headed along an interior road. Aristotle's phone buzzed and he checked the message. 'Taz is at the border.'

'Already? Isn't that tight?'

'You'll have plenty of time. He usually spends several hours there getting drunk.'

Bethan sat at her kitchen table working on her laptop by the light of a lamp, sipping a cup of tea and eating a sandwich.

Her mobile chirped and she picked it up. 'Hello, boss.'

'S C & O 19 won't give you access,' Dillon said.

She slumped with disappointment.

'They expect to be able to release information on the case in the next week or so.'

'That's it?'

'I'm afraid so.'

'Did you find out if there is a suspect at least?'

Dillon went silent.

Bethan grew hopeful. 'There is, isn't there?'

'Yes.'

'A week could be too late.'

'That's irrelevant.'

'His life is irrelevant?'

'S C & O 19 is mounting an important operation based on elements of the case. That operation takes priority.'

'To a human life? Did you tell them he was in danger?'

'It's only a theory and not a very tight one either.'

'This is a Catch 22. You realise that, don't you?'

'It's a significant operation as I understand it.'

'We're missing an opportunity to solve several murders and by doing so prevent others. We're talking about organised serial killings.'

'I was going to trust you with a name but I'm not sure I will now.'

'You have the rapist's name?'

Dillon goes silent again.

'I promise you I can be trusted with it.'

'If I give it to you it has to be for research only. They'll release the name in a week but you'll have the jump.'

She perked up. 'Absolutely. Of course. I understand completely.'

'I want your word,' Dillon insisted. 'Your solemn promise not to share it with anyone or act on anything you find without consulting me.'

'I promise. I won't do anything with it other than background research.'

He hesitated.

'I won't do anything that will raise a flag,' she insisted. 'I promise.'

'Your friend Jedson is the field manager on this.'

'Jedson? He's an imbecile.'

'Apparently not as stupid as he appears. His undercover work has provided a lot of significant operational data. They're actually talking about a promotion if he pulls this one off.'

'Oh dear. He'll be more insufferable than he is already, if that's possible.'

'You ready for the name?'

'Yes.'

'Milo Krilov.'

Bethan tapped the name onto her computer screen. 'Krilov with a K?

'Kilo, Romeo, India, Lima, Oscar, Victor. Russian. Former Russian Special Forces.'

'Special Forces?'

'Extremely dangerous.'

'Any idea why he wasn't charged?'

'He's essential to the operation.'

'Is he aware of that? I mean, is he volunteering info?'

'No. Even more reason why we must respect the confidentiality. He doesn't know we're onto him.'

She typed his name into her police data portal. 'Thank you, sir.'

As Dillon disconnected his call a picture of Milo Krilov appeared on her computer screen. A heavy set, balding man who looked every bit an Eastern European thug.

The two MI6 4x4s drove towards an aircraft parked alone and away from the terminal buildings, a British Airways Boeing 777. There was another 4x4 parked in front of the aircraft. Two men wearing overalls were beneath the front wheel arch shining lights up into it. As the 4x4s arrived, Gunnymede watched them place a ladder that reached up inside the wheel bay and one of them climbed inside.

'The crew will be here in about thirty minutes,' Aristotle said. 'Soon as the guys attach the harnesses you'll get into position. The pilot may shine a light on you while he carries out pre-flight inspections. He'll know you're there of course.'

'What's the drill if he misses the drop?'

'Your only option is to release over Kazakhstan. Unless you want to continue all the way to China. Landing in Beijing would not be a good idea.'

No kidding.

Gunnymede watched the engineers faff around in the wheel housing, attaching straps and what looked like an oxygen bottle.

'You're not English,' Gunnymede said.

'Do I sound English?'

'No. But then not all English sound English.'

'I'm Greek.'

'I had my suspicions,' Gunnymede said, rolling his eyes.

'Aristotle's not my real name.'

'Seriously? And there was I thinking you were related. So what's a Greek doing working for 6?'

'It's complicated.'

'I would hope so.'

'My relationship is with Harlow. Call it a special relationship. His father and my father worked together in the Second World War. My father was with the resistance. Harlow's father was with the SOE. You know how nepotistic MI6 is. Wasn't your father in the firm?'

Gunnymede glanced at him.

Aristotle moved on. 'Harlow's father parachuted into Greece one day and stayed for more than a year fighting the Germans and Italians. They became good friends. After the war Harlow's father often came to visit. I knew Harlow as a child. I used to beat him with a stick. He wasn't a very nice boy. Spoilt. Typical upper class wanker.'

'And now you like him?'

'He's tolerable.'

'How'd you end up working for him?'

'I was a Greek civil servant for thirty-six years.'

'Secret services?'

Aristotle shrugged without denying it. 'Part of the time. I was stationed in many embassies around the world. When I retired, Harlow asked if I'd like to work with the British. I saw it as a kind of family tradition.'

'You were working for 6 while a Greek civil servant?'

'I never said that.'

'You didn't need to. So, what exactly is your position in the firm?' Gunnymede asked.

'I'm nothing but an oily rag to a very large engine.'

Gunnymede looked at him, unsure if he could believe any of it. The floodlights went off, plunging the area in darkness.

'They're ready for you,' Aristotle said.

There was a knock on the window. One of the MI engineers gave them a thumbs up and they climbed out.

Gunnymede awkwardly made his way to the foot of the ladder in his cocoon and an engineer attached clips to hoops on the back of it. 'Pure silicon carbide,' the engineer said as he tightened a drawstring. 'Best RAM there is. You familiar with RAM?'

'Radiation absorbent material,' Gunnymede said.

'It won't conceal you completely but it shouldn't raise any alarms. Just another dead bird.'

'Dead bird?' Aristotle asked.

'His radar reflection won't be much greater than that of a goose,' the engineer explained. 'You'd be surprised at the number of birds that die while flying. A normal flying bird has a pattern anomaly that is ignored by radar tracking algorithms. Otherwise early warning systems would be triggering every minute. But when they die and drop it's out of rhythm and they can attract attention. Russian radar will track him falling but the operator will assume it was a bird strike because of the stealth image.'

'What kind of bird?' Gunnymede asked.

'What?' the engineer asked.

'What kind of bird? I'm dropping at 36,000 feet.'

'Geese?' Aristotle suggested.

'Geese fly at 36,000 feet?' Gunnymede asked, unconvinced.

'Actually no,' the engineer said. 'Geese are around 30,000. I looked it up. The highest ever recorded bird was at 37,000 feet.'

'What was it?' Gunnymede asked.

'A Rueppell's vulture,' the engineer replied with some satisfaction.

'A vulture?'

'That's right.'

'What time of year?'

The engineer was suddenly not quite as confident. 'I don't know,' he said. He held the parachute up for Gunnymede to pull on and buckled it up around his chest and thighs.

'Do you think the Russians know about Rueppell's vultures?'

The engineer gave him a pathetic smile.

The final touches were oxygen bottle and mask, a pair of goggles, his helmet and an altimeter which Gunnymede strapped to his wrist, all coated in tiny silicon carbide cones.

'Up you get,' the engineer said as he zipped up the final flap of the stealth suit. 'Good luck.'

'Enjoy your trip,' Aristotle said.

'I'll bring you back some fake caviar.'

Gunnymede climbed the ladder. The engineer inside the wheel housing attached the harness to the ceiling and helped Gunnymede into position. 'I don't suppose you've done this before?' he asked.

'Nope.'

'It's basic enough. The harness'll hold you into the ceiling. Once the doors close it'll be like lying in a hammock. Your O_2 is here, enough for twenty-four hours. Your suit heater plugs in there.' He plugged it in. 'Refreshments here. If you need to take a piss, just do it through this flap onto the door. If you want to take a dump you're on your own - design budget didn't stretch that far. A couple of minutes before the drop, the doors'll open. Pull this toggle here and the harness'll disconnect you. Position yourself on the wheel, which will be here. The pilot'll give the wheel a jerk a minute before you reach the drop zone. Your backpack is clipped to the parachute harness as per normal HALO jumps. When you're over the drop point the pilot will give the wheel another jerk. That's your signal to release. Don't hang about. Every second is about two hundred and fifty metres off your landing point. Six seconds a mile. He will've allowed for wind speed and direction so that wheel jerk will be three seconds from smack above your landing point. Is that all good for you?'

'So, from the second wheel jerk I've got three seconds to fall out,' Gunnymede said.

'Thousand and one, thousand and two, thousand and three,' the engineer said as he tightened the straps and made a final check of everything using a flashlight. 'You got your ear defenders?'

Gunnymede held them up.

'That's your harness release toggle.' He pointed to a strap above Gunnymede's face. 'Right then. You're good to go. Good luck. Safe journey.' The engineer struggled to give him a smile as if that was all he could offer. He was clearly concerned yet also impressed with the stranger and could only wonder who he was and what his mission was. He removed the ladder and walked away with it.

Gunnymede made himself comfortable. His only view was the ceiling. He heard vehicle doors close, engines gun to life and drive away. A few minutes later the floodlights came back on. It was business as usual for the aircraft.

Gunnymede closed his eyes. It was comfortable if nothing else. Butterflies flew around inside his belly but not as badly as before. He was handling it. Kind of. Half an hour later the beam of the pilot's flashlight fluttered above him. The man had no idea what to expect when he shone his torch up into the darkness. He knew someone would be up there but nothing else. He was uncomfortable knowing someone would be hanging beneath him for several hours and that he'd drop him away at thirty-six thousand feet while they were doing six hundred miles per hour. And like the MI6 engineer, he could only wonder who the person was and what they were going to do when they landed in Russia.

Thirty-five minutes later, the plane taxied towards the runway. Gunnymede looked down at the tarmac. The engines roared to full power and he jolted in the harness as the aircraft accelerated. Turbulence filled the cavity with increasing ferocity. Something was flapping madly at Gunnymede's feet. The aircraft rumbled along. From his perspective the runway surface was surprisingly uneven. The wheel structure bounced violently at times, finding dips and bumps as the aircraft picked up speed. When the wheel left contact with the tarmac it continued to spin. The hydraulics immediately kicked in, there was a loud clunk as the suspension elbow disengaged and the wheel supports folded inwards and rose up towards him.

The wheel stopped a few inches short of Gunnymede's back and the double doors began to close. As the gap got smaller the turbulence, which had reached hurricane proportions, reduced proportionally. The sprinklings of lights on the ground were gradually shut out until, with a final clunk, it went completely dark and the wind abruptly ceased.

It wasn't as loud as Gunnymede thought it might be, to the extent that he didn't use his earplugs, the hooded part of the stealth suit providing enough protection. He couldn't see a thing at first, but within minutes, his eyes adjusted to what little light there was coming from various LEDs dotted about, not that there was much to look at.

He felt a vibration in a trouser pocket. His phone. With some contorting he managed to retrieve it and checked who it was. Bethan.

'Hello,' he said, closing the top of the stealth suit to reduce the noise.

'Have I caught you at a bad time? I can barely hear you.' She was at her desk, one of the few at work.

'I'm at an airport?'

'Will you be coming back to London any time soon?'

'I'll give you a call.'

'I look forward to it.'

The signal suddenly dropped. Gunnymede jolted around in his cocoon as the aircraft hit a pocket of turbulence. The hammock setup was actually soothing. He closed his eyes and concentrated on relaxing, a practice he'd perfected in prison. Within minutes he fell into a light sleep.

Mahmoud sat in one of the little cafes in the lower level of the Galata road bridge that connected old and new Constantinople. He'd been there for almost an hour. When his time was up, which would be soon, he'd head back into the old town near the railway where he shared an ISIS safe house with several other young men. They all seemed to be waiting to head into Syria, unlike him who was waiting to head further west, but to where he had no idea. His orders were to go to the cafe at 9pm where he was to wait to be contacted. If no one showed by 10pm he was to go back to the house and repeat the procedure every evening until his contact arrived.

Each time someone entered the cafe he looked at them in the hope they were the one. This was the third night of the routine. He was bored in Turkey and wanted to get on with his life. He had been assured that as soon as this deception was over he'd be reassigned, which probably meant going back to Syria. One of his concerns was that his passport was not really his. He didn't think he looked much like Saleem although he was enough, it seemed, to convince the Turkish border guards.

An Arab man entered the cafe and sat at a table across from him. He ordered a coffee and concentrated on his phone. Mahmoud watched him for a while before deciding the man wasn't interested in him. Another five minutes and he'd leave.

What Mahmoud wasn't aware of was that the new arrival was photographing him. The recognition images were messaged to GCHQ in England and within a few minutes it was confirmed that Mahmoud was not Saleem.

When Mahmoud left the cafe he was too inexperienced to notice the Arab man follow him or the two other men that tagged along from wherever they'd been waiting. Mahmoud had done the journey several times already and would do it again the following evening. All he wanted to do was get back to the house.

As Mahmoud made his way through dark, narrow streets his followers came together, caught up with him, pounced on him from behind and dragged him into an alleyway. They held him down, covering his mouth to keep him quiet while one of them injected a fluid into his neck. They kept their firm grip of him for almost a minute while he went limp and his eyes changed from frantic to relaxed and then shut. A car pulled up. Mahmoud was tossed into the back. The others jumped in and the vehicle drove away.

Gunnymede was abruptly woken up by a combination of the scream of hydraulic motors, a burst of bright sunlight and a fierce wind. The air circled inside the small space like an entrapped tornado and rapidly reduced in violence to severe wind as the bay doors opened beneath him. The sun was low in the sky and directly ahead of the plane.

He'd fallen into a deep sleep, no doubt assisted by the pure oxygen, and fought to switch himself on. He quickly unplugged the oxygen umbilical from the main supply and plugged it into the small bottle attached to his harness. The hammock release cord dangled above his face. He took a moment to ensure his gear was secure, his kit between his legs. All seemed good. Time to drop into the gap between the wheels. He gave the toggle a yank.

Nothing happened.

He gave it another sharp tug but the hammock remained locked into place. He quickly checked the cable, where it went through the rings along the aircraft body but he couldn't see an obvious jam. He pulled hard on it with both hands, acutely aware the second hand was ticking, tugging at it violently but still it remained jammed.

The wheel suddenly jerked upwards a few inches hitting him in the back before returning to its position. Signal number one. A minute to go. Another tug and still nothing. This was not good. He wrapped the toggle around his hand, gripped it with the other and pulled as hard as he could. He paused a moment, positioned himself better and pulled on it again until he needed to relax. What the hell!

The wheel jerked again. Holy shit! He had three seconds to drop.

He mustered all his strength, raised his feet to the ceiling, pulled hard on the toggle and held the pressure. This was his last effort. The seconds were flying by, as was the plane over his target. He pushed as hard as he could with his feet, yelling out loud with the effort, his thighs taking the strain.

Something snapped! He flew back, the chute on his back hitting the wheel, flipped onto his side, dropped into the gap between the wheel and the left door and out of the plane in a single, slick movement. His head hit the slipstream first and he tore along the bottom of the aircraft as if it was sucking him up to it. The plane's skin was millimetres from his face but before he could make contact with it, it disappeared in a snap and he spun like a rag doll in the aircraft's slipstream. He fought against the g-force, pushed out his arms and legs, spreading like a starfish. Within seconds the spin was broken and he went stable on his back, nothing but blue sky in his vision. The plane was already a mile away.

He remained in that position for a short while, taking a moment to recover. Any elation that he felt having managed to survive was overshadowed by a fear he'd gone too far off course. He checked his altimeter. Three minutes before his chute opened. The backpack was still between his legs. The chute square on his back. The stealth suit flapping wildly. He hoped it was doing its job. If so, some Russian radar technician somewhere was seeing a dead bird plummet having struck a passenger plane bound for Beijing.

The blue sky instantly disappeared and everything was bright white. Keeping his arms outstretched he pulled in his knees. The move flipped him over and seconds later the cloud disappeared and there was the planet. He checked the compass beside the altimeter and turned himself to face north. The terrain was sandy brown with clumps of dark foliage and snaking streaks of black and grey. On the western horizon he could make out the rectangular patterns of cultivated fields. To the north was the salt lake of Elton ten miles across. It was supposed to be north east of him. He was way off.

He turned to face west and adopted the tracking position, keeping his body as thin as possible, his arms by his sides and legs straight, forming a saucer curve with his arse higher than his head. The wind tore at him but he didn't experience any obvious sense of forward movement. He knew that in theory, in that position, his vertical drop would be around 120 mph while his horizontal speed should be 70 mph.

He concentrated on the area directly ahead. It was slowly moving towards him and began to fit the map he'd memorised. He could see the winding road with a distinctive loop in it that he needed to be inside. He adjusted his aim towards it, willing himself forward. 8,300 metres high. He kept the position. He was getting closer.

Gunnymede watched the altimeter spin through the numbers. As it closed on 3,000, his concentration grew more acute. He needed to be another click or so. He would keep tracking until the auto pull released his chute. At 1,500 meters the ground came into sharper focus as it accelerated towards him. The gauge passed 800, 700, 600. Heading for critically low! Had the auto pull failed? He flared out, halting the track, his hand quickly searching for the ripcord. As his fingers found it Gunnymede felt the heavily loaded spring in the release mechanism pop. His body jerked hard as the chute opened, like crashing into a wall, his chin hitting his chest, every bit of air knocked out of him, the harness straps biting into his thighs. Just as suddenly he was upright under a rectangular canvass, the ground almost within reach.

There wasn't much time. Whoever had configured the barometric pressure reading had cut it fine, no doubt because the lower the opening the less chance there was of being picked up by radar. He grabbed both steering toggles and yanked down on them. As they came level with his chest he felt the chute move back. He released them to prevent it stalling. The ground was rocky. It quickly rose up to meet him. A broken leg would end the operation and probably his life. A couple of metres from impact he shut the cells. The chute stalled as his feet hovered above the ground and he touched down lightly. As the chute collapsed ahead of him he unclipped it and it fell away.

Holy mother of God, I'm alive!

He had no time to waste as he pulled his way out of the stealth suit and harness and unstrapped the assault rifle from his side. After collecting the chute, he folded it into a bundle along with the stealth suit and covered it with rocks. It wasn't perfectly hidden but then it was unlikely that the location saw any human traffic. The position was miles from civilisation and not exactly attractive hiking or hunting country. There was no indication of the country of origin on any of the gear if it was found anyway. He pulled the pack onto his back, cocked his assault rifle and climbed onto a rock to inspect the direction he needed to head. A check through the scope gave him a finer view. The sun remained behind the cloud he'd passed through and the air was chilly with a slight breeze. It didn't look like rain. Perfect conditions.

Gunnymede unlocked his phone, pulled up the SIS app, used the fourth fingerprint of his left hand to open it and selected the satellite image he'd been sent. He zoomed out the image until the Spice Road came into view and orientated it to fit his position. The nearest point of the road was five clicks south. Another satellite image opened showing five seconds of footage of three vehicles driving along a dirt road. Taz's convoy. The footage had been taken minutes before and relayed to him. The lead vehicle looked like a Toyota Hilux. The map showed Gunnymede's position relative to the convoy. Taz was on his way.

Gunnymede took a slug of water from the bladder, had a pee, adjusted the pack on his back and headed off at a good pace.

The terrain was rough going and an hour later he caught sight of the road which was on lower ground a couple of hundred metres away. He removed the pack and gave the area a 360 through the scope. There wasn't much in the way of cover between his position and the road so he decided to stay where he was. He didn't need to be any closer to achieve his aim anyway.

He removed the bags from his pack containing the Rapto technology and within a minute had attached the antenna and battery to the control box. When he switched it on, an amber LED flickered before turning green. The device made a soft noise followed by a READY message on a screen. Gunnymede checked the network indicator on his phone. It had changed from the Russian network it had been using to searching which meant the Rapto was doing its job. Seconds later, it went back to the Russian network.

A series of numbers appeared on the screen. It was his phone's ten digit MIN. All appeared to be working.

A sound drifted to him on the breeze and he looked towards the eastern approach expecting to see the three 4x4s. There was nothing there. He looked west to see a vehicle heading east along the road. A 4x4. Through the scope, he could see it was a black Ford.

Another engine sound and he looked east again to see three vehicles come into view. Taz's convoy. Gunnymede checked the Rapto to see it was already busy loading numbers onto the screen. Within seconds it had recorded seven different MINs. No doubt they included any phones in the Ford. Not that it mattered. GCHQ could track a hundred thousand numbers and match the right one with Taz using a facial recognition system at the first opportunity.

Gunnymede's job was done. A boy scout could've done it.

He connected his phone to the Rapto which automatically connected to GCHQ and relayed the data while watching the vehicles move along the road. As he dismantled the gear, he glanced at the Ford and Toyotas as they slowed to pass each other on the narrow road. As he watched, the Ford swerved to a halt, blocking the road causing the Toyotas to brake hard kicking up a cloud of dust, four men with assault rifles leapt from the Ford and opened fire, running along the sides of the convoy, concentrating their fire into the cabs. Gunnymede was stunned. It was an ambush.

Saleem had been seated in the front passenger seat of the rear Toyota, staring out over an uninteresting landscape of brittle bushes, rocks and sand. It'd been a similar view all the way from the Kazakhstan border. He was still cold. The driver, Ibrahim, had asked him if he minded not turning on the heater because it made him sleepy. Saleem had no problem with that. The man had fallen asleep once already while driving. They were crossing Turkmenistan at the time. Saleem had to grab the wheel to prevent what could've been a disaster. If he had died, the operation would've been cancelled, or at least, just as bad for him, given to someone else. Since then, Saleem didn't sleep while Ibrahim drove. Saleem was the most important item on the convoy as far as he was concerned.

Saleem and Ibrahim had no knowledge of the black Ford heading towards their convoy. With the dust being kicked up by the lead Toyotas they could see little beyond the vehicle in front. Ibrahim kept pretty close to the tail of the other Toyota. That particular habit had irritated Saleem from the start of their journey and after the first few hundred miles he asked Ibrahim why he drove so close. Ibrahim said he had a fear of another vehicle cutting in to try and separate them. Saleem accepted that as a sound strategy on a busy road. But when Ibrahim continued to do it on narrow dirt roads in the middle of nowhere where the chance of someone cutting in was zero, Saleem asked him again. Ibrahim's excuse in that case was the concentration helped keep him awake. Saleem philosophised that any help in that department was welcome. He'd more chance of surviving a collision with the back of a vehicle than driving off a cliff.

The Toyota in front stopped suddenly on the packed sand. Ibrahim hit the brakes and skidded into the back of it. They never wore seatbelts and so both men slammed into the dashboard, Saleem hitting his head on the windshield. Neither was badly hurt. Just stunned. But what followed was unexpected and far worse.

Machine-gun fire.

Ibrahim froze as his brain struggled to process what was happening. It was the same for those in the other Toyotas. Saleem, however, was a veteran of vehicle ambushes. The majority of his experiences had been from the air but he'd survived a few ground attacks. Despite being in the drug smuggling business, Ibrahim and the others had never experienced anything like it. Saleem had learned that in a vehicle ambush, if the vehicle you're in isn't moving, then get the hell out of it because it's the vehicle that's attracting the bullets. And you'd better move really fast!

Saleem barged open the door. Bullets slapped through the Toyota in front as the attackers, on the other side of the vehicle, blasted it on full automatic fire. Saleem saw blood literally spurt out of the metalwork and shattered windows as the driver and passenger were riddled. The attackers would soon be upon the last vehicle. Saleem had seconds. For half of one he remembered his shoulder bag on the floor that contained his personal effects. But even the time spent grabbing for it would likely mean his end. As it was, he probably wouldn't make it.

Ibrahim was still in his seat as he looked over at Saleem climbing outside. For a slender moment he realised he should be doing the same. Then bullets shredded his head and torso. Those same bullets flew within inches of Saleem who took off with all his might and ran as hard as he could between rocks.

More bullets splattered and ricocheted to his sides as the shooter saw him run. Saleem changed direction as another burst smashed into stones around him. He scrambled up a short incline, rolled over the top and down the other side as bullets flew above him.

Silence fell as the shooting appeared to stop but he continued to run as hard as he possibly could. He would keep running and scrambling until his heart failed him. If there was one thing members of Daesh had learned over the last few years in Iraq and Syria when under attack it was how to run, and run and run.

Gunnymede watched the ambush unfold before his eyes. In less than a minute all three Toyotas were neutralised. One of the attackers looked like he was pursuing someone. He gave chase for a short distance before giving up.

When the firing ceased, the men moved in to open the doors. A shot rang out as a survivor was executed. Silence descended except for the wind gently blowing through the brittle foliage.

Gunnymede processed the situation as he watched the attackers ransack the vehicles, opening up the backs and hauling boxes onto the ground. To do absolutely nothing and stay completely still was his initial choice. Safest. Wisest. Smartest. Stay put until the attackers had gone then get out of there.

He considered the implications of the unfolding incident, the positives and negatives. Lamardi had suggested there was a significant component in the convoy connected to Saleem's threat against the homeland. Worst case scenario, it could be a bio-chemical substance or dirty bomb material. A nuclear bomb was a distant possibility. There had been rumours for years about a few old Russian miniature suitcase nukes running about from the Cold War. It wasn't worth thinking about. If there was anything, it was going to be bio-chem. If so, it was now in the hands of a bunch of unknowns. But then, on a positive note, GCHQ would be able to track the MINs and eventually put faces to the men. On the other hand, that might not happen until after they'd handed the device over to other players.

Gunnymede didn't want to face what was swiftly emerging as a problem for him. He really couldn't sit back and do nothing as these clowns walked off with what might well be a serious WMD. The main reason he couldn't do nothing was because he was the only person who could. If the device left this location, it could end up anywhere. It could kill a lot of people.

'Shit!' he muttered softly. He had to make an effort at least. It wasn't worth dying for since there might not be a device. But he couldn't take the risk there was.

Four to one. If he was going to have any chance at all he needed them all together. It would have to be a surprise. An ambush. Swift and decisive. No chance for them to retaliate.

First thing first, he needed to get to the road and ahead of them. But which direction should he go? Would they head east towards Kazakhstan or west back into Russia? The Toyotas were shot to bits and would have to be moved for the Ford to get past. Very unlikely. And since the attackers came from within Russia the chances were they'd be returning.

West it was.

He scrambled over the rocks, keeping low as he hurried along, confident the men were too busy to watch the countryside. He soon came to the road. The vehicles were out of sight around a slight bend. But a couple of steps onto the sand and he could see the back of the Ford. It hadn't moved.

He quickly crossed over and stepped into a rocky outcrop. It was a good position, feet from the road with cover from view and fire. He reminded his hands where everything was – pistol in side trouser pocket, spare rifle mags in left jacket pocket, spare pistol mags in right. This was crazy. He was going to do it. He knew himself well enough. Once he was in the right position he would go for it. He knew he would. Shit!

An engine revved! He craned to get a look. The Ford was moving back and forth, turning around in the narrow road. Shit! They were coming his way. This was it. He was going to do it. The adrenaline started to shoot through him.

As the Ford moved off towards him he brought the scope up to his eye. Two men in the front. The back was in darkness. The other two had to be there. Where else would they be?

The vehicle gradually accelerated towards him. Going through the gears. His finger rested on the trigger. There was an optimum moment. Not too far away. Not too close. He had to have time to get everyone.

When the Ford was twenty metres away Gunnymede squeezed the trigger releasing a long, sustained burst. He aimed for the driver first, holding the barrel on him for several bullets then moved it left, right, left, easing it from side to side, keeping all the rounds in the vehicle. The magazine emptied. He moved his fingers as fast as he could. Ejected the empty mag, dug another out of his pocket and shoved it in, hit the breech mechanism and the spring slammed it forward. By the time he'd changed mags the Ford was level with him. He fired into its side, raking back and forth between the front and rear seats. He ran out of bullets again as it rolled on past him, left the road, bumped into a mound of rocks and stalled.

Gunnymede replaced the magazine and moved in. The vehicle was motionless apart from steam hissing from the ruptured engine. There was no other movement. Every window was shattered. The doors were heavily punctured. He could see all four men inside, the two in the back clearly dead, their heads ripped open, brains spilled out. The driver was the same. It had been overkill. A blitz. But he'd got the job done without a shot being returned which was the plan.

To his surprise, the front passenger, however, was not dead. He had somehow miraculously survived. The man turned his bloody face to look at Gunnymede through one good eye and stared, unblinking, his breathing laboured, as if waiting for an answer to a question. Gunnymede couldn't let the man survive. There were too many reasons to kill him and not one to let him live. Gunnymede drew his pistol and aimed. The man didn't flinch. He'd just executed the survivors of his own ambush and knew what was coming. He understood.

Gunnymede fired a single shot into the man's head which flew back against the door frame. And that was that.

He went to the back of the vehicle and opened it. Several shoe-sized boxes fell out. The entire back was crammed full with more of the same. He opened one. It was tightly packed with brown paper packages.

There was a sudden roaring scream and two jet fighters shot low overhead. Gunnymede dropped to cover as his eyes shot skyward and his heart leapt into his throat. He watched as they disappeared beyond the horizon. It was time to go. He speeded up and unwrapped one of the packages. The paper was stiff and coated in a thick brown wax. Inside was a firm, lightly tanned, rectangular doughy lump. He knew what it was before he picked at a corner and it crumbled into sugary granules. Afghan heroin. He removed the lids of several of the boxes. They all contained the same packages. There must've been a couple hundred kilos of the stuff. He looked back towards the Toyotas. The attackers appeared to only want the heroin. There was nothing else in the back.

The sound of jet fighter engines suggested they were circling far away. He soon found them. Seems like the dead bird didn't fool the radar operators for too long. Gunnymede was confident he had a little time. This was a remote location to get any response to other than aircraft.

He jogged along the sandy road to the Toyotas as the fighters continued their circle. The driver and passenger of the leading vehicle were hanging out of the open doors washed in blood. Inside the back were various boxes that had been opened to reveal pistols, magazines and ammunition. The ground was littered with more of the same. A wooden crate lay open with packets of plastic explosives. He inspected the other two vehicles to find similar items. Grenades, mortars, pistols, rifles, bullets. But no heroin. It was all in the back of the Ford which seemed to prove it was the target booty for the gang. He looked in the cabs, front and back. Everything was soaked in blood. He checked under seats looking for concealed compartments. He pulled off any panel that looked like it might be capable of hiding a specially sealed, ominous looking container designed to carry hazardous material. Nothing.

In the open passenger door of the trailing Toyota he noticed a shoulder bag on the floor, its flap open and the contents spilled out. He might've moved on had he not caught sight of a British passport lying amongst the trash. He opened it. The name was different but he instantly recognised the face. The jets screamed overhead. They'd seen the vehicles.

Gunnymede checked the dead driver. Not Saleem. He hurried to the other vehicles to check all the bodies. Taz was amongst them but none of the others was the English-born terrorist. He faced the countryside in the direction he'd seen the man run. It had to have been Saleem. Somewhere out there was the Daesh commander. If he had survival instincts, he'd still be running and Gunnymede suspected Saleem wasn't short of any.

Gunnymede went back to the shoulder bag. There were various currencies including British pounds. A phone which suggested Saleem probably didn't have one on him. There were pens and paper and a well-worn map of London. Did Saleem have the WMD with him? He'd been running for his life. He would've taken his satchel if he'd had the time to grab anything. But maybe the WMD was more important. He remembered what Saleem had said about the UK task being simplicity itself, without WMD or explosives.

'Saleem was the cargo,' Gunnymede realised. That's what Lamardi was giving to Jervis.

Inside the backs of two of the Toyotas were bicycles. Useful if they broke down. Gunnymede lifted one onto the ground. It would do nicely. He looked to find the jets again. They were still circling.

He dumped his rifle, shouldered Saleem's bag and cycled away. He reached the Ford and as he caught sight of the heroin he slowed to a stop. He moved the bicycle backwards until he was able to see all of the heroin in the back of the vehicle. There certainly was a great deal of it.

He climbed off the bike and picked up a block of the sugary substance. He went to the side of the road to examine the terrain once again, even though he knew it well enough by then. He was hoping it might offer hope of providing a hiding place for the stuff. But there wasn't. And even if there had been, there was far too much of it to move and conceal against the elements in the time that he probably had, bearing in mind the aircraft and the likelihood of imminent visitors.

It was a missed opportunity for sure.

He climbed back onto the bicycle and pedalled on down the road.

Chapter 18

Gunnymede entered the Heathrow arrivals hall carrying Saleem's shoulder bag. He stopped to one side and ran his eye along the waiting people as other arriving passengers walked through the exit from the customs and baggage hall and past him. He wasn't surprised to find Aristotle staring at him from the back of the hall. The tall Greek made his way over as Gunnymede headed towards him.

'I didn't know you were so competent in battle,' Aristotle said. 'I watched the satellite display. Impressive.'

'Fish in a barrel.'

They walked outside to a waiting car.

'We traced the MINs of the four Russians you ran into,' Aristotle said. 'They were members of a cartel from Kiev.'

'They were there for the heroin.'

'Did you find a weapon?'

'Nothing. Did you see the one who escaped the ambush?'

'Yes.'

'Did you place a track?'

'We were focused on you.'

Gunnymede held out Saleem's shoulder bag. 'This belonged to him.'

Aristotle looked inside the bag, took out the passport and opened it.

'Lamardi was giving us Saleem,' Gunnymede said.

Aristotle nodded as he thought about it. He climbed into the car. Gunnymede got in beside him and it pulled away.

'He still has to make his way to London,' Aristotle said.

'My money's on him getting here.'

They sat back in thought.

'Where are we going?' Gunnymede asked.

'Jervis wants a personal debrief.

'Will Harlow be there?'

'No.'

'What's the relationship between those two?'

'Jervis is technically superior to Harlow. But Harlow doesn't work directly for him.'

'Are they close?'

Aristotle stifled a chuckle. 'It's safe to say they don't like each other.'

'Why?'

'The same reason I don't like you. One of us is a snake in the grass.'

It was getting dark by the time Gunnymede left his debriefing in Legoland. As he headed along the pavement overlooking the Thames he pulled out his phone and made a call.

Bethan was at her desk in Scotland Yard staring at a sheet of paper with a picture of Megan on the top half, the bottom dedicated to Milo Krilov and a short summary on him.

Her mobile rang. She answered it. 'Hello?'

'Bethan?'

She smiled. 'Devon. Are you back?'

'I am.'

'To what do I owe the pleasure?' She tried not to sound as hopeful as she suddenly felt.

'I'm sorry about the other night,' he said.

'We were cut off.'

'I meant the hospital.'

'What are you sorry for?'

'I left without an explanation.'

'I think you were entitled.'

He went silent.

'Do you want to talk about it?' she asked.

'Is that meal still on offer?'

'Sure. When did you have in mind?'

'Well ...'

'Tonight?'

'It's late ...'

'Tonight's fine,' she said.

'You sure?'

'Got to catch you when I can. Technically we're still partners. The case isn't solved.'

'That's right.'

'I'll send you the location.'

'You're sure it's no big deal?'

'Nope.'

'I look forward to it.'

'Bye.'

She grabbed her coat and headed for the elevator.

Gunnymede arrived at Bethan's house holding a bottle of wine and knocked on the front door. It opened and Bethan was standing there with a smile.

'I'm looking for Captain America's sister,' he said.

'Shh. Not so loud. The neighbours have no idea.' She let him in and closed the door.

He pulled off his coat. 'It's nice to be here.'

'A rough one?'

'Challenging.'

'We'd better begin the treatment then. Wine or whisky?'

'I'd prefer to start with a fine Albanian sheet-pees.'

'I'm afraid we're out. Would sir make do with a scotch?'

'Damn it all, if I must.'

She poured two glasses and handed him one. They clinked and took sips.

'Perfect,' he said. 'As a wise person once said to me in Albania recently, has there ever been a better all-round medicine in the history of the world?'

She saluted that and went back into the kitchen. 'When's the last time you had a home cooked meal?' she asked.

'Years,' he said.

'Can you actually remember?'

He took a moment to think about it. 'My Aunt Grace. At her cottage. The last meal I had with Mcgan.'

He didn't see her pause before scooping food onto a couple of plates. 'How long were you together?' she asked.

'Altogether ... I suppose, eight years.'

'That's a long time.'

'She was too good for me,' he said, more to himself.

'Why do you say that?'

'Lots of reasons. I was hardly ever home.'

'She would've understood that, her father being SAS.'

'How did you know that?'

'A nurse at the hospital. I suppose it's tough on both parties, a relationship in your business.'

'It can be a distraction.'

'Having a girlfriend?'

'Having someone you care about. What about you? What's your excuse?'

'What do you mean?'

'Well, I'm alone because my girlfriend hanged herself.'

She came in with the plates of food and put them on the table. 'I don't know why exactly. The right man hasn't come along. I'm too particular. I rate myself higher than I am. Choose one.'

They tucked into the meal. 'Why was it years since your last home cooked meal with Megan?' she asked.

He carried on eating while considering her question. 'That was a bit of a slip, wasn't it,' he eventually said. 'I expected you to know anyway.'

'That you spent time in prison?'

'Is that all you heard?'

'I didn't dig if that's what you mean.'

'If you did, you'd find I was convicted of stealing twenty kilos of heroin.'

'Wow. That's a lot of heroin. So how come you work for military intelligence if you have a criminal record?'

'MI has a long history of employing criminals.'

'Really?'

'Didn't you hear the story about the Nazi safe that needed to be cracked during World War Two without the Nazis knowing and the only man who could do it was languishing in Wandsworth prison doing a twenty year stretch for a string of bank robberies? His employment by the SOE kicked off a long history or utilising underworld skills.'

She was impressed. 'Why'd you do it?'

He shrugged. 'Moment of weakness. Greed. Or maybe it was a cunning plan that went horribly wrong and left me high and dry. Choose one.'

She contemplated his answers as she sipped her drink. 'What are your particular skills?'

'Luring.'

'What?'

'I'm a lure. Bait.'

'Can you elaborate?'

'A decoy.'

'As in, expand on.'

'No.'

She reached for a bottle of wine and unscrewed the top. 'Wine?'

'Sure.'

She poured a couple of glasses and they took a sip.

'Can I ask *you* something about your work?' he asked.

She shrugged. 'Sure.'

'Do you know anything about Megan's case?'

She paused to look at him. He was staring at her as if studying for signs. 'I'm not involved with that case,' she said, going back to eating.

'I'm surprised they've no suspects.'

'That's how it goes sometimes.'

'Is it possible they have a suspect and aren't telling anyone?'

'If that's true it's because they don't have the evidence to get a conviction.'

'So, no one was brought in for questioning?'

'Like I said, I'm not involved in the case.'

They ate the rest of the meal in silence.

'Thank you,' he said, sitting back. 'That was very nice.'

'You're welcome.'

She got to her feet and went to pick up his plate. He put his hand on hers. She didn't pull away. He put his other on her hip as he looked into her eyes. She leaned down and kissed him on the lips. He got to his feet without disconnecting and they kissed deeply.

Bethan's bedroom was dark but for a shaft of light from a streetlamp finding its way through a small gap in the curtain and cutting across the bed. Gunnymede and Bethan lay naked together, content in each other's company.

'You said he died in Lebanon while in the military.'

He glanced at her. They'd been lying in silence for some time. He looked back at the ceiling in thought.

'What was he doing in the British military in Lebanon?' she asked.

'Do you ever stop working?'

'I stopped for the last couple of hours. This isn't work anyway. I'm interested in you – I hope you don't mind.'

He didn't. 'He was working in the British Embassy.'

'In Beirut?'

'Yes.'

'How'd he die?'

'A bomb as he was leaving the embassy. It was during the civil war.'

'I'm sorry. And you went to live with your aunt.'

'She always looked after me when he was away. I think I spent more time with her than him anyway.'

'How many other staff died?'

'None. The embassy had already been evacuated.'

She looked at him questioningly.

'He wasn't an ordinary member of staff,' he admitted. 'I don't know what he did, exactly.'

'Where's he buried?'

'He's not.'

'His body was never repatriated?'

'Never found.'

'Seriously?'

'Big bomb. Disrupted country in the middle of a civil war. No-one from our side in country to take care of things. I can understand.'

'You could find out more if you wanted to, couldn't you?'

'It's not that simple.'

'You've never been interested enough to try? I'd be dying to know.'

'Time out. Loo break,' he said as he climbed off the bed and stepped out of the room into the dark hallway.

There were three doors suggesting three options to the bathroom. He went to the nearest and opened it. It wasn't a bathroom, but it wasn't a bedroom either. There was no bed at least. He was about to close the door when a wall with several pictures stuck to it caught his attention. He stared at them and, in the dim light could make out the word ALBANIA hand written on a card. There were other labels with strings connecting them to the various pictures.

His curiosity got the better of him and he moved inside to take a closer look. The matrix included the Afghan Lamardi shot in Macedonia with a piece of string linking it to the Albania killings. There was a floating label with British Special Forces/SAS on it. But what got his attention was a picture of Megan linked to a picture of a Russian called Milo Krilov.

Gunnymede unpinned the picture of Krilov.

Bethan stepped into the doorway behind him. 'I forgot to lock this room,' she said.

'Milo Krilov is the rapist?'

'I couldn't tell you. I'm not supposed to know.'

'Why not?'

'It's a confidential case.'

Gunnymede weighed his feelings. 'I'm not angry,' he decided. 'But I do feel betrayed.'

He walked past her and went downstairs. Within a couple of minutes he was dressed and out the door.

Bethan sat on the top stair and held her head in her hands.

Gunnymede walked along the street studying the picture of Krilov. He pulled out his phone, placed the paper against a wall and photographed it. He searched his contacts for a number and hit the call button. It took a while for it to pick up.

'What do you want?' Aristotle asked.

'How do I check a name and face these days?'

'You don't.'

'What do you mean, you don't? I don't? We don't?'

'You don't. You don't have access to that facility.'

'That's a part of my job.'

'You want to know something, you ask me.'

'Where's the love?' Gunnymede muttered, rolling his eyes. 'I'm sending you a name and a face.'

The phone went dead. Gunnymede sent the picture as he entered Hampstead underground station.

Chapter 19

Bethan walked into her busy office, slumped into her chair, opened her laptop and, after a long moment of indecision, closed it and looked over at Dillon's office. The pain of having to go and see him drained her.

Jedson stepped out of the elevator wearing an outfit that suggested homeless. He looked for Bethan, as he always did on arriving at that floor, made his way over and sat on the edge of her desk. 'Hey.'

She didn't appear to see him despite him practically breathing down her neck.

'Heavy night?' He nudged her.

'Not now, Jedson, please.'

'Why don't we skip this place and get an early one? Hair of the dog and all that.'

'What part of your ridiculously small brain informs you that I'm remotely interested in even talking to you?'

'Hey, calm yourself. No need to be rude.'

'Go away or I swear I'll scream.'

The people nearby glanced at Jedson, of whom they appeared to share the same low opinion.

Jedson eased himself to his feet. 'I can see I've caught you at the wrong time of the month. I'll return when you're in a better mood.' He made his way out of the room.

Bethan's phone chirped and she answered it. 'Trencher.'

'Bethan. It's Ardian Kostag.'

'Hello, Ardian.'

Ardian was on his computer at his desk in a large, crowded office. There was a lot of noise coming from outside, like people shouting.

'Did you receive the forensics on the PAD device I sent through a couple days ago?'

'Yes. Also the results of all foreigners passing through ports and border crossings in the last nine months. No flags though.'

'And no further progress this end. Anything your end?' Someone walked into Ardian's office and while the door was open the sound of shouting increased.

'What's all that noise?' she asked.

'Those are protestors. Families of the officers killed. They're demanding to know what is happening. We've had demonstrations for several days. They are angry we haven't named those responsible. Some are saying there's a cover up. We're getting pressure to come up with answers. The conspiracy theorists are causing lots of problems. Some say it's the Russians. Others it's the Americans.'

'I'm sorry to hear that.'

'You know, world wars have begun with much less in the Balkans.'

'Indeed. I'd dearly love to see this case resolved, if only for your sake. I do have some questions for you,' she said, consulting her notes. 'I'd like to ask you about K-17. I'm interested in the team's history.'

'Go ahead.'

'How long have they been together? Do individuals move between teams regularly?'

'Actually, the teams can be very, um, *nepotizum*. Sorry, I don't remember the word in English.'

'Nepotistic?' she guessed.

'Nepotistic. Thank you. Many of the men are related. They can stay in the same team for years.'

'Can you tell me how long the current K-17 team has been together?'

'I would have to check. But as I said, I would not expect to find many transfers between the teams.'

'Do you know if K-17 was involved in any incidents?'

'There are often incidences at the checkpoints. Many go unreported. Only the serious ones tend to get filed. How far back do you want to go?'

'Five years.'

'Five years?' Kostag seemed daunted by the request. 'That's a long time.'

'Three then. As far back as you can.'

'Are you looking for anything in particular?'

'I'd be very interested in any incident involving a British subject.'

Her comment got Kostag thinking. He accessed the police data on his computer.

'Ardian?' Bethan wondered if she'd lost the connection.

'I'm just checking something,' he said. 'There was an incident involving a British person. There are not many incidences involving British people at border checkpoints so it should not be difficult to find. Give me a moment.'

Bethan waited patiently while Kostag went through a list of files. The noise grew louder and then quieter again as someone left the office.

'Here we are,' he said. 'Interesting.'

'What is?'

'I have an incident. And it was involving K-17. Eight months ago. I wasn't in this department then. A car was passing through a checkpoint. The passenger was a United

Nations lawyer, a Brazilian. The car was driven by his bodyguard who was British.'

'Bodyguard?'

'Yes. One minute ... a man named Alan Masters. Scottish. There was an argument between the lawyer and the border police. The report states the lawyer was arrogant and aggressive and fuelled the argument. Things became physical. Masters stepped in to separate them.'

There was a moment of silence while Kostag read the rest of the report.

'And the outcome?' Bethan asked.

'Not good. Masters was shot by one of the border police. He died the next day in hospital.'

'Where did this take place? The checkpoint?'

'The same checkpoint where K-17 was executed,' Kostaq said.

'Can you send me Masters' details?'

'I have a copy of his passport page. I'll send it to you ... are you onto something, Bethan?'

'I don't know. I have a few thoughts I'd like to pursue. Hopefully they'll shed some light.'

'I hope so too. As always, if I get anything else I'll pass it on. I would appreciate it if you would do the same. I would very much like to close this case more than any other I think I have had.'

'I completely understand, Ardian. I'll be in touch.'

'You have a good day, Bethan. And good luck.'

'You too. Thank you.'

Bethan disconnected and scribbled some notes into the file. A flag popped up on her computer screen indicating an email. It was from Kostag. She opened the attachment. A copy of the British bodyguard's passport filled the screen. She copied the significant information into the police database and seconds later a window displayed a picture of Masters and his biography. He was a former member of the British Army, notably the Green Jackets, and also served eleven years in the Special Air Service.

She looked towards Dillon's office. He was at his desk. As she got to her feet to head over there, Dillon stepped out of his office and walked towards the elevators. 'Everything okay?' he asked her.

She forced a smile. 'Fine, thanks.'

'It's lunchtime,' he said, hitting the elevator call button. 'Go and grab a meal. You look pale.'

'Will you be back this afternoon?'

'Yes, but late. Got a working lunch.' He stepped inside the elevator and the doors closed.

Gunnymede sat in a cafe sipping a coffee as he watched the world go past the window. His phone chirped and he answered it.

'It's me,' Aristotle said. 'Do you know Krilov?'

'No.'

'You never heard of him before?'

'Nope.'

'You sure about that?'

'You don't need to get me interested in him more than I am.'

'What *is* your interest in him?'

'He's the man who raped Megan.'

'I see. Why do you want to know about him?'

'Why do you think?'

'You want revenge?'

'If you don't want to give me the info I'll find it elsewhere.'

Aristotle went silent for a moment. 'Krilov is former Spetsnaz,' he finally said.

'Spetsnaz?'

'He's a specialist thug. An assassin. The type the GRU uses to kill people with nerve agents in foreign countries.'

'Is he still serving?'

'Hard to say. He joined the civilian security circuit eight years ago. Spent a couple years running armed security against Somali pirates. Some close protection work in Chechnya. Then he disappeared for three years. There's no record of his employment. Like he was dead. He closed his bank account even. Then a year ago, he showed up in Kabul. Face recognition picked him up arriving at the international airport. There was no reason to monitor him, so he was left alone. They think he went to Helmand Province. He left two weeks later. Nine months ago he turned up in the UK as a visitor. Lots of cash. Investing in property using various offshore accounts. But he was clean and so he was left alone.'

'Anything on the rape – why he wasn't charged?'

'I couldn't find out. I have an interest in your intentions,' Aristotle said. 'Are you going to tell me them?'

'I don't have any at the moment.'

'I hope that's remains the same. You cannot afford to have any problems with the police. The lifeline keeping you out of jail is a thin one.'

'Then tell me.'

'Tell you what?'

'Why a former Spetsnaz raped my girlfriend?'

'I grant you that's an interesting question.'

'You think Spangle had anything to do with it?'

'How do you connect him to Spangle?'

'Who was it said Spangle is everything?'

'She was raped while you were in jail in the USA.'

'I don't believe it was a coincidence.'

'I'll send you what I have,' Aristotle said and disconnected.

Great.

As Gunnymede sat in thought, his phone vibrated and a banner showed a file from Aristotle. Gunnymede clicked it open. To his surprise it included Krilov's UK home address, vehicle details and a mobile number.

Bethan walked up the street away from Scotland Yard, her mind in turmoil. She took several turnings and found herself walking past a familiar pub. She had a sudden thought and paused to look at the entrance. It was an idea worth pursuing.

She pushed her way inside and scanned the moderately busy place at the tail-end of the lunchtime rush and found who she was looking for. Jedson was in a corner clutching a pint and chatting with two other men. She looked away as if she hadn't seen him and headed towards the bar.

Jedson stopped in mid conversation as he saw her cross the room. 'Target front,' he said.

'Isn't that the analyst on the third floor?' a colleague asked.

'You still trying to corner her?' the other said with a chuckle.

'She's a long term project,' Jedson replied without taking his eyes off of her. 'Had her claws out earlier. Softly, softly, catch a tiger,' he added with a wink before heading off on an interception course.

Bethan sat on a stool a second before Jedson arrived.

'I come in peace,' he said, hands up, putting on a clown smile. 'I want to apologise for being rude earlier.'

She put on a tired expression and backed it up with a heavy sigh. 'No, it is I who should apologise. I was out of place talking to you like that.'

Jedson was surprised to hear that. 'We'll call it quits then. I was just saying to the lads, we don't often see you in the staff canteen.'

Bethan glanced at the two men who looked as socially retarded as Jedson, forced a smile and turned her attention to the row of bottles on the shelf at the back of the bar. 'I've had a long and frustrating day and it's only halfway through,' she sighed.

'You need some medicine. Allow me to fill your prescription. Bartender?'

'I can get my own drink.'

'Come on. It's not a sexist thing. You can get the next round.'

'I'll have a scotch,' she said, conceding.

'Single malt?'

'A cheapy will do fine.'

'Nonsense. Only the best for you,' he insisted and looked for the bartender. 'A single malt, please mate. Make it a double. On the rocks?'

'No ice. Just some water, thanks,' she said.

Jedson looked pleased with himself as the bartender placed the whisky in front of her along with a jug of water. She poured some water into it, took a sip and expressed her deep appreciation of it.

'Cheers,' Jedson said, raising his glass.

They touched glasses.

'There was a reason I came to see you earlier,' he said.

She gave him a warning look.

'No, nothing naughty. It was to do with work.' He moved a little closer to her in order to lower his voice.

'Am I right in thinking you might fancy joining our little gang?'

'What, S C & O 19?'

'Yeah.'

'Where'd you hear that?'

'Your boss Dillon's been down to the office. He was talking about you as I understand it.'

'I don't think he was there to see if I might join.'

'You sure?'

She shrugged. 'News to me.'

'No? Pity.'

'But then again, all that cloak and dagger Serpico undercover stuff does have a certain attraction.'

'Like a bit of danger, do you?'

'A little bit of excitement might improve the job.'

'You'd be perfect for it.'

'Why's that?'

'We're short of women. Quality that is. The ones we have look like blokes. I think they're all bloody dykes.'

She humoured him with a smile and took a sip of her drink. 'What sort of cases are you working on?'

'All sorts. Anything that requires an undercover element. Surveillance and technology. Working against seriously bad guys. Drugs. Guns. Organised crime. Stuff like that.'

'Sounds exciting.'

'You'd need to learn how to shoot a pistol and SMG.'

'Really? That would be different. What attracts me to S C & O 19 is how laidback it is.'

'It's how you've got to play the game. It's a tough job but you don't see me getting stressed.'

'And you don't have to put up with all the red tape I'm always coming up against.'

'Na. We're usually the ones making the red tape.'

'Tell me about it. I run into it all the time. Your latest red tape has been a pain.'

'Mine?'

'Not you personally I'm sure.'

'What was that then?'

'Maybe it was you.'

'Go on.'

'Let's enjoy the drink and leave work out of it,' she insisted.

And he did. Not what she was really hoping for.

'I can't resist the opportunity,' she had to finally say. 'It was to do with a case I'm working on.'

'What was that then?'

'It's probably small fry for you.'

'That's what relationships are for, aren't they? Helping one another.'

'Okay. I'm looking into unsolved British military related homicides.'

His brow wrinkled as he thought on that one. 'Unsolved soldier deaths?'

'No. That was a bit vague of me. Homicides directly connected to the military. Where the perpetrators are military personnel.'

'I see. I've never heard of that. How did we get in the way?'

'One of the cases involves someone your people are interested in.'

'Who would that be?'

'A Russian. Milo Krilov. As soon as I started to dig I ran into the wall.'

Jedson gave her a sideways look. His gormless expression had hardened a little.

'There, you see. That's the wall I ran into earlier. Let's just forget it.'

His tone subtly altered from buffoon to something more serious. 'How does this Krilov person relate to unsolved military homicides?'

'You know him, then?'

'I'm wondering how the military related homicide fits in.'

'He raped a girl who subsequently committed suicide,' she said. 'Hence the homicide.'

He nodded. 'What's the military side?'

'Her father is former SAS.'

Jedson sipped his beer while considering her comment.

'But then, you knew that,' she added.

He looked at her again, into her eyes as if searching for something. 'So, where'd you come across this Russian?'

'It came up in a search I was doing.'

'The name Milo Krilov just popped up when you were doing a search? Search of what?'

She suddenly felt uncomfortable with his darkened response. 'I'm going to have to tell you a secret,' she said in a low voice.

'Go on.'

'Could get me in trouble.'

'You can trust me.'

'Okay. I will. I was researching the rape and I hit the red wall, restricted access and all that and so I went to Dillon and told him what I was doing and what I'd run into and he checked for himself.'

'And he told you about Milo Krilov.'

'Not directly. I was naughty and took a look at his screen when he had his back turned.'

'And you saw the name, Milo Krilov.'

'I'd like to know more about him.'

'Like what?'

'Why he hasn't been charged.'

Jedson looked around to ensure no one was within hearing distance. 'You think I'm pretty stupid, don't you?'

She felt the serrated edge of his irritation. 'What do you mean?'

'You've always taken me for a numpty. All those snide comments you make in the office in order to entertain the other idiots. A bit too close, you and Dillon. Thick as thieves, aren't you?'

Bethan was unbalanced by his aggressive posture.

'Let me tell you something,' he said, leaning closer. 'I've always had a thing for you. Something about you always gets me going. No one else does it for me the way you do. I'd tell you anything you want in the right circumstances.'

'What circumstances would they be?'

He grinned. 'Ever play strip interrogation? I tell you something, you take a piece of clothing off, and we keep on going. You'll know everything you need to by the time you're bollocky buff.'

'I'll never be that desperate,' she said, getting off the stool. 'Thanks for the drink.'

As she turned to leave he took a hold of her arm. 'Yes, you run along,' he said. 'And I'll decide whether to report this conversation to my boss or not.'

Bethan pulled her arm away and walked out of the bar.

'Tiger's getting away,' one of Jedson's colleagues called out to the tune of laughter.

Jedson was too thick skinned to let it bother him. He watched her leave with snake-like eyes.

Chapter 20

Gunnymede sat on a low garden wall in front of a terraced house in a dimly lit residential street in West Winchester. He'd chosen the darkest part, a section not covered by the handful of street-lamps and from where he had line of sight to a specific house along the other side of the street. The number of cars that tightly lined both sides suggested it was a busy neighbourhood although in the hour he'd been there only a couple of pedestrians had gone by.

Gunnymede took a final draw on a cigarette and tossed it. He got to his feet and stretched his legs that had begun to stiffen. He'd been there several hours and the question was how much longer would he give it.

As he sat back down, the front door to the house he'd been watching opened and light filled the small yard. Gunnymede crouched a little to ensure he was out of sight behind a car. The light went out seconds later and a man stepped into view. It looked very much like Krilov. Balding, six foot six, broad and hard to miss. He paused at his gate to look up and down the street. The man had awareness. Gunnymede kept sight of him through the car windows.

Krilov stepped through the gate to a Mercedes SUV, climbed in, started the engine and drove away. Gunnymede had identified the car on an earlier walk past based on the info from Aristotle and stuck a lump of chewing gum onto one of the rear lights. As the car headed away Gunnymede could clearly see the gap in the curved LED strip where the gum covered it.

He climbed onto a powerful motorbike, the pool bike Aristotle had been driving a few days before, pulled on a full-faced helmet, started the throaty engine and eased away from the kerb. Half a minute later he arrived at a busy T junction and searched the tail lights of the cars driving away left and right. The broken line of the LED light stood out and he followed it.

Gunnymede maintained several cars between him and Krilov. It wasn't long before the Russian turned onto a main road and Gunnymede dropped back even further. Several miles from the city the Russian left the highway onto a country road. Two cars ahead of Gunnymede took the same turn to help maintain his cover.

Another turn onto a less busy road and Gunnymede found himself with nothing between him and the Russian. He slowed down to put himself out of direct line of sight. The road was twisting and Gunnymede could only keep track of the Merc by its headlights reflecting off the countryside.

As Gunnymede came out of a long bend he saw a vehicle turning off the road up ahead. He couldn't be certain it was the Russian as it passed between trees and climbed a hill. As he drew level with the lane he caught sight of the tail lights a second before they disappeared over a rise. It was the Merc. What's more, the lane was signposted as a dead end.

Gunnymede drove on for another half mile before pulling off the road under a line of trees and turning off his lights and engine. The silence was abrupt as he removed his helmet. There were no other vehicles on the road. He accessed a 3D map on his phone. The lane Krilov had turned into went steeply up hill, down the other side and quarter of a mile later reached a small collection of structures.

Gunnymede climbed off the bike and walked to a hedgerow to find a way through.

The elevator doors opened on the third floor of Scotland Yard and Dillon stepped out reading his phone. A handful of officers were at work. He entered his office and closed the door behind him.

Bethan sat in the shadows watching him. She took a deep breath and got to her feet. Time to face the firing squad.

She knocked on Dillon's door and walked in.

'What are you doing here so late?' he asked.

'I believe I've added a few more links to my theory regarding British military related homicides.'

'Can it wait until tomorrow? I'm leaving to meet my wife for dinner.'

'It won't take long,' she said, aware she sounded anxious.

He smiled. 'Burning to tell me your theory. I can't dampen your enthusiasm.' He sat back. 'I'm all ears.'

She groaned inwardly, knowing the smile would soon be gone. 'I think we're looking at a British Special Forces and military intelligence organised reprisal.'

'A what?'

'A revenge squad.'

'Go on.'

'Here's how it works. If a member or former member of British Special Forces or military intelligence is murdered and the perpetrator escapes justice, the organisation will take revenge.'

Dillon stared at her as if waiting for more.

'That's it in broad terms,' she added.

'Sounds quite serious.'

'Yes.'

'Are these avengers serving members or former?'

'I'd say both ... I don't think it's a small group of people either. I think it's structured.'

'What do you mean, structured?'

'Some of the killings appear to have benefited from sophisticated intelligence resources. Lamardi, for instance. He could've been killed in revenge for the deaths of two SAS operators and a Military Intelligence officer. Finding his home in Macedonia required state sponsored levels of intelligence. Another example is moving individuals and weapons across distant foreign borders without detection. There's also access to current British ordnance, items only Special Forces use such as sophisticated mines. Financing is another factor. The Albanian and Lamardi operations must've been expensive. One might expect such incidences to have a financial justification but many of them appear to be purely revenge.'

'You're suggesting these avengers includes personnel within British military intelligence, the military and the Ministry of Defence?'

'There is no other explanation.'

'Are you also suggesting this is state sponsored?' Dillon asked.

'I wouldn't make that accusation for the purpose of initiating an investigation. But I wouldn't rule it out in some form or other. Lamardi's death would've been privately applauded by certain members of the MoD. But then we have the two lawyers who were murdered because they were responsible for Peters' son committing suicide and the Albanian border guards who were assassinated for killing a former SAS trooper eight months ago. They both sound like private vendettas. I suppose I would describe the avengers as a private clique with those involved having access to MoD assets.'

Dillon mulled it over. 'How do you think one gets access to this organisation?' he eventually asked. 'How did Peters know who to contact for instance? How does a qualifying individual get their case heard?'

'The organisation has to be secret, obviously. It wouldn't be if people knew how to contact it. But what if it's the other way around? What if you don't find it? It finds you. What if "they" decide which murders should be avenged? The relatives don't need to know. Their permission isn't required. The organisation can just go ahead and do it.'

'But Peters knew how it happened. He probably knew who did it.'

'Perhaps he's old enough and well connected enough to know someone in the organisation. That would explain why he got revenge for his son who wasn't Special Forces.'

Dillon went into thought again.

'British Special Forces is sending out a message,' she pressed. 'If you mess with us, then if the law doesn't punish you, we will.'

'Any proof?'

'Not yet. I've just been looking for the right direction in which to focus.'

'It must sound a bit fantastic even to you.'

'Fantastic?'

'Remote from reality.'

'It's extraordinary but not impossible.'

'Possible is not probable. What's your next step?'

'I need help. This could be enormous. It needs a dedicated investigation team.'

'I can't go upstairs without evidence. Not something on the scale you're proposing.' Dillon made ready to get back to work. 'If we're going to implicate the Ministry of Defence, the Army and Navy we'd better have a damn sight more to show than an unsupported theory. Get me some evidence, and I mean serious evidence, and we'll take another look at it.'

She sighed and leaned back against the wall.

'Was there something else?' he asked.

'Gunnymede found out about Milo Krilov.'

Dillon stopped dead. 'What?!'

'The man who raped Megan Henderson, Gunnymede's former girlfriend.'

Dillon's eyes darkened. 'And how, pray tell, did Gunnymede find out?'

'I screwed up.'

'How exactly did you screw up?'

'He went into the wrong room in my house looking for the bathroom and found my matrix.'

'For Christ's sake! I gave you Milo Krilov in the strictest of confidence!!! The implications for the classified operation surrounding Krilov could be catastrophic. And catastrophic for me and therefore for you!'

'Only if he acts upon it.'

'Acts upon it! For God's sake! He's not some ordinary Joe in the street. He's an MI6 operator, a dysfunctional one at that and of dubious background! Are we to wait until he does do something?'

'Give me time to fix this,' she pleaded.

'Fix what? Remove it from his memory?'

'Ensure he doesn't act on the information.'

'The fact is, he knows. What if he's doing something right now? What if the police operation is in progress right now? A senior officer in S C & O 19 gave me Krilov's name as long as I assured him I'd give it to no one. I now have to tell him the boyfriend of the woman Krilov raped has that information, and that he works for MI6. Thank you very much! Now get out of my office.'

She walked out of the room close to tears, went back to her desk, grabbed her bag and left the office.

Gunnymede made his way up a grassy slope heading for a line of trees. At the crest he could see the lights of the only collection of structures in sight in a valley running across his front. There was a main house and a couple of long, windowless buildings. Woodland folded around the far side and beyond. It begged a closer inspection and Gunnymede made his way down a large field towards it.

He reached a wooden fence fifty metres from the first long building and paused to take a look at everything now that he was closer. Krilov's Merc was parked outside the house alongside two other 4x4s. The ground floor lights were on. Several exterior lights illuminated the complex but there were plenty of dark corners and shadows to hide in. What Gunnymede didn't notice was a 360 CCTV dome on the end of a long pole that reached above the haze of lights rendering it near invisible at night time.

The place looked like a farm but not a lot of farming went on anymore, if any. There was an absence of machinery and accessories, no barn, no hay, no fertiliser or animal feed. It didn't even smell like a farm.

Gunnymede climbed over the fence and made his way to the nearest storage building, a white painted concrete block, single storey, windowless construction with a metal corrugated roof. He walked to one end and looked around the corner. No door suggested it was the back end of the building and he continued to the next corner to look across a yard where he could see the other similar building. To the left was the small hut surrounded by fencing. A large dog stepped out to look about as if it had heard or smelt something. A Rottweiler. Another one joined it and they stared in Gunnymede's direction. A moment later they lost interest and went back inside.

Gunnymede went back the way he'd come, around to the opposite end and peered around that corner to find the building entrance. A large metal door secured by a sophisticated keypad system. Such an expensive lock looked out of place on such an ordinary farm building.

He stepped back and studied the roof construction, a common security weakness. An oil drum against the building provided a perfect platform. He found a short length of iron piping, climbed onto the drum, pushed the pipe under the roof corner and levered it up. A couple of nails popped loudly and Gunnymede paused, worried about alerting the dogs. They didn't make a sound and he eased the edge up further. When the corner was high enough he jammed the pipe in the gap so that it held up the corner like a tent pole and he took a look inside. There were electrical devices like battery chargers throughout giving off enough light to show the building was one large space. It was filled with shelving and tables randomly arranged with boxes large and small, stacked and opened with items everywhere like a poorly managed storeroom. Gunnymede used his phone light to illuminate the contents of an open box directly beneath him. Interesting. It was filled with assault rifle magazines. A closer look was indeed required.

Gunnymede eased himself beneath the ceiling, reaching for a beam that took his weight and swung inside landing lightly on a concrete surface.

He moved about the room inspecting as he went. There was a variety of military paraphernalia; weapons cases, magazine pouches, chest harnesses, pistol holsters and fighting knives. On a stack of shelving, he found blocks of plastic explosive, sheets of Semtex, rolls of detonation cord and fuse wire. A stack of small black boxes with red warning symbols caught his eye and he unwrapped one to find a dozen detonators. There were cartons of hand grenades, a shelf dedicated to claymore mines and crates of M4 assault rifles. This was a serious arsenal.

The central part of the room was dedicated to a large table covered with files, paperwork, a couple of laptops and a box of mobile phones. Taped to a wall was a photograph of a ship, a map and a sea chart. The map was cut to include Southampton and Winchester while the chart focused on the Port, Southampton Water and the Solent. There was Cyrillic hand writing on the chart which he couldn't read. The ship in the photograph was a medium sized cargo carrier. Sketching on the chart showed its track past Cowes on the Isle of Wight, along the estuary and into Southampton port. The map had a road route highlighted from Southampton to Winchester and this location.

One thing seemed obvious. He was looking at a plan of some sort. The ship was to sail into Southampton Docks where, it had to be assumed, its cargo would be unloaded and driven to this farm. Looking at his surroundings one had to wonder what the cargo consisted of.

Gunnymede examined the chart more closely to find a circle drawn around a large oil refinery south of

Southampton on the west coastline of the estuary. There was nothing to suggest its significance. The refinery was also circled on the map. He examined the papers on the table. On top of one pile was a photograph of a bearded Arab with his name and date of birth in English. There were six more head-shots and details, all Arabs. The last page froze him. It was Saleem. The name was different but it was him without doubt.

Krilov was bringing in more than drugs.

Gunnymede took photographs of everything and searched through the rest of the papers in case there was anything else. The door to the building suddenly flew open and Gunnymede saw a big man wearing thick goggles holding what looked like a large flashlight. It emitted an incredibly intense strobe light. Gunnymede immediately began to lose control of his body. He struggled to turn away but the light came at him from every angle. He closed his eyes. Bumped into a shelf. Opened them and was hit again by the strobing light. He started to suffer an epileptic fit as his knees gave way and his body convulsed violently. The man with the strobe walked over, struck Gunnymede's head with a cosh and he dropped to the floor near unconscious.

The man switched off the powerful strobe, leaned over him and removed the heavy goggles. It was Krilov. 'You like that? It's British. We stole it in the seventies. Works even better underwater.'

A couple of thugs came in and dragged Gunnymede along the floor to the far end where there was a small workshop and a single metal bed without a mattress which they unceremoniously dumped him onto.

Krilov inspected him. 'Now we have some fun.'

Chapter 21

Bethan walked through the underground car park to her car, climbed in behind the wheel and sat in thought. She brought up Gunnymede's number on her phone and hit the call button. It went straight to an electronic voice.

She took another moment to consider things then keyed in another number. This one picked up.

'Bethan,' a man answered.

'Hi, Jordan.'

Jordan was pure geek, a junk-food specialist, sunshine averse and in dire need of professional wardrobe advice from any nation. He was sitting in a swivel chair inside his usual and most preferred habitat which was a windowless, air-conditioned room filled with ultra-modern technology that only the most advanced of nations could afford. He didn't use a phone, he was way beyond them. Bethan's voice, which filled the room, brought a smile to his pasty face.

'You're finally calling to ask me to dinner. How nice.'

'I'm still considering your marriage proposal. Please don't think I've forgotten.'

'Don't take too long or someone else is going to snap me up. What do you need?'

'A track.'

He glanced at a spreadsheet on a monitor. 'When did you put in the request?'

'I didn't. There's no paperwork with this one.'

'I didn't know you did naughty.'

'It's a friend. I'm worried about him.'

'Competition?'

'Hardly.'

'Send me the number.'

Bethan messaged it to him and he copied it to a tracking system.

'You want history or current?' he asked.

'Current.'

'History's interesting.'

'What's interesting?'

'The SIM began life a few weeks ago in London. A visit to Russia. Starts in the middle of nowhere before departing Volgograd airport. Currently static north west of Winchester for fifty-seven minutes.'

He touched a key and pulled on his headphones. 'You want to hear the audio? It's more interesting than the history?'

'Okay.'

A series of male screams followed by shouting.

'Sounds Russian,' Jordan said.

'Shit! He's killing him.'

'Who's killing who?'

Bethan started the engine and screeched out of her parking spot towards the exit. 'Can you send me a fix?'

'On its way.'

Within seconds she was on a main road and heading towards the M3. Gunnymede's coordinates came up and a tap transferred them to her GPS. The congestion frustrated her. She hit the emergency switch and the emergency lights came to life.

Gunnymede screamed as his body went rigid on the springs of the metal bed, his hands and feet secured by plasticuffs, his shirt removed and trousers pulled up to his knees. One of Krilov's thugs, Ashio, a large fellow wearing a gas-mask and thick rubber gloves, stood over Gunnymede holding a sophisticated, modified liquid dispenser, a fine green florescent fluid not unlike anti-freeze dripping from a nozzle.

Krilov watched from the comfort of a tattered armchair a few feet away while he played with Gunnymede's phone. 'Choba,' he said, ordering Ashio to repeat the treatment.

Ashio sprayed Gunnymede's shins with the liquid that seemed to glow momentarily on contact with air. It immediately bubbled and Gunnymede screamed uncontrollably once again as his entire body tensed, his veins bulging under his skin. As the bubbling reduced, so did the pain and Gunnymede's body gradually relaxed leaving him panting for air.

'Explain to me something,' Krilov said. 'You have no identification and your credit card is assigned to anonymous.'

Gunnymede could do little else but breathe hard, his body drenched in sweat.

'That doesn't look like the credit card of a cop or anyone normal in fact. Open your phone for me.'

Gunnymede ignored him.

'Please. Open it.' Krilov sighed and gave his man a nod who responded by generously spraying Gunnymede's legs again.

Gunnymede screamed, even louder than the previous time, the veins on his throat close to bursting.

'We can do this all night if you want,' Krilov said. 'Open the phone and I'll give you a break.'

Gunnymede held up a shaking forth finger on his right hand. Krilov leaned forward and let the finger touch the phone, activating it and then sat back to explored the various apps.

'The only time I've seen a phone as sanitised as this was in the GRU. Nice software. Very practical for someone who works for military intelligence. Is that what you do?'

Gunnymede blinked heavily as the sweat ran into his eyes.

Krilov nodded to Ashio who sprayed Gunnymede again. Gunnymede screamed in utter agony as soon as the liquid touched his skin. His body arched on the bedsprings, his mouth wide open. The green substance bubbled, dripping onto the floor where a whiff of mist floated from it.

'You know this stuff?' Krilov asked him. 'You play with it before? In Afghanistan or Iraq maybe? Yeah, Maybe you Brits don't have it yet. Americans have it. They call it speak juice. We call it *dopros vody* – interrogation water. It's the new water board. Our boys came up with it when cooking up new assassination compounds. It don't kill but it sure as hell hurts. But you know that already. Somehow makes nerves ten times more painful. Bad stuff, eh?'

Gunnymede regained composure as the pain subsided.

'What you doing here?' Krilov asked him.

'You raped Megan Henderson,' Gunnymede said between panting.

Krilov chuckled. 'You here 'cause I raped Jack's daughter. That's funny 'cause I raped Jack's daughter 'cause he wanted to kill me. Wait, I change that. I didn't rape her. Ashio did that. Ashio had the fun. I gave the order. You know, Jack, right? SAS.'

'Yes.'

'So you know Megan? How is she?'

'She's dead.'

Krilov's expression turned thoughtful. 'Dead? That's tough. How'd she die? Ashio wasn't that hard on her.'

'Suicide.'

Krilov gave Ashio a chastising look. 'That's bad news. That was not the plan. So tell me. Why did Jack want to kill me? He was snooping round my house. Same as you. I found him the same way I found you but he wasn't so nosy to break into my stuff and he got away before I could catch him. So I punished him. Ah. I know. You're an assassin. Jack sent you to kill me. Revenge for his daughter. That's why you have no ID.'

'No one sent me.'

'No? So why you here?'

'Megan was my friend.'

'Friend? Ah. So this is personal.'

He studied Gunnymede. Considering something. He said something to Ashio. Ashio put down the interrogation juice, removed his gas-mask and gloves and walked out of the building.

'I want to find out who you are but I'm bored with the modern methods. I like the old fashion ways. We have all night.'

Krilov dug out his own phone to make a call and walked away.

Bethan drove hard along the M3 motorway, past a sign for Winchester. Her emergency lights strobed brightly, motorists moving over to let her whiz along the fast lane.

Krilov sat talking into his phone while Gunnymede lay in front of him. He was in serious trouble and talking wasn't going to get him out of it. Krilov finished his call, got to his feet, stretched his back and walked towards the far end of the building to make another.

Gunnymede shook the sweat from around his eyes to take a thorough look at his surroundings. The plasticuffs securing his hands looped through the curved bar that served as the headboard. The right end slotted over the horizontal post that supported that corner of the bed. A bolt passed through holes in both of them, the only thing holding the bar in place.

Gunnymede shuffled the plasticuffs along the bar, around the curve and down to the bolt where he contorted to get a hold of both ends of it. The nut turned and he started to unscrew it.

Krilov reached the end and turned to walk slowly back, still on the phone. Gunnymede watched him as he turned the screw. Krilov glanced at him. Gunnymede stopped. Krilov went back to his call. Gunnymede felt the screw thread. There was a good centimetre left to undo.

Ashio returned carrying a large moulded plastic box, a roll of plastic sheeting and a bucket. He put them by the bed and took a moment to place a cigarette between his lips. He was about to light it when Krilov ripped it from his mouth, slapped him around the face, knocking the cigarette away, and verbally abused him, pointing to the explosives in the room.

Ashio looked most apologetic as Krilov shook his head and went back to his phone. Ashio spread the plastic sheeting beneath the bed and positioned the bucket directly under Gunnymede's head. He removed a well-used electric chain saw from the plastic box, unravelled the cable and plugged it into a socket in the wall. A quick flick of a switch and the roar filled the room as the tooth-covered chain spun around the chain guide. He grinned at

Gunnymede as he gunned the motor. Krilov appeared in front of him holding up his phone and looking irritated.

Ashio turned off the chain saw, put it down and Krilov went back to his call.

Ashio looked around aimlessly. Nothing to do. He took out his cigarette pack, looked at Krilov, and walked the length of the building and outside.

Krilov was walking away. Gunnymede shuffled his hands back to the bolt to continued unscrewing it. Krilov reached the end of the room and turned about, pausing as his discussion became heated. Ashio walked back inside exhaling smoke. Gunnymede turned the nut furiously. Ashio was halfway along the building when the nut flew off and bounced along the floor. Gunnymede rolled onto his back.

Ashio stood on the nut, picked up the chainsaw and looked at Krilov who had just finished his phone call. Gunnymede looked at the bolt that was still through the holes. Ashio held up the chainsaw to Krilov who signalled him to commence. Ashio started the chainsaw, revving it for affect and closed on Gunnymede. The teeth rattled around the end of the saw. Gunnymede didn't take his eyes off it. As Ashio lowered it to cut off one of Gunnymede's hands the chainsaw jerked in his grasp and died. The thug looked back to see the plug had come out of the socket. The cable had looped around a chair.

Ashio un-looped it resignedly and went over to the plug to push it back in. Gunnymede deftly removed the bolt. The chainsaw burst into life and Ashio advanced on Gunnymede once again. The thug leaned above him and lowered the spinning chain towards his hand. Gunnymede pushed up the bar disconnecting it from the bed and swung it across his body to block the saw. Sparks flew wildly as the teeth struck it. Gunnymede heaved up with all his strength, snapping the other end of the bar from the bed post and pushing the chainsaw upwards. Ashio's foot slipped on the plastic sheeting and he fell back, losing his grip on the chainsaw which fell onto his neck, cutting into it. His scream lasted but a second as blood filled his throat. He threw the saw aside but the damage had been done. Blood gushed through his fingers as he held his neck in an attempt to stem the flow.

Krilov was the other end of the room and unaware of what had happened at first. When he saw Gunnymede sitting up and struggling to release his feet he ran towards him.

Gunnymede could see he wasn't going to free himself before the Russian arrived. He grabbed up the roaring chainsaw and swung it over his body to sever the bonds securing his feet. As Krilov closed in, Gunnymede sprang off the bed and extended the chainsaw to meet him but as he made his lunge the plug popped out of the socket, killing it. Encouraged, Krilov closed the gap with malice in his eyes. Gunnymede threw the chainsaw at him, looked around, grabbed the interrogation water and as Krilov came at him he squeezed the trigger sending a jet of liquid into the Russian's face. It glowed fiercely for a few seconds. Krilov screamed like a banshee and fell to the ground as the liquid bubbled his flesh. He shrieked as he held his face, the liquid covering his hands, adding to his pain. Gunnymede picked up the headboard bar and raised it to bring it down hard on Krilov's head. At that very moment, somewhere in Gunnymede's consciousness, he was aware of movement at the building entrance. He paused long enough to look and saw Bethan, her taser in her outstretched hands aimed at him. Before he could process another thought she fired and a dart flew into him on the end of its fine wire. The shock tore through his body and he dropped the bar and fell to his knees as he went into spasm.

Krilov scurried away on his hands and knees until he could get to his feet and stumble through the room, bouncing off shelves and boxes and out the door.

Gunnymede ripped the dart from his body with a shaking hand as he fought to recover. 'What are you doing?!' he shouted.

'Stopping you from killing him!'

Gunnymede fought to get to his feet. 'Jesus Christ!' he yelled at the top of his voice, as much to deal with the pain as well as his frustration.

'You need to calm down.'

'He was killing me!'

'That's not what I saw.'

Gunnymede looked for Krilov. 'He got away?'

'This is not the way to solve this, Devon.'

Gunnymede tottered towards the entrance.

'Don't, Devon. I'm prepared to stop you,' she said, reloading her Taser. 'Frankly I thought better of you.'

Gunnymede ignored her.

'I'm warning you,' she called out as she brought the taser up on aim.

He reached the doors.

'Stop right there!' she called out.

He stopped. But not because she told him to. The pair of Rottweilers were bearing down on the entrance at full speed. Gunnymede grabbed the door and only managed to slam it shut as the beasts threw themselves at it with a heavy thump, snarling and growling in murderous frustration. He pushed against the door, barely keeping it closed while he looked for a way to lock it. There was a bolt at the top. He threw it across.

Bethan held her fire, confused by his actions.

He stepped back. The door was holding. He hurried to his clothes and pulled on his shirt and jacket. 'We have a problem.'

'What's going on?' she asked.

'We need to get out of here. What are you doing here? Doesn't matter,' he said, grabbing his phone.

'I'm sorry, Devon, but I'm going to have to arrest you.'

'He's coming back and with friends.'

'Are you surprised he's angry? I'll talk to him. He'll be fine when I explain I'm taking you into custody.'

'He's coming back to kill us,' Gunnymede said in exasperation as he grabbed a pistol off a shelf. 'You and me both. Can you see any 9mm ammunition?'

'Put that down! Are you insane?'

'Listen to me. That is not an ordinary man.' He continued to look through the shelves.

She followed him, trying to get his attention. 'No, you listen to me. It doesn't matter who he is. We're not in a war zone. This is England. You can't solve your problems this way. Oh my God!' She exclaimed as she almost stepped on Ashio's lifeless body. Ashio's hands were around his throat, his eyes open wide and blood everywhere.

'That would've been me seconds before you got here,' Gunnymede said as he considered some grenades and changed his mind.

'Who is he?'

'I didn't catch his name.' Gunnymede found a box of magazines that fitted his pistol and continued to look for bullets.

'You killed him?'

'Are you taking anything in?'

'Dear God! You're out of control!' She aimed her taser at him. He grabbed it, tossed it away and held her shoulders to face him. 'Take a look around you. This isn't a normal man cave. Krilov is Russian special forces. He probably works for the GRU. And he's coming back here with friends to kill the both of us. Am I getting through to you?'

Bethan took a closer look at a shelf packed with guns and explosives. The penny dropped. She pulled out her phone. 'I'll call my people.'

He stopped her with a raised hand as he tried to listen.

'Let me call my boss,' she insisted.

'Shh! The dogs have stopped barking.'

The sound of an electric motor came from outside. It became a heavy, gnawing buzz as it touched the brickwork of the building. A big drill.

'What is that?' Bethan asked.

'They're drilling a hole.'

'Why?'

'They want to kill us without setting off the munitions.'

'I don't understand.'

'What comes through a hole and kills everyone inside a confined space and isn't water? Add to that he's Russian, he's not subtle and has access to a lot of bad toys.'

She took a second to think. 'Gas?'

'You're catching on,' he said regarding the mere pistol in his hand and threw it down. It wasn't going to be enough.

He grabbed a block of plastic explosives, detonators, fuse wire and matches, found a knife, cut off a piece of fuse wire, pushed the end into a detonator and crimped it with his teeth.

'What are you doing?'

'Trying to get us out of here,' he said as he pushed the detonator into the explosives.

She got back to her phone and started to key in a number as a drill bit burst through the far wall. The drill wiggled about a bit before it was withdrawn.

'Block the hole,' Gunnymede ordered urgently. 'Quickly!'

She hurried off as he went to the opposite end of the building and cleared away a pile of crates to expose the wall. He dug Ashio's lighter from his pocket and got to work.

Bethan went to the drill hole, looked around, found a piece of cloth, shoved it into the hole and got her weight behind a crate and pushed it in front of it.

A moment later a metal rod shot through the hole, dislodging the cloth and punching the crate back. She looked back at Gunnymede for help but he was busy with his own task.

She needed something more effective. A box of tools was by the door and she sorted through them, found a screwdriver and a hammer and went back to the hole. She placed the screwdriver into the hole and hammered it home as hard as she could.

It looked solid.

Seconds later a sledge hammer slammed against the outer wall and a large scab broke away to fall at her feet. She stepped back as another blow sent more shattered brickwork into the room. Another and a hole appeared, large enough to place a hand through.

Outside, Krilov stood back watching three of his men at work against the wall, all wearing Russian made military biological and chemical warfare suits. One of them was preparing what looked like a sophisticated high pressure gas bottle system with a rubber hose attached to a complex valve head. They fed the hose in through the hole and turned the valve.

Bethan stepped back further as the end of the hose poked through the hole. It was certainly ominous. An orange gas gushed from the hose, slowly at first then increasing in volume. It was heavier than air and gathered on the floor in an ever increasing cloud. As the gas accumulated it began to spread like a thick ground smog.

Bethan backed away and hurried down the room, stepping over the dead thug to join Gunnymede. 'Whatever it is, it's coming,' she said.

Gunnymede concentrated on what he was doing.

'It's an orange gas,' she said.

'Got it,' he said putting the finishing touches to his work.

'What is it?'

'No idea,' he said as he propped the lump of explosive against the wall and straightened the trailing fuse wire. He placed boxes and furniture against it and held up the lighter. 'When I light it we have a minute before it goes. Understood? Go to the corner behind those boxes.'

She quickly obeyed and crouched behind them.

He lit the fuse and joined her, pulling more crates in front of them and using his body to protect her. He leaned round to look for the gas but couldn't see anything from where he was. Not at first. Then a wisp of orange mist drifted between shelving halfway down the room and oozed along the floor towards them.

'I take it that will kill us?' she asked.

'I don't think it's going to make us laugh.'

The gas spread the width of the room as the leading edge rolled towards them.

'How much would we need to breathe before it kills us?'

'If it's nerve gas, none. A droplet on the skin will be enough.'

The hissing fuse burned smokily and went out of sight behind the boxes. It was too slow for Gunnymede's liking, the gas moving far too quickly. When it was metres from their outstretched feet they instinctively pulled them in.

They pressed themselves against the wall as the orange wave drew closer. The charge should've detonated by now. The gas was within a fingers-reach of their legs.

The explosion was ear-splitting in the confined space and rocked the building so violently it felt like the entire structure might collapse. The blast reached out, the shockwave throwing back everything in its path, including the gas. Debris hit Gunnymede's back as he shielded Bethan. Most importantly, the blast created a large hole sending bricks across the farm yard.

Smoke and dust filled the room. Gunnymede grabbed Bethan's arm and yanked her with him. Unable to see much, both coughing, Gunnymede felt his way along the wall, stumbling over rubble until he reached the edge of the crumbling hole and stepped through it.

Gunnymede kept hold of Bethan's arm as he broke into a run, out of the dust and into the night air.

'My car,' she said, pointing.

They ran towards it and climbed in. She struggled to find her key. Gunnymede looked over his shoulder anxiously. There was no sign of pursuers. She found the key, dropped it on the floor, scrambled to pick it up while he bit his lip in an effort to resist offering encouragement. She started the engine and screeched away, turning in a tight circle and towards the lane that ran up the hill into woodland. Gunnymede looked back again to see if they were being followed but there was nothing but smoke.

She drove as fast as she dared along the lane, up the hill through the trees and down the other side.

'Left,' he said as she reached the main road which she turned sharply onto. 'That's my bike,' he said a few hundred yards later.

She pulled over and stopped, leaving the engine running while she gathered herself.

'You okay?' he asked.

'I think so. You?'

He opened the door, climbed out painfully and stretched his back. He pulled up his trouser legs to inspect his skin by the glow from the car's lights. The skin was red, covered in a rash, but otherwise it seemed okay.

She stopped the engine and climbed out. 'Would we know right away if any of that stuff touched us?'

'No idea.'

'Should we go to hospital?'

'If you start feeling weird maybe you should.'

She was still frustrated with him. 'If you didn't go there for revenge what were you doing there?'

'I just wanted to check him out and it kind of escalated.'

'Why did he want to kill you?'

'You know he's a major heroin dealer?'

'I didn't. I'll have to tell my boss about tonight ... I'll obviously have to tell him about you. Will that be a problem for you?'

'Don't worry about it.'

He finished stretching and made his way over to his bike. When he looked back at her she was still by her car, watching him. 'You should get going.'

She didn't move.

'What is it?' he asked.

'You remember the trend I told you about? British military homicides?'

'Yes.'

'I have a theory. They're not all random killings. Many of them are connected. Organised. An organised group of revengers made up of British military. They avenge the deaths of soldiers where the perpetrator hasn't been brought to justice.'

He didn't answer.

She suddenly realised something. 'You know about it, don't you?'

'There've been rumours.'

'What rumours?'

'They're years old.'

'Like what?'

He sighed. 'That's the point. None of them are meaningful. No names or places. Just anecdotes.'

'So you knew about it when we went to Albania?'

'I never made any connection.'

'What kind of intelligence officer are you?'

'I'm not an analyst. Or an investigator.'

'What are you then?'

'I'm a field operator.'

'You're allowed to think, though, right?'

'There's no need to be insulting.'

'I believe these avengers were behind the Albania border guard killings and also your Afghan security director, Lamardi.'

He studied her as he thought of something. 'You think I'm a part of it?'

'Why would you say that?'

'You just said I was allowed to think.'

'Are you? Part of it?'

'I get the feeling you wouldn't believe me if I said I wasn't.'

'Actually I would. I don't believe you are a part of it.'

'Why not?'

'You have a motive for killing Krilov. If you were a part of the organised revenge you wouldn't be here. Someone without a motive would've come in your place so as not to implicate you. That's how it works.'

'So why're you telling me about this revenge mob?'

She shrugged. 'It's going to come out. I wanted you to know.'

'Why?'

'I feel protective about you.'

'You just tasered me.'

She stifled a smirk. 'Was it painful?'

'Actually, it was pleasant compared to the *dopros vody*.'

'The what?'

He looked around, conscious of where they were. 'You should get going.'

She nodded. 'Sorry and thanks,' she said. 'Sorry for suspecting you and thanks for saving me.'

He came over to her. Stepped closer. She looked into his eyes. He kissed her softly and they had a much needed hug.

'I don't suppose you'd like to come back to mine?' she asked.

'I would. But I've got some things to do.'

She understood and let go of him. 'Be safe.'

'I'm in the wrong job for that.'

She climbed into her car.

'I'll call you,' he said.

She smiled, started the engine and drove away.

He watched her go.

As he walked to his bike he opened the photo file of Krilov's plans on his phone and sent them to MI6 Ops. He climbed stiffly onto the machine, pulled on his helmet, started the engine and drove onto the road.

A few miles down the road his phone chirped and he touched the hands free button.

'Devon Gunnymede,' Simons said in his patronising manner. 'You've had a busy evening. What's Krilov like?'

'He's an arsehole.'

'I hope he's not a dead arsehole.'

'He's a pissed off arsehole.'

'I hope you didn't put him off his plan. We need that ship to come in. Interesting connection, Saleem and Krilov. It ties Saleem into the heroin convoy.'

'What about the ship?'

'The police have known about it for a week. It's scheduled to arrive tomorrow evening. Saleem could be on board.'

'If Krilov suspects I know about it, he'll warn it off.'

'Do you think he does?'

'I don't know. We should board it now.'

'Not my first option. We're putting a bird on it. If it stays on course and nothing comes alongside it we'll let it run its course and the police can do their job in Southampton. Otherwise we'll take steps. Let's see what the next twenty-four hours brings. With luck we can wrap up this part of it.'

'Krilov could be a link to Spangle.'

'I'm sure he is. Have a good night.'
The phone went dead.

Chapter 22

Krilov leaned over a kitchen sink, dabbing his face with a wet cloth. The flesh around his eyes was tender. He examined himself in a mirror. Krilov was not the prettiest of creatures but that didn't hinder his vanity. He poured himself a vodka with a heavy hand and downed it without a wince.

One of Krilov's men came over and placed a freshly printed photograph in front of him. It was an isolated still from a CCTV camera. A clear picture of Bethan and Gunnymede.

'Send it to the policeman,' Krilov said in Russian.

Krilov took another drink and accessed a number on his phone.

A man answered with a simple 'Hi'.

'I send you a picture of a man and a woman. I want their details – home, car, location, everything.'

Jedson sat on his black leather couch in his small, poncy-looking London flat talking to an iPad on his coffee table. 'I'm just looking,' he said as he opened Krilov's message and Gunnymede and Bethan appeared.

'You can do this now?'

'That won't be a problem. What do you want to do with them?'

'Kill them.'

'I want the woman.'

'What for?'

'I just do.'

'There's plenty woman where you're going.'

'I want this one.'

Krilov disconnected.

Jedson checked his watch, picked up a glass half filled with a dark liquor and took a long drink as he studied the picture.

Gunnymede pulled the bike to a stop outside a large Georgian house in a residential street in Holborn. The engine went silent and he climbed off stiffly, pretty sure he heard a creaking sound come from his bruised frame. He was all cleaned up and looking quite presentable, except for the grazes on his face and hands. He took a bunch of flowers and a box of chocolates from a pannier and walked up a short flight of steps to the front door which was standing ajar and stepped inside the tasteful contemporary flats conversion. He climbed a staircase, faced the door of an apartment and, after a brief tidy up of his hair and clothes he knocked on it. A moment later it opened and a slender woman in her sixties stood there looking at him with a blank expression.

He smiled at her despite her air of indifference. She was on the frail side but the sparkle in her eyes left no doubt about the quality of her inner strength and cognisance.

'How did you get in downstairs?'

'The door was open.'

'You didn't break in?'

'I didn't.'

'You took your time coming.'

'I've been busy.'

'Flowers *and* chocolates are a sign of guilt.'

'They're not for you.'

'Who are they for?'

'A sweet, kind, loving lady who I'm hoping to find somewhere in there, if I can ever get through the access control.'

She gave in, smiled and reached out to him. 'I just needed to make sure it was my Devon. Give me a hug.'

Gunnymede held her while she patted his back. When he stepped back she took a look at him. 'You've put on some muscle.'

'I had a lot of recreation time.'

'You probably didn't get a decent cup of tea.'

'It's criminal what they serve as tea.'

'I'll put the kettle on,' she said as she headed down the hall into the kitchen. 'Have you had breakfast?'

'Tea would be great.'

'Rubbish. You'll have something to eat with it.' She opened the fridge and pulled out a plate of sausages and bacon, tomatoes and mushrooms and a carton of eggs. She sniffed the meat. 'I bought these expecting you a few days ago. They'll do. A little bit of gangrene never hurt anyone.'

'Do you need a hand?'

'You never started asking me that until you left home. You didn't mean it then either. You look like you've got a few aches and pains.'

'I'll be good to go in a few days.'

'They got you in the wars already.'

'Well, you take the Queen's shilling, you take your chances with it.'

'I'm betting on the Middle East.'

'For what?'

'That's where you've been, isn't it?'

'How do you know that?'

'Well, it's too early for North Korea, too late for North Africa and everywhere else can manage without you for the time being.' She paused. 'Unless of course it's those pesky Russians.'

'Our favourite bad guys.'

'They've always been jerks,' she said, putting the sausages and bacon in the frying pan. 'Putin's still trying to finish off what Ivan the Terrible's grandfather started. Borders and buffers. They respect nothing but severity. They'll evolve one day, I'm sure, but not in our lifetime.'

She poured a cup of tea and put it in front of him as he sat at the table. 'I heard about Megan,' her face darkening.

He looked into her eyes and nodded, as if they were passing data between them. Nothing more was needed to be said and she went back to the cooker. 'So tell me then.'

'What subject are we on to now?'

'How did you get back into the firm?'

'They needed me.'

'Not because they thought you were innocent.'

'You know I wasn't.'

'I know you're not a bad person. You weren't a thief as a boy and that's where the foundations are laid. You were up to something and it went wrong is my guess.'

He smiled at her, appreciating her.

'So they need you for something that was going on when you left. Unfinished business.'

'You know them as well as I do. Better I expect.'

'They won't have changed. Never trust any of them. Not that they're wrong. They just don't care about collateral damage. It's what they're taught in school. Or they used to be. I despair, wondering where our next generation of ruthless bastards will come from. This country produces such bleeding heart liberal pussies these days.'

'Language.'

They chatted while she made breakfast, while he ate it and while he had his post breakfast cup of tea. After the meal, Gunnymede cleared up and sat by the window that looked down onto the street while she sat at the dining table.

She opened a wooden box, removed a packet of filtered cigarettes, an ashtray and lighter and lit one up. She inhaled deeply and blew the smoke out in a long stream, thoroughly enjoying it. 'I've decided that more than five cigarettes a day is unhealthy for the body and less than five is unhealthy for one's contentment. No point being alive if you're unhappy.'

He poured himself a glass of water and looked at her as if measuring her up. 'Aunt Grace.'

'Something important coming,' she said, drawing on the cigarette. 'You have about five ways of saying Aunt Grace and that's one I don't hear often.'

'Tell me about the death of my father.'

She exhaled, filling the air between them with smoke. 'The last time you asked me about your father you were eleven years old.'

'I'm looking for the adult version.'

'What do you want to know?'

'Tell me how he was killed.'

'He was caught by a roadside bomb as he was leaving the embassy.'

'You told me that much when I was eleven.'

'Why the sudden interest?'

'It's not so sudden. It's just time to ask.'

'You're more cynical now.'

'I think there was more to it than just a roadside bomb. Was it bad luck or was he the target?'

'You're looking for bad guys.'

'I'd like to know who was responsible.'

'Then you'll want revenge.'

'That's not what's driving my curiosity.'

'What is?'

'I'm in the business. I know a lot of people who were killed and I know why. But I don't know why my own father died.'

She stubbed out the cigarette. 'Of course you have a right to know. But if you want details I'm not the person you need to ask.'

'You never told me he was military intelligence.'

'Didn't I? I suppose it was obvious. He was always doing his own thing in the name of the military. He never wore a uniform. He was a hammer like you, not one of the academics. He got his hands dirty and liked it.'

'Was he targeted?'

'That was the question on everyone's lips at the time. You know I was just MI6 administrative.'

'To a department director.'

'There was nothing conclusive. There were rumours, but they were coming upstream, from the ranks. Unreliable. There was one rumour, however, that came downstream, several years later, a few months before I left – I'm going to have another cigarette,' she said, lighting up. 'I suddenly feel like I'm back in the office. We smoked like chimneys in those days.'

'What was the rumour?'

'The device was Hezbollah, the bomber was Hezbollah, but the request was from outside Hezbollah.'

'Who?'

'I don't know. The suggestion was it wasn't local.'

'You mean not from within Lebanon?'

'That was the suggestion.'

'So, outside of Lebanon was the Russians and allies.'

'And the rest,' she said, staring ahead at nothing, deep in her own images.

'Was there an enquiry?'

'If there was I didn't get sight of it. You can understand why of course. He was my brother. They would have made a point of me not seeing it ... if there was one.'

'What would you have done if you discovered foul play?'

'That would depend on who was behind it. There were a lot of players in that conflict. Russians. Syrians. Israelis. Palestinians. Americans. Iranians. Christians. Muslims. Amal. Druze. Maronites. Us. And more ... I suppose, when you boil it all down you could say it was essentially West v Soviet. What would I do if I thought there'd been foul play? Are you asking me as a hammer or a pen? We use the skills we have, Devon. I would've written, internally of course, in the hope that someone might do something. But it was just a rumour. And now, a long time ago,' she said with some finality, taking another deep drag and blowing the smoke into the room.

An hour later she walked with him to the front door. She smiled at him. 'I'm sorry I called you a hammer. You are a hammer. But everyone thinks that's all you are. Let them think that. It's to your advantage. Because you're much, much more.'

They hugged affectionately. As they parted, Gunnymede remembered something. 'Harlow sends his regards.'

'Harlow?' She looked surprised.

'I didn't know you knew him.'

She didn't smile and looked into the distance as if in thought. 'He was already in the firm when I arrived. A skinny whippersnapper.'

'What was he like?'

'A twit at first. But he became amusing. Not my type really though he thought otherwise.'

Gunnymede kissed her on the forehead. 'See you.'

She watched him walk down the stairs. Her smile remained until he was out of sight and then faded and disappeared.

Bethan bit into a piece of toast followed by a sip of coffee and pulled on her jacket, all in one fluid motion as she picked up her phone and laptop bag.

The front door knocker sounded. She took another sip of coffee and went to see who it was. Jedson was standing on her doorstep looking sheepish.

'What do you want?' she asked coldly.

'To apologise. Again. Twice I've been really very rude and I don't have any excuses.'

'Go away,' she said and started to close the door.

'Wait.' Jedson stopped the door from closing. 'I've decided to tell you everything you need to know about Milo Krilov. No strings.'

'I don't need to know anything about him. Now go away.'

'Please, Beth. I also want to apologise for threatening to go to my boss. I didn't mean it.'

'I don't care.'

'Does Dillon know you went to Krilov's farm last night?'

'What?'

'With that MI lad you went to Albania with?'

'How did you know that?'

Jedson took a sly look to his side, along the street, out of sight to Bethan. Three thugs climbed out of a parked van. 'I told you. I'm very special.'

He shoved the door hard, the edge catching Bethan on the side of her head knocking her back. Jedson pushed into the house, sealed her mouth with a hand and pulled her to the floor. As she struggled, the thugs stepped in and closed the door. One of them produced a roll of masking tape and wound it around her head several times to cover her mouth. Another secured her hands and feet with plasticuffs and within seconds she was trussed up like a calf ready for branding. The third extended the blade of a builders knife. Bethan's eyes widened and she tried to scream. He knelt down over her, cut into the carpet along the length of her body and continued to score a large rectangle. They pulled up the corners and rolled her in the carpet like a hand-made cigarette, picked her up and carried her out of the house.

The back doors of a van were opened and the carpet roll was unceremoniously thrown in. The thugs climbed in and it drove away. Jedson stood in the doorway waving at the van. He looked up and down to see there was no-one about, not that he particularly cared, closed the door and walked off.

Chapter 23

Gunnymede parked the bike in a residential street and switched off the engine. Narrow terraced houses lined both sides of the street. A couple of kids were kicking a ball about. An old man cycled past with a basket of groceries hanging off his handlebars. The light was fading. It would be dark in less than an hour.

Gunnymede walked a short distance along the pavement to a house and studied the front door. A most familiar door. In his mind's eye, he saw it open and a beautiful girl with a broad smile stand in the doorway, anxious to hug him.

Poor Megan.

He rang the doorbell. A light came on in the hallway and a figure could be seen through the thick smoked glass panels marching along it from the back of the house. The door opened and Jack Henderson stood there. 'I didn't expect to see you here.'

'We need to talk, Jack.'

'This isn't a good time.' Jack was distracted. 'Can you come back tomorrow?'

'It's important.'

'Surely it can wait a day.'

'It can't.'

'It will have to. Sorry Devon. I'm really busy.' Jack started to close the door.

'It's about the Becket Approval,' Gunnymede said.

Jack froze. A moment later he opened the door. 'Where did you hear those words?'

'The first time was from Megan.'

'Megan?'

'You didn't think you could keep secrets from her living in the same house, did you?'

Jack had to concede that point.

'She told me because she was worried for you. She thought it would lead to serious trouble for you.'

'I see ... can we meet up later? I'll be free in a couple of hours.'

'Jack. The secret's out.'

'What do you mean?'

'I came here to warn you.'

A couple walked past the house making Jack suddenly conscious of how public their conversation was. 'Come in.'

Jack closed the door but remained beside it.

'The police know,' Gunnymede said.

'How?'

'The organisation has been busy lately ... It was only a matter of time.'

'What do they know?'

'Enough to take a lot of cases off the unsolved shelf and start taking a closer look at them.'

Jack was vexed. 'How do you know this?'

'I've been working with Scotland Yard.'

Jack shook his head. 'I don't believe they have anything we need to worry about.'

'A dozen Albanian border guards ... Mustafa Lamardi in Macedonia. A couple of lawyers in London last week ... The police are talking about them.'

The cases clearly meant something to Jack. He sighed deeply as he looked down the hallway towards the other end, his mind churning. He finally came to a decision. 'You'd better come with me.'

Jack led the way down the hallway to the back of the house and into a large kitchen. Half a dozen men were gathered, all waiting silently for Jack to return. They were surprised to see Gunnymede, as much as he was to see them. Peters the farmer, Charlie, Boris the Bull, three other hard looking men and a woman Gunnymede didn't recognise.

'What's 'e doin' 'ere?' Boris asked angrily.

'Easy, Boris,' Jack said.

'This is a surprise, Gunny,' Charlie said.

'He's a police officer,' Peters said.

'He's MI6,' Charlie explained.

'He came round my farm with a female copper,' Peters chimed.

'Calm down, everyone,' Jack said. 'He's got something to say I think we all need to hear.'

'I don't care what 'e's got to say,' Boris said, his tone aggressive.

'Shut it!' Jack interrupted in a raised voice, glaring at Boris. 'He came here with something important to say and it will be said. Go on, Devon.'

They all looked at Gunnymede with suspicion.

'I've been working with the police as a consultant,' Gunnymede said. 'Peters was one case. The two lawyers killed in London. Another was in Albania. A dozen border guards killed by a sniper.' Gunnymede didn't miss that one of the men he didn't know reacted ever so slightly to the comment. 'Mustafa Lamardi was killed in Macedonia, by the same sniper.' The same man blinked again in a way that Gunnymede couldn't ignore. 'You a sniper?' he asked the man.

Charlie looked between the man and Gunnymede. 'Sidney was "M" Squadron's best,' he said. 'But so what?'

'M' Squadron was SBS. 'Nice shooting,' Gunnymede said.

Sidney looked away sheepishly.

'The police are working on the premise they were the work of a single organisation,' Gunnymede continued. 'A group of revengers made up of special forces and military intelligence.'

'What's that got to do with us?' Peters said.

'Yeah, why you tellin' us?' Boris asked.

'No reason. I just thought I'd drive all the way down here and mention it,' Gunnymede said.

'Okay. So just because you think you know where to come, it doesn't mean the police do,' Charlie said. 'Or does it?'

'I don't believe they do right now,' Gunnymede said.

'How do they know?' Peters interrupted. 'Someone must've said something.'

'Good detective work,' Gunnymede replied.

'Bollocks,' Boris said.

'Does it really matter?' Gunnymede argued.

'They got any names?' Charlie asked.

'I don't think so.'

'So no one knows it's anything to do with us, except you,' Charlie said.

'I believe so.'

There was a long silence as they considered the implications.

'I'll do 'im in if no one else wants to,' Boris said.

'Shut up,' Jack said scornfully to Boris, treating him like a fool. More important things were on his mind. 'I'm not so concerned about the past as I am the future.'

'Why should we worry?' Charlie asked. 'Okay, so they've figured out it's soldiers doing the hits. That's not such a genius conclusion to be fair, is it? I would've expected someone to figure that out by now.'

'He's right,' one of the others said. 'Knowing it's soldiers doesn't point the finger at anyone specific.'

'There's hundreds of possible suspects,' Charlie said. 'Thousands.'

'Why do you trust 'im?' Boris asked Jack. 'He's a thief.'

'So are you,' Jack said.

'I didn't take twenty kilos of heroin.'

'Because you're not smart enough to,' Gunnymede said.

Boris moved to lunge at Gunnymede but Charlie and another stopped him.

'Easy, Boris,' Charlie said.

'Shut it. Everyone,' Jack snarled. 'Let's calm this down. Maybe we should thank him for coming to us. He could've said nothing.'

'I did what I came here to do. You do what you want with it,' Gunnymede said before walking out of the room. Jack followed.

As Gunnymede reached for the front door, Jack put his hand on it. 'Thanks, Devon. I appreciate it.'

Gunnymede took a moment to look at Jack, into his eyes. 'There is something else ... Milo Krilov.'

The name had an immediate impact on Jack.

'You knew about him before he kidnapped Megan.'

Jack looked immediately guilty.

'Why were you doing a recce on him?'

'He killed two SBS lads in their mini-sub in a Swedish Fjord ten years ago. There was no threat to him on the task. It was cold blooded murder. We wanted revenge.'

Gunnymede understood. 'He suspected you were targeting him so he punished Megan as a warning to you.'

Jack hated to hear it from Gunnymede. 'I know ... How do you know all this?'

'I met Krilov last night.'

'What? You talked to him?'

'It wasn't exactly a social.'

Jack was racked by his own guilt. 'I wake up every day knowing what he did to Megan was my fault. That's when I can get to sleep ... I didn't know he saw me. I did the recce. Got what I wanted. Then a week later, he took Megan.'

'Megan is dead because you chose to play judge and jury. You don't deserve to sleep.'

'I won't apologise for what we do.'

Gunnymede opened the door and paused as something occurred to him. 'How'd you know Krilov was in the UK?'

Jack was deep inside himself.

'Jack?'

Jack shook his head, refusing to say.

'You don't run the Becket Approval, do you?'

Jack didn't answer.

'Who's above you?'

Jack looked him in the eyes. 'You'll find out one day. I'm sure of it.'

Jack walked away down the corridor.

Gunnymede could only wonder what the man meant as he left the house and headed back towards his bike. He didn't see three men climb from a parked van further down the street. Only when they were closing in did he notice them and that one was carrying an iron bar by his side. Gunnymede kept on walking as his mind flipped to crisis mode.

He arrived at his bike. A car door slammed behind him and he looked over his shoulder to see two more men walking towards him. Jesus! Five. This was a serious situation.

Gunnymede stepped between his bike and a car, onto the road, crossing to the other side. The men followed, stepping between vehicles in a pincer movement to keep Gunnymede contained. As Gunnymede reached the opposite pavement he grabbed a bottle from a bin.

The group of three formed a single file to pass between the tightly parked vehicles. The other two were still crossing the road. Gunnymede went for the three, launching the bottle at the leading thug hitting his hands which he'd brought up to protect his face causing him to drop his iron bar. As the others backed out to take another route, Gunnymede carried on forward, grabbed the iron bar and slammed it into the side of the thug's head. The man went down and Gunnymede hurried to intercept another.

The next thug to step between cars was wielding a hand axe which he raised to engage. Gunnymede ran at him and jabbed the bar as if it was a sword, catching the thug in the mouth, breaking several teeth. The thug behind drew a pistol and as he reached out to shoot, having to lean around his colleague, Gunnymede managed to knock the barrel with the bar as the gun fired. The bullet missed Gunnymede's head by inches, ricocheting off a wall and smashing through the window of a house. The thug lost grip of the gun when it fired and it fell between the cars.

The situation was getting even more desperate. Gunnymede dropped the bar and went for the gun but before he could reach it he was grabbed by one of the men, brutally thrown back to the ground and punched and kicked repeatedly. Gunnymede swung his feet and fists wildly but others joined in, their combined boots and fists raining down. A machete was raised. Gunnymede saw it in time to move his head to one side as the blade struck the pavement. A thug held Gunnymede's head steady while the machete was raised for another blow. As it came down towards the centre of Gunnymede's skull the man was grabbed from behind, his head yanked back by his hair with great force. Boris the bull savagely illustrated his nickname by pounding the man's head against a lamppost cracking it loudly. Charlie kicked a thug in the testicles hard enough to drop him to his knees, raised a brick he'd carried across the road and brought it down onto the man's head making a cracking sound that could be heard up the street. Jack swung the edge of a cricket bat into a face. Other members of the kitchen meeting joined the melee with vigour and within seconds all five thugs were laid out. It was carnage.

Gunnymede got to his feet feeling his bruised face and cut lip having fared well considering. People stepped from front doors or looked through windows, wondering what had happened. Jack picked up the pistol in a handkerchief.

'Krilov's people,' Gunnymede said.

'They come for me?' Jack asked. 'Or you?'

A thug rolled onto his back, unable to get to his feet, moaning in pain. Gunnymede crouched over him. 'What are you doing here?'

The thug shook his head.

'I asked you what you're doing here.'

'Come for you,' the thug said in a Slavic accent.

'You came to kill me?'

'No kill. Take you.'

'Take me where?'

The thug looked away.

'Boris is very good at getting answers out of people,' Charlie offered.

Indeed, Boris looked enthusiastic at the mere suggestion. The thug recovered enough to sit up and wipe blood from his nose. The only other conscious colleague said something in Russian which the one sitting up found amusing.

'What's so funny?' Charlie asked him.

'He said we should've got girl. Much easier job than this one.'

They chuckled in pain. Hard bastards.

'What girl?' Gunnymede asked. 'What girl?'

The thug continued to chuckle. Gunnymede dug out his phone and brought up Bethan's number.

The phone rang. And rang.

Gunnymede grabbed the thug by his hair. 'What girl?'

'Police girl,' he said.

'Where is she?'

The thug's response was to stare coldly at him.

'Who's he talking about?' Jack asked.

'A police officer I was working with. She helped me find Krilov. He's kidnapped her.'

'He'll tell Boris,' Charlie said.

Gunnymede took the thug around the throat. 'Tell me where she is.'

The thug simply stared at him as if enjoying the attention.

'Shots were fired,' Jack said. 'The police'll be here any minute. Get him in the house. Sid, Billy. Keep the police happy. Show them the gun,' he said, handing it to them. 'Keep them away from the house.'

Charlie and Boris hauled up the thug and helped him across the road. Gunnymede and Jack followed. They guided him into Jack's house, along the corridor and into the kitchen.

'Clear the table,' Boris said.

Charlie moved the mugs and plates away. Boris took the thug by his hair and pulled him onto the table, laying him flat on his back.

Gunnymede leaned over the thug. 'Where is she?'

'We need to prep 'im,' Boris interrupted. ''Old 'im down.'

They held the thug down by his arms while Boris searched through Jack's kitchen drawers. Boris returned holding a meat hammer and a fork.

The thug nervously eyed Boris and his tools but remained defiant. 'I tell you nothing,' he said.

'I ain't asked you nothin' yet 'ave I?' Boris replied testily.

Boris took a firm hold of the thug's head, positioned the hammer above his mouth and hit his front teeth. The thug wriggled hard.

'Hold 'im,' Boris ordered.

They pinned the thug down and Boris set to with the hammer, tapping away until he'd broken several of teeth. The thug struggled in excruciating pain, blood and mucus spurting from his mouth as the others kept a firm hold of him.

Gunnymede leaned over to say something to the thug but Boris interrupted him again. ''E's not ready.'

Boris took the fork, bent one of prongs to isolate it, grabbed the thug's jaw to hold it steady and placed the tip of the prong into a broken teeth shoving it brutally inside and deep into the nerve. The thug screamed so loudly he could be heard beyond the walls of the house.

Boris removed the bloody fork and looked into the thug's eyes. The thug was shaking with pain. 'You don't answer the questions, you get this all day.'

Boris stepped back. ''E's ready for the first question.'

Gunnymede was impressed with the simplistic brutality of it all and leaned over the shaking thug. 'Where is she?'

The thug hesitated.

Boris leaned in with the fork. 'It can sometimes take several nerves to get them going?'

The thug shook his head and did his best to talk with his smashed teeth. '*Nietsiperigon zavod.*'

'What'd he say?' Charlie asked.

'Dunno,' Boris said. 'Where is she?' Boris shouted.

'Re ... refin ... nery,' the thug said.

'Say it again,' Charlie asked him.

'Re ... finery.'

'Refinery,' Charlie said.

'Refinery?' Boris echoed.

The thug nodded.

'Mean anything?' Jack asked.

Gunnymede needed more. 'What refinery?' he asked.

'*Masla,*' the thug said. 'Oil,' he translated, keen for them to understand.

'Oil refinery,' Charlie said.

Gunnymede took out his phone and brought up the shots of the map and chart from Krilov's man cave. The oil refinery was circled on both. 'Where is the refinery?' he asked. 'Where?'

'Sooth ... oom ... toon,' he said.

'Southampton?' Gunnymede clarified.

The thug nodded enthusiastically. '*Da. Da.*'

'Why? Why is she at the refinery?'

The thug shook his head.

'Tell me why she's at the refinery.'

'Not know.'

Boris pushed through, shoving the fork deep inside a freshly broken tooth and wiggling it around for good measure while the thug wriggled and screamed frantically.

''E asked you why?' Boris shouted after removing the prong.

'Not know,' the thug shouted back. 'Not know! Not know!'

'I don't think he knows,' Charlie said.

'Is Krilov at the refinery?' Gunnymede asked.

'Krilov. *Da*! *Da*!'

'Da's yes in Russian,' Boris offered.

'*Armia*,' the thug said.

'What did he say?' Charlie asked.

'Say that again,' Boris said.

'Krilov has army,' the thug said.

'Krilov has an army,' Boris clarified.

Gunnymede leaned over the thug again. 'If the girl isn't there you'll belong to these men for the rest of your short and painful life.'

'She there,' he insisted. 'She there.'

Gunnymede left the kitchen and walked out of the house.

Charlie and Boris went to the front door to watch Gunnymede go.

'Where's he going?' Boris asked.

Charlie shrugged. 'Take on a Russian army by the sound of it.'

Boris nodded approvingly. 'Got balls.'

As Gunnymede climbed onto his bike, several police vehicles arrived at the end of the street and armed officers got out. Gunnymede started the engine and drove away.

He turned onto a main road, his mind buzzing, trying to understand what could be going on. He accessed his phone and called Bethan's office number. A moment later the operator picked up announcing he'd reached Scotland Yard.

'I want to speak with DCI Dillon.'

The operator asked him to hold. A moment later she came back to tell him Dillon was unavailable.

'It's an emergency,' Gunnymede stressed.

The operator asked him to hold again. A moment later a man's voice came on the line asking how he could help as Dillon was unavailable.

Gunnymede hung up. There was no point. He turned onto a main road and bombed along it.

He hit another phone contact. It picked up. 'Aristotle?'

Aristotle was in a dark 4x4 parked in a deserted section of a dock. 'Yes, Mr. Gunnymede.'

'I need help.'

'With what?'

'Last night I met Milo Krilov.'

'I heard.'

'I was with a police officer. The one I went to Albania with. Krilov has kidnapped her.'

'That's unfortunate.'

'He's taken her to an oil refinery down the estuary from Southampton Docks. Fawley refinery.'

'Why?'

'I don't know.'

'We expect Krilov to be in Southampton Docks for the arrival of his vessel.'

'So why's he at the refinery?'

'Perhaps you have your information wrong,' Aristotle said.

'I don't think I do. You need to send a team to the refinery to check it out.'

'I will ask the police to send a patrol to investigate.'

'No. Krilov is armed and dangerous. You have to send an armed response team.'

'That's not possible.'

'Why not?'

'Because we will need all our resources for the ship. You yourself reported there will be ISIS members on board. They could be armed. The crew could be armed and hostile. We have armed response teams and special forces here.'

'Is that where you are right now?'

'Yes.'

'Something's happening at the refinery and we haven't got it covered.'

'I'll report what you have told me but I don't think anything will happen at such short notice and without evidence.'

Gunnymede understood the dilemma.

'Why don't you go and check it yourself?' Aristotle suggested. 'Report what you see. If it's significant perhaps that will convince superiors to send assistance.'

'It's a big place. I've got no gear.'

'I don't have any other suggestions for you.'

'Great.'

Aristotle looked through his window at a SAS command station with troopers preparing their assault equipment. 'I can meet you and bring you some "gear",' he said.

Gunnymede thought about that.

'That's all I can do for you, Gunnymede.'

'Okay. I'll meet you outside the refinery. I'll send you an RV.'

Gunnymede disconnected and took a moment to think things through. There was nothing else for it. He opened a map app on his phone and searched the refinery perimeter. He found a location, pinned it and sent it to Aristotle.

He veered the bike across the road, took a sharp turn at a junction going through a red light and speeded away.

A line of vans drove along a disused road, the lead vehicle's headlights cutting into the darkness. They passed through a pair of rusting, disfigured gates into a derelict section of Fawley oil terminal on the west coast of the Southampton estuary. Manning the gates were two men armed with AK47 assault rifles. When the last vehicle passed through they struggled to close them.

The vans followed the heavily potholed perimeter road, past a block of empty storage containers daubed in graffiti and over a pair of rusting railway tracks, the gaps between the rails filled with old sleepers to allow the vehicles to cross easily.

The road passed through a large, open space with warehouses dotted around its edges and to a ramp that climbed onto a long, poorly lit jetty that carried miles of piping between the terminal and the estuary landing stage. One of the vans remained at the bottom of the ramp long enough to unload armed men while the rest continued along the pipe jetty road above the salt marshes and over the shallows until they reached the landing stage suspended high above the water on dozens of concrete pillars.

'Get the forklift truck,' the leader barked and two of the men ran off towards the main terminal.

The vans that continued on came to a halt in a line at the end of the pipe jetty where it connected to the landing stage and a dozen more armed men dismounted. Krilov climbed out wearing a black one-piece and looked across the estuary, breathing in the air deeply as if savouring it. The sky was clear with a gentle breeze. The air smelled of salt and kelp, the dominant sound the estuary water lapping against the legs of the landing stage.

The landing stage was a long narrow platform a couple of hundred metres from the shore in deep water, designed for large vessels such as oil tankers to come alongside and discharge their cargo. Krilov walked onto it and climbed a large valve head in order to better observe the estuary in all directions. The waterway was busy with a sprinkling of coloured navigation lights from channel markers and boats.

One of the men escorted Bethan, her hands tied in front of her. Krilov looked down on her. She scowled at him, her eyes filled with defiance.

'Take the little bitch over there,' Krilov ordered, indicating the parapet at the land side of the landing stage.

Her handler yanked her over and forced her to sit on the crumbling tarmac. When he walked away she lowered her head, desperate and despondent.

Chapter 24

Gunnymede drove along a narrow, poorly maintained tarmac road that was in complete darkness beyond his headlights. He'd left the main road half a mile behind. A dirt track led through a line of trees into what looked like an access to the salt marshes but it ended in an empty clearing a hundred metres further on. Parked at the back of the clearing was a 4x4. Gunnymede stopped beside it and turned off the engine.

The driver's window slid down to reveal Aristotle. 'I talked with Simons and his response was as I expected. With no evidence he cannot divide what forces they have to come here.'

'Would a sighting of Krilov be enough?'

'I should think so.'

'Isn't anyone a little concerned that if Krilov is in the refinery and not in the docks, then we don't have full control of what's going on.'

'If Krilov is indeed here then it would be a cause for concern. But this is a police operation and they don't know that Krilov might not be at the docks.'

'Why not?'

'Because we haven't mentioned it to them.'

'Why not?'

'Because we don't know for sure. You don't know for sure. Remember, the police don't know about Saleem.'

'Why not? They're going to know about him when the ship docks.'

'No they're not. They're going to have six members of ISIS on their way to UK.'

'Why don't they know about the threat to London anyway?'

'Come on, Gunnymede.'

'Because that's our route to Spangle.'

'Correct.'

'A high price to pay for Spangle.'

'I don't think anyone is suggesting that. The longer we can keep a lid on the operation the more chance we have of flushing him.'

'You know an awful lot about the engine for an oily rag.'

Aristotle treated the comment with his usual contempt.

'What about Bethan Trencher?' Gunnymede asked. 'The police officer who's been kidnapped.'

'Again. No proof. I'm surprised a person of your experience in the business has not considered the information you've gained about Krilov and the police woman could be disinformation designed to throw us off the real operation.'

'I don't believe it is. Why are you here if you don't believe me?'

'Because there's always a chance. And what else do you have to do tonight.'

Asshole. 'What did you bring me?' Gunnymede asked.

Aristotle climbed out of the cab and opened the back of the vehicle. Inside was a large black plastic box. He raised the lid to reveal that it was filled with a variety of assault equipment. 'Compliments of the SAS.'

Gunnymede looked through the box. 'Shit. This is everything.' He removed his jacket and pulled on a moulded torso armour with high velocity plates front and back. Over that he fitted a weapons harness with various pouches filled with munitions and a pull-down knife in a sheath on his left shoulder. He lifted out a rubber pack and examined it.

'What's that?' Aristotle asked.

Gunnymede opened a flap to expose the innards. As he thought. 'A drone. Nice toy.'

He looped the strap over his head and placed it on his back where it was designed to sit. Next was a helmet with a dropdown screen and a pair of tight leather gloves.

The final items were weaponry. Gunnymede loaded a semi-automatic pistol, cocked it and placed it into a thigh holster. He lifted out a G36 rifle with underslung grenade launcher and suppressor, attached a 100 round twin drum to it, placed a 40mm grenade into the grenade breech and hooked the tail of the hands free rifle sling to the centre of his chest harness. He was good to go.

'You look like the real thing,' Aristotle said.

'Let's hope anyone I meet is as dumb as you.' Gunnymede looked in the direction of the refinery. 'Now all I have to do is find that son-of-a-bitch and Bethan.'

Aristotle closed the back of his 4x4 and climbed back behind the wheel. 'Good luck,' he said as he started the engine.

'Wait a minute,' Gunnymede said going to the cab window. 'That's it. You're just driving off.'

'Did you want me to come with you?'

'I didn't mean that. This is a big deal. What happens if I do find Krilov?'

'Let us know. Oh, and, please keep in mind you're breaking a large number of laws and you're on your own if caught. All of that equipment is deniable.'

'But if anything happens to me, doesn't that scupper your plans for Spangle?'

'We can't wrap you in cotton wool. Spangle expects to see you operating as normal. Let me tell you a truth, shall I? There's little chance of Spangle going for the bait anyway. He's sure to see through you. But the small chance is still worth it.'

'You don't believe Krilov's here, do you?'

Aristotle just looked at him.

'It's me you don't trust, isn't it? I keep forgetting. I'm just a low-life heroin thief whose only purpose in life is bait for Spangle ... with a small chance at that.'

'You're not the smartest operator in the box but you always get there in the end, don't you?' Aristotle smiled and drove away.

Gunnymede watched him go. Fucking Greek wanker.

He sighed heavily and looked at himself in his war gear. This was ridiculous. He should dump this shit, climb back onto his bike and ride off to the nearest pub. Who cared about Krilov? But he couldn't. Because he cared about Bethan. Arguably it was his fault she was in the mess she was. He had to try at least.

He cocked the G36 and set off along the track back to the narrow tarmac road. Once he reached it he headed south. The salt marshes were on one side and the sprawling refinery on the other with dozens of huge, drum shaped containers spread around like giant draughts on a board. The breeze played with the tops of trees and the broad carpet of marsh grass, the shimmering rustle providing cover for his footsteps.

Gunnymede had gone a couple of hundred metres when vehicle headlights appeared behind him. He ducked into the marsh reeds as it went past.

A car. With just one person in it.

Gunnymede carried on while watching the car's tail lights move away. A little further on they glowed brightly as the brakes were applied. The vehicle had come to a stop.

As Gunnymede got closer he could hear voices above the idling engine. A moment later, the car continued on its way into the refinery. Gunnymede dropped the screen over his left eye. He could hardly see through it. He found the switch on the thermal that turned it on. The imager kicked into life and within seconds revealed two figures. They looked like they were carrying rifles.

He continued forward, cautiously, bringing the rifle into his shoulder. The thermal images grew sharper. It crossed Gunnymede's mind they could be a couple of local poachers. As he closed on the gate the men remained engaged in conversation. It didn't sound like English. He needed to find a way around these guys. That would mean pushing through bushes and climbing fences. Boring and time consuming.

The gods solved the problem for him. As he took a step closer, he accidentally toed an empty beer can that rattled as it rolled away.

He froze, as did the two men now looking in his direction. Gunnymede took a slow step backwards and stopped. They were probably unable to see him but then they might if he moved again. This was an impasse. Not a good start.

Gunnymede watched one of them bring his rifle into his shoulder. He wasn't prepared to take any risks with them and so he aimed his rifle and fired several silent bullets into the thermal shadows. They dropped like sacks, their weapons clattering on the road.

Gunnymede moved forward and eased through the gate to check on the bodies. They were both dead. And the two AK47 assault rifles were proof enough they weren't poachers. It also lent credibility to the possibility that Krilov was somewhere nearby. He thought about calling Aristotle to let him know but changed his mind. It wasn't concrete proof Krilov was at the refinery. And there was no time to lose.

He broke into a jog along the road. The lights from the vehicle that had past moments earlier followed the perimeter of the refinery, keeping close to the water. Gunnymede followed it.

Krilov sat on a bollard on the landing stage looking onto the estuary, patiently waiting. His men lounged around, quietly chatting, smoking, some of them dozing. Bethan sat back against the rails, looking at Krilov, hating the man and fearing for herself at the same time.

A pair of headlights illuminated the landing stage. A vehicle was coming along the pipe jetty. Bethan heard it stop. The engine died and a door slammed shut. She saw a figure step onto the landing stage carrying a suitcase and move between the down lights towards Krilov. It was Jedson. Another loathsome individual.

Jedson wore a look of triumph as he closed on Krilov. The Russian ignored him and went back to gazing on the estuary. Jedson looked like he was going on holiday, dressed in a snazzy shirt and jacket. He put down his suitcase and held out a police radio for Krilov to hear. Police chatter filled the air, snippets of voices declaring various teams were moving into position, covering this section and that.

'All good,' Jedson said with a grin. 'Over a hundred officers and other agencies. And all in Southampton Docks.'

Krilov nodded. 'You done good job, Jedson.'

Jedson appreciated the compliment as he looked around for something specific and found it.

Bethan watched him as he walked over to her.

'How's it going?' he asked, crouching by her.

She turned away, unable to look at him she felt so disgusted.

'I always wanted to go on holiday with you. Never thought of a cruise though. We'll share a cabin. It'll be nice. Don't you want to know where you're going?'

'I know where I'm going.'

'Where's that then? Oh, I see. You mean you're not going across the ocean but under it. Well, we'll see. That'll be up to me. Depends on how well you treat me. I'm moving to Russia, you see. Won't be able to stay here now. Not after this little caper. I didn't think it was going to end up this way, me going to Russia and all. Not when I was first offered the job. One thing led to another. You know how it is. Sneaky little Cossacks probably knew all along. But I don't mind. I'll just have to get used to vodka that's all, once I run out of bourbon.' He tapped a shoulder bag he was carrying. 'Fancy a drop now?' He opened the bag, pulled out a bottle and offered it to her.

'What is your reality?' she asked. 'Is everything just one big fantasy to you?'

'If you mean, do I take everything seriously, obviously not. What's the point?' He smirked and took a swig.

'You're a child.'

He stood up. 'Well. Be a good girl and you can join us. If not, then it *will* be the bottom of the big blue for you.'

Krilov's team leader walked by.

'Where's the ship, comrade?' Jedson asked him.

'There,' he said, pointing to a cluster of lights in the estuary.

'There you go,' Jedson said to Bethan. 'All going smoothly to plan. Up you get.'

She reluctantly got to her feet and they walked to the estuary side of the landing stage to look at the ship.

'That's the cargo ship?' she asked.

'Yep.'

'The one going to Southampton Docks?'

'Yep. Except it ain't,' he said with a smirk.

Gunnymede arrived at the corner of a building breathing hard and crouched to inspect a wide open space the size of a football field. Several warehouses and pieces of heavy machinery were dotted around. Lights outside warehouse fronts and above signs provided patches of illumination.

He took a sweeping look through his imager and found several figures beyond the far side of the clearing on the top of an elevated road. It was the pipe jetty that ran from the centre of the terminal to the landing stage six hundred metres further on. Gunnymede could make out rifles in the hands of the figures. It certainly required investigating.

He cut directly across the open ground setting off at a brisk walk. He was halfway across when the throaty sound of an engine starting up inside one of the warehouses paused him. A light came on as a vehicle drove out. Gunnymede dropped to a knee, looking for somewhere to head for. There was nowhere nearby and he decided to remain still in the open rather than risk being seen while moving.

It was a forklift truck with a single headlight, two men on it and headed in the same direction as Gunnymede. As it drew parallel, Gunnymede could see one of the men was holding a rifle. The passenger caught sight of him and nudged the driver to make a turn. The forklift swung sharply round and Gunnymede was bathed in its headlight.

Shit!

He started to run. The vehicle followed. Gunnymede changed direction but the driver adjusted. It was getting closer. Gunnymede ran backwards, aimed above the headlight and fired a short burst of bullets that were silent above the sound of the vehicle. The forklift continued to come at him. Gunnymede changed direction but this time the forklift didn't adjust. As it drove by the men were slumped over the controls.

He expected it to slow to a halt but it continued on at full speed. A swift projection of the vehicle's route was a sudden cause for concern. It looked like it was heading towards a telegraph pole. Gunnymede concentrated on willing it to miss but it struck the pole with a wallop, snapping it at the base with a heavy crunch that would've been heard by those on the pipe jetty. The pole toppled but then stalled, the high tension wires holding it off the ground. But the collision didn't halt the vehicle. It merely altered its direction.

Gunnymede groaned as he projected its new path. The bloody thing was heading towards a large propane gas container behind a flimsy wire fence. He considered running to it in the hope of stopping it but it quickly became obvious he'd never make it in time.

The forklift ripped through the fence and one of its prongs pierced the tank. Liquid gas burst out as the forklift ground to a halt. And then the really *really* bad news came.

Several of the high tension cables holding up the pole snapped and sparks cascaded as the electrical cables fell across the tank.

You have to be kidding me!

Gunnymede hit the ground flat. The explosion was deafening as the tank blew apart and an intense white flame shot into the night sky, bright enough to be seen from the space station.

Gunnymede hugged the ground as the fiery blast ripped over him followed by pieces of debris dropping all around. When the intensity subsided he looked up to see the forklift consumed by a roaring fire.

He got to his feet and ran hard to get off the open space, ducking amongst a collection of machinery. The explosion would no doubt alert the terminal security who would more than likely contact the emergency services.

So much for sneaking.

Krilov was watching the ship close on the landing stage when the explosion occurred, Jedson and Bethan nearby. They all turned to face the distant boom and see the incandescent plume reach into the night sky.

Krilov shouted for his lieutenant to call the checkpoints and find out what it was.

'What the bloody hell was that?' Jedson said as he turned up his police radio. Comments were exchanged between various police teams reporting the distant fireball but no one seemed to know what it was.

Krilov's lieutenant jogged over with a phone to his ear. The team on the ramp didn't know what had caused the explosion and he couldn't get a reply from the men at the gate.

Krilov ordered the ramp team to check it out and barked a command to the others to stay alert. He turned his attention back to the ship but a feeling of concern nibbled at him. Something wasn't right. The tediously slow process for the vessel to come alongside was suddenly irritating him.

Gunnymede stepped out of his hiding place to take a look towards the pipe jetty. He could see figures moving about but not very clearly. He needed a bigger picture.

He reached behind his neck and pulled a toggle. The cover of the pod dropped away to reveal a drone the size of a dinner plate. Its four small propellers burst into life, automatically unlocking it and it zoomed skyward, ascending to a hundred feet above him where it remained. His flip down screen switched to drone view.

A ball on the end of a cable attached to the drone pack hung over his shoulder. On it was a toggle that altered the drone's direction. A push brought it into static hover wherever it was and a double push brought it back to its default position above Gunnymede. After some fumbling and direction challenges he managed to send it towards the pipe jetty.

As it arrived, his drop down showed the drone's point of view – a handful of men heading down the ramp to ground level. Two of them left the group and jogged in Gunnymede's direction. He stepped back into cover as they passed him by, heading towards the burning propane tank. He turned his attention back to the ramp and pipe jetty. Since it led to the estuary and the men appeared to be guarding the route, it was probably where he needed to be. Question was, how could he avoid the men.

He checked the map on his phone that showed the landing stage and the pipe jetty road leading to it. His location was marked. The pipe jetty was the only way to the landing stage since it was suspended above ground and the water.

The pipe jetty it was going to have to be and, therefore, through the men.

Gunnymede took aim on the cluster of figures arriving at the bottom of the ramp, exhaled, paused his breathing, and fired a series of silent shots. One of the figures dropped and the others scurried for cover firing randomly in all directions. After some indecision, they all ran beneath the pipe jetty to the other side. Which actually wasn't too helpful because they were still in the area and he needed to get by them.

He sent the drone to the other side of the pipe jetty and saw where the men had gone to ground in a group. They needed flushing. He raised the end of the G36, assessed the angle and fired the grenade launcher. The weapon popped loudly as it recoiled sharply. The high explosives shell landed this side of the pipe jetty exploding on the road.

Crap.

Gunnymede shoved another shell into the breech and angled the weapon again, adjusting for the drop of the last shot. He fired while looking through the drone's imager. The shell landed several metres behind the men splattering them in shrapnel. When the flash dissipated it didn't look as if the grenade had inflicted much damage because they all seemed to be moving and firing their rifles, again in every direction.

Krilov stood on his bollard facing the sound of gunfire and explosions. It was clear that whatever was happening was a direct threat to his operation.

Krilov's lieutenant was on the phone nearby. 'They're under fire,' he called out.

'I know that, idiot,' Krilov shouted. 'Give me the situation? Who is attacking? Numbers? Vehicles? Jedson!'

'It's none of our people,' Jedson shouted from where he could see the flash of gunfire.

'How is that possible?' Krilov shouted back.

'I don't know but it's not the police or military.'

'They don't know who it is or how many,' the lieutenant called out. 'They say they're surrounded.'

'Tell them they must hold that road!' Krilov faced the ship that was closing in on the landing. 'Throw the lines!' he yelled at the crew lining the deck.

Gunnymede edged closer to the ramp. He could see men running but not away from the pipe jetty as he'd hoped. The ones that had gone the other side were coming back and heading up the ramp. He fired a burst into them. One of them went down and the others found cover behind a stack of oil drums and pallets. They would have to be dealt with before he could pass.

He moved the drone above the men and studied the bird's eye view, comparing it to his own. From the air he could clearly see each man but not from the ground. He came up on aim for the first of them and fired a series of bursts into an oil drum. The drone image showed the man fall and lie still. He moved to the next behind some pallets. A couple of short bursts dropped him. He shot the last two with the same ease and searched the drone's image for any signs of life. There weren't any and he moved the drone to the top of the jetty to see the remaining figures running along it towards the landing stage. As far as he could see there was no-one left alive at the ramp.

He was about to set off when he heard the crunch of footsteps behind him. He ducked behind cover as the two men who'd passed by earlier were heading back, clearly unaware of what had happened to their colleagues. Gunnymede waited for them to pass and shot them in the back.

He took a moment to inspect them. They looked like ordinary civilians dressed for an evening in the countryside.

With one eye ahead and the other on the drone, he made his way to the pipe jetty and up the ramp, ready to engage anyone still up for it. Several men lay dead. He took another close look at one of them. A young man in rugged civilian clothes who couldn't have been more than eighteen years old, an M4 assault rifle still in his hands, his weapons harness filled with spare magazines. Amateurs. They probably knew as much about soldiering as the pope.

Gunnymede sent the drone ahead as he made his way up the ramp. It revealed those running towards the landing stage. The drone continued on to show a line of vehicles parked at the end of the pipe jetty where it connected to the landing stage. The stage was well lit with several figures on it. Gunnymede could only hope that was where he'd find Krilov and therefore Bethan.

The drone continued on to reveal a large ship coming alongside the landing stage. Gunnymede could only wonder what was going on. Was it the cargo ship with Saleem on board? Surely not.

Krilov gauged the distance between the vessel and the landing stage, inch by inch, anxious for it to come alongside. 'Throw the lines,' he shouted impatiently.

Several lines flew into the air. One of them reached the landing stage where it was hauled in connected to a heavy mooring warp.

Krilov's lieutenant came running. 'Boss, I can't get hold of any of the men at the ramp.'

'None?'

'None.'

'Who are they?' shouted Krilov angrily. 'Who's attacking us?'

'I don't know, boss.'

'What about the road, our route out of here?'

'It looks clear. There's no sign of the attackers. I don't understand.'

'When the vehicles are loaded I will lead the men ahead to clear the way,' Krilov said as he pulled on his body armour. 'Get everyone loading the cargo as quickly as possible!'

Jedson crouched behind a bollard. He realised Bethan was standing in the open beside him and pulled her down. 'Where's our boat, Krilov?' he shouted.

'Who makes this attack?' Krilov shouted back.

'I told you I don't know!' Jedson looked for Krilov's lieutenant, saw him the other side of the stage and hurried over to him. 'Where's our boat?' he asked. 'The one that's supposed to take us to Russia?'

'Other side of ship,' the man informed him before hurrying away.

Jedson went back to the cargo ship as it closed on the landing stage, all the warps now attached to bollards. He hurried back to Bethan. 'I think the bloody wheels are falling off this one.'

The ship's crew started handing crates to Krilov's men on landing stage.

'Get everything into the vehicles!' Krilov shouted.

Saleem sat in the bowels of the ship in a grimy storage room illuminated by a bulb in a wire mesh on the wall. The room was beside the engine room and vibrated constantly. Not only was it noisy, the air was just about breathable. Five Daesh colleagues were waiting for him to give the word to disembark. None dare speak. They'd been on the vessel for two days having boarded in the English Channel from a fishing boat. They'd met for the first time in a house on the outskirts of Ostend, having travelled from various parts of Europe and the Middle East. Saleem arrived just in time to catch the boat. They'd been told he was a great commander with much battle experience and he was to be obeyed without question, on pain of death. Other than that, they had no idea what they were doing in England.

There was a heavy jolt and the room shook as the vessel bumped alongside. Saleem remained seated, staring at the air. He'd become far more serious since leaving Syria. During the worst madness of the desert campaign to capture Mosul followed by the retreat to Syria, he'd always been able to produce an amusing quip. But the weight of this task had grown heavy on him. Confidence in himself and his passion for the mission had not diminished. If anything, they had strengthened. His survival of the ambush in Russia had reinforced his belief that Allah was with him. He knew he'd succeed if he kept his nerve. This operation was the greatest single attack

ISIL had ever put into execution phase since 9/11. Weeks ago it had still seemed like a fantasy. Now he was back in England. But he also knew the closer he got to the climax, the greater the obstacles would be.

The deck would be busy for the first few minutes of docking, the Russians unloading their contraband. On leaving the ship, he wanted to go directly to the vehicles and depart right away. No hanging around. Therefore he'd wait until the bulk of the cargo had been unloaded. He would give it a few more minutes and then order the move to the main deck.

Gunnymede was crouched behind a heavy valve, looking down the length of the pipe jetty towards the landing stage trying to decide what to do. The firing had stopped but he would be seen as soon as he tried to make his way forward. He couldn't stay there for long either. Those vehicles were there for a reason. The pipe jetty was the only way off and there was no way Gunnymede was going to stop them on his own.

He took out his phone and made a call. It rang several times. 'For fuck's sake pick up.'

'Gunnymede?' It was Aristotle.

'The bloody ship is here!'

'What ship?'

'Are you insane? *The* ship!'

'Are you sure?'

'Am I sure?! Aren't you monitoring it?!'

'The police pulled off all surveillance when it entered the estuary as a precaution.'

'What precaution?'

'They didn't want to take the risk of the ship detecting them.'

'Whose brilliant idea was that?!'

'One of the police undercover people said the ship would have sophisticated surveillance detection systems on board. If they knew they were being monitored, they'd dump their cargo. We would also risk losing Saleem. Where exactly is the vessel?'

'The landing stage of the refinery. You need to get everyone over here now!'

'I'll get back to you,' Aristotle said and the phone went dead.

'Morons!' Gunnymede shouted as he put the phone away.

Time was the factor now. Krilov might get off the landing before the police turned up. What that would mean for Bethan he could only guess. He had to slow down the show.

Oil was pouring out right in front of him from a bullet hole in one of the pipes that ran along the jetty. It wasn't under much pressure but there was enough inside the pipe to keep it flowing. And that was only the one pipe. There were a couple of dozen of them. The pipes went all the way past the line of vehicles to the landing stage.

He checked his pouches for grenades. He had six left. He loaded one into the breech, closed the housing and held the rifle parallel with the pipes. The vehicles were easily in range. He just had to get the trajectory right. There was a slight breeze left to right. He made a fine adjustment and fired!

The round thumped into the night sky. Seconds later there was a splash as it missed the jetty altogether and landed in the water.

Useless twat!

Gunnymede loaded another. Aimed. Adjusted. Fired! The shell took a couple of seconds to arc back down and landed amongst the pipes beside the nearest vans where it exploded. He couldn't see the oil spilling out of the torn pipes but knew that had to be happening and quickly loaded another shell. Oil didn't burn. It was the vapour that came off it that burned and so it needed to be heated up. A couple of shells would do the trick.

He concentrated on replicating the same angle and fired. The shell landed further on but amongst the pipes again. This time the explosion ignited the oil. The interesting thing about oil fires is they can begin very small. As the temperature increases the more gas evaporates, the larger the fire becomes, the greater the temperature increases and so on, a vicious escalation where the heat becomes so intense the metal pipes themselves will melt.

The blaze quickly spread. Gunnymede fired another shell that hit its target sending globs of burning oil in all directions. Several men were hit by the stuff. Those on fire had little choice but to jump into the water. Some weren't so lucky and were consumed before they could escape. One vehicle after another, including Jedson's, caught fire as burning oil spread across the narrow road.

Gunnymede held his second to last shell. He loaded it, lowered the elevation to extend the range and fired. It exploded on the landing stage amongst those carrying heroin boxes, killing and injuring several of them. To add to the confusion he aimed the rifle in the general direction of the flames and shot through them with long bursts of automatic fire. Several of Krilov's men and a couple of crewman were caught in the hail and went down. Heroin boxes were dropped as men scurried for cover.

Krilov was crouched in a cluster of valves when he heard his name being called from above. He looked up at the ship's bridge. The captain was on the bridge wing shouting at him. He wanted Krilov to release the lines so that the ship could get away.

Krilov ignored him. He couldn't care less about the ship. His heroin crates were scattered all over the landing. Most of the consignment was still on the ship's deck. His men were either dead, wounded or had taken their chances to escape by jumping into the estuary. It was over. He needed to save himself. The only thing keeping him there was an intense hatred for whoever was responsible for this attack.

Krilov's lieutenant scurried over with a rifle to report something but he seemed ambivalent. Krilov could read it in his eyes. 'You want to go?' Krilov shouted. 'Go! I give you permission.'

'It's only one man,' the lieutenant said.

'What?' Krilov asked, unsure if he'd heard correctly.

'I've been watching. It's only one man, boss. I'm sure of it.'

'Rubbish.'

'It's too late. We cannot get the cargo off the jetty. I see you, boss.'

And with that the man left his rifle, ran along the jetty and jumped off the end.

Krilov was left staring at the flames wondering if his lieutenant could possibly be correct. The question was, who was crazy, or angry enough to attempt such a thing?

The thug Boris had tortured was lying on a hospital bed, a nurse seeing to his wounds. A police officer was on guard outside the room.

The nurse left the room leaving the thug alone. He checked to see the policeman wasn't looking, retrieved a phone from a pocket, brought up a number with bloody, shaking fingers and put it to his ear.

Jedson made his way over to Krilov with Bethan in tow. 'We have to go,' he said to the Russian. 'Let's get on the escape boat. This has all gone tits up.'

'Who attacks us?' Krilov asked.

'I told you! Not the police!'

'You are sure?'

'We don't have bombs for a start.'

'Then who is it?'

'It has to be a rival gang. We're dead if they catch us.'

'That's no gang-man,' Krilov said. 'It's Special Forces.'

'I'd know if the bloody SAS were here!'

Krilov's phone chirped. He wanted to ignore it but reluctantly answered. It was the thug in the hospital.

Krilov listened, his mouth hardening with anger as the thug told him what had happened with Gunnymede. He put the phone down, got to his feet and stared beyond the flames, along the pipe jetty. 'It's the intelligence officer,' he said.

'What intelligence officer?' Jedson asked.

'The one from the farm. Last night.'

'Gunnymede?'

'Yes. Gunnymede?'

'Gunnymede?' Bethan echoed in a mixture of disbelief and hope.

'Bollocks,' Jedson said. 'On his own? Impossible.'

'Not impossible,' Krilov said, a hint of admiration in his tone. 'I could do it.'

'Whoever it is, we're out of here,' Jedson said, making ready to go with Bethan.

She remained where she was, looking defiant.

'Don't even think about making it hard for me. You either come with me,' Jedson said, picking up a shackle. 'Or I crack your skull open right here.'

He grabbed her tied hands and yanked her up. 'You coming, Krilov?'

Krilov didn't hear him, his gaze fixed towards the pipe jetty.

'Suit yourself.' Jedson grabbed his suitcase and dragged Bethan to the side of the ship. 'Get on board,' he shouted angrily. She climbed over the side. Jedson threw his suitcase after her and followed it.

Krilov stepped onto the valve to look through his binoculars. His angle allowed him to see the road beyond the flames. He saw a figure moving towards the burning vehicles. Krilov wanted to kill him so badly he could taste it.

Jedson could see the roof of a cabin cruiser and dragged Bethan across the ship's deck to the other side to find it's narrow bows touching the side of the ship where a man was waiting. He shouted something in Russian on seeing Jedson and appeared anxious to get going.

Jedson dragged Bethan to a short rope ladder down to the cruiser's bows. 'Climb down!'

Bethan didn't move. Jedson lifted his suitcase onto the rail, shouted to the man to catch it and tossed it at him. The man ducked out of the way as the suitcase bounced off the side of the boat, the impact smashing it open and it fell into the water along with its contents.

Jedson was livid. He faced Bethan with a snarl. 'Get on that boat!'

'No.'

'If you don't, I'll throw you over.'

She stood defiantly, her tied hands clenched in solid fists.

Jedson lunged at her. She swung wildly at him, catching him on the side of his face. The blow stalled him. Out of the pain grew a very much darker Jedson. A murderous Jedson. He straightened up. This was her end.

Gunnymede ran down the pipe jetty and stopped in front of the flames. Bethan was the other side. So was Krilov and Saleem. He could wait for the police to arrive but that might be too late.

He went to the rails the opposite side of the road to the piping and looked along it. He could see the landing, on and off, between gouts of flame. He put down the rifle and emptied the pouches of explosive ordnance. He held the last grenade and decided he might as well use it. He loaded into the G36, raised the barrel and fired. As the shell sailed through the air, Gunnymede dropped the rifle, pulled the webbing up around his face, pulled down his helmet and charged into the flames.

The shell landed on the deck a few metres behind Jedson sending him flying. Bethan was knocked back by the explosion but was unhurt save a few scratches. The grenade had punctured several oil drums on the deck, at the same time igniting a pile of canvas beside a poorly maintained lifeboat.

Saleem and his men, in their room below, looked up at the sound of the explosion. Those with experience of war had no doubt what it had been. Saleem grabbed his backpack and hurried out of the room followed by the others.

A copy of the Koran remained on the table.

Saleem led the way along a narrow, dingy corridor to a set of stairs. One of the men realised he'd forgotten something and stopped.

'What is it?' a colleague asked.

'I left my Koran.'

'Leave it!'

'No!' he said and hurried back.

The colleague frowned and went with him.

Gunnymede ran through the blaze keeping a hand on the rail using it as a guide. Seconds later he emerged the other side, smouldering but otherwise undamaged. He pulled his pistol and aimed ahead as he panned left and right. The only people he could see lay still on the ground. Scattered around the landing, between the ship and the vehicles were boxes, some spilled open. Much of it was heroin.

He removed his helmet and moved closer to the ship. A shout came from above and he aimed his pistol at the bridge. It was the captain, directing his crew to deal with the fire. Several crewmen hurried across the deck towards the flames. Gunnymede saw someone beyond the fire. The far end of the deck. It was Bethan. A man was facing her.

Gunnymede ran to the ship's side to climb over when four men hurried through a door at the base of the superstructure a dozen metres away and climbed over the side onto the landing. Gunnymede and Saleem stopped dead on seeing each other. Smoke drifted between them but they knew each other instantly. Their images were ingrained. Saleem couldn't believe his eyes. It wasn't possible. His colleagues also stopped. The man was holding a pistol towards them.

Gunnymede's finger tightened on the trigger. Saleem's head was in his sights.

Saleem could see it coming. He stood his ground, unable to do anything, refusing to run.

Krilov stood up from where he'd been crouching on the deck of the ship and with hatred in his eyes, sprang over the side hitting Gunnymede as he fired. The bullet missed Saleem by an inch and slammed into the body of a man behind him, killing him.

Krilov had hit Gunnymede like a charging bull. He could've chosen to shoot him but he wanted to tear him apart with his hands, break his bones, rip out his eyes, cut off his face, slice open his body, pull out his organs and watch him die slowly, knowing who'd killed him. It could be no other way for Krilov.

Gunnymede hit the ground beneath the weight of the Russian with such force it concussed him. His pistol bounced out of his grip and tumbled away. Russian spetsnaz were trained in the art of unarmed combat. Krilov's speciality had been jujutsu and he relished it. As Gunnymede fought to recover, Krilov punched him in the face. Another blow struck his ribs. Krilov slipped around his back, gripped him with his legs and looped his arms around his neck to place Gunnymede in a powerful stranglehold while at the same time trying to push his eyes into his brain. Gunnymede grabbed one of Krilov's little fingers and ripped it sideways, breaking it at the knuckle joint which released the grappling hands from his face. But it was a minor defence as Krilov's muscular limbs tightened around Gunnymede like a boa-constrictor and he brought all his power to bear in order to suffocate and break Gunnymede's bones at the same time.

Gunnymede could feel the life draining from him as he struggled to breathe. He grabbed at Krilov's arm in a futile attempt to prevent it from crushing his throat. He couldn't budge it. Krilov was too strong by far.

Saleem stood watching, enjoying the fight. Gunnymede's eyes started to bulge and his face swell. Saleem didn't notice his men had all but hurried away. One of them tugged at him and urged they get going. Saleem looked to see the others were already climbing over the rails. He wanted to watch the end of Gunnymede. There was something extremely satisfying about seeing this man die. His colleague tugged him again anxiously, urging him to get going.

Saleem had to pull himself away. He disconnected from the execution and followed the others over the side and down a ladder to the water.

Gunnymede began to lose consciousness. The Russian was too strong, the stranglehold too perfect. Stars filled his eyes as his brain began to close down. He made one last effort to pull Krilov's arm from around his throat. His fingers touched the knife at his shoulder below Krilov's forearm. He ripped it from its sheath and shoved the blade into Krilov's arm with every ounce of strength he had left. The blade went through the arm, the tip digging into Gunnymede's kevlar vest. Krilov howled in pain and although his grip weakened he held on. Gunnymede twisted the knife to one side and yanked it down hard with his final effort, cutting through arteries and tendons. Krilov's grip failed.

Gunnymede pulled himself free and rolled away to draw in deep breaths as blood began to flow back into his brain.

Krilov's hate and tenacity drove him on and he got to his feet. Gunnymede looked up at the beast, a wall of roaring flames behind him, and from his crouched position, launched himself with everything he had left. He struck Krilov below his chest with his shoulder in a classic rugby tackle and propelled the man backwards. Gunnymede released him at full stretch and fell to the ground. Krilov tumbled backwards into a puddle of burning oil that immediately soaked him. Flames licked at him. He screamed as he ignited, rolling out of the oil but by then he was a human torch. Unable to see, his eyes shut tight against the flames, knowing there was water in every direction, he ran, hit a rail, somersaulted over it and, in a fireball, plummeted to the water.

Gunnymede immediately flipped his focus to Saleem but the Daesh commander was gone. He hurried along the landing, searching over the side in every direction but there was no sign of him. The water was a rippling black emptiness. The beach was a few hundred metres away and in complete darkness. If there was anyone there he would not have seen them.

He suddenly remembered Bethan and spun around to look towards the ship. He hurried to the side and climbed onto the deck. The fire still burned. Crewmen had broken out hoses and were throwing burning debris overboard. There was no sign of Bethan.

Bethan was in fact below decks fighting for her life.

Jedson had recovered from the explosion without serious injury and had come at her with a pole, ready to bash her, his eyes filled with malice. As he lunged at her he slipped on an oily patch and fell. At the same time she stepped back to avoid his blow, her ankles hit the raised rim of a hatch and she fell into it and down a flight of stairs. With her hands still tied she'd been helpless to stop herself.

She struck the lower deck which knocked the wind out of her. Two men hurried along a corridor and stopped on seeing her. Arabs, one of them holding a copy of the Koran. He said something in Arabic to the other and they stepped over her and quickly climbed the stairs.

Bethan got to her feet while deciding where to go. On deck was Jedson. The only other option was to hide on the ship. She faced a long corridor with doors left and right, hurried along it to the end, down a flight of steps and through a metal door into a noisy room filled with machinery.

To one side was a greasy workshop. She grabbed the first tool she saw, a pair of pliers, and tried to cut her bonds. She couldn't grip them well enough and they fell to the floor. As she picked them up she peered round the doorway and up the stairs in fear Jedson might be there. It was clear.

Frustrated, she looked around for something better and saw an electric grinder. She rubbed the plasticuffs against the stone wheel but it turned with every movement. She found a switch and the motor burst into life. She touched the plastic against the spinning stone which cut it instantly. She pulled her hands apart with relief. As she turned to leave she stopped dead. Jedson was in the doorway, his eyes filled with murder.

He lunged at her. She sidestepped, pushing him to one side. His back hit the spinning grinder cutting into him, his jacket getting sucked around the stone, jamming it to a stop. He yelled in frustration as he reached for her unable to advance. As he fought to release his jacket she grabbed a metal rod and slammed his shoulder with it, snapping his collar bone. His reaction was even wilder rage and he swung out a fist that connected with her face sending her flying back into shelving.

Bethan was rocked by the blow and staggered out of the room with a bloody nose while Jedson fought to free himself. She pulled herself up the stairs but as she reached the top, Jedson stepped from the workshop in time to grab her trouser belt. With all his might he wrenched her down, flinging her to the metal floor.

The effort sent a bolt of pain through his broken collar bone, delaying him long enough for Bethan to scramble up and stagger away along the gangway, through a steel doorway and into the engine room.

Jedson grabbed a long hammer from the workshop and went in pursuit of her.

Bethan hurried along a narrow bridge suspended between the two main engines, one silent, the other rumbling away, its camshaft spinning rhythmically as the piston arms pushed it around. She went through a door at the end, into the steerage locker, but there was nowhere else to go.

She stepped back into the engine room as Jedson entered from the other side, hammer in hand. She looked around for a weapon. There were bits and pieces everywhere. A bin of rags, cans of various oils and lubricants, tools and an iron bar. She went for the bar, gripping it with both hands like a baseball bat as she faced him.

He stepped onto the bridge, smirking with confidence. 'I should be on my way. But I just can't leave you. It's true. I'm obsessed with you. I always have been. From the first time I ever laid eyes on you I wanted you. Strange how I'm just as eager to break you into pieces. What kind of love is that, do you think?'

'It's called a mental disorder.'

He came at her, swinging the hammer wildly. She managed to block it with the bar but the blow was painful. She sidestepped his next awkward swing, the blow striking the engine with a heavy clang. He swung again and missed. Growing frustrated, he changed tack, swinging across his front. She blocked it but the bar was slammed out of her hands. Seeing her defenceless, he came at her for the death blow. She grabbed up the lid to the rag bin and held it like a shield. He swung at her head. The hammer glanced off the lid and went into the spinning camshaft where it was ripped from his grasp, almost breaking his wrist, and thrown back at him with double the force, hitting him in the chest. He lost balance and fell against the engine, inches from the spinning camshaft.

She seized her chance and lunged at him with the bin lid in an effort to push him into the cams. He held on. She slammed the lid into his face. He weakened. Again she hit him. Another blow and his grip loosened. Another and he fell back, his head dropping between the cams where it was instantly crushed. Blood and brains spurted over her as she looked away, horrified.

She sensed someone nearby and spun round, bin lid at the ready. Gunnymede, out of breath, was looking at her from the doorway.

She dropped the bin lid, went over to him and hugged him desperately. The emotion flowed out of her.

'It's okay,' he said. 'It's over.'

She looked at his battered face and scorched clothing. 'Are you okay?'

'I feel worse than I look.'

She smiled for a second before growing serious again. 'Krilov?'

'Gone. Come on.'

They climbed through the ship and onto the main deck where the crew had the fire under control. The vehicles were still burning, the air thick with smoke. Gunnymede climbed over the side and helped her down onto the landing.

'How did you know to come here?' she asked.

'They tried to kidnap me too.'

She looked around at the bodies. 'Why are you alone?'

'You're not very popular. I couldn't get anyone else to join me. You would've done the same for me.'

She looked down at a box of heroin, the broken packets strewn around. 'This was about something more than just drugs wasn't it?'

He didn't answer.

'There were Arabs on board,' she said. 'Were they illegals or something more?'

'Something more.'

A distant thud of rotors grew louder. A pair of helicopters were coming along the estuary, low above the water. At the same time, a line of blue flashing lights could be seen moving through the terminal towards the pipe jetty.

Gunnymede watched the helicopters describe a wide arc over the water to line up for an approach to the landing stage. 'I'd rather not be here when they arrive,' he said, picking up his pistol. 'It will only complicate things for me.'

'How do I explain all of this?'

He tossed the pistol into the estuary. 'Just say you slept through the whole thing.'

He went to the rail, found a ladder and climbed onto it. 'You going to be okay?' he asked.

'Yes.'

'I'll be in touch,' he said with a slight smile and climbed down out of sight.

A fierce wind thrashed at her as the first of the large helicopters came into a hover, its searchlight finding her. As it touched down a dozen armed police in black leapt from the open door and spread out in teams.

Dillon climbed out and hurried over to her.

'My dear girl,' he said, examining her, her bruises and bloody face. 'Are you alright?'

'I'm fine.'

'What are you doing here?'

'Krilov kidnapped me.'

'I don't understand,' he said, looking around at the dead bodies, burning vehicles, heroin. 'What happened? Who did all of this? Who killed all these people?'

'Southampton was a decoy. Jedson was working for Krilov.'

'Jedson?'

'He's dead?'

'Jedson's dead?'

Her emotions started to get a hold of her.

Dillon put his arms around her as he continued to take in the mayhem that surrounded him. 'I really don't understand what happened here.'

Chapter 25

Jack Henderson walked briskly along the path that ran along the top of the ridge towards Pen Y Fan. He was feeling the pace. Breathing hard. It'd been much easier in the old days, even with a rifle and pack. A large cloud scraped over the peak but otherwise he could see for miles in all directions. Hardly a breeze. Most importantly, there was not another human in sight.

He took advantage of the privacy, pulled his old SAS beret from a deep pocket of his camouflaged windproof jacket, reverently touched the famed cap badge, the gently embossed wings of the dagger, and placed it on his head. His thoughts turned to his early days wearing the coveted beret. A young, slender, determined Jack. A thick, handlebar moustache grew over his top lip. He could see the lads he'd completed his selection with. The pleasure of learning he'd passed. He saw himself trudging along the very same track, perspiring, in pain, weighed down by a heavy pack and rifle, filled with resignation. He was never going to fail. It was cold and drizzly that day with low cloud reducing visibility to a handful of metres. It seemed like a long time ago. It was.

Jack shaped the beret onto his head as he pressed on.

When he reached the Pen he walked around it. Still no sign of another soul in any direction.

He sat himself down and removed his beret to look at the cap badge once more, rolling the rim through his fingers as he contemplated his life.

'Enough,' he said.

He laid the beret on the grass, bottom up, and removed a photograph from his breast pocket. It was of Megan, smiling, young, her beautiful face, auburn hair just like her mother's. As always, she made Jack smile. But the memories of the last few months were too bitter to bear. The most painful of them her death. And he was to blame.

He placed the photograph in the beret, stretched out on his back and looked at the sky. He removed a pistol from his pocket, held it above him. Cocked it. Placed the end of the barrel under his chin. His final thought. If there was a God, the bastard had better let him see his Megan one last time.

The shot rang out across the Beacons and like Jack, it was gone. A gentle breeze picked at Megan's photo and yanked it out of the beret. It rolled away and caught the breeze as if it was his very soul leaving his body.

Chapter 26

Gunnymede lay on the couch in his apartment looking at the Thames, the wind and rain beating at the glass balcony doors. He delicately sipped a mug of tea, trying to avoid touching his lips with the hot cup where they were tender.

His phone rang and he stiffly reached for it. The number was withheld but he answered it anyway.

'Hi.' It was a girl's voice.

'Hello,' he said back.

'I don't suppose you recognise my voice.'

It was a soft voice with the hint of a southern Irish lilt to it. It didn't trigger any immediate memories for him though. 'Sorry, I don't.'

'We worked together. Briefly. Eight years ago.'

It hit him like a slap and he sat up stiffly. He'd never forgotten her. She had been brand new, straight out of the recruitment box. It was her first operation. Gunnymede had been brought in to help boost the numbers for just one night. He was partnered with her because he had operational experience and they also looked like they could pass as a couple. Two complete strangers thrown together. They spoke hardly a word to each other throughout the operation. He wasn't the chatty type with strangers anyway. The fact that he found her quite beautiful the first time he set eyes on her had to be ignored. It had been an effort for him not to take another look at her face. She had been painfully aloof, as if she had a wall around her. He did his best to ignore her and let her stay behind her wall. They were on task and that was that. There was no need for chat. They were on a stake out.

They were in a car in the old city of Prague pretending to be a couple hanging out after the bars had closed, quietly watching and waiting while listening to the operational radio chatter through hidden ear pieces. And then the target suddenly appeared. The man they'd been waiting for. Their job was to trigger his move for the team. He looked directly at them, the only other people around. The man stopped to scrutinise them. And so they did what a couple were expected to be doing in a car at night parked in a dark, quiet side street after the bars had closed. They embraced and kissed deeply. The bad guy continued to watch. They kept on kissing. But then something happened between them. Something deep within them both. The moment became mutually magnetic. They grew more passionate.

At some point they were no longer acting. It was as if they'd forgotten why they were there. Their fervour grew. The man stepped closer as the windows were coated in steam.

Convinced of their ardour, he stepped back and walked on. They continued to kiss and explore each other, neither wanting to separate. It was the most passion-filled moment he'd ever experienced. She smelled and tasted like nectar.

Voices began to break through. The ops officer was calling for Gunnymede to assist the follow. When they finally separated they were out of breath. He climbed out and hurried away.

On completion of the task, he went to his hotel and hung around the lobby until the small hours hoping she'd turn up. The next day he was gone. Sent somewhere else on another task. He never saw or heard from her again. He never knew her real name or anything about her and it was inappropriate to ask about another operator.

'I remember you,' he said. 'Not your name though. I don't think I knew it.'

'It's Neve.'

'It's been a long time.'

'It seems it.'

'It was ...' he began, then stopped himself.

'What was that?'

'Memorable. That time together.'

'I wasn't calling to reminisce.' There was a sudden chill in her voice. 'I'm running the team to find Saleem.'

Gunnymede went silent as he digested that.

'Did you exchange any words with him?' she asked.

'There's a team?'

'They didn't tell you? Need to know I suppose.'

Gunnymede contained his surprise as well as a level of embarrassment.

'When Saleem came off the ship? At the oil terminal. Did he say anything to you?'

'No.'

'But he knew it was you.'

'Who set up the team?'

'Jervis. Maybe they just haven't told you yet. I think you should be at the next meeting.'

'If I'm invited I'll come.'

She chuckled softly. 'That sounded petulant.'

'I'm hurt.'

'You'll get a message.'

The phone disconnected. Gunnymede remained sitting up.

That was a surprise. Neve. Jesus.

Bethan was in her Dartmoor cottage sitting in front of the fire reading a book when her phone chirped. It was Dillon.

She picked it up. 'Take all the time off you want. Relax and ignore all phone calls. Forget about work. Yet here you are.'

'I didn't say forget about work altogether.'

'I think you did.'

'How are you?'

'Bored.'

'You're ruined, then.'

'Why?'

'Your job was never supposed to be that exciting. You'll always be bored now ... Are you alone?'

'Is this you being fatherly again?'

'Can you talk, is what I meant.'

'Yes.'

'When do you think you'd like to return to work?'

'What's come up that can't wait for me to heal naturally?'

'Looks like you've come under the gaze of the cloak and dagger brigade ... SIS. Secret intelligence services.'

'I'm already less bored.'

'They want you to consult.'

'On what?'

'There's a team.'

'What kind of team?'

'That's why they're called the secret services. Don't know why they're called intelligent though. A little bird told me the whole Southampton cockup was because of them. Rumour has it that battle at the ship was their people. I'm surprised you didn't see any of them.'

She didn't say a word.

'There's something else,' Dillon said. 'Your friend Devon Gunnymede. Regarding your military revenge conspiracy. He's top of the list of suspects.'

'I explained why I thought he couldn't be a suspect.'

'I'm unconvinced. Have you heard from him?'

'No.' She masked her disappointment.

'Well, I recommend you keep well away from him if he tries to make contact. I'm putting a request into MI6 to present him for questioning.'

'I think you might be wasting your time.'

'They're not a law unto themselves you know, even though they might think they are.'

'I meant, I don't believe he's a bad guy.'

'We'll see. Can I reply to this SIS request and tell them you're available?'

'Yes. I can leave any time.'

'You're sure? It means coming back to London tomorrow.'

'I'm sure.'

'Okay. Well. See you soon.'

''Bye,' she said and put down the phone.

She sat back in thought a moment before heading into her bedroom to pack.

Gunnymede left his apartment, down the stairs and through the lobby of his apartment block on his way outside when he noticed something in his mailbox. He opened it to find an envelope addressed to him. It was the first piece of mail he'd received at the apartment.

He opened it. All it contained was a small piece of paper with bright yellow stripes across it.

Gunnymede walked into the ante room of Harlow's office to find Aristotle sitting and reading a newspaper. There was the slightest hint of surprise on the Greek's expression when he saw Gunnymede.

'Is the old man in?' Gunnymede asked.

Harlow's secretary gave him her usual look of disapproval before picking up the phone. 'Mr Gunnymede is here.'

She replaced the phone, walked to Harlow's door and opened it. Gunnymede walked through. Aristotle put his newspaper down and followed.

Harlow was behind his desk. 'Gunnymede. How are you feeling?'

'I'm fine, thank you?'

Aristotle closed the door.

'If you're looking for an update, we've nothing on Saleem. We think Krilov has left the country. Spirited away by his master. I have my doubts Krilov could've helped us identify Spangle anyway. Krilov was merely the UK manager of Spangle's heroin empire. We might've gained some understanding of Spangle's relationship with Saleem but there you go.'

Gunnymede didn't acknowledge any of the information, as if it was inconsequential.

'What is it?' Harlow asked, seeing something in Gunnymede's look.

Gunnymede dropped the envelope onto Harlow's desk. Harlow looked at him enquiringly before picking it up. He tipped the yellow striped piece of paper onto his blotter.

Aristotle leaned in to take a look, raising an eyebrow. He looked at Gunnymede and Harlow who were both looking at each other. 'I don't know the significance of this.'

'It's a Spangle wrapper,' Harlow said, examining the envelope address.

'Did you send it?' Gunnymede asked Harlow.

'Why would I send it to you?'

Aristotle touched it with a finger. 'You said it was a boiled sweet from the 1980's.'

Harlow took a closer look at the sweet paper. 'It is.'

'So how did he get it?' Aristotle asked.

'Is that relevant?' Gunnymede said.

'What's relevant is he knows where you live,' Harlow said.

'Not only that,' Aristotle said. 'He's also telling us he knows where Gunnymede lives.'

Harlow turned the wrapper over but it looked very ordinary.

'Maybe there's something embedded in it,' Aristotle suggested.

'We'll have it examined of course,' Harlow said.

'If it really was from Spangle, how did he know his codename was spangle?' Gunnymede asked.

'Ah. That would be my fault,' Harlow said. 'Three years ago we attempted to employ the resources of our allies, the Germans and the French. It didn't reveal anything particularly useful and it left Spangle's codename exposed. Once again demonstrating the porosity of our dear European friends.'

'How would he know where I live?'

'The police I expect. When we lent you to Scotland Yard, you were exposed to the police administrative system.'

'Another reason why you sent me to Albania.'

'Yes. A positive development don't you think?'

'So Spangle just sent me a message saying hello, I know you're back in the game and I know where you live.'

'This time it was hello. Let's hope next time it will be a question and a means by which to answer it. Meanwhile, the priority is Saleem. Jervis has put together a team that will work parallel to the police. Despite your knowledge of Saleem there was some resistance to inviting you further into the fold. We managed to get you a special dispensation to work with the team.' Harlow opened a drawer and removed a cardboard box. Inside it was a plastic card and a small red box, both of which he placed in front of Gunnymede. 'Your ID.'

Gunnymede picked up the card to examine it. 'That's my prison mug shot.'

'It's the only recent picture of you we had on file.'

Gunnymede opened the small red box to find a coveted MI6 badge.

'Bet you never thought you'd ever hold one of those again,' Harlow said. 'Something else.' There were several post-it note blocks in various colours on his desk. He pulled the top note off the pink block and handed it to Gunnymede. 'You asked for that?'

Gunnymede read it. 'Thanks.' As he put it in his pocket his phone beeped. A message from Neve.

'Am I allowed to have dinner with a colleague on my company card?' Gunnymede asked.

Harlow pushed a button on his desk phone. His secretary looked in.

'Has Gunnymede got a bank account yet?' Harlow asked.

'It will be ready in three working days,' she said.

Harlow looked at Gunnymede. 'You may. But it will be deducted from your salary.'

Gunnymede left the room.

Harlow picked up the spangle wrapper and looked at Aristotle who raised his eyebrows at him.

Gunnymede used his new ID card to gain access to the MI6 headquarters building and took an elevator to the fourth floor. He walked along a wide corridor to a door labelled F42, inserted his ID card into the keypad and tapped in a number. It unlocked.

Inside was an operations room with a large screen on one wall, a dozen monitors and computer terminals, several of them occupied, and a spacious worktop in the centre. The walls were lined with panels designed to hold paperwork without pins or adhesive, several of them already populated with photos and labels.

Leaning over the worktop, poring over several satellite pictures was Neve. As the door closed behind Gunnymede she looked up at him. He felt that same sudden impact he'd felt on seeing her for the first time eight years ago. There was something magically magnetic about it. It wasn't anything like love or even desire. It was like a rush. A sparkle that tingled in the pit of his stomach. Like tasting something delicious that required immediate examination, and another taste. The ardour he felt in the car had not changed in all that time. Their eyes locked. He started to smile but checked himself. She was without expression.

A woman seated at a computer terminal turned in her chair to look at Gunnymede. It was Bethan. She smiled broadly and got to her feet.

Gunnymede was unbalanced by her unexpected presence but recovered to smile broadly. Neve didn't miss the exchange between them.

Gunnymede walked over, unsure who to greet first. Bethan intercepted him, clearly wanting an embrace but mindful of their surroundings. 'Hello,' she said, somewhat shyly. 'Nice to see you.'

'This is a surprise,' he said.

'I didn't know you were part of the team,' Bethan said, looking into his eyes. 'I was hoping you would be.'

'Hi,' Neve said, joining them, seeing the sparkle in Bethan as she looked at Gunnymede.

'Hello. You haven't changed at all,' Gunnymede said to Neve. 'We last met years ago on a task,' he explained to Bethan.

Bethan looked between them, suddenly sensing something but unsure quite what. Neve wasn't smiling.

'I'm surprised you remembered what I looked like,' Neve replied. 'It was dark and brief.'

Bethan could only wonder what she meant.

'We met on a stakeout,' Gunnymede explained.

Bethan nodded. 'Thank you,' she said to Gunnymede.

'For what?' he asked.

'For inviting me onto the team.'

Gunnymede looked between Bethan and Neve. 'I didn't.'

Bethan was confused.

'I invited you,' Neve said. 'Jervis asked me to.'

'Oh. Who's Jervis?'

'My boss,' Neve said.

'He's the operations director,' Gunnymede explained. 'He must've been impressed with your work.'

'What work?'

'The military assassination theory you're working on for one,' Neve said.

'How do you know about that?' Bethan asked her before looking at Gunnymede for an answer.

'I never said anything to anyone here,' Gunnymede said in his own defence.

'Jervis mentioned it,' Neve said. 'He also gave you credit for assisting Devon in flushing out Krilov.'

'I didn't do anything,' Bethan said. 'In fact I almost screwed it all up.'

'He likes your intuition,' Neve said. 'Whatever.' She was eager to move on. 'We're here to find Saleem. Let's talk about how we're going to proceed.'

Neve led the way to the worktop.

'Be flattered,' Gunnymede said to Bethan as they followed Neve. 'Jervis is hard to please.'

Bethan forced a smile.

Neve leaned over various maps and photographs of players that covered the worktop. 'The police and border forces were briefed yesterday about Saleem which kicked off a nationwide hunt. The media are being kept out of it for the time being. London is obviously the prime location. The main areas of focus are: Where he is; What the target is; and his Methodology. Search lanes will include Saleem's history and associates, communications, data analysis, financials tracking and foreign intelligence liaison. Monitoring will take up the bulk of the task with the police and GCHQ sharing comms, facial and DNA tracking.' Neve looked at Bethan. 'Be aware, elements of this operation may overlap other operations and there may be information that you are not cleared to know. You may be excluded at times. I don't need to tell you not to discuss anything you learn in here with anyone out there.'

Bethan nodded understanding.

'The focus of this operations room will be on finding Saleem's target. My approach will be to look at Saleem's task from his point of view. We need to examine his aims and objectives, identify the obstacles he will want to mitigate and hopefully cross a point where he's been and find a thread. All we have at the moment is his threat to kill thousands of people. That ambition in itself narrows down his target. It also narrows down the methodology. It's not vehicles running through pedestrians for instance.'

'What about his threat to achieve his objective without WMD?' Gunnymede asked.

'That would certainly narrow it down further but I don't think we should take that seriously. I don't see how he can achieve the death of thousands without chemical or biological weaponry, can you?'

'Not yet.'

'We may be able to form an idea of his objective if we can create an accurate profile,' Bethan said.

'You're obviously not the only profiler working on this,' Neve said. 'You'll have access to everything that comes in.'

'How much time do you think we have?' Gunnymede asked.

'I don't think we have long. Days perhaps.'

'If we spread our theories too broadly we'll miss him,' he said.

'Meaning?' Neve asked.

'I believe he's using brains over brawn. I think he's using creativity over WMD.'

'You think he's that smart?'

'No. It's not his plan.'

'Keep your theories narrow and you'll also risk missing him,' Neve said.

'I've met him. I've heard him talk. I've looked into his eyes and seen his passion. He's no genius. There's something simple about what he wants to do. He has no history of operational command. He's relatively inexperienced for a job of this importance. He was selected because he's low profile and can be trusted to execute a simple plan. That's why we won't pick up trails of RDX or fertiliser or radioactivity or encrypted messages and complex manpower management. His mission is analogue not digital.'

'I don't buy it,' Neve said. 'Especially the bit about his selection because of inexperience. That doesn't make sense to me.'

'You said you wanted to look at this task from their point of view.'

'His.'

'His. Theirs. But you're not. You're looking at it from our point of view.'

'Let me remind you you're not the ops officer on this,' Neve said firmly. 'I am. We'll look for fertiliser and radioactivity and bombs and guns and encrypted messages because that's how we're going to find him.'

Bethan looked between the two, wondering what was going on between them.

'Fine,' Gunnymede said stepping back, doing his best to control his irritation. 'Let's go for a drive,' he said to Bethan.

'Devon?' Neve said as he started to walk away. 'Jervis told me something you should know. He doesn't have much confidence in you.'

Gunnymede stopped before leaving the room. 'Why's that?' he asked.

'Your only incentive for doing this job is to stay out of jail.'

'Isn't that good enough?'

'Not if you don't want this job to end.'

'What's that supposed to mean?' Gunnymede asked in a sarcastic tone. 'If I see Saleem I'll say to him, shh, keep going, I won't tell anyone.'

'You know they can't keep you out of jail forever,' Neve said. 'You're on a temporary pass. Once this operation is over you're going back to prison.'

Bethan looked at Gunnymede who was staring coldly at Neve. She felt horrified for him.

'Well, that's positive incentive, isn't it,' he said and walked out the door.

Bethan studied Neve for a second as if trying to figure her out. Neve looked her in the eyes coldly. Bethan didn't hold her gaze and left the room.

Chapter 27

Gunnymede and Bethan climbed into her car in the Legoland car park. He slammed the door and stared ahead in silence.

'I'm going with former girlfriend, acrimonious split but lots of residuals, not all of them bad. Well, until just now.'

'Just drive, please.'

She started the car and headed out of the car park. 'Where too?'

He held out the pink post-it Harlow gave him. She read it and carried on.

Twenty-five minutes later they arrived in a residential street in Clapham. Bethan turned off the engine and looked at Gunnymede questioningly. He was staring at a terraced house.

'Are you going to tell me what we're doing here?' she asked.

Gunnymede didn't respond.

'Need to know,' she quipped. 'Got it.'

Gunnymede climbed out, walked to the front door and pushed the doorbell. It chimed somewhere inside.

The door opened and an Arab woman in her fifties pulling a scarf over her head looked him up and down. 'Yes,' she said, smiling politely.

'I was a friend of Nahim's,' he said.

Her smile disappeared.

'Can I come in? I won't keep you long.'

She took a moment to decide before stepping back and letting him in.

Bethan watched the front door close behind him and took her phone from a pocket. She hit a memory dial and waited for it to answer.

'Not working you very hard if you've got time to call me,' Dillon said.

'I missed you.'

'Of course you did. What do you need?'

'Who's taking over the military homicides case?'

'No one. I don't have anyone to spare. Besides, it's your case. I can't believe you have so little to do with this current threat you're thinking of that case.'

'It's not that. I just wondered why I'm here.'

'What do you mean?'

'I don't know what I mean exactly. It's just that I don't know why I've been attached to MI6. I'm not that wonderful. They don't need me for anything specific. They have their own profilers. And then they mentioned the assassination case and I wondered...'

'Wondered what?'

'It will sound stupid.'

'Tell me.'

'I suddenly wondered if I was attached to 6 so that I couldn't work on the assassination case.'

'You're right. That does sound daft. For one, they can't keep you in the funny farm forever.'

'I know. That's the obvious answer.'

'Mind you, now that you mention it, there was something that, well, I didn't think was odd at the time. All of your current files were accessed by MI6. I thought it was you at first, trying to do some homework, you know what a workaholic you can be. But it wasn't you, was it?'

'No.'

'They're permitted access because of the relationship with the Albanian case. But with all that's flying around with this terror threat, why do they want to look at your files? I suspect it was that chap, Gunnymede. Have you seen him since joining them?'

'It's not him.'

'How can you be so sure?'

'I just am. Thanks. I'll talk to you later.'

'Okay. Take care of yourself. Remember that lot don't care about anyone. Not even their own people.'

''Bye.'

''Bye.' She put the phone down and stared into space.

Gunnymede followed the woman into a reception room. It was neat and tidy with simple furnishings. His attention was immediately drawn to a large framed picture on the mantelpiece of a young man he recognised. A black ribbon was draped around it with plastic flowers either side in small, golden vases. Gunnymede took a closer look at the young man, who was smiling broadly with large, bright eyes.

'You worked with Nahim?' the woman asked.

'No. Not exactly.'

'When did you last see him?'

'A few days before he died.'

'Do you know how he died? They won't tell me.'

'I don't.'

'He never told me anything about his work. I didn't even know he worked for the government. I thought he was with ISIS.'

Gunnymede looked at her. She was smiling but she looked like she might start crying any moment.

'I asked him before he left if he was a member of ISIS and he didn't deny it. He spent the last months before he left in a local mosque. But at school he wasn't interested in religion. He had his prayer mat in his room in the correct gibla, his Koran by his bed, but he never performed wudu at home or prayed. It was for show. He never mentioned any friends. He was living a lie to protect his secret. His last year alive I thought he was an extremist but he wasn't. He was a good boy. That's all they would tell me. That Nahim was a good boy.'

'He saved my life. I came to pay my respects and tell you how very sorry I am that I am unable to thank him in person.'

She seemed touched by Gunnymede's sincerity. 'I'll thank him for you. In my prayers. What is your name?'

'Devon.'

'I'll thank him for you, Devon.'

Gunnymede could see a light in her eyes. Despite her pain there was some kind of positive resignation in them. 'You see him, don't you?'

'I see him,' she said, smiling. 'He was a lovely boy. He still is a lovely boy. He is with Allah now. He is happy.' She made him feel somewhat more at ease about her son's death.

When he climbed back into the car he was lost in thought. Bethan sat silently, aware he was going through something deep and personal.

'Can I ask if that was her?' she eventually asked.

'Who?'

'Saleem's mother?'

'No. It wasn't her.' Something occurred to Gunnymede. 'She lives near here though. Head towards Wandsworth.'

'Are we going to see her?'

'Yes.'

'Do we need to check if she's been interviewed already? It's a normal procedure with us.'

'No. Let's go. I'll get the address.'

She drove off as he tapped a message into his phone.

Twenty minutes later she turned into a street lined with narrow terraced houses and packed with cars.

'Pull in at the end,' he said as he eyed a particular house they passed.

Bethan parked the car and turned off the engine.

'Saleem's mother was interviewed this morning by the police,' Gunnymede said. 'I wouldn't be surprised if there isn't some form of surveillance on the place.'

'Is there a particular reason we're here? I mean, apart from the obvious profiling.'

'I'd like to meet her. You coming?'

They climbed out and walked down the street to the front door.

'Would you do the badge thing,' Gunnymede said as he looked around.

Bethan knocked on the door. A man in his sixties opened it. He wore a crisp white shirt and looked at them severely. Bethan held up her badge.

'Who are you?' Gunnymede asked.

'I'm the uncle,' the man said. 'Did you forget something? The police were just here.'

'Is Mrs Saleem in?' Gunnymede asked.

The man frowned and stepped aside as they entered. He led the way down the hallway to a door and indicated they should go in. 'Would you like me to come in?'

'I'll call you if I need you,' Gunnymede said.

The man walked away and Bethan and Gunnymede entered the room.

Mrs Saleem was seated on a stool in front of a coffee table where there was a picture of Saleem with a black ribbon draped around it. She looked as if she was grieving but there was a hint of theatrics about her posture. Gunnymede and Bethan exchanged looks. She'd also read the insincerity.

Gunnymede nodded to Bethan to take over.

'Mrs Saleem?' Bethan said.

Mrs Saleem looked up at Bethan as if she wasn't aware they were in the room. Her sunless expression brightened. 'Hello.'

'I'm with the police,' Bethan said.

'Of course. Can I offer you some tea?' she said, getting to her feet.

'No thank you. I'd like to ask you some questions?'

'Are you different police to the ones who were here earlier?'

'Yes.'

'The same questions or different questions?'

'Let's see shall we. When's the last time you saw your son?'

'They asked me that question.'

'I suppose we're not so different then. When's the last time you saw your son?'

'Christmas four years ago.'

'Are you sure?' Bethan asked.

'I'm sure.'

'How can you be so sure?'

'Because it was Christmas. We don't celebrate Christmas but it's impossible to miss it in England.'

'Why are you sure it was four years ago?'

'Because I count the days and weeks since he left.'

'To join ISIL?'

'I don't know where he went.'

'You don't know he went to join ISIL?'

'Eventually. Yes. But I don't know where he went at first. I don't think he joined ISIL as soon as he left home.'

'When's the last time you heard from him?'

'A year ago. Last November.'

'How did he contact you?'

'He telephoned me?'

'What did you talk about?'

'He didn't have long to talk.'

'What did you talk about?'

'He talked about how he was feeling. How he hated the food and the heat. He mostly called to say goodbye.'

'Why goodbye?'

'Because he knew he was going to die.'

'Why was he going to die?'

'He said he was joining a big battle and he didn't think he would survive.'

'But he did.'

'No, he did not.'

'Why do you say that?'

'My son is dead. He died in that battle as he predicted he would. All this talk about him coming back to England is lies. Or they have made a mistake.'

Gunnymede looked at the photo of Saleem, the cold, unholy eyes he knew so well. 'That's your son?' he asked.

'Yes,' Mrs Saleem said dramatically as she looked upon it.

'Do you pray for him?'

She looked at Gunnymede as if he was odd. 'Of course I pray for him. Many times each day.'

'Where do you pray for him.'

'Here of course.'

'Do you see him when you pray?'

'See him?'

'Yes. Do you see him?'

'Of course I see him.'

'I mean, do you see him?'

'Yes, I see him.'

'Next time you see him can you send him a message from me. Tell him the one he tried to kill in Syria a few weeks ago is alive and well and I'm going to find him and kill him.'

Her eyes darkened as she stared at him.

'I'm going to kill him slowly and painfully, with these.' He held up his hands. 'Tell him,' Gunnymede said before heading for the door.

He stepped onto the street and did his best to calm himself down. Bethan remained inside for several more minutes. When she came outside they walked back to the car.

'Wasn't that a bit obvious?' she asked.

'What?'

'Goading her into making contact with him.'

'I got angry. That old bitch knows he's alive. She's spoken to him since he's been here.'

'How do you know?'

'I'm sure he didn't tell mummy where he's staying in England. But he has an ego the size of Iraq. I'm assuming he got it from her.'

They climbed into the car and sat looking towards the house as Gunnymede's mind churned.

'What now?' she asked.

His phone chirped and he answered it.

It was Neve. 'Where are you?'

'Saleem's house.'

'Did you just talk with his mother?'

'Yes.'

'I'm assuming you tried to wind her up.'

'I did my best.'

'She just posted a message on Telegram.'

'What was it?'

'No words. They think it was an emoji.'

'She told him something,' he said and disconnected. 'Told you. Ego the size of Iraq.'

Gunnymede and Bethan sat in a quiet corner of a pub nursing a couple of half pints. He was nibbling from a plate of fries. It was dark outside.

'Can I ask you a personal question?' Bethan said.

'No.'

She looked at him with a frown.

'Do you always have to be analysing people?' he asked. 'Can't you take a day off now and then.'

'Yes. No.'

He ate a couple of chips while she stared at him. He sighed. 'What kind of personal question?'

'Is it true what Neve said about you going back to prison when this task is over?'

'I was treading on her ops officer toes. She was putting me in my place.'

'Is it true, though?'

'I have no control over that.'

'Can I ask why you're not in jail anyway?'

'Not really.'

'Can I ask why you went to jail?'

'I told you.'

'Heroin thief.'

'What's your problem?'

'You don't like it when I call you that, do you.'

He stuffed another chip in his mouth.

'You're not comfortable with that label,' she said. 'I can't tell whether it's because it doesn't really fit or it makes you feel guilty.'

He put on a false smile as if inviting her to guess. A second later it disappeared.

The door to the street opened and in walked Neve. She came over and sat opposite them.

'You look the perfect couple,' Neve said playfully but the barb was obvious.

'Have we got our bird up yet?' Gunnymede asked, ignoring her quip.

'Only just. It was getting a bit crowded up there. We've got priority now. What exactly did you say to her?'

'Something about wringing her son's neck when I got a hold of it.'

'Can I get you a drink?' Bethan asked her.

'No thanks. If I drink I have to pee and things always seem to kick off when I go for a pee.'

'Then have a bloody drink,' he said.

Neve looked pleased she was winding him up. 'Good point,' she said as she picked up his drink and took a sip.

They all sat uncomfortably together for a long, quiet minute.

'Why did you do it?' Neve eventually asked Gunnymede.

'Do what?'

'Steal all that heroin.'

'Christ! What is it with you two?'

'I was disappointed when I heard.'

'You were disappointed,' Gunnymede said mockingly. 'My old headmaster would've been disappointed.'

'So why'd you do it?' Neve persisted.

Gunnymede rolled his eyes. 'Why is it so difficult for you people to understand the simple concept of temptation. I was in a bad place. I was pissed off with the job. With my life. I was going nowhere. A few million quid might've fixed it.'

'You knew you could never get away with it,' Neve said.

'At the time I clearly thought I could. Let me ask you something. You too,' he said to Bethan. 'What do you do all this for? Risking your life. Patriotism? Queen and country? Your political party? Your God because you think he's on your side? What drives you? You have no idea of the depths of my cynicism. I look back on conflicts like Vietnam, the Falklands, Northern Ireland and wonder why anyone thought they were worth the effort of getting up in the mornings, never mind dying for. I visited a mother today. Mother of a bloke who died for who knows what. I wanted to ask her why he did it, but I'm damned sure she wouldn't have been able to tell me. People knew what they were dying for centuries ago. Maybe all the way up to the Second World War. But after that? I don't know why they bothered. I know why the people at the top bother. Luxury. We secure their luxuries. So there I am, looking at twenty kilos of a substance that would buy me lots of luxury and I went for it.'

'You never got it, yet here you are,' Neve said.

'Maybe I want a second try.'

'What do you think?' Neve asked Bethan.

'I find you both fascinating,' Bethan said, taking a sip of her drink.

'Why *are* you here?' Neve asked her. 'That was a rhetorical question because I know you don't know. So, tell me about the assassination program.'

'You've read the file,' Bethan said.

'I've read nothing,' Neve said. 'Jervis mentioned the title and nothing else. Sounds interesting though.'

'Military personnel killing people who killed military personnel and got away with it,' Bethan explained.

'And that's why you went to Albania together?'

'That's right,' Bethan said.

'And Jervis sent you on that,' Neve said to Gunnymede.

'Harlow,' he replied..

Neve studied him, looking for something. Gunnymede stared back at her.

Bethan looked between them. 'Excuse me, I'm going to the loo,' she said, getting to her feet and heading away.

Gunnymede waited until Bethan was out of the room. 'Why are you bringing her in on this?' he asked.

'She's already in on it.'

'No she's not. She's an analyst. A profiler.'

'Why's she here?'

'You keep asking that.'

'What's Jervis up to?'

'Maybe it's Harlow.'

'Maybe it's Spangle.'

'Are you involved in the op too?'

'No one's involved in the Spangle op but you. And Jervis and Harlow and that strange Greek bloke who hangs around him. Who is he, anyway?'

'Harlow's dad and his dad were mates.'

'And the assassination case is about Spangle. I'm not asking. I'm just curious.'

'Everything's about Spangle,' he said. 'This operation is somehow about Spangle. He's the most dangerous single person on this planet.'

'There's a lot of competition out there. North Korea. Iran. Russia. China.'

'Those leaders are all accountable to someone eventually. Spangle isn't.'

'Do you really believe you're the bait?' she asked.

'You're another well-informed oily rag aren't you,' he said, staring at her.

'Echo is foxtrot,' came a voice over their ear pieces.

They went to their phones and accessed apps as Bethan returned. 'I heard the message,' she said.

'Turns out everyone was waiting for *you* to go for a pee,' Gunnymede said to Bethan.

A bird's eye view of Mrs Saleem's terraced house came up on Gunnymede's phone showing someone leaving the front door. It zoomed in to reveal Saleem's mother wearing a head scarf and zoomed back out to follow her along the pavement.

'She's heading in this direction,' Neve said.

They watched her walk along the residential street, make a right turn at the end and cross the road. At the next junction she turned onto a busy commercial street lined with shops, the pavements heaving with pedestrians. The screen split as a static CCTV joined the follow. It split again as another contributed to the shot.

Saleem's mother walked down the street, threading her way between shoppers.

'She knows where she's going,' Gunnymede said.

After a few hundred metres she stopped by the kerb, between a lamppost and a phone booth and faced the traffic.

'That's a stop, stop,' a voice said over the radio.

She removed her hands from her pockets.

Gunnymede concentrated on the various views of her. 'It's a DLB,' he said.

'What's a DLB?' Bethan asked.

'Dead letter box,' he said.

'She's going to leave something for someone to pick up,' Neve added.

Saleem's mother put her hands back in her pockets and walked back the way she came.

'That was a drop,' Gunnymede said.

'I never saw anything,' Neve said.

'Neither did I but that was a drop,' he said.

The various cameras watched her walk down the street.

'She's going home,' Gunnymede said. 'Her job's done.'

Neve was on her phone to the control room. 'Play back her static position and examine in slow time. Zoom in.'

The screens remained split, one was a view of the CCTV following Saleem's mother back down the street while another replayed her at the phone booth and lamppost.

'There,' Gunnymede said. 'On the lamppost. She stuck something to it. Go!' He hurried out the pub. Bethan followed. 'You take beyond the booth. I'll take this side. And make sure mummy Saleem doesn't see you!'

Bethan hurried down the street searching for Saleem's mother the other side. She saw her heading along the busy pavement and looked away as they drew opposite each other. Saleem's mother was focused on returning home. Bethan carried on until she could see the phone booth, went past it and into a shop from where she could see it.

Gunnymede meanwhile stepped into a department and went to a display window from where he had eyes on.

They waited. Eyes flicking between the lamppost and people approaching it from both directions.

As Bethan watched, a man stopped outside her window. She took little notice of him at first until she realised he was also looking towards the phone booth. He was shorter than her with jet black hair. She moved to get a better angle while keeping an eye on the phone booth.

'I have a possible,' she said.

The man turned around for a second to look at the window Bethan was behind. She froze, fearing he was looking directly at her then realised he was looking at the reflection. She could see his face clearly.

'It's him. From the ship.'

'Saleem?' Gunnymede asked.

'No. When I was on the ship I saw two Arabs. This is one of them.'

The man set off across the street.

'He's crossing towards the booth,' Bethan said.

The drone picked up the Arab approaching the lamppost and watched as he deftly removed something and walked away.

Bethan looked at her phone screen. The man headed down the street and into a shop.

'Take him,' Gunnymede said as he ran across the busy road.

Bethan hurried out of the department store, across the road and into the shop. It was a busy market hall with dozens of independent booths. Bethan kept walking, looking in all directions. She stepped onto a box and looked towards the back of the hall just as the Arab went through a door.

'He's out the back!' Bethan said as she hurried after him.

Gunnymede carried on along the street, bumping into people as he watched the drone view on his phone. The operator moved it to the back of the store but it was a confusion of partially covered narrow walkways with people moving in all directions.

'We've lost him,' Gunnymede said angrily, breaking into a run.

He ran into an alleyway, turned the corner at the end hoping to see far enough ahead but there were too many obstacles. 'Bethan?'

'I'm out the back heading north along a narrow walkway.'

'Do you have?' he asked, craning to try and see her.

'Negative. Wait. I have. I have!'

Bethan could see the Arab coming to the end of the walkway. He ducked under an awning and out of sight. She sped after him, reached the awning and went under it. The alleyway carried on for a bit before reaching a street but it was empty. She hurried to the end and into the street. It led back to the busy shopping high street. There was no sign of the Arab.

She looked back to see Gunnymede stepping under the awning.

She went to him. They met in the middle and looked at the only door in the alleyway. Gunnymede took a hold of the handle and turned it. The door was unlocked. He eased it open to reveal a yard filled with household junk and old building materials. It was the back of a three storey house that looked as if it had been abandoned in the middle of a refurbishment. There was scaffolding and building materials but everything looked in a state of decay.

Bethan followed him across the yard to the back door that was ajar. He reached inside his jacket for a semi-automatic pistol which he tugged out of a shoulder holster as he eased the door open. It led onto a dark, dingy landing. A rusting wheelbarrow sat in the hallway alongside cement bags that had long since solidified.

They eased their way along the concrete floor to a flight of steps. Further ahead was the front door.

'Check it,' he whispered.

She went to the door and examined it. It was shut solid. She shook her head. They looked up the stairs.

Gunnymede led the way, easing up each step, keeping to the wall to reduce the chance of noise, ears and eyes fine-tuned to the space above. The second landing was equally trashed, dirt and cobwebs everywhere, thick sheets of plywood covering the floor that didn't creak when stepped on. There were several doors to choose from but before they could inspect them a noise came from above. And again. The top floor. Like furniture being moved. Gunnymede and Bethan barely breathed in an effort to concentrate their hearing.

Voices trickled down to them. They focused above as they ascended the last flight of stairs, one careful step at a time. A creak forced Gunnymede skip a step. Bethan followed.

There were only two doors on the top landing and it was obvious which was the one they wanted. Gunnymede signalled Bethan to keep away from the door as he levelled the pistol and gripped the handle.

In a single swift movement he turned the knob and pushed the door open to reveal two men. Saleem and the Arab from the street. For a second they were frozen still. The Arab then lunged for a pistol on a table and Gunnymede fired. The bullet slammed through his head spraying Saleem in blood and he dropped dead to the floor.

Saleem remained still in his chair other than his empty hands that very slowly rose into view. Gunnymede stepped inside and checked behind the open door. The small room was sparsely furnished. A table and a few chairs. A single window was ajar leading onto a flat roof with scaffolding.

Bethan stepped in behind Gunnymede.

'The tide has turned again,' Gunnymede said. 'I would really like to shoot you in the head right now and save all the aggravation of a trial and prison.'

'Then you'd never find out about the attack.'

'Don't need to now.'

'Someone else will come.'

'Good piece of bargaining for your life.' Gunnymede said. 'Kind of relies on me giving a fuck. So tell me?'

'Where the attack will be? You don't seriously expect me to tell you right away do you?'

Bethan walked over to the table and looked at various items on it, one of them a map of London which she opened up.

'You won't find any indication on that map,' Saleem said.

Bethan sorted through the other documents.

'You'll find nothing here.'

'There's a clue in here somewhere,' Gunnymede said. 'There always is. And you know it too, don't you. Empty out your pockets.'

Saleem did as he was told, placing items on the table. There wasn't much. Bethan went through them. She unfolded a piece of paper. 'It's an invoice for ten tons of quick dry cement.'

Gunnymede looked at Saleem for an explanation.

Saleem shrugged.

'That's got to be a clue to something, right?' Gunnymede said. 'Ten tons of quick dry cement.'

Bethan found nothing else of interest.

'Since this is the only chance I'll get, what I'd like to do is start shooting you through your limbs while you try and remember anything relating to the attack,' Gunnymede said, aiming the pistol at one of his knees.

Bethan glanced at him, wondering if he was serious.

'I'll have to send the lady out for some tea of course,' Gunnymede added.

'I'll tell you nothing,' Saleem said. 'But if you must torture me then go ahead.'

Bethan nosed around the room, inspecting a picture on a wall, flicking through a copy of the Koran on a window ledge.

'Bethan. Would you give us a moment, please.'

'You're not serious, are you?'

'Of course I am.'

'I can't tell if you're bluffing or not.'

'That's supposed to be his line.'

'I'm sorry, Devon, but I can't be a party to you torturing him. Not like that at least.'

'Which is why I'm asking you to go and get a cup of tea.'

She frowned at him as she pushed on a wooden panel below the sloping ceiling that followed the shape of the roof. It moved easily. She leaned on a chair in front of it and pulled at the panel. It slid to one side. 'One moment,' she said as she removed it completely to reveal a small safe on a stand.

'What have we here?' Gunnymede exclaimed.

Bethan picked up the chair, moved it to one side and stepped on the wooden floorboard. As she did so there was a subtle click from beneath the floor.

'Don't move,' Saleem said to Bethan. 'Please stay perfectly still.'

Gunnymede instantly flicked the end of his pistol towards him.

'No, please. You're standing on a boobytrap. A pressure release trip. If you step off that floorboard we're all dead.'

Bethan froze to the spot, a hand on the sloped ceiling to keep her balance. Gunnymede was unsure what to do for a moment, expecting some other surprise to follow. 'Your turn to bluff, is it?'

'I'm not bluffing, I assure you, mate.'

Gunnymede knelt beside her, keeping the gun on Saleem. She was twisted slightly and turned her foot a little to straighten up.

'Easy,' Gunnymede warned.

Saleem slowly got to his feet.

'Give me the slightest excuse to kill you and I will,' Gunnymede said.

'You know how fond we are of boobytraps. There's a pound of plastic underneath her. I'm a little nervous myself. It's a Russian device and a bit sensitive.'

'Stay exactly where you are,' Gunnymede said threateningly. He inspected the floorboards either side of the one she was on. One of them was loose. He dug a finger under an edge and eased it up.

He checked to ensure Saleem was still then used the light on his phone to see under the floorboard. The mechanism was clear. An igniferous device with the detonator fixed directly to it and wrapped in what looked like a large slab of plasticine.

'Very deceitful,' Gunnymede said as he inspected it.

A sudden loud crash and Gunnymede rolled to his side and aimed his gun towards Saleem who was no longer there. Saleem was halfway through the window. Gunnymede fired but Saleem was already through.

Gunnymede scrambled up and went to the broken window frame hanging off its hinges to see Saleem drop over the side of the flat roof.

He pulled himself through the window, onto the roof, aiming his gun as he hurried to the edge in time to see Saleem leap from a small balcony back into the house through another window. Gunnymede hurried back into the room, out the door as Bethan watched anxiously, and down the stairs several at a time. On reaching the bottom he sprinted out the back but Saleem had already made it across the yard and was in the alleyway. Gunnymede ran into the alleyway and spun in both directions, gun outstretched, but Saleem was gone.

'Shit!'

Moments later Gunnymede came running back into the room where Bethan was standing. 'I'm sorry,' he said.

'I take it he got away.'

'He's a swift little bastard.'

'You should be after him.'

'Don't be ridiculous. What if something happened to me. It could take hours before someone found you here.'

'I have my phone.'

'I didn't think about that.'

'I'm touched.'

'Attention seeking.'

'I was kind of joking.'

'I do care.'

'Yes, but I meant in a more personal way.'

'For God's sake.'

'Let's not have a row,' she said, still trying to be amusing.

Gunnymede considered her position. 'This is what we're going to do. I'll put my foot beside yours and keep the weight down and you step off.'

'I'd rather not if you don't mind.'

'It will work.'

'I don't care to try. It sounds dodgy'

'It's only a little dodgy.'

'You have called someone I take it.'

'Of course. They'll be here soon. I'll wait right here with you.'

She moved slightly.

'Easy.'

'I've got cramp in my foot.'

'Ignore it. Try and relax. Breathe. What would your father say if he could see you now?'

'He'd probably be quite philosophical about it. Part of the job and all that. My mother on the other hand would be hysterical.'

She moved again, grimacing as she dealt with the cramp.

He grew anxious. 'Please don't move.'

'At least we'll go together.'

'What?'

She chuckled. 'Sorry. I have a wicked sense of humour at times. Keep talking. It does take my mind off it. I saw something in your eyes when you came into the operations room and saw Neve. When's the last time you saw her?'

'Eight years ago.'

'That's right. A long time. Were you in a relationship?'

'No. It was a very brief encounter.'

'A one night stand sort of thing?'

'We were on a task together. We ended up kissing.'

'You were on a brief job together and kissed. I see.'

He rolled his eyes. 'We were on a stake-out. In a car. It was late. We were playing the role of a couple parked up after the pubs closed. The bad guy came along and saw us and, well, we had to kiss.'

'Nice work if you can get it.'

'Someone's got to do it.'

'That does sound romantic though. Did you have sex?'

'No,' he said emphatically. 'It was really nothing.'

'I'm jealous, obviously. But I'm not going to commit suicide over it, don't worry. You're not that wonderful.'

'I really am not.'

Gunnymede hit a key on his phone. 'This is Gunnymede. Where's ATO? What's taking so long?!'

He listened for a moment before putting the phone down. 'They're a few minutes away. The bomb disposal officer said try not to move.'

It served to amuse them.

'Have you seen your aunt yet?' she asked.

'Aunt Grace?'

'Yes.'

It was an unexpected question. He shrugged. 'Yes.'

'Did you ask her about your father?'

'My father?'

'For God's sake I'm trying to make small talk here,' she said frustratedly.

'Sorry – yes, I did in fact.'

'What did she say?'

'Nothing really.'

'She doesn't know anything?'

'I don't think so.'

'But you're not sure?'

He sighed, tired of the subject.

'Sorry, but I just can't believe you're not interested in your own father's mysterious death.'

'It's not that I'm not interested.'

She became distracted by something at her feet.

'What is it?' he asked.

'It feels like it's getting warm down there.'

'What?'

'My foot. It's getting warm. Perhaps you should leave.'

'It's your imagination,' he said, dropping to his knees to feel the plank beneath her foot. 'It's not warm,' he said with some relief. He stood up and looked into her eyes. 'You're very brave.'

'Why? I don't have much of a choice.'

'I know you're brave.'

'What do you think's in the safe?' she asked.

'Probably nothing.'

'I hope this wasn't all for nothing.' She stared into his eyes. 'Devon – would you kiss me.'

'What?'

'Kiss me.'

'Are you sure?'

'Why wouldn't you?'

'I don't want you getting all wobbly kneed. You know how weak you get when I kiss you.'

'Please.'

He moved close to her. Smiled. And kissed her softly on the lips.

'You can do better than that,' she said.

They kissed again, a lingering, gentle kiss.

When they separated she inhaled with deep satisfaction. 'There was something very special about that.'

'Snogging on a bomb does lend a certain je ne sais quoi,' he said.

They smiled, inches apart.

'That beats ours by a mile,' Neve said from the doorway.

She surprised them both. Gunnymede had to steady Bethan.

Footsteps on the stairs grew louder as several men hurried up them. One of them came in carrying a bag of tools.

'Which one is it?' he asked with urgency.

Gunnymede stepped back to allow the man access to Bethan.

'I don't need to tell you to keep perfectly still,' the man said as he dropped to his knees.

'Can we talk,' Neve said to Gunnymede as she left the room.

Gunnymede followed her onto the landing.

'Tell me you didn't let Saleem escape in order to save her.'

'I pursued Saleem until I lost him.'

'For God's sake. A couple thousand people versus one cute girl?'

'Don't even go there.'

'How did he escape you?'

'The bomb was a distraction. He took his chance and legged it. Where the fuck were you lot anyway? Some back up.'

'The drone lost sight and neither of you called in your location.'

'Once we got here we couldn't talk. Why didn't you track us?'

'The house shadowed your signal. They showed you across the road. Okay, let's not turn this into a slanging match. Do we have anything?'

'Nothing obvious. An invoice for ten tons of quick dry cement. There might be other stuff.'

'Jervis thinks the attack will happen in the next twenty-four hours.'

'How does he know that?'

'He's looking at it from their point of view. They either call it off or do it now.'

'Saleem won't want to delay it or let anyone else do it another time,' he said. 'I agree. If he had a choice he'd push for hitting it now.'

'We're running out of time,' she said.

'Did you ever do one of those post-traumatic stress courses?'

'Everyone does,' she said. 'Why?'

'I missed mine. Take care of Beth's repatriation, would you?' He walked down the stairs.

Neve looked as if she'd been left holding the baby. She leaned into the room.

The bomb disposal officer was on his knees and reaching under the floorboards. 'I'd appreciate it if you left the room please, miss,' he said as he fiddled with something.

Bethan looked at Neve who returned her gaze for a moment and stepped back into the hallway.

Ten minutes later Bethan stepped out of the room and rested against a wall somewhat exhausted as several MI6 analysts went into the room.

'Stressful?' Neve asked.

Bethan smiled politely.

'You're going to need therapy,' Neve said.

'I agree. My bartender or do you have one I can use?'

Neve looked into the room as the bomb disposal expert placed the components of the device into plastic bags. One of the analysts opened the safe and searched inside it.

'Empty?' Neve asked him.

The man nodded.

Neve headed down the stairs. 'Come on,' she said to Bethan. 'We keep a bottle in the office for such occasions.'

Bethan followed.

Chapter 28

The 194 ton aggregate carrier, the *Polo Harrow,* was moored alongside a floating pontoon adjacent to the Port of London Authority utility offices on the south side of the Thames, 300 metres from the Thames Barrier. It was dark when a minibus drove into the industrial estate and along the poorly lit road to the Authority centre. Following the minibus was a lorry carrying a dozen pallets topped with cement bags. The minibus reached the end of the road turnabout and came to a stop. The lorry parked behind it and engines and lights were turned off. The area was well lit but devoid of life.

A dozen men climbed out of the mini bus and three more from the lorry. They were all British Arabs. Four of those who had arrived on the ship with Saleem set off through the Authority yard and up a zig-zag ramp to a long, covered walkway suspended above the water. They paused at the end to observe the *Polo Harrow* the other side of the floating pontoon. Lights were on inside the superstructure at the back of the boat.

The leader drew a long knife from a sheath under his jacket. The others did the same and they crossed the pontoon and stealthily climbed on board. They went directly to the back of the superstructure and after a brief pause to ensure all were ready, they opened the door into a small crew room. A young man in grubby overalls was making a cup of tea for himself. Two of the ISIL fighters quickly set upon him with their knives, stabbing his body and slitting his throat while the other pair headed through a door and up a narrow flight of stairs.

They paused at a door to look at each other and synchronise their thoughts. A second later they pushed open the door to find an engineer leaning against the wheel watching the river. The killers made swift work of him and left his body on the floor oozing blood from the slice across his throat.

The one in charge shouted for the others to return to the vehicles while he made his way along the narrow side of the aggregate storage compartments to the front of the boat. He hauled open the bosun's locker hatch and shone a torch inside. It would do nicely.

Within an hour a timber framework had been constructed inside the bosun's locker and a large number of the cement bags had been carried on board and dumped by the hatch. The chain of bag carriers made their way between the boat and the lorry well into the night as the bags were emptied into the wooden framework followed by buckets of river water.

Bethan sat in the dimly lit operations room reading her emails on her phone. Two analysts were at computer terminals.

The door opened and Neve walked in with a bottle of Scotch. 'Harlow's office,' she announced. 'He always has the good stuff.' She cracked open the top. 'He won't miss it. He seems to prefer his Temple office these days anyway.'

She poured two glasses and handed one to Bethan. 'Welcome to the madhouse,' she said, taking a sip.

'Is this a normal day in the life of a secret squirrel?'

'Most of the time it's boring as hell. You've been lucky.'

Bethan held up her glass. 'Lucky in something at last. Can't wait for tomorrow.'

'I was serious about a therapist.'

Bethan raised her glass to her, took a good sip and sat back to enjoy it.

'Are you and Devon an item?' Neve asked.

'I don't know. I was hoping we might be. You weren't expecting me, were you?'

Neve shrugged.

'Sorry.'

'I have no interest in Devon.'

Bethan looked at her, unsure about her. 'Did you know Megan?'

'Megan?'

'His fiancée.'

'He had a fiancée?'

Bethan decided not to get into it. 'I never met her.'

'What happened to her?'

Bethan was reluctant but answered anyway. 'She died.'

'Oh,' Neve said, looking genuinely sorry.

They sipped their drinks in silence for half a minute.

'I was curious to see him again,' Neve said.

'You knew each other for just a moment.'

'A couple of hours, max. We barely exchanged a word.'

'But something happened.'

'Yes. Something happened.'

'What?'

'Who knows? I likened it to a holiday romance.'

'Aren't you supposed to never try and recreate those?'

'It's good advice.'

The door opened and Gunnymede walked in. 'I thought I'd find you here,' he said, walking over to the Scotch and pouring himself a glass.

'Who?' Neve asked. 'Us or the scotch?'

He smiled at them as he took a drink. 'Right. Let's get down to this. How do you kill a couple thousand people in London?'

'We could be asking Saleem that right now,' Neve said.

'But we're not, are we,' he replied.

'Go over your conversation with him,' Bethan said. 'The one in Syria.'

'It was short and sweet. He was going to kill thousands of people in London without explosives or weapons of mass destruction.'

'You're absolutely certain of that?' Neve asked.

'I can't remember the exact words. I had a rope around my neck while balancing on a log at the time. But that's the thing. He spoke to me softly so that no one else could hear and he was expecting me to be dead minutes after. So there was no reason for him to misinform me.'

'He could've been exaggerating,' Neve suggested. 'Bragging.'

'Yes, he was bragging but he was excited about it.'

'It might've been the truth that day,' Bethan offered. 'But is it the truth today?'

'Does anyone mind if I smoke?' he asked. 'I think better with a cigarette.'

The girls shrugged. He lit one up and took a long drag. 'Want one?'

'No thanks,' Bethan said.

Neve shook her head.

'That's a good point though,' he said.

'What is?' Neve asked.

'Is it true today? He was excited about the pure simplicity of it. That's why I'm stuck on no explosives or WMD. I mean, that's how we always find these people.

They make or acquire weapons and explosives and leave trails for us to follow. No ordnance makes it very difficult for us. It's almost impossible to stop them from hiring vans and driving into people, or buying knives and stabbing them. He's found a weapon that we won't notice until it's too late.'

'Why thousands of people?' Neve asked. 'Why not a specific number?'

'That's another clue,' he said. 'The number is dictated by the method. Maybe he can't kill more or less than that number. He has no control over numbers. It's at an event or location where there could be or will be thousands of people. Maybe they'll all die or only a portion of them.'

'How can you kill a thousand people without a bomb or chemicals?' Neve asked.

'They would have to be confined,' Gunnymede said. 'In one location. Just for a moment, take away bombs and anything else. What kills thousands of people and is natural, for instance?'

'Earthquake,' Bethan said.

'Tsunami,' Neve offered. 'Fire?'

'Two hundred thousand people were killed in the 2004 tsunami,' Bethan offered.

'How do you make a tsunami?' Neve asked.

'In London?' Gunnymede added.

'What's the capacity of Wembley?' Bethan asked, tapping the questions into her phone. 'Ninety thousand.'

Gunnymede emptied his glass and sat on the couch. 'There's a clue staring at us. I'm sure of it.'

Bethan and Neve sipped their drinks in silence.

Gunnymede stretched himself out on the couch and put a cushion under his head.

A few minutes later Neve stood up and looked in Gunnymede's direction. His eyes were closed and he looked asleep.

She went to the only other couch and stretched out on it.

Bethan continued reading her phone. When she next looked up they were both sleeping soundly. The two analysts were quietly tapping away at their consuls.

Bethan got to her feet, stifled a yawn and left the ops room.

Five minutes later she was driving along the river embankment in the rain. The roads were practically empty.

The two analysts turned off their computers, collected their coats and went to the door. The last one to leave looked at Gunnymede and Neve asleep, switched off the lights and left, closing the door.

Bethan glanced at the river as she drove along it. Something was on her mind and she pulled over. She climbed out and went to the parapet to look down onto the river. The vast body of black water was high and moving slowly. She stared at it in thought.

Neve opened her eyes and sat up, remembering where she was. She lowered her feet to the floor and looked around the room, rubbing her tired eyes. She checked her watch.

She got to her feet and faced the door. She didn't move other than to look over at Gunnymede sleeping soundly.

Bethan walked along the embankment, pausing every now and then to look at the river.

Neve walked over to Gunnymede and looked down on him. He looked peaceful. She started to turn away when he took her hand. She stopped and looked at him. He looked serious as he stared at her.

Bethan took a last look at the water before walking back to her car. She climbed in, started the engine, pulled a U-turn and drove back in the direction she'd come.

Gunnymede sat up and placed his hands on Neve's hips. She put her hands on top of his to stop him. He squeezed her, his hands moving back slightly, his fingers touching her bottom. She gritted her teeth as she squeezed his hands. He didn't remove them. She grabbed a hold of his hair with both hands and held him strongly. He didn't take his gaze from her eyes. She could've wrenched herself free but she didn't. She looked into his eyes. Her jaw grew less tense. Her grip on his hair slowly loosened. He got to his feet and wrapped his arms around her. She struggled without making a sound as he held her firmly. His hand went to her face. She tried to turn away but it was a weak effort. He moved her head to face him and kissed her on the lips. She didn't struggle. Her mouth slowly opened and her breathing quickened.

She put her arms around him as they kissed deeply. He pulled off his jacket and yanked hers of her shoulders. She helped undress him while he undressed her. They grew feverish for each other. Rapacious.

She stepped out of her trousers as did he. He pulled away her panties, lifted her onto the worktop and they began to make passionate love. As she wrapped her legs around him the door opened and the light came on. Gunnymede and Neve froze, entwined, and looked towards the door to see Bethan standing there, looking at them.

Bethan took a second to take a hold of herself. She managed to make no outward signs of her shock. She let the door close and crossed the room to the coffee machine, placed a cup in the holder and selected a latte.

Gunnymede and Neve fumbled to get dressed.

'Drowning,' Bethan said.

'What?' Neve asked as she fastened her bra.

'Drowning,' Bethan repeated. 'He's going to drown them.'

'How do you drown thousands of people?' Neve asked.

'It helps if they're below ground level,' Bethan said.

'River level,' Gunnymede added, catching on as he pulled up his trousers.

'The London underground,' Bethan said. 'How many people in the underground during a busy work day?'

'Thousands, easily,' Neve said.

'Saleem said he could do it any time,' Gunnymede remembered.

'The underground's empty when it's closed,' Neve said, tucking in her shirt.

'But any time could also mean any time of convenience,' Bethan said.

'Any day,' Gunnymede said, pulling on his shoes.

'Any time of day,' Bethan added. 'But how do you get the Thames into the underground?'

'Make a hole,' Gunnymede said. 'In the embankment.'

'You couldn't do it without explosives,' Neve said. 'Could you?'

Gunnymede went to the worktop computer and pulled up a map of the London Underground system. He searched along the river looking for underground tunnels.

'Blackfriars. Victoria embankment. It's the closest the underground gets to the river.'

'How close?'

'I don't know. There's an underground operations room at Charing Cross,' Gunnymede said taking a step towards the door and pausing to see if the others were coming. 'We should go check it out.'

'Would anyone like a coffee?' Bethan asked.

Gunnymede and Neve glanced at each other, both still very much off balance.

'I'll have one,' Neve said. 'White, no sugar.'

'Me too,' Gunnymede said.

'Help yourself,' Bethan said, heading for the door. 'I'll see you in the car park.' Bethan paused as she opened the door and looked at Gunnymede.

He held her gaze, his eyes filled with schoolboy guilt.

'Your flies undone,' she said and let the door close behind her.

Gunnymede did up his fly as he glanced at Neve who couldn't hold his gaze.

Bethan walked to the elevator and pushed the call button. Her eyes began to water. The elevator doors opened. She wiped a tear and stepped inside.

Gunnymede, Neve and Bethan were escorted to the control room of Charing Cross underground station and introduced to the two men running it early that morning, Bob and Tyrone. The room was surrounded by half a dozen monitors of various sizes attached to wall brackets above a worktop tailored to fit inside the angular walls. The top sections were glass providing a view of the main station access to the ticket machines, barriers and escalators that led down to the trains.

They stepped inside, closing the door behind them and with it shutting out the noise from a floor washing machine making its rounds.

'How can we help?' Tyrone asked with a welcoming smile.

Gunnymede looked to Neve who invited him to take the lead. 'I'll get straight to the point. Our department deals with anti-terrorism and today we're looking at theoretical attacks on the underground system.'

'This sort of thing's not new to us,' Tyrone said. 'We often work with the police on their terrorist exercises.'

'We had one two weeks ago in fact,' Bob remembered. 'Do you work much with the met police?'

'Sometimes,' Gunnymede said, anxious to get on with it.

'This a bombing, shooting or stabbing?' Bob asked.

'We had a nerve gas exercise two years ago,' Tyrone reminded Bob.

'Oh, yes. Based on that Japanese attack,' Bob said.

'None of those,' Gunnymede said. 'My first question. Where does the train line run closest to the river bank?'

Bob and Tyrone looked at each other with questioning frowns and returned their gazes to Gunnymede. 'What do you mean exactly?' Bob asked.

'The TFL accurate tube map shows the circle and district line running along the Victoria Embankment to Blackfriars. It's the closest point a train tunnel gets to the river that I can see.'

'I see what you mean,' Tyrone said, reaching for a long map roll which he unrolled on the table. 'That's right. The closest point that any underground rail tunnel gets to the river is here, near the Blackfriars underpass.'

Gunnymede, Neve and Bethan closed on the map. 'How close does the tunnel get to the riverbank wall?' Neve asked.

Bob exhaled through pursed lips as he considered the question. 'About ten metres I'd say.'

'Ten?' Gunnymede asked. 'How accurate is that?'

Tyrone took a ruler and placed it on the map, measuring the gap between the wall and the tunnel. 'You've got about a metre of stone wall and then about nine metres of earth. Another metre of tunnel wall. Ten or eleven metres.'

Gunnymede, Bethan and Neve looked at each other.

'How do you get through ten metres of that?' Bethan asked.

'Without explosives,' Neve added.

Bob and Tyrone glanced at each other, a little confused. 'I don't follow,' Tyrone said.

'We're looking at ways a terrorist might breach the riverbank and flood the tunnels,' Gunnymede said. 'I'd like to explore the possibilities a boat could ram a hole through the embankment.'

'You'd need a bloody big boat to do that,' Bob said.

'How big?' Neve asked.

'Christ. Two thousand tons going at twenty knots maybe,' he said. 'Maybe more.'

'Never make the turn though,' Tyrone said.

'It'd take up the width of the river standing still,' Bob said with a chuckle.

'I don't know too much about boats,' Tyrone added. 'But I know something about heavy objects going at speed and ramming into things, such as trains hitting barriers. Half a dozen carriages would run at two hundred and fifty tons. At thirty miles an hour it would only make a dent in a ten metre thick wall of soil. A boat at ten or twelve knots, not a chance. Anyway, the biggest boat you're going to get coming up the Thames might be a hundred tons. Two at the most. And it wouldn't be able to make the turn at top speed to line up to the embankment anyway. The river's only two hundred and fifty metres wide at that point.'

Gunnymede sat back in thought.

'How much explosive would you need?' Neve asked.

'Don't know anything about explosives,' Tyrone said.

'Ten thousand pounds of ampho might do it,' Gunnymede said.

'As far as the non-explosives theory goes this looks like a non-starter then,' Bethan said.

'It would seem so,' Gunnymede said, taking a last look at the map before leaving. Something caught his attention and he took a closer look. 'What's that? The circle. There's another one here and here.'

Tyrone examined the map.

Bob joined him. 'Those are bore holes,' Bob said.

'Bore holes?' Gunnymede asked.

'Water wells,' Bob explained. 'That's how Londoners got their water before the days of piping it in.'

'They stopped using them by the early nineteen hundreds when water mains were put in,' Tyrone added.

'This one is between the underground tunnel and the embankment,' Gunnymede said.

The others took a closer look.

'That's right,' Bob said.

'What's the diameter of the bore hole?' Gunnymede asked.

'A couple of metres at least,' Bob said. 'Maybe four.'

'And what's the gap between the bore hole and the embankment?'

'Don't know,' Tyrone said. 'Couple of metres I suppose.'

'Would flooding the bore hole impact the train tunnel?' Gunnymede asked.

'Sure. If the bore hole was open to the river the tunnel would get flooded too,' Tyrone said.

'Would a two hundred ton vessel going 15 knots bash through a metre or two of embankment?' Gunnymede asked.

'The boat would have to hit the embankment smack on the bore hole,' Bob said.

'But if it did?' Gunnymede asked. 'In theory.'

Bob and Tyrone looked at each other. They nodded in agreement. 'I expect so,' Tyrone said.

'Certainly possible,' Bob said. 'And then we'd close the gates,' he added.

'The flood gates,' Bethan said.

'That's right,' Tyrone said. 'We can seal off the tunnels.'

'How long would that take?' Neve asked.

'About ten minutes,' Tyrone explained.

'Would that be enough time?' Gunnymede asked.

'That would depend on how much water was coming in,' Bob said.

'A high tide would be quite serious,' Tyrone explained.

'Spring tide even worse,' Bob added.

'Add to that an easterly wind,' Tyrone said. 'And we'd be in a pickle.'

'How often does that happen?' Gunnymede asked.

'You've got one today,' Bob said. 'They're talking about closing the Thames barrier.'

Gunnymede, Neve and Bethan looked at each other.

Bob and Tyrone both smiled, feeling they'd been more than helpful.

Chapter 29

Saleem arrived at the Port Authority building as the sun broke the horizon and made his way along the gangways to the *Polo Harrow*. He was greeted by each fighter he passed as he climbed on board and made his way to the bow.

The forward deck and aggregate storage was littered with empty concrete bags. A hose hung over the side with water pouring from it. One of the men was poking into the boatswain's storage hatch with a long pole. Saleem joined him and looked down into the hatch. The wooden framework was complete and the triangular space it created behind the nose of the vessel was filled with the quick-setting concrete. The bows had in effect been turned into a battering ram. Saleem took the pole and poked it into the concrete for himself.

'It will be solid soon,' the fighter assured Saleem.

Saleem looked over the side to see the water was a couple of metres below the freeboard. 'We need to get going,' he said, making his way towards the stern.

He entered the superstructure and climbed the narrow steps. The engines were gunned as he entered the wheelhouse where one of his men had control of the vessel. Saleem paused on entering to look down at the body of the engineer lying in a pool of blood in a corner.

'Let's go,' Saleem ordered, joining his colleague. He looked through the bridge windows at the wide open river, the Thames Barrier clearly visible up ahead.

The fighter went to the side door that opened out onto a short wing and shouted orders. The lines were cast and the boat drifted from the pontoon. Two fighters remained on board as the rest watched the boat leave.

'Allahu akbar!' They shouted several times in unison.

'When does the barrier close?' Saleem asked.

'We have time,' the pilot said as he throttled the engine to pull power.

Water lapped over the bows with each wave it struck.

'Isn't the front a bit low?' Saleem asked.

'It will be fine,' the pilot assured him. 'We could do with more water in the storage compartments to balance it better. But it will be fine.'

Red crosses on each pier of the Thames barrier began to flash, warning the gates were closing. The two fighters joined Saleem and the pilot as the boat sailed between two of the piers. Saleem stepped out of the side door to look back at the barrier. Several dams had already been raised into position. The two remaining gates that were still open would soon be closed.

Saleem looked ahead. The river was clear with only a handful of boats moving on it. He went back into the bridge.

'We will cover the fourteen kilometres in plenty of time, boss,' the pilot assured him.

'We need to hit the bank a good half hour before high tide.'

'We will, in sha Allah. We don't want the tunnels to run out of water,' the pilot said with a smile that the fighters shared.

Saleem stared ahead. He was so close to immortality he could taste it.

An MoD car pulled to a stop on the Victoria embankment and Gunnymede and Bethan climbed out.

Gunnymede looked about to get his bearings as Bethan crossed the pavement to the parapet. He joined her, pausing to reflect on her as she looked down onto the water.

'I'm sorry,' he said.

'Nothing to be sorry about,' she said, trying to ignore him. 'Where's this bore hole?'

'I'm very sorry,' he insisted. 'Truly. You're the last person in the world I'd want to hurt.'

'Well you did. But that doesn't matter. I have no claim on you. This is hardly the time.'

He reluctantly turned his attention to a metal bench on a raised section of pavement. 'Beneath the bench,' he said, walking over to it. 'They said it pretty much sits directly on top of the bore hole.'

He faced the river and stepped to the parapet.

She joined him to look down onto the water. 'I don't remember seeing it this high before,' she said.

'Eleven times a year on average. And there's another hour to go,' he said, stepping back to look around.

'You've got paint on your jacket,' she said.

He looked at the front of his jacket to see a large red smudge and realised he had some on his hands too. It was on the parapet.

He leaned over the parapet to see red paint had been coarsely brushed in a circle on the water side of it. Gunnymede assessed the position of the red blotch. 'It's directly in line with the bench,' he said. 'It's a marker.'

She leaned over the parapet to look for herself. 'It's happening today!'

He scanned the river. There were a handful of boats in transit, none of them big enough to be a threat.

He took a hold of Bethan's shoulders while looking her square in the eyes. 'You have to get to Blackfriars station and get them to shut it down! I'll tell Neve. You have to close the station and get everyone up from the tunnels. Go!'

Bethan hurried to the car.

Gunnymede pulled out his phone and hit a number.

Neve was in Charing Cross Station reading a newspaper when she answered her phone.

'It's happening today!' he shouted. 'There's an aiming point on the parapet right in front of the bore hole.' He went to the parapet to search the near side bank in both directions and saw a jetty a hundred metres away with couple of men loading canoes onto the back of a rubber inflatable. 'I'm heading onto the river. Bethan's gone to close down Blackfriars station. We need help!'

He pocketed the phone as he ran along the embankment, clambered over a set of steps, down the other side onto a landing and towards the boat where the two young men were loading canoes.

Gunnymede held out his ID as he approached out of breath. 'I'm with the security services. I need your boat. This is a national emergency.'

They practically ignored him. 'Yeah, right,' one of them said.

Gunnymede took out his pistol and fired a round into the planking between the men, both of whom leapt back in complete shock.

'I'm sorry. I don't have time to fuck about. I'm security services. This is a life and death emergency! Get your boat started! Now!'

One of the men dived into the water and swam away.

Gunnymede addressed the other. 'I'm not going to shoot you! I just want your boat. And I need you to drive it. Please.'

The man nodded quickly.

'Let's go!'

The man obeyed and jumped into the boat. Gunnymede untied the lines and climbed in as the engine started.

'Main channel,' Gunnymede shouted. 'Quickly!'

The young man turned the throttle to full power as he deftly spun the nose around towards the centre of the river.

The MoD car came to a halt outside Blackfriars underground station. Bethan leapt out and ran inside. She paused in the cavernous hall to get her bearings. A member of staff directed her to the station manager's office. By the time she got there, he was on the phone talking with the security services who had called him. She showed her ID as she explained who she was and he informed her police and anti-terrorist units were on their way. He agreed the first thing they had to do was evacuate the station, get everyone up from the tunnels and shut the watertight doors.

She followed him as he hurried along a landing to the control room.

Gunnymede squatted at the front of the inflatable searching in every direction for any boat that might look big enough to ram a hole through a couple of metres of embankment. There weren't any such vessels motoring along the river within view but after a couple of minutes going east at full speed a large work boat appeared heading towards them. Gunnymede indicated to his driver to head for it.

His phone chirped and vibrated in his pocket. It was Neve.

'The big red button has been pushed,' she said, still in the Charing Cross control centre.

'I'm on the water.'

'I can see you.' She was looking at his marker on a tracking app.

'When can I expect assistance?' he asked.

'Police boats are on their way. Helicopters have gone up. I have no ETA yet.'

'We need to block the embankment at the marker. A boat. Anything.'

'It's all in motion.'

The inflatable closed on the approaching work boat. 'Go around the front!' he shouted.

'What?!' Neve asked.

'I'm talking to my driver.'

The inflatable cut across the front of the work boat and down its starboard side while Gunnymede inspected it. It didn't look big enough to be a threat and he signalled the driver to continue east.

'That's a negative!' Gunnymede said into the phone.

'There's a police boat five minutes from you.'

Gunnymede saw another workboat heading his way. An aggregate carrier. This one was longer, broader and heavier in the water, particularly the bows.

'Did you hear me, Devon?!'

'I'll get back to you,' he said and pocketed the phone.

'Excuse me,' the coxswain called out.

Gunnymede looked back at him.

'We've only got about half an hour of fuel,' he said.

'Keep going,' Gunnymede shouted and signalled him to go down the port side of the oncoming boat.

As the boats closed on each other Gunnymede got to his feet to get a better look, keeping his balance by holding onto a bow line. He couldn't see any crew. It certainly looked big enough to make a good dent in the embankment.

As they passed each other a guff of wind whipped up some trash at the back of the boat, some of which blew into the water. Gunnymede signalled the driver to turn about, vectoring him onto the trash. He leaned over the side and grabbed it up. It was an empty cement bag.

'Go!' Gunnymede shouted. 'Catch that boat!'

The driver opened up the throttle and the inflatable shot forward. Gunnymede hit a key on his phone.

'Neve! I've got a possible! The *Polo Harrow*! An aggregate carrier!'

'The police can't be more than a minute away!'

'So's the bloody embankment!'

Gunnymede put his phone away. 'Get me on that boat!'

The driver was up for it and powered the inflatable closer to the stern. Gunnymede signalled the starboard side and the driver accelerated over the work boat's bow wave to come alongside.

Bethan was in the control room of Blackfriars station watching the dozen screens showing various locations from the ticket hall to the escalators, tunnels and platforms. Staff members were busy blocking routes down to the platform and ordering people to leave the station. Down escalators had been switched off. Loudspeakers continually broadcast warnings for everyone to exit the station in an orderly manner. People were streaming for the exits.

The senior controller looked at a screen showing dozens of people in a hallway at the bottom of a staircase. 'What are those people doing?' he asked no one in particular. There were half a dozen operators in the room. 'They should be heading up.'

'Disorientated,' a controller suggested.

'Tell them to take the stairs,' the senior controller said, exasperated.

'I've been trying,' another controller said.

'Maybe they're foreigners,' another suggested. 'Can't speak English.'

One of the screens showed a dozen young school children and a couple of supervisors heading along an access tunnel.

'Why are those children not hurrying?' Bethan asked a controller.

'Not only that, they're going the wrong way,' he said. He pushed a series of buttons and pulled a microphone to his mouth. 'This is an emergency announcement. Will all passengers please make their way up to the station entrance in an orderly manner. I repeat. This is an emergency announcement.'

Several of the children were holding hands and skipping as the others ambled along as if they hadn't heard the announcement.

'They can't hear,' the controller said.

'The speakers must be down in that tunnel,' another offered.

'They'll hear the announcement when they reach the platform,' another said.

Gunnymede grabbed the vessel's side at the rear, pulled himself up and scrambled onto the narrow deck outside the superstructure. He pulled out his pistol and stepped to the door at the back, gripped the handle, pushed it open and charged in, gun levelled. The small crew room was empty except for a man lying on the floor, soaked in blood, his throat cut open. Gunnymede needed no further evidence and moved to the internal door that led to the stairs up to the bridge. He made his way carefully up them, the end of his gun leading the way and stood outside the only door. He checked the hinges to confirm which way it opened, gripped the doorknob and, taking a breath, yanked it open.

Standing inside, less than two metres away with their backs to him were four men, all looking ahead through the bridge windows. The sound of the engines at full speed directly below filled the room. Saleem was first to look around and see Gunnymede pointing his gun at him.

'I'm making the turn in ten seconds,' the pilot said. When Saleem didn't answer he glanced at him and then at Gunnymede. The other two fighters did the same.

One of them reached for a knife on the bridge dashboard.

'Make the turn,' Saleem said.

'Turn that wheel and I'll kill you,' Gunnymede warned.

'Turn,' Saleem ordered. 'Allah will protect you.'

The pilot looked through the window for the red marker on the embankment. It was then or never. He spun the wheel. As the boat lurched over Gunnymede steadied himself in the doorway and shot the pilot through the side of his head. The man slumped lifelessly over the wheel and dropped to the deck.

'Go!' Saleem yelled and the other two charged.

Gunnymede shot one in the chest but the other reached out and slapped the gun out of his hand before he could get off a second shot. They all fell back through the door to the floor at the tops of the steps.

Saleem grabbed the wheel and spun it round to complete the turn. The boat lurched heavily to one side.

Gunnymede battled with the remaining fighter, punching and kicking him while defending against the knife. As the boat lurched over, both men rolled into the bulkhead. Gunnymede punched him several times as hard as he could before he realised the man had gone limp. Gunnymede pushed him back to find the knife deep in the man's chest.

The boat continued to lean hard over. It felt like it might capsize. Gunnymede struggled to his feet, fighting against the force of the turn and sloping floor. He pulled himself into the doorway and saw Saleem straightening the wheel. The Arab was lining the boat up with the red target on the embankment that was barely a length away.

As the boat levelled out, Gunnymede threw himself at Saleem. Saleem grabbed a hold of the wheel and held it firm as Gunnymede reached around his neck from behind and tried to pull him off. Saleem was choking, his face turning red, but he held on with grim determination. Gunnymede was facing the window. He could see the red painted parapet closing in fast. He pulled at Saleem with all his might even though he knew it was too late. He watched the bank get closer as if in slow motion.

The bows struck the parapet with tremendous force. Saleem and Gunnymede were pressed into the wheel which snapped off and they hit the consul. The bows blew through the parapet like it was made of cake and ploughed deep into the pavement, cutting the bench in two. The momentum pushed the bows up and as it reached the road it came to a screeching halt at a steep angle. The bow was smashed open with pieces of concrete crumbling out of it.

More significantly, the river poured around the boat and into the exposed bore hole.

The flow was tremendous and only increased as the rushing water quickly eroded the soil. The surface of the river was a good metre above the bore hole and it poured in with ever increasing volume like a burst dam.

Gunnymede and Saleem had fallen back as the boat had risen up but as it tilted over to one side, Saleem fell out of the shattered side door.

Gunnymede had rolled to a stop at the same opening door and saw the Arab flip over the side. He pulled himself up onto his knees and edged outside to see Saleem holding onto the twisted rail, most of his body in the water that was pouring into the bore hole. If he were to let go, he would not be able to stop himself from following it. The embankment continued to erode, increasing the flow which would only get worse as the river level rose. The sound of the water rushing into the hole was almost too loud to speak over.

Gunnymede dropped out of the bridge to the rail where he only just managed to stop himself from following Saleem over the side.

Saleem mustered all his strength to try and heave himself out of the water but it pulled at his body and it was all he could do to hang on. Gunnymede reached out and grabbed his hands in an effort to help keep his fingers wrapped around the rail.

They looked into each other's eyes through clenched jaws.

'Who did you speak to in Syria?!' Gunnymede shouted. 'In the desert! Who did you speak to?!'

'Save me and I'll tell you!' Saleem shouted back.

Gunnymede looked into his eyes. 'You don't know, do you?'

'I know who gave him the plan!' Saleem shouted.

'Who?!'

'Save me!'

'Tell me and I'll save you!' Gunnymede shouted. He could feel Saleem's fingers loosening their grip. 'Tell me!'

'He's British!' Saleem shouted.

'You're lying!'

'No! A politician!'

'Who?!

'Save me!!!'

The boat suddenly jolted heavily as a piece of it broke off. Gunnymede lost his footing. One of Saleem's hands gave way and he hung on desperately with the other. Gunnymede fought to help him.

Saleem tried to reach the rail again with the free hand but the angle would not allow it. 'Save me!!!' he shouted.

It was a final desperate cry for help as he felt his grip fail. The hand left the rail but Saleem was still there. Gunnymede had a hold of his wrist. But he was never going to keep it for long. Seconds later, Saleem's hand popped from Gunnymede's grip and he shot away with the flow and into the yawning gap in the embankment where he disappeared inside a vast suction of water.

Gunnymede watched the point where Saleem had disappeared, his only regret he didn't get the name.

'Dear God!' one of the station controllers called out and everyone looked at the monitor he was watching. Water burst into one of the platform access tunnels through a disintegrating wall that quickly eroded the ceiling along its length. Another screen showed a different section of tunnel with dozens of people hurrying along it as a side of it burst open with tremendous force slamming them back the way they were going. Within seconds the tunnel was filled with water and the CCTV camera submerged for a few seconds before it failed.

'It's happened,' Bethan muttered.

'How long before the rail tunnel doors are closed?' the senior controller shouted.

'Three minutes,' came the reply.

'We need to close the internal doors to level three,' the senior controller urged. 'Get those people out of the tunnels!'

'Where are those children?' Bethan asked, pointing to the monitor that showed them still walking along in ignorance of any danger.

'That's here,' a controller said, pointing to a tunnel on a station map.

Bethan took a second to memorise it, ran out of the room, along a walkway and down a set of stairs. At the bottom she sprinted towards the barriers and scrambled over them.

'Stop!' one of staff cried out but Bethan barged past him, ran to the escalator that wasn't moving and bounded down it, several steps at a time. When she reached the bottom she paused long enough to work out where she was and set off at a sprint along a tunnel.

Back in the control room, they watched various CCTV cameras showing people frantically wading through water. Some views showed people finding flights of stairs to escape. One group reached a stairwell only to be thrown down them by the arrival of a wall of water.

The river gushed into the tunnel the children were in and the adults quickly grabbed the smallest ones and hurried back the way they came. Everyone in the operations room anxiously watched the monitor.

'How far are they from the internal doors?!' a controller asked.

One of them indicated the map. 'They're here. The doors are here,' he said concerned. It was not a short distance for children in those conditions.

'Close the doors to half way,' the senior controller ordered. 'Start with doors A1 and A2. C3 and 4 standby!'

Bethan hurried along a corridor knee deep in murky water that was flowing towards her. She paused in shock as a section of the wall started to move before realising it was one of the watertight doors shifting out of its recess. She stood in the opening and shouted for anyone to head towards her.

The door was halfway across the tunnel when it came to a stop. She heard echoing screams along the tunnel. The water was rising to her waist. She pushed on beyond the watertight door and down the tunnel.

She came to a short staircase going down with water flowing over the steps like a waterfall. The screams of children came from further below. She held onto the rail as she made her way down the steps. She could see several children hanging onto the rails at the bottom. Adults appeared carrying as many children as they could and Bethan let herself ride the fall to the bottom as she held onto a rail.

'This way! Hurry!' Bethan shouted as she grabbed a couple of children and began to pull herself back up the stairs using the rail. The adults followed. A child lost her grip and screamed as she was swept away and out of sight. There was nothing the adults could do but press on.

Bethan made it to the top of the stairs and around the corner. The water was still rising but the force of the flow had reduced.

Back in the control room they could see Bethan carrying children with others behind her.

'They'll make it to the doors,' someone muttered.

'No they won't,' another controller shouted. 'The doors are closing!'

They could all see the monitor showing the massive doors moving to the closed position.

'Keep them open!' the senior controller shouted.

A controller kept punching a button but to no effect. 'It's not working!' she shouted! 'I can't stop them.'

'For God's sake open them,' the senior controller pleaded.

'They're being overridden at the TFL HQ,' an operator shouted.

The senior controller picked up the phone and desperately punched in a number.

Bethan reached the door as it sealed shut. She banged on it, shouting for it to be opened. She looked around for a CCTV camera and waved frantically at it while holding the children.

A controller buried her face in her hands, unable to look as the water quickly rose to Bethan's shoulders. Seconds later it was lapping against her face as she trod water. Bethan had to release one of the children in order to keep afloat. Everyone in the control room who dared to watch could not believe what they were seeing.

Minutes later the tunnel was full and Bethan held tightly to the child as they struggled to suck air from the gap at the ceiling. The gap quickly disappeared and she was completely immersed. Seconds later Bethan succumbed and released the dead child in her final throes.

It was over. Bethan floated lifelessly. The senior controller was the only one who could stomach watching the monitor. Not that he was really focused on anything. He was in total shock.

Epilogue

Gunnymede stood on a bridge over the Thames up the road from the Legoland building holding what was left of the bottle of Scotch while staring down onto the water.

Aristotle walked up the street and stopped a few metres from him.

Gunnymede held out the bottle to him.

'I won't, thank you,' Aristotle said.

'I'm trying to imagine being under there right now. It's very cold and lonely.'

'They estimate two hundred dead.'

'Not a bad day's work for Saleem.'

'Two hundred is a lot better than a few thousand.'

'I only care about one of those,' Gunnymede said, taking a drink.

'There's been no explanation for the doors yet. No one is owning up to closing them. There's a suggestion it was a technical problem. The failsafe position for the doors is closed.'

'We'll have to blame someone. It'll probably fall at the feet of some engineer currently on holiday somewhere who hasn't even heard of this yet.'

'Harlow told me to tell you that despite everything, it was a job well done. You must accept it could've been a complete disaster if you hadn't worked it out when you did.'

'I didn't. Bethan worked it out. She's the hero of the hour.' He took a drink. 'Saleem told me the source of the plan was a British politician.'

'Saleem?' Aristotle found that interesting. 'I don't suppose he told you who.'

'He was about to but he had to shoot off. A meeting in hell he had to attend.' Gunnymede looked beyond Aristotle to see Neve approaching. 'Ah! Neve. Step into my office. The Greek was just leaving.'

Aristotle decided that was probably a good idea and walked away.

'Arsehole,' Gunnymede muttered, taking a sip.

Neve took Aristotle's place and leaned against the parapet to look at the water.

'I'm sorry,' she said.

'We covered all of that. Two hundred dead. Faulty watertight doors. Congratulations to me.'

'She was very brave. I didn't appreciate her.'

'You didn't have to. I didn't either. Actually that's not true. I just didn't want to. So, there's a vacancy if you want to fill it.'

'I think I'll pass if that's okay.'

'Wise choice. Life expectancy is not too great for the women in my life.'

He held up the bottle. 'To Captain America's sister!' He emptied the last of the Scotch into his mouth and threw the bottle as far as he could into the river.

'If you want to blame someone, blame Spangle,' she said.

'Of course. Spangle is everything. But there is a positive side. As long as he's free, so am I.'

Gunnymede walked away.

Gunnymede was sprawled on his couch in his clothes. Several empty bottles of assorted alcoholic beverages littered the coffee table, a full ashtray and empty fag packet amongst them.

A persistent knock on the door eventually woke him up and he struggled to sit up. The knocking continued and he checked his watch. It was a bright day outside which he far from appreciated.

He got to his feet, stumbled to the door and opened it.

Charlie was standing there.

'What the fuck do you want?' Gunnymede asked.

'I need to talk to you.'

'I'm not in the mood,' Gunnymede said, closing the door.

Charlie stopped it from closing fully.

Gunnymede opened it again and looked at him coldly. 'If I could attempt it without falling over I'd punch you.'

'It won't take a minute ... please.'

'What is it?'

'Can we talk inside?'

'What is it?'

Charlie sighed, controlling his frustration. 'Jack's dead.'

'Jack Henderson?'

Charlie nodded.

'How?'

'He shot himself.'

Gunnymede considered the news. 'I can understand that. Is that it?'

'I need to ask you something,' Charlie said. 'But not out here.'

Gunnymede sighed heavily and stood back to let him in. 'Wait a minute. How did you know where I live?'

Charlie shrugged.

Gunnymede shook his head, made his way unsteadily into the kitchen and set about making himself a cup of coffee. 'I'd offer you a tea or coffee but as you're not staying long, I won't.'

'You know about Jack.'

'Not until you just told me.'

'I didn't mean that.'

'For fuck's sake. I can't handle anything cryptic right now. If you want to communicate with me you're going to have to keep it very simple.'

'The Becket Approval,' Charlie said, studying Gunnymede.

Gunnymede poured boiling water into a mug and stirred it. 'That is a statement?'

'You know Jack was the operations officer for the Becket Approval.'

'Not exactly.'

'The position needs to be filled.'

Gunnymede sipped the drink which was too hot. 'Why are you talking to me about that organisation?'

'Like I said. The position needs to be filled.'

'You're asking me?' Gunnymede said.

Charlie stared at him by way of an answer.

'First of all,' Gunnymede said. 'Forgetting how utterly bizarre that concept is. Why are you asking? I mean, who the fuck are you?'

'It's not my idea.'

'It's not your idea to come here and ask me to take over Jack's, what is that, a murder squad. Is that a hobby? Who's idea was it?'

'I can't say.'

'You can't say.'

'I don't know exactly.'

'Exactly?'

'I don't know.'

'I'm still asleep and dreaming, aren't I? There's a technique I read about that you can use to test if you're in a dream or not ... what was it? Oh yes. Bite the end of your fingers.' Gunnymede bit the end of a finger. It hurt. 'You need to leave,' he said to Charlie. 'Please. Now.'

'This wasn't a good time.'

'It will never be a good time.'

'I was told you'd be interested.'

'By a hidden voice? Please go.'

Charlie rolled his eyes and went to the front door. Gunnymede opened it, Charlie left the flat and Gunnymede closed it behind him.

Gunnymede went into his lounge and to the balcony windows where he sipped his coffee and looked at the Thames, shaking his head in disbelief as he looked back towards the front door.

He put a hand in his pocket, felt something and retrieved it. It was his ornate SIS badge.

He opened the balcony doors and held it as if he was going to toss it. And he might've done had something deep inside not stopped him.

He dropped the badge onto the coffee table and went back to watching the Thames.

Printed in Great Britain
by Amazon